THE WITCH'S TALE

THE WITCH'S TALE

Stories of Gothic Horror from the Golden Age of Radio

by Alonzo Deen Cole

Edited, with Introduction and Program Log
by David S. Siegel

Dunwich Press
An imprint of Book Hunter Press
Yorktown Heights, NY 10598
1998

THE WITCH'S TALE

THE WITCH'S TALE by Alonzo Deen Cole. Edited by David S. Siegel.

Cover by Alice Pfeiffer

Printed and bound in the United States of America

Library of Congress Catalog Card Number 98-071725

ISBN: 1-891379-01-1

Dunwich Press
An Imprint of Book Hunter Press
PO Box 193
Yorktown Heights, NY 10598
(914) 245-6608
bookhuntpr@aol.com

For Susan, Jennifer, Edward, Robert, Jessica and Gabriella.

Dedicated to the memory of
Alonzo Deen Cole (1897-1971)
Without whose imagination this book would not have been possible.

And with special appreciation to
Dorothea Cole

Acknowledgments

I would like to express my gratitutde to the following for their enthusiasm, encouragement and assistance: Arthur Anderson, Jackson Beck, Rob Imes, Charles Michelson, Raymond Schnitzer, Robert Schultz and Miriam Wolff.

Thanks also to my wife and partner, Susan, who typed the thirteen radio dramas that appear in this book. Without her, this book would be impossible. Moreover, without her (and sometimes, even with her), I would be impossible.

Table of Contents

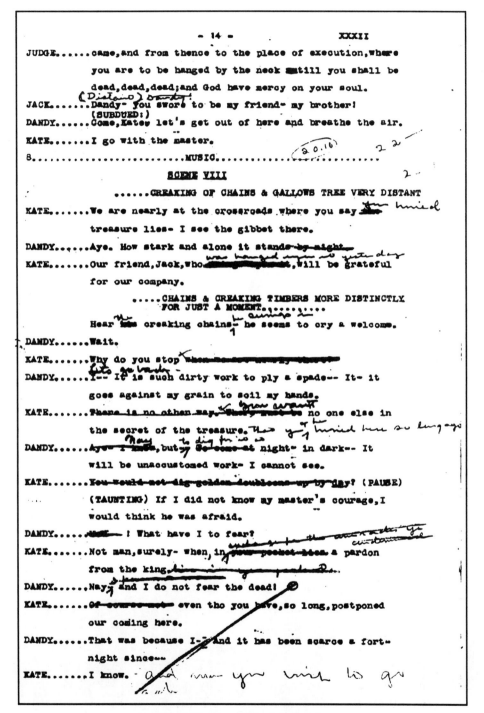

- 14 -   XXXII

JUDGE......came,and from thence to the place of execution,where
            you are to be hanged by the neck ~~until~~ till you shall be
            dead,dead,dead;and God have mercy on your soul.
            (Distant) Dandy!
JACK......Dandy- you swore to be my friend- my brother!
            (SUBDUED:)
DANDY......Come,Kate, let's get out of here and breathe the air.
KATE.......I go with the master.
8........................MUSIC........................   *20.16   2 2*

                          SCENE VIII   *2*

            ......CREAKING OF CHAINS & GALLOWS TREE VERY DISTANT
KATE.......We are nearly at the crossroads where you say ~~the~~ *buried*
            treasure lies- I see the gibbet there.
DANDY......Aye. How stark and alone it stands ~~by night.~~
                                  was hanged upon it yesterday
KATE.......Our friend,Jack,who ~~~~,will be grateful
            for our company.
            .....CHAINS & CREAKING TIMBERS MORE DISTINCTLY
                 FOR JUST A MOMENT...........
            Hear ~~the~~ creaking chains- *the swinging in* he seems to cry a welcome.
DANDY......Wait.
KATE.......Why do you stop ~~when~~ *into the barn*
DANDY......I-- It is such dirty work to ply a spade-- It- it
            goes against my grain to soil my hands.
KATE.......~~There is no other way,~~ *you aren't* no one else in
            the secret of the treasure. ~~The~~ *you buried here so long ago*
                   May to dig for us so
DANDY......~~Aye- I know~~,but ~~to come~~ at night- in dark-- It
            will be unaccustomed work- I cannot see.
KATE.......~~You would not dig golden doubloons up by day?~~ (PAUSE)
            (TAUNTING) If I did not know my master's courage,I
            would think he was afraid.
DANDY......~~Bah~~! What have I to fear?
                                      would you get the own naked so circumstance
KATE.......Not man,surely- when, in ~~your pocket lies~~ a pardon
            from the king ~~~~.
DANDY......Nay, and I do not fear the dead!
KATE.......~~Of course not~~ even tho you have,so long,postponed
            our coming here.
DANDY......That was because I-, And it has been scarce a fort-
            night since---
KATE.......I know. *and now you wish to go*

Introduction

Before *Tales of the Crypt*, before *Halloween* and *Friday the 13th*, before even the original classic film versions of *Frankenstein* and *Dracula*, and certainly well before the advent of modern television, the medium of radio provided its audiences with a healthy share of goosebumps and chills.

Fans of radio's Golden Age recall programs like *Lights Out, Inner Sanctum, The Hermit's Cave, Quiet Please, Suspense* and *The Shadow*. The great granddaddy of them all, once heard, not easily forgotten, was a program called *The Witch's Tale*, written and conceived by Alonzo Deen Cole who also starred in and directed the program. (Orson Welles had nothing on Cole.)

Born in St. Paul, Minnesota on February 22, 1897 to Daniel and Grace McHenry Cole, Cole didn't lose any time launching his career as a writer. At the age of 11, in a state-wide competition among school children, he won first prize at the Minnesota State Fair for a scenario for a military pageant. Later, while in high school, he wrote, directed and starred in many plays presented by the school's dramatic society. After graduating from high school at age 16, Cole enrolled in The Minnesota Academy of Arts but his initial interest in drawing was overshadowed by his penchant for acting and he was soon to take on a succession of small roles, first with a Minneapolis stock company and later with a rival St. Paul company for the munificent salary of $15.00 per week.

Cole's stage career was progressing modestly when it was interrupted by his enlistment in the medics during World War I. After serving in France he transferred to the Entertainment Division A. E. F. and, after the Armistice, was assigned to a repertoire company composed of professional actors in uniform.

Returning to civilian life in 1919, Cole encountered the infamous theatrical strike that pitted performers, represented by Equity and led by Ed Wynn, against the big wig producers and theater owners of the day. He was, nonetheless able to secure an Equity approved contract and, until the stock market crash and ensuing depression of the 1930's, worked steadily in both the legitimate theater and vaudeville.

Marie O'Flynn, the actress who was to become Cole's vaudeville partner and later his wife, came on the scene during the 1925-26 season when the couple first appeared together in an act called *The Honeymooners* (shades of Jackie Gleason). Cole later adapted these skits for his and Marie's first major radio appearance, a program called *Darling and Dearie*. The 15 minute serial ran for 74 consecutive weeks over radio station WOR in New York beginning March 6, 1931.

Several months later, on May 28, 1931, *The Witch's Tale*, made its debut performance, also on WOR. The program was to become the premier horror radio series of it's day.

How Deen Cole (Alonzo was only used by folks who did not know him) came to write the initial script for *The Witch's Tale*, put together a cast and sell the idea of a radio series devoted to stories of the supernatural to the management at WOR is somewhat speculative. A prodigious reader and natural raconteur, Cole possessed a charismatic personality that enabled him to persuade station executives that a series of dramatized creepy stories in the late evening hours would attract listeners away from some of the more traditional musical interludes being broadcast by rival stations at that hour.

At the time, radio was dominated by David Sarnoff's National Broadcasting Company which ran two networks, the Blue and the Red, and William Paley's Columbia Broadcasting Company. The third, and much smaller network, Mutual, was owned by Louis Bamberger, a Newark, New Jersey department store owner, and did not have the finances needed to attract the big names in early radio entertainment. As a consequence, many of the Mutual's programs were produced by local affiliates like WOR, the network's New York City outlet, and sold to other stations on the network. (Perhaps the most famous of these local programs was the *Lone Ranger* produced in Detroit.)

Cole's instincts were on target and before long, *The Witch's Tale* began to pay off for both Cole and the station. Indeed, the program was shortly to become the talk of the local tabloids. Following the program's third broadcast, Dorothy Kardel wrote in the *New York Daily News* of June 12, 1931:

"For the third time old Nancy told her Witch's Tale and succeeded in working me into a sweat. Thrill seekers miss plenty when they fail to hear this new dramatic series."

On the program, Cole played the male lead in every broadcast and Marie O'Flynn always played opposite him. The rest of the cast was made up of a three actor ensemble that was only occasionally added to. Cole also played the part of

Satan, the black cat, and did so with great relish.

Anyone who has ever listened to a broadcast of *The Witch's Tale* will remember the cackling voice of Old Nancy, the witch of Salem, whose job it was to introduce each program. Nancy was originally portrayed by stage actress Adelaide Fitz-Allen, who took on the role at age 75, and who also played occasional minor roles on the program. When Fitz-Allen passed away at age 79 on February 26, 1935 (never having missed a performance), Cole auditioned several actresses for the role. Thirteen performances and three "try out" Nancys later, Cole discovered thirteen year old Miriam Wolff who had been playing witches on the CBS Saturday morning series, *Let's Pretend*. (It was Nila Mack, the producer-director of *Let's Pretend*, who had worked with Cole on the vaudeville circuit, who brought the teenage "Nancy" to Cole's attention.)

In addition to Cole, his wife and Fitz-Allen (and later Wolff), two other actors rounded out the company's ensemble cast: Mark Smith and Alan Devitt. Wolff recalls being awed by Smith's imposing size (a six feet eight inch tall frame carrying two hundred and eighty pounds) when, as a teenager, she had to share a microphone with him. She also remembers Devitt as an enthusiastic actor who would sometimes become so involved in his role that he had to struggle to keep his false teeth from falling out of his mouth while reading his lines.

The character of Nancy was a true stroke of genius. It is no accident that later radio programs would use similar characters to introduce the mayhem that they would dramatize. Who can ever forget Raymond (Edward Johnson) of *Inner Sanctum* fame, the Mysterious Traveller (Maurice Tarplon) who would tell frightening stories to train passengers into the night, the Man In Black (Joseph Kearns) who would introduce us to stories of *Suspense*, and of course, the Whistler (Marvin Miller). These well known hosts and several more (the Hermit of *The Hermit's Cave* fame, the Bell Toller of *The Weird Circle*, Arch Oboler telling us to put our *Lights Out*, etc.) all helped to set the mood for the programs that were to follow.

It would be a mistake to take Nancy too seriously. As regular listeners noted, at each broadcast she announced her birthday and it could be a hundred and eleven one week and a hundred and eight the following week. (Some weeks, in the same introductory monologue, she was two different ages.) Those privileged to read some of the early scripts for which recorded episodes do not exist, find that Nancy herself explains her penchant for fibbing about her birthday as an excuse to receive gifts (sweets) from her visitors in exchange for which, she weaves a tale. In some of the early programs, Cole gave Nancy the surname "Holcomb," a name which Wolff found amusing as Cole used the word "holcomb" (hokum) to mean "bull."

Even before Nancy made her appearance, listener's would hear long-time WOR personality Roger Bower begin the program by announcing: "The Witch's Tale" followed by the mysterious theme music *Orgie and the Spirits* by Leginski. At that point, listeners to an early program would hear something like:

> Do you believe in ghosts, goblins and those strange spirits of evil that sometimes leave their home in the darkness to walk the day with men? Before you say "No," turn down your lights, mount a broomstick and come with us to the little tumble down shack in Salem, Massachusetts where an old, old woman lives alone with a coal black cat. Her name is Nancy Holcomb and they say she is a witch; her cat is known as Satan. The broomstick travels fast— we're at her door—and if she'll let us in, perhaps we shall hear that which will make the phantom spirits of evil seem real to us—terrible—very terrible.

As the music ended, there was a knock at the door and after a brief conversation with the visitor (Tom), Nancy proceeded to tell her yarn.

In later episodes, Cole shortened the announcer's role and would simply begin each program with: "Again we bring you The Witch's Tale written and produced by Alonzo Deen Cole. And now let us join old Nancy and Satan her wise black cat."

No matter what the announcer had to say, it was Nancy who listeners remembered, and for that reason, each of the scripts in this collection includes Nancy's very unique style of welcoming her guests and telling her story. We suspect that our friend the Crypt Master grew up at old Nancy's knees. (The editor is pleased and privileged to have Miriam Wolff who portrayed Nancy write the Prologue and Epilogue for this collection.)

Throughout its seven year run, *The Witch's Tale* underwent numerous scheduling changes, including more than 28 changes in the day of the week it was broadcast, plus countless changes in the times the program was broadcast. These changes would often occur without notice and were usually caused by the need for the station to give the time to either a special (musical, political or social) event or because a paying sponsor might decide to buy that time slot for a different program.

The program was heard most frequently on Mondays (144 programs) and Thursdays (89 programs), occasional Tuesdays, Wednesdays and Fridays and once on a Saturday.

The programs also underwent a number of time schedule changes and could be heard as early as 8:00-8:30pm and at other times as late as 10:30-11:00pm. The most frequent time slot (102 episodes) was 9:30-10:00pm, followed by 9:00-9:30pm (55 episodes) and 10:00-10:30pm (54 episodes). Loyal listeners had to be careful, though, because the program aired at other times as well.

The log that appears at the end of this book illustrates the nature of the many scheduling changes the program went through.

That the program survived these changes AND retained a core of loyal listeners is certainly a tribute to the quality of the weekly dramas and the acclaim it received from local critics. On November 14, 1932, Nick Kenney of the *New York Daily Mirror* wrote: "Boyoboyoboyoboyo!!!! Alonzo Deen Cole's Witch's Tale of last evening was one grand piece of radio drama!!"

While the vast majority of the stories told by Nancy were original plots, Cole also did a number of adaptations of classics such as Robert Louis Stevenson's *The Wonderful Bottle*, Alexander Dumas' *The Corsican Brothers* and Nathaniel Hawthorne's *Rapaccini's Daughter*, as well as adaptations of a number of stories based on legends, including The Golem, Tanhauser, The Flying Dutchman, Faust, etc.

Most of the programs ran thirty minutes in length although there were a few two-parters and even one or two three-parters. What is interesting is that many, if not all, of the two-parters began as single programs that Cole realized toward the latter part of the live broadcast were running too long. Rather than cut, he would quickly write new dialogue for the actors that had the effect of extending the program and a new epilogue for Nancy announcing that the program would be concluded the following week. That, of course, meant that Cole would have to create an entirely new program for the following week bringing the story to a satisfactory conclusion. Somehow, despite cast frustration, it seemed to work. Radio veteran Jackson Beck, who appeared in at least two episodes of the program, recalls Cole frantically rewriting and handing changes to the actors in mid broadcast.

A number of programs were repeated, some more than once. The first program to be repeated, "The Were-Wolf" (Program #2), was later repeated as Program #216. Other programs were repeated at more frequent intervals and a few, e.g., "The Confession" and "The First Of June," were repeated more than once. Sometimes, there were modifications in the second script and in some cases, different titles were used for the second broadcast (Program #33, "Kamohoalii" is the same story as Program #207, "The King Shark God.") Specific data regarding the programs that were repeated is included in the log.

While those who knew Cole attest to the fact that he was well read, and today's horror aficionado can recognize the literary sources for many of his radio plays, one can only speculate as to his tastes for the more lurid pulp magazines of his day as so many of his plots derive from the same fountain of eeriness that filled the pages of such classic pulps as *Weird Tales*.

Mad scientists, haunted houses, ghosts seeking revenge, ancient curses, creatures out of control (insects, tigers, wolves, snakes, etc.), witches, magicians, vampires, were-wolves, The Reign of Terror, tales of African or Latin American jungles, the Wild West, statues coming to life and simply bloody murder were the stuff that made *The Witch's Tale* plots flow. It was no surprise when the May 1933 issue of *Science Fiction Digest* noted: "The Witch's Tale, written by the versatile Alonzo Deen Cole, is rated by radio critics as one of the five leading acts on the air."

It should also come as little surprise that in 1936, during the actual run of the program, an attempt was made to launch a monthly pulp magazine based on the series. The magazine, *The Witch's Tales*, listed Alonzo Deen Cole as editor and author but also featured stories by other pulp writers. Only two issues (November and December) were to see the light of day. Years later, in 1951, a comic book publisher, the Harvey Features Syndicate, would publish at least five issues of a comic book entitled *The Witches Tales*.

Also in 1936, the Tom Moore Cigar Company published a 38 page pamphlet containing four stories taken from *The Witch's Tale* ("The Spirits Of The Lake," "The Were-Wolf," "Graveyard Mansion" and "The Gypsy's Hand.") The publication may have been a "giveaway tie-in" for the radio program, which was a common practice of that period. (As Cole's sister Muriel was the inspiration for the then well known Muriel cigar, one can only wonder if there was some tobacco connection there.)

While the last live performance of *The Witch's Tale* took place on June 13, 1938, Cole had managed to record enough of the programs to sustain sales of the show to regional advertisers for an additional six years. During its initial live broadcasts the only sponsorship that has been documented was that of the L. Bamberger Co. (owner of both the station the program was broadcast from and the department stores) and, for a very brief period (September to October, 1935), The Joseph Martinson Coffee Company.

For fans of The Golden Age Of Radio, especially those who revel in listening to recorded broadcasts of that period, the news is mixed. The good news is that about thirty programs of *The Witch's Tale* survive; a few of these are Australian versions as Cole sold the rights to the program to agents down under. The bad news is that the sound quality on these recordings is generally rather poor. Hobbyists "in the know" attribute this to the poor quality of the original material used to make the actual recordings. Nonetheless, fans who want to listen to an early *Witch's Tale* and who don't mind filtering out the crackling sounds and other imperfections, can certainly do so.

Cole himself withdrew the series from the market in 1945 and in 1961, when he moved to California, he destroyed his own recordings of the program feeling they had lost any further commercial value.

After taking *The Witch's Tale* off the air, Cole wrote scripts for *Seth Parker, The Hour of Charm* and *Gangbusters*. He also wrote specials for the *Kate Smith Hour* and contributed several scripts for *The Shadow*. In addition to writing, he was also involved in acting and tried his hand at more than one audition record for new radio shows that failed to attract sponsor interest.

In the summer of 1943 Cole signed a contract with the Columbia Broadcasting System as its chief writer of a new crime detection series. Originally entitled *Flash-Gun Casey*, the series was based on stories written by mystery writer George Harmon Coxe. The title was soon changed to *Casey, Crime Photographer* and ran from August 19, 1943 to April 22, 1955. The program was highly rated by both listeners and sponsors. According to Cole's personal notes, he was the sole author for the series' run of 384 scripts, quite an accomplishment by any standard.

Over the course of his career as an author, Cole is credited with having written close to 900 radio plays that were produced, in addition to some screen plays and documentary films.

After the conclusion of *Casey, Crime Photographer*, and after taking a well earned vacation, Cole returned to work hoping to sell *The Witch's Tale* as a television series. While a pilot for the show was shot, Cole himself admitted that because the product had been done so cheaply it lacked quality and never sold.

Cole's marriage to his long time *Witch's Tale* co-star, Marie O'Flynn, ended in divorce in the early 1950's and in 1955 he remarried. In October, 1961 he moved his family from their comfortable home in Scarsdale, New York to Glendale, California, where he hoped to find work in the television and movie industry. In the process of packing and moving he developed a hernia and shortly after his arrival in California began to experience chest pains and difficulty breathing. His physicians advised him that he had a vastly enlarged heart and a life expectancy of about two years. That was in 1962. While he remained relatively inactive following that prognosis, he lived for another nine years with the aid of a salt free diet and the use of digitalis and other drugs. He died on March 31, 1971 at the age of 73 of an acute coronary occlusion, leaving his widow

Dorothea, who was 21 years his junior, and a daughter by his second marriage.

Considering the availability of some 332 *Witch's Tale* scripts, the selection of which radio plays to include in this anthology presented quite a challenge. Even after the fairly large number of repeated scripts were eliminated, there remained a healthy number of scripts from which to chose. Ultimately, several factors were used in making the final selections: The collection does not knowingly include programs that are adaptations of the works of others or of popular legends since such stories are already well known and available in other anthologies. It was also decided to omit programs that are two or three parters since the length of such plays would be double or triple that of the length of the typical half hour program. Finally, as the plots to the 30 odd programs of *The Witch's Tale* that are in circulation among collectors of The Golden Age Of Radio are known, these scripts were not considered.

The thirteen radio plays that follow are all believed to be the original creative works of Alonzo Deen Cole. Readers must be prepared to suspend their belief in the rational and embrace old fashioned "melodrama" at both its best and its worst.

Those not familiar or comfortable with dialogue written in "dialect" are reminded that without the visual stimulation of television, radio, particularly radio drama that was being broadcast in the 1930's, depended to a large extent on the broad dialect that was viewed as typical of the various ethnic groups who were being portrayed.

Read these plays as though you were visiting Nancy, and as she begins each tale do your best to picture yourself (remember, radio has always been called *The Theater of the Mind*) as each character who is being portrayed. If you are successful, you will appreciate the fear that so many felt late at night as they cuddled under their blankets listening to these tales of fright.

David S. Siegel
September 1, 1998

PROLOGUE

by Miriam Wolff
"Nancy" 1935-38

NANCY: Heh Heh Heh Heh Heh! Hunner an' sixty nine year ole I be today, yessir, hunner an' sixty nine year ole!! Weel, Satan...

SATAN: (*A long, welcoming howl of a cat call, perfectly timed by actor Alonzo Deen Cole, in his weekly feline role.*)

NANCY: ...this being a very special birthday, I'm going to share the spine tingling present I just received from our weird and magical master, writer, director, fellow yarn-spinner, Alonzo Deen Cole...

SATAN: (*Prolonged and proud MEEEEOW!*)

NANCY: A special-bound volume of thirteen of our very favorite spooky sturries of The Witch's Tale that we spun for you these past hunners of my birthdays.

SATAN: (*Another very proud meow.*)

NANCY: Now, Satan, I want you to mind the timing of those cat calls! You know, that if you add a sound that's not in the script, it ruins the rhythm and pace and our director will go into a screaming rage (scary enough to make you lose your calm) and we will just disappear into dust...So, no extraneous "now's, and's, but's, or's or err's," please. Read the yarns as written. We're gettin too old, too rich and too talented to change the past.

SATAN: (*Timid meow.*)

NANCY: So...now, you tell these folks to douse out them lights...A'settin' quiet in the dark is the way to be part of our perty tales.

SATAN: (*Satan tells them,* "LIGHTS OUT!!")

NANCY: That's right. Now...Draw up to the fire and gaze inter the embers...gaze inter them deeeep! And soon, ye'll be shaking with fright in the land of devils and evil spirits, blood-thirsty screams and horror.

NANCY: Soon ye'll be in the fantasy land of ghosts and goblins...and THE WITCH'S TALE...Heh Heh Heh..THE WITCH'S TALE.

(Fade out with a blood-curdling laugh from Nancy and a long devilish wail of a meow from Satan.)

Alonzo Deen Cole, Adelaide Fitz-Allen (top), "Nancy" 1931-35, and Marie O'Flynn

Miriam Wolff, "Nancy" (1935-38)

The Image

Monday, February 8, 1932

(Musical theme.)

ANNOUNCER: And now let us make our way to that eery, windswept corner of historic Salem, where stands the ghostly little home of old Nancy and her black cat, Satan. There, from out the strange and fearsome shadows that seem ever to hover within its single ancient room, we shall hear another story of forbidding mystery.

(Music swells...wind whistles...)

PROLOGUE

NANCY: He he he... *(CAT meows.)* Yes'r, Satan—yew an me is havin' anuther buthday. Hunner an twen'y one year ole, I be t'day—almos' a hunner an twen'y tew! He he...'spose, in exchange fer th' nice presint these here young good-fer-nuthins brung us, we'll haf t' tell em anuther ov our cheerful leetle stories.

DICK: If you'd really like to, Nancy.

TOM: But you know we don't bring you birthday presents just to get something in return.

DICK: Oh, perish the thought!

NANCY: Humph—wonder how long ye'd bring em if ye didn't tell ye yarns! But me an Satan ain't th' kine whut 'cepts suthin fer nuthin. No, sir— not in th' hull hunner an thutty four year sence we wus bornd! We wus brung up right—t' be allus perlite an tell th' truth, an never t' look at th' vally o' presints whut's gave us s' much es th' sperrit t' which they iz sent. 'Course, when we gits a nicer presint, we do feel like showin' a leetle more 'preciation.

TOM: I hope you liked this one tonight, Nancy.

NANCY: Oh, this un's fine! C'mon, Satan—we'll show our gratty-tood with a yarn that'll give these young know-nuthins nightmares fer a week!

DICK: Now, Nancy—

TOM: Nancy—

NANCY: He he...douse that candle! It's more cheerful in th'dark. Now draw up t' th' fire an gaze inter th' embers—t' a cheerful leetle town, t' Noo York City we're a goin'—where cheerful lookin' houses stan' in cheerful lookin' groun's. An in one o' these houses, we're goin' t' call on sum cheerful lookin' peepul. He he...ever'thin' 'bout this stury's nice an cheerful at th' start—an mebbe—meebe— it'll stay that way. Mebbe! He he he he...

(Music: light, modern theme.)

SCENE 1

CLAIRE: *(Distant)* Hawkins!

HAWKINS: *(Distant)* Yes, Miss Farnum?

CLAIRE: *(Closer)* Has uncle returned yet?

HAWKINS: *(Closer)* Not yet, Miss.

ANNA: *(Distant...German dialect.)* Iss dot you coming down de stairs, Miss Farnum?

CLAIRE: *(At mike.)* Yes, Anna. Do you want something?

ANNA: *(Coming up.)* Vhat should I do? Your uncle's lunch I can keeb no longer! For de bast half hour it iss been getting bad, und now id iss ruined combletely!

CLAIRE: Don't bother about it. He's probably having something to eat in the city—if he remembers to eat at all.

ANNA: Budt he said he vas coming back from New York py noon und I fixed all his vegetables.

CLAIRE: Something has evidently delayed him—order him some fresh ones for dinner.

ANNA: Jah. *(Going away.)* Such a mans—only vegetables he eats, und den he don't come home to eadt dem!

CLAIRE: Where has Mr. Corbett gone, Hawkins?

HAWKINS: Back into the library, Miss.

CLAIRE: So?? I'll fix that!

(Knock at door.)

     (Peremptorily) Terry! Terry!

TERRY: *(Inside)* Come in—come in, dear!
(Door thrown open.)
CLAIRE: Ah ha—going back to work!
TERRY: *(Laughing)* That's what your uncle pays me for, you know.
CLAIRE: And you will be a conscientious secretary! Look here, young man, I've already told you our afternoon was all planned. It's much too beautiful to stay indoors, so you're going to chuck those old notes and smelly books and take me for a nice long drive.
TERRY: If I take you for many more afternoon drives, this book of your uncle's never will be finished.
CLAIRE: What if it isn't? Nobody will want to read anything so frightfully uninteresting, anyway!
TERRY: Be careful! I shall probably be writing ponderous volumes about ancient things myself some day—and, as a dutiful wife, you won't be allowed to skip a single syllable. I'll even dedicate them to you.
CLAIRE: What a frightful prospect! After living with uncle all these years, I should have realized the dangers that lurk in the vicinity of an antiquary—yet I become engaged to one who will follow in his footsteps!
TERRY: *(Laughing)* You were blinded by my youth and beauty to the awful future.
CLAIRE: *(Laughs)* And I'll have to remain that way to keep my sanity. Come on—get your hat. You can drive with one hand and we'll be romantic in the sunlight.
TERRY: I can't—honestly, dear. Just look at this desk—it's piled with work that must be done. Your uncle's been too kind to me—I can't throw him down.
CLAIRE: I suppose you're right—it is important to him.
TERRY: And to me, too. You have no idea what I'm learning by association with him. Why, on folklore, he's the foremost authority of the age. And this library and museum he's collected of ancient customs and beliefs would drive any student mad with envy.
CLAIRE: I know—but. I've simply never become very interested in the things that—to you and him seem so important. Don't look shocked, Terry! Why should I become excited, because a lot of stupid savages believed in spells, and magic, and such preposterous things as—as vampires for instance?
TERRY: These stupid savages, dear, were our ancestors—not very far removed.

CLAIRE: But why not just let the modern world forget they had such insane delusions, instead of writing books about them and hunting everywhere for new evidence of their silly practices.

TERRY: For one thing: they may not have been silly practices nor insane delusions!

CLAIRE: You don't mean you believe—

TERRY: No—no—I keep—Of course your uncle and I are mainly interested from a historical standpoint; but we are both persuaded that behind every superstition there lies a grain of truth. Sometimes, by the harnessing of obscure—but very real forces—that grain has been cultivated to tremendous proportions. Those forces are what men called "magic."

CLAIRE: But science says—

TERRY: Science too readily denies that which it cannot explain. It cuts the knot, but leaves it still untied.

CLAIRE: If I thought there was any truth in some of those ancient ideas— Ugh! It gives me the shivers.

TERRY: *(Laughs)* Don't worry—the only magic we have around here is the sort you practice. And by your uncanny charms you've succeeded in getting the thoughts of a serious scholar entirely off his work.

CLAIRE: Then you will take me for a drive?

TERRY: Come on. But there'll be no romancing this evening young lady! I'll have to wade into this desk after dinner and make up for lost time.

(Automobile comes to a halt outside.)

CLAIRE: *(Laughing)* It's your own fault if I take you away—you made me love you with your youth and beauty.

TERRY: *(Seriously)* Do you really love me, Claire?

CLAIRE: Uh huh. Oh, I'm so happy, Terry. *(Quickly)* Let me go and come on—it's much more fun in the car, where you try to kiss me and watch the road at the same time.

TERRY: I won't do that long—we'll find a parking place!

(Outside door opens.)

FARNUM: *(Distant)* Thank you, Hawkins—thank you.

CLAIRE: Uncle!

FARNUM: *(Outside)* Oh Terry! Terry where are you?

TERRY: Excuse me, dear. Coming, Dr. Farnum!

CLAIRE: There goes my drive.

FARNUM: *(Outside)* Oh here you are Terry! My hat, Hawkins. No, not this package—it's precious! Terry, my boy, come back in the library.

	(Coming up.) Just wait till you see what I have in this package.
CLAIRE:	Uncle Malcolm—why did you have to come home just at this moment? Now, I'll never get him out of the house.
FARNUM:	*(Surprise)* Claire, my darling—what's the matter?
TERRY:	*(Laughing)* I had just been tempted from the path of duty—for a drive.
FARNUM:	Good thing for you—beautiful day—you work too much inside. But wait till you see what I have in this package, Terry—we'll spend all afternoon on it.
CLAIRE:	Oh! Have you had your lunch, Uncle?
FARNUM:	Lunch? No, no—no time for trifles.
CLAIRE:	You're going to take time! You'd never eat if I didn't stand over you.
FARNUM:	Really, Claire, darling—
CLAIRE:	I'll have Anna get you something.
FARNUM:	Only vegetables—no meat, remind her!
CLAIRE:	She's cooked here long enough to know you're another dietary Bernard Shaw. Now show Terry what's in your package quick, for when I come back he's going out with me.
FARNUM:	That—that girl just runs me, Terry. You see what you're getting into when you marry her.
TERRY:	*(Laughs)* She runs me now.
FARNUM:	*(Laughs)* But she's right! I need lunch. And you need air, Terry. But wait till you see what I have in my package!

(Package unwrapped.)

TERRY:	Where did you get that??
FARNUM:	He he...thought it would make your eyes open!
TERRY:	Lord! It's one of the most astonishing wood carvings I've ever seen!
FARNUM:	Isn't it perfect? Thing seems alive.
TERRY:	Ye—es. I'm glad it isn't—it's positively repulsive.
FARNUM:	He he...that's what the woman said at the little curio shop I found it in—she was glad to get rid of it. Isn't it marvelous? I got it for twenty dollars—only twenty dollars.
TERRY:	About sixteenth century, I should say—the work is too fine for an earlier period. Where did it come from originally?
FARNUM:	They didn't know at the shop—they received it in a mixed shipment of odds and ends from France. The woman in charge called it "The Man-Beast."

TERRY:	That's as fitting a name as any. But it's different from most half-human, half-animal figures like the centaurs and satyrs. Why it's man and beast at the same time!
FARNUM:	That's what fascinates me so. And have you ever seen such an expression of cruelty as the artist carved into that face?
TERRY:	No—it's bestial—obscene. This image was probably used in devil worship—perhaps in connection with the Black Mass.
FARNUM:	Yes—undoubtedly a figure out of demonology. And you've noticed the base is carved with cabalistic symbols?
TERRY:	I noticed that at once. But, aside from the pentagrams, I don't recognize any of them.
FARNUM:	Nor I. That is going to be our task, my boy—to find out their source and meaning. Ah, it's been months since I've had a real problem like this!
TERRY:	Say—we'll have a splendid time!
FARNUM:	I thought you'd be delighted! The books I want are upstairs in my study. Come, son.
CLAIRE:	*(Coming up.)* Uncle—your lunch is ready.
FARNUM:	Just one minute, my dear—I'm taking Terry—
CLAIRE:	Not one second! You haven't eaten—and you mustn't keep Anna waiting—and you're not taking Terry anywhere!
FARNUM:	But, my dear—
CLAIRE:	No!
FARNUM:	Oh—these women—
CLAIRE:	*(Curiously)* What's that you have in your hand?
FARNUM:	Claire—I must show you! The most remarkable carving—a find! Here, hold it carefully—don't drop it. He he...the woman at the shop wanted to get rid of it! She said—
CLAIRE:	Take it away!
TERRY:	Claire??
CLAIRE:	*(Frantic)* Take it away! Take it out of my hands! Quick!!
TERRY:	Yes, dear! I have it! Darling—what's the matter?
CLAIRE:	*(Dazed)* It—it seemed suddenly to move—as though it were alive—and I couldn't let it go.
FARNUM:	My dear?
CLAIRE:	Put it away—out of my sight! It's the most evil obscene thing I've ever looked at!
TERRY:	Darling—what's come over you? Why—that's funny.
FARNUM:	What's the matter with you?

TERRY:	There is something strange about this little figure to the touch.
FARNUM:	What do you mean? I've just carried it all the way from New York.
TERRY:	It may be only when it's held a certain way.
TERRY:	Let me have it!
TERRY:	Take it like this—with both hands—here—and here. There is a slight resistance when you let it go.
FARNUM:	Hmm—the wood seems—soft.
CLAIRE:	And there's a—a pulsation underneath.
FARNUM:	It's illusion—crazy illusion!!
CLAIRE:	Put it down on the desk—don't hold it any more, Uncle. Put it down—please!
FARNUM:	Certainly—if you're going to be childish. By golly—it doesn't want you to let it go! There. Terry, if I can read those symbols, we may be on the verge of a great discovery!
CLAIRE:	*(Gasps)*
TERRY:	Darling?
CLAIRE:	Look! On the wall! That shadow!
FARNUM:	Shadow??
TERRY:	I see what she means, sir—no light in this room should cast a shadow there!
FARNUM:	That of the image is the only one there!
CLAIRE:	And it seems more than shadow—it's so huge—life-like—as though it were something real, half-man-half beast!

(Music: mysterioso.)

SCENE II

(Dinner scene. Occasional clatter of silver and dishes.)

FARNUM:	*(Peevish and irascible, in contrast to previous scene.)* I've had enough of this, Claire! Once and for all, I'm not going to let that image out of my possession—much less destroy it! This dinner is atrocious! *(Calls)* Hawkins! Salt! There's no flavor in anything tonight.
HAWKINS:	Yes, sir—here, sir.
CLAIRE:	Then if you will insist on investigating it, uncle—bring it down in the library and work with Terry. Don't stay up in your study alone, as you have all afternoon.
FARNUM:	Terry has his own work to do. And what does he know about cabalistic symbolism?
TERRY:	Your uncle's right dear. And I think you are making a mountain

out of a mole hill. Some trick of light undoubtedly caused that queer shadow—

CLAIRE: And some other trick imposed on our sense of touch, I suppose—all three of us!

TERRY: Yes, dear. I think the novelty of its excessive ugliness imposed upon our imaginations. You thought you felt something strange, and by suggestion, fostered the same illusion in your uncle and me. You'll agree that's a practical explanation, Doctor.

FARNUM: *(Shortly)* Yes.

CLAIRE: *(Doubtfully)* I—I suppose you're right—Yet, this afternoon, you said that behind every superstition there was an underlying truth. Someone once believed that little wooden demon had power—

TERRY: *(Laughs)* Now, dear, you've furnished the explanation of your primary illusion! That rather rash remark of mine was fresh in your memory.

CLAIRE: That may have had something to do with it. You haven't noticed anything more—strange—about it, uncle, since you took it upstairs?

FARNUM: No. Let's drop the subject. Oh—I can't make this food taste like anything! *(Calls)* Anna! Mrs. Hoffman! Bring me that cook, Hawkins! Mrs. Hoffman!!

CLAIRE: Uncle??

ANNA: *(Outside)* Jah—jah—I vas coming!

(Door opens.)

You vas calling me, Doctur?

FARNUM: Yes. What's the matter with your dinner? It's rotten!

ANNA: Rhotten—de dinner??

CLAIRE: No, Anna—there's nothing the matter with it. Uncle—

FARNUM: You keep out of this. These vegetables—they taste like hay!

ANNA: *(Simply)* Vhat do you eggspect from spinach und carrots? Und dey iss alvays vat you vant.

FARNUM: That'll be enough of your impertinence!

CLAIRE: Uncle Malcolm—you've never—

FARNUM: I'm running this! Either you prepare me something fit to eat hereafter, Mrs. Hoffman—or I get another cook!

ANNA: So?? Den dots joost what you can do! For twenty years haf I cooked for de besdt famblies und—

FARNUM: That's enough—get out!!

ANNA: Jah—you pet I gedt oudt! *(Going)* I pack ride now und leave diss blace!!! My dinner iss rhotten! Oh!!

(Door slams.)

CLAIRE: Anna—wait!

FARNUM: Sit down!

TERRY: Dr. Farnum!

FARNUM: If you two don't like the way I do things you can get out, too! Pay this woman, Claire—and get a new cook tomorrow. Hawkins, can you prepare a steak?

HAWKINS: Steak, sir??

FARNUM: Steak—rare!

HAWKINS: Yes, sir.

FARNUM: Do it—and bring it to my study!

(Chair scrapped back.)

CLAIRE: Uncle—you can't eat red meat! Your diet—

FARNUM: I'm hungry! Do as I tell you, Hawkins! *(Going)* I'm going upstairs.

HAWKINS: Yes, sir.

CLAIRE: Terry— what's come over him?

TERRY: He's always been so gentle—I never saw him act this way before.

CLAIRE: He was perfectly beastly! His eyes looked wild—feverish—You don't think he's ill?

TERRY: I hardly know what to think.

HAWKINS: Shall I prepare a steak—rare—for the doctor, Miss?

CLAIRE: Certainly no—He's been a confirmed vegetarian for years. I'll be responsible, Hawkins.

HAWKINS: Very well, Miss.

CLAIRE: I must go out to the servant's quarters and appease Mrs. Hoffman— she can't leave after being with us so long.

TERRY: I'll go with you.

(A savage growl.....distant.)

CLAIRE: What was that?

TERRY: Sounded like an animal.

(Dog howls outside.)

(Laughs) Oh, it was old Pete growling! The chauffeur probably left him chained to his kennel again and he's making a complaint.

CLAIRE: *(Doubtfully)* It might have been a dog Pete's size, but—that growl seemed to come from upstairs.

(Dog howls.)

TERRY: No question about that being Pete.

(Dog howls with fear.)

Say, there's something the matter with him—let's see!

CLAIRE: Come on!

(Door thrown open.)

TERRY: He's not tied—there he goes across the lawn towards the servant's quarters!

CLAIRE: That's not Pete—it's too big,

(A howl closer.)

               And he is chained to his kennel! Look.

TERRY: Something has frightened him. Pete!!

(Distant...screams.)

CLAIRE: Terry!!

ANNA: *(Distant)* Ach!! Help! *(Screams)*

CLAIRE: It's Anna!

TERRY: Something's happened! I'll see—you stay here!

CLAIRE: No—don't leave me! Anna! Anna! We're coming!

(Running feet.)

TERRY: The door's open—let me go alone!

CLAIRE: No! Here comes Hawkins and John!

VOICES   *(Out of breath.)* What is it, Mr. Corbett? What's the mater?

TERRY: I don't know yet! Here!

CLAIRE: *(Screams)* Terry!

TERRY: God!

HAWKINS: She's dead!

TERRY: Her throat ripped open!

CLAIRE: *(Screams)* Terry—Running across the lawn!

TERRY: The animal we saw before!

CLAIRE: It's like that image—like a human beast!!!

(Music)

SCENE III

FARNUM: I—I fear I can add nothing to your investigation, lieutenant. As my niece has already told you, I was lying upstairs unconscious while this terrible thing transpired.

CLAIRE: Terry—Mr. Corbett here—had to burst open his study door. We—we were afraid whatever it was had attacked him, too.

LIEUT: And you say this strange animal the rest of you saw disappeared in the direction of the house here, Mr. Corbett?

TERRY: It was running in this direction, lieutenant. Then Miss Farnum fainted, and I didn't see where it disappeared.

LIEUT: Hmm—butler and chauffeur aren't very clear on that point, either. Miss Farnum's description of it is rather extraordinary—half-human-half-animal.

TERRY: It—it was quite dark. We couldn't—

CLAIRE: But Terry—We both—

TERRY: Dear—

LIEUT: There's no doubt it was an animal of some kind—or a maniac. I'll have the asylums and zoos checked up first thing in the morning. But the only throat wound I ever saw similar to that on the victim was made by a wolf.

TERRY: *(Pause)* Yes—I, too, have thought of that.

CLAIRE: This creature ran on all fours, like a wolf—but it was too big. It was—

FARNUM: Pardon me. But if you have no further questions to ask me, lieutenant—I am very faint.

LIEUT: No, no—That's all. Thank you, Dr. Farnum.

CLAIRE: Can I help you to your room, Uncle?

FARNUM: No thanks, my dear. Hawkins, will—

HAWKINS: Here, sir.

FARNUM: Goodnight—all of you.

ALL: Goodnight, uncle...Goodnight Doctor...etc.

LIEUT: I guess there's nothing more to be done—unless you can think of anything further you have neglected to tell me, due to the natural excitement.

CLAIRE: *(Slow)* Terry—

TERRY: There is nothing further, lieutenant.

LIEUT: Then we'll let the matter rest until morning. Lightning is hardly apt to strike twice in the same place, but I am leaving one of my men on the grounds however for your protection.

TERRY: Thank you. I'll show you to the door, lieutenant.

LIEUT: Much obliged. Come on, Fallon.

FALLON: Yes, sir.

TERRY: This way.

LIEUT: Goodnight, Miss Farnum.

CLAIRE: Goodnight.

LIEUT: 'Night, Mr. Corbett.

TERRY: Goodnight, lieutenant. Sergeant.

FALLON 'Night.

(Door closes.)

CLAIRE: Terry—you wouldn't let me speak about the image.

TERRY:	Shh. No, dear—they would have merely laughed at you. And it's ridiculous! For—forget that image.
CLAIRE:	No. While my uncle lay upstairs unconscious, that thing in his study—
TERRY:	This frightful affair has unnerved you—you don't know what you're saying!
CLAIRE:	Terry—look at me! You believe the same as I do that that wooden figure—
TERRY:	No.
CLAIRE:	You do. And through your work—your studies—you have an idea what that repulsive little figure represents. You know—or think—it has some supernatural power!
TERRY:	No!
CLAIRE:	You do! Tell me, Terry! I'm afraid!
TERRY:	There's nothing to tell—nothing to fear—only—Wait here! I'm going to get that image from your uncle's room!

(Music)

SCENE IV

CLAIRE:	He wouldn't give it to you. I heard you talking.
TERRY:	He—he's irritable, as he was at dinner. He's locked himself in his bedroom and won't let me in.
CLAIRE:	And that—thing—is locked in with him.
TERRY:	Yes—Let's go back downstairs, dear.
CLAIRE:	I suppose we may as well. I—I went into his study while you were talking to him through his bedroom door. Terry, on the table where that little image had stood, there is a stain—like blood.
TERRY:	Dear, your nerves are completely frayed by this horrible night. Won't you go to bed and get some rest?
CLAIRE:	No, no—how could I? Let's go outside—in the air—and think.
TERRY	A walk about the grounds may do you good. Come on.
(Door opens.)	
CLAIRE:	The air smells fresh—it's good after—
TERRY:	I'll leave the door open behind us. Hawkins has probably gone to bed.
CLAIRE:	There's the policeman standing over there, that the Lieutenant said he'd leave.

TERRY: The sight of anything so prosaic and twentieth century looking as his nightstick and brass buttons should calm your fears about—

CLAIRE: It doesn't. Terry, we simply must find some way to get that thing out of uncle's room.

TERRY: I'll manage it in the morning.

CLAIRE: But morning may be too late. That thing is wicked, evil! You fear it too—and won't admit it to me! You know as well as I—that thing is death!

TERRY: I'll get it in the morning, dear—destroy it—I promise you. There's nothing to fear tonight. The Lieutenant was right when he said lightning never struck twice in the same place!

(Dog howls.)

CLAIRE: Terry!

TERRY: Pete!

(Dog howls.)

CLAIRE: That's the way he howled before when—

TERRY: Good god!

CLAIRE: The beast! The man-beast!!

TERRY: It's running toward that policeman!

CLAIRE: His back is turned—He can't see it! *(Shouts)* Officer!! Officer!!

TERRY: *(Shouts)* Behind you, man! Your gun—quick!

OFFICER: *(Distant)* I see it!

CLAIRE: *(Screams)* Terry—it's turned back—this way!

TERRY: It's after us! Run!!

CLAIRE: It's coming too fast!!

TERRY: Get behind me—here! Your gun, man—for God's sake, shoot!!

(Two shots.)

CLAIRE: Oh!!

TERRY: He hit it!

OFFICER: *(Distant)* Stay where you are! Out of the line of fire!!

CLAIRE: He hit it again—it staggers!

TERRY: It's only wounded. Shoot again—it's getting away!

OFFICER: Watch where it goes—I've gotta reload!

TERRY: Stay here with him, dear!

CLAIRE: No! Terry—it's going in the house!! Uncle!!!

TERRY: Come on, officer!

OFFICER: I'm with you!

CLAIRE: Up those stairs!

(Running feet.)

OFFICER: I hit it bad—it's left a trail of blood!
CLAIRE: Uncle! Uncle Malcolm!!
TERRY: Gad! The blood drops lead to his room!
CLAIRE: And his door is open!!
OFFICER: Let me go first, Miss—with the gun! *(Pause)* Jees!!!
CLAIRE: *(Screams)*
TERRY: Dr. Farnum!!
CLAIRE: It's killed my uncle!!!
OFFICER: But where did it go? The bloodstains end but the beast ain't here!
TERRY: Claire—darling—come away!
CLAIRE: *(Sobbing)* No.
OFFICER: Wait! No animal has killed this man—he's been shot!
CLAIRE: That image—it's clutched in his hand!
TERRY: Yes—and the blood trail ends at his side.
(Music)

SCENE V

CLAIRE: Terry, you know the explanation of this awful thing—you must tell me!
TERRY: Yes—you'll have to know now.
OFFICER: And if there is an explanation, I want it! I couldn't have shot this man. You saw that thing outside—it wasn't human.
TERRY: But the blood trail it left ends here. Yes—you shot this man.
OFFICER: Then he wore a disguise—and that ain't here!
TERRY: Yes—it's there—still clutched in his hand.
CLAIRE: That image!
OFFICER: That—that's a statue of the thing we saw!
TERRY: It's a little more than that, I'm sure—now. Look.
CLAIRE: The figure opens!
OFFICER: Like a box!
CLAIRE: There's something in there!
TERRY: Yes—something he just had time to replace before he fell.
OFFICER: What is it?
TERRY: Don't touch it! I think it's a girdle of human hide. Have you ever heard of were-wolves?
CLAIRE: Were-wolves—men transformed by witchcraft into beasts!

TERRY:	In every country, in every age, men have believed in their existence. It was thought the transformation was effected by means of a magic belt of human skin.
OFFICER:	You mean to say that belt in there—
TERRY:	Yes. In a measure, it's properties passed through the image itself—as when we felt we held a living thing; as when, before your uncle discovered the secret opening in this figure, he became dissatisfied with his diet of years. The were-wolf's appetite can only be appeased with flesh. And, when once the transforming belt is girded on, it can only be satisfied with blood.
OFFICER:	Let me see that belt!
TERRY:	Look out!
OFFICER:	I didn't mean—I'll pick the box up!
CLAIRE:	The girdle fell out—I've got it.
TERRY:	Claire—don't touch that girdle!
CLAIRE:	Why—I can't let go!
TERRY:	Don't touch it with your other hand, too—it completes the circuit! For God's sake—Claire!!
CLAIRE:	(A growl.)
OFFICER:	Jees! She's changing!
TERRY:	Keep away from her—she'd kill you now! I'll try to hold her from behind! I've got her!
CLAIRE:	(Screams and growls like a beast.)
TERRY:	Get that belt! Not with your hands—use those fire tongs! Quick! She's trying to get at my throat! She'll kill me! Claire!!
OFFICER:	I got it—struck it from her hands!
TERRY:	Thank God! Claire! Claire!!
CLAIRE:	(Sobbing) Oh Terry—Terry—I knew what I was doing—and couldn't help myself!
TERRY:	There, there, darling! That's what happened to your uncle.
CLAIRE:	Throw that thing in the fire!
TERRY:	With the tongs, officer!
OFFICER:	Yes sir. Look at the flames catch it!
CLAIRE:	And that image with it—that image of the demon who gave it power!
OFFICER:	It's in—the fire's taking it!
(A beastly cry.)	
	Jees—hear that!
CLAIRE:	Terry! Look—that shadow rising from the fire!!

TERRY: But now it's only a shadow; the power of the human beast is at an
                end!

(Music)

EPILOGUE

NANCY: He he he...an th' moral o' this yarn is: that th' nex' time yew young
                know-nuthins buy yerself a belt t' keep yer pants up, ye wanta
                make good an sure it ain't made outa human hide—an alser, that
                it dunt cum in too fancy a box. Well, we got bizness t' ten' tew
                now, Satan. 'Portant bizness, Satan—near midnight, Satan. He he
                he he...

(Musical theme.)

From Dawn To Sunset
Monday, February 15, 1932

(Musical theme.)

ANNOUNCER: Since the first long distant dawn of thought, man has peopled the night with terrors. Of the thousand shapes of fear his frightened eyes have seen in shadows, old Nancy and her black cat, Satan, have a thousand tales to tell. And they should know whereof they speak, for they—so the credulous believe—are themselves allied with the Powers of Darkness. If you are not afraid of ghostly things, come now to that ramshackle little house in ancient Salem where this strange pair reside, and hear with us another haunting mystery of the uncanny and the weird.

(Music swells...wind whistles...)

PROLOGUE

NANCY: He he he *(CAT meows)...* 'nother stury these here young knownuthins want we shud tell em, Satan—yes'r...he he...'nother yarn they're askin fer 'bout things t' ha'nt their dreams.

TOM: We didn't ask for anything like that, Nancy!

DICK: You misunderstood us. We thought you might have a nice cheerful story to tell us for a change.

TOM: You must know some cheerful ones, Nancy—even though you've never told us any.

NANCY: He he...sure we knows cheerful ones—Satan an me knows all kines! A long time we were alearnin' em. Hunner an twen'y fi' year old, I be t'day—yes'r, hunner an twen'y fi year ole! Did yew say "much obleege" t' these young good-fer-nuthins fer th' nice buthday presint they brung us, Satan?...*(CAT meows)...*Acourse ye did! I mighta known ye wouldn't fergit yer manners—yew an me allus makes it a p'int ter be perlit—even t' nubudies like these here.

TOM: Yes, Nancy.

NANCY: 'Sides, this here presint they brung us t'night is reely better'n th' one they give us fer our buthday last week...he he. Whut kine ov a cheerful stury'll we tell em, Satan—t' show our 'preciation?...(*CAT*) He he...that's a good idee! A fine idee!!

DICK: What has Satan suggested this time, Nancy?

NANCY: Oh, he's thought o' jest th' thing fer t'night! Th' full moon outside reminded him...(*CAT*)

TOM: Moon? Then it's going to be a romantic story?

NANCY: He he...that's it, Satan—a romantick stury!...(*CAT*) Douse that candle—blow it out! 'Snicer sittin in th' dark t' heer r'mantick yarns like this. Now draw upter th' fire an gaze inter th' embers. Tha's right, Satan—jump up here b'side me...(*CAT*) Gaze inter th' embers while I stirs m' caldron. Up t' th' North we're atakin' ye t'night—up t' th' North, in Canadee. In a fine ottymubill, we're agoing' with a happy boy an gurl, who's aridin' in th' moonlight— th' romantick moonlight! He he he...th' romantick moonlight! He he he he...

(*Music*)

SCENE I

(*Automobile effect. High powered car.*)

AGNES: Don't you think you'd better drive a little slower, dear—and watch out for a marker? We may be on the wrong road again.

DONALD: (*Laughs*) I don't believe there can be any more wrong roads. Since we left Three Rivers, we must have—have tried every one in Canada.

AGNES: (*Laughs*) We've certainly explored the Province of Quebec thoroughly. I'll say—thanks to my genius for always turning left when I should turn right and right when left is the proper direction. But it's been fun—I've never driven all night before.

DONALD: It must be nearly dawn.

AGNES: (*Yawning*) The rooster'll start to crow at any minute now.

DONALD: Don't you think you'd better lie back in the seat and have a cat nap? If we ever do find Claude's chateau, you'll be too sleepy to see it—

AGNES:	I'm not sleepy— much. Besides, as long as we have to be out like this, it would be a shame to nap and waste what's left of this gorgeously romantic moonlight. *(Giggles)*
DONALD:	Romantic moonlight. I'm surprised at you—an old married woman becoming romantic.
AGNES:	*(Giggles)* A matron—of a month.
DONALD:	It's been a wonderful month, hasn't it? Sweetheart—
AGNES:	Now, now, keep both hands on that wheel! Oh, look, dear—we are on the right road! There's that big yellow barn the man told you to watch for.
DONALD:	At last! Then if the fellow knew what he was talking about, Claude's chateau is only a mile from here! We'll make that mile in nothing flat.

(Motor accelerates.)

AGNES:	DONALD! Not any faster!!
DONALD:	*(Laughs)*
AGNES:	Oh! After promising your brother we'd be here three weeks ago, you would try to make up our delay by gaining thirty seconds now!
DONALD:	We are a mere three weeks late. But if Claude expected promptitude from a man on his honeymoon, he's crazy.
AGNES:	A bachelor like him—Claude isn't apt to make allowances for that. You know that you should have written him of our change of plans.
DONALD:	Then he would have been sending me telegrams and letters. I didn't want anyone to know where we were—I just wanted to be entirely alone with you.
AGNES:	I've been completely lost in a world of our own.
DONALD:	I hate to come out of it.
AGNES:	I wish we never had to come out of it.
DONALD:	Sweetheart—
AGNES:	The WHEEL, Donald! Watch your wheel!!!
DONALD:	Oh yes—yes! 'Salright.
AGNES:	*(Faintly)* Oh—my heart! *(Suddenly)* Dear—I think that's the chateau beyond those trees!
DONALD:	That stone tower answers Claude's description all right.
AGNES:	I'm sure this is the place. Turn in the driveway, dear. Every window in the house is dark, of course. This is a fine hour to be arriving anywhere!

DONALD: Nevertheless, we're arriving—right now.

(Motor stops.)

AGNES: At last—

DONALD: Sit still—I'll try and wake someone up.

(Honks motor horn....Stop at her speech.)

AGNES: Donald—stop! You'll wake up everyone for miles around. Get out and ring the door bell.

DONALD: Alright. You want to stay in the car?

(Car door opens.)

AGNES: No—I'm stiff from sitting so long. Dear—there's someone who isn't in bed and asleep. Over there among those trees—Or do I just see shadows?

DONALD: No—that's a man, and—

AGNES: Is that a woman with him?

DONALD: Can't make out. Might be another man, wearing a long overcoat or—robe of some kind. Say—this fading moonlight and the shadows of those trees play funny tricks.

AGNES: Donald, does—does it seem to you that those people are—are floating over the ground instead of walking?

DONALD: Yes—funny. *(Laughs)* Oh, Lord—we're both so tired we're beginning to see things! *(Calls)* Hey! Hello back there! Is this Claude Grahame's place?

CLAUDE: *(Very distant.)* Yes! Hello!

DONALD: Dear—It's Claude! Wait here.

AGNES: Donald—Dear, don't leave me!!

DONALD: I haven't seem him for over a year. Come with me.

AGNES: No—Not back there among those trees!

DONALD: Why?

AGNES: I don't know. Besides, he's coming here to us.

DONALD: What's he doing, prowling around out here this hour of the night—or morning?

AGNES: Who—whoever was with him has gone back into the woods. Darling—look at Claude's face in the moonlight.

DONALD: He must have been ill—he's white as—

AGNES: And his eyes—they gleam like a cat's. There's something about him—I don't want him to come close!

DONALD: My brother?

AGNES: No! Come away, Donald! Come away! Don't let him come near me!

CLAUDE:	*(Coming up.)* Agnes! Agnes!!
DONALD:	Claude—What is the matter with you?
AGNES:	Keep him away from me—Don't let him touch me!
CLAUDE:	Agnes!
DONALD:	Claude? CLAUDE!
AGNES:	*(Screams)*
DONALD:	Let her go! Are you mad? Take your hands from her or—
CLAUDE:	*(A snarl.)*
(A blow.)	
DONALD:	*(Cry of pain.)*
(Falling body.)	
AGNES:	Donald! Claude, you've knocked him down. *(Terror)* Don't touch me. No, No—let me go! Let me go!
CLAUDE:	Blood!
AGNES:	*(Screams)*
(Cock crows.)	
CLAUDE:	I come! *(Going away.)* I come! I come!
AGNES:	*(Faint)* Ohh!
FRANCOIS:	*(Distant)* What de mattair dere? What ees? *(Pause)* What de mattair dere, I say?
AGNES:	*(Weakly)* Help! Whoever you are, come quick! Donald—Donald, Claude's gone. *(Alarm)* Donald, are you—
DONALD:	*(Dazed)* What—Oh! Agnes, you're—
AGNES:	I'm alright. Suddenly, he let me go and ran.
DONALD:	Must have knocked me out. I—
FRANCOIS:	*(Coming up.)* What ees? What have happen here?
AGNES:	My husband's brother—gone suddenly insane. He seized me, and when my husband tried to stop him, he struck him.
FRANCOIS:	Where dees man now?
AGNES:	Why—he ran into those woods, I think. He—he just disappeared.
DONALD:	Mad—ill—No telling what he may do. He's my brother—I must go after him!
AGNES:	No, no Donald—he'd kill you!
DONALD:	Are you a servant here?
FRANCOIS:	I am concierge.
DONALD:	Then you can tell me what has happened—if this madness has just come upon him—Mister Grahame, your employer—the owner of this estate—
FRANCOIS:	Monsieur Grahame?

DONALD: Yes, I'm his brother.

AGNES: It was he who—

FRANCOIS: You—you do not see Monsieur Grahame tonight?

DONALD: Yes! Can't you understand?

FRANCOIS: Sainte Vierge—

AGNES: Why are you crossing yourself?

FRANCOIS: I fear dees ting happen when de moon she's full. De dead hav come back to walk alive!

DONALD: What are you saying? What—

FRANCOIS: Monsieur Grahame, your bruddair—Two week ago he died.

(In the distance a cock crows.)

(Music)

SCENE II

DONALD: Monsieur Daignault, all day I have been trying to find someone in this village who would talk sensibly to me. As my brother's attorney here, I expected—at last—some help from you.

DAIG: I am sorry, Monsieur, that I must reiterate the fact: your brother die two weeks ago.

DONALD: Yet, last night, both my wife and I saw him—heard his voice— felt his hands upon us! Don't you, like everyone else we've talked to, say we saw the dead alive as a vampire. It was my brother, I tell you! A mad man but a man of flesh and blood!!

AGNES: Donald—please—

DAIG: Monsieur Grahame, we here in French Canada are bequeath traditions, beliefs, knowledge from an older land which you Americans have never learn, or have forget. Madame, your husband's brother, when he seize you in his arm last night—what was it his attempt to do?

AGNES: He tried to—to kiss me.

DAIG: On the throat?

AGNES: Yes. Oh, it wasn't as though he was your brother, Donald—or even a—a man. There was something—horrible—about him!

DONALD: He was mad—that's all.

AGNES: It isn't all. It was something more—worse—and when first we saw him with that other—that figure in the cloak, who disappeared—You, too, noticed how they seemed to glide—to float through the air—instead of—

DONALD: We had been driving all night—our eyes were tired—

DAIG: Pardon Monsieur. When your assailant released you, Madame—fortunately unscathed—it was just at the break of dawn.

AGNES: Yes. We heard a rooster crow—it seemed to be—He seemed to receive a summons.

DONALD: What is all this leading to? Any madman might have done the same erratic thing!

DAIG: Monsieur Grahame, you have been show the certificate of your brother's death. Did you note the cause?

DONALD: Yes—pernicious anemia. A disease impossible in one of my brother's constitution—another reason I know he is not dead! Who is this Dr. Hugo, who signed that certificate? I have tried all day to find him at his home.

DAIG: You will soon meet him. I have invite him here.

DONALD: I want to meet this Dr. Hugo! And I want you, Mister Daignault, to secure a court order for the opening of the tomb which bears my brother's name.

DAIG: That shall be done at morning, even had you not request it; because, Monsieur Grahame, there are certain things that must be done to destroy that body which, in death, becomes a —vampire's.

DONALD: What?

AGNES: Donald!

DAIG: I have said it—vampire! Of your brother's death, you do not yet know all. Upon his throat was a little mark—blue: the sign of the vampire kiss. From there his blood had been slowly drawn until there was no more in his vein. And they who are kiss by the dead alive, Monsieur, become themselves the dead who live.

DONALD: You—you can't expect us to believe such rot as that?

DAIG: When tomorrow is open your brother's tomb, you will see I do not lie.

DONALD: What do you mean?

DAIG: That, though he has been bury fourteen day, his body will be whole—there will be color in his cheek. In this village, we have seen such thing before—too many time.

DONALD: I am going to that cemetery! Your court order can come later or not at all—I'm going to open that grave which bears my brother's name!

DAIG: No, no, you cannot now!—The night is here!

DONALD: I'll leave you at the hotel, Agnes. Come on.

DAIG: Wait, Monsieur—It may be death to go at night. From dawn to sunset those undead lie helpless in their graves; but from dark to morning they can walk in human form, searching for the blood their lust demands!

DONALD: So now I will find the tomb empty. Mister Daignault, you should have attempted to deceive me with a less childish story. I shall find that tomb empty because my brother is alive! Come, dear.

(Door opens.)

DAIG: Monsieur, I beg—you must not do this thing tonight!!

DONALD: No? Watch me!

(Door slams.)

DAIG: *(Low)* Go on then, fool—and see what you will find.

(Music)

SCENE III

HUGO: How fortunate we met so opportunely as you were leaving our good friend, Daignault's, Monsieur Grahame! As a physician, my experience among cemeteries cannot fail to exceed your own— and, while I do not approve of your intention, I feel it is my duty to assist.

DONALD: *(Shortly)* That is very good of you, Dr. Hugo.

HUGO: Not at all. As I was not available when you tried to reach me at my home today—I feel that now I owe you something for your wasted time. I doubt if you would find anyone else to accompany you here at night.

DONALD: Where is my brother's tomb? In this moonlight, things look different than in the day.

HUGO: I will show you.

DONALD: You are not credulous like Mister Daignault, Dr. Hugo.

HUGO: Dear me, no! As I have already assured you, Monsieur, your brother died of a perfectly natural complaint; and that which you saw and felt last night—Well, if it was not a product of tired nerves and imagination, you may have been deceived in the darkness by a man bearing a resemblance to your brother.

DONALD: You assure me that my brother is dead—really dead? Not the horrible thing that Daignault said?

HUGO: You have had time to think about your conversation with him— to wonder if strange things cannot be true.

DONALD: He—he seemed to believe it so thoroughly—it did make an impression, I guess. Oh, it's these graves all about—this shadowy moonlight!

HUGO: Perhaps you would rather return to your hotel and your charming wife—and reconsider your decision to violate a tomb.

DONALD: No. I'm going through with it—I must find out!

(A metal door breaks open.)

DONALD: Doctor—this door has already been forced!

HUGO: Flash your light inside!

DONALD: A coffin—open on the floor! Come! AHH!

HUGO: Your brother, Monsieur.

DONALD: A wooden stake driven through his breast—his head here—has been severed from his shoulders!

(Music)

SCENE IV

DONALD: Who could have done that thing? Who could have done it?

HUGO: Who can say? Graves have been violated thus before in this village! Monsieur Daignault's views are shared by many here. And by the sharpened stake and severed head, they believe a vampire is destroyed.

DONALD: It was too horrible—hideous—my brother.

HUGO: But now you know that he is dead.

DONALD: But was he dead last night—

HUGO: He died two weeks ago. Had you not been in such haste to leave the tomb, I would have been glad to point out the natural proofs of dissolution.

DONALD: How can you talk like that? Like a ghoul—a—forgive me, doctor. Your profession has made you careless of death. And you have been very kind. Here is my hotel. Goodnight.

HUGO: Let me accompany you to your room. You have had a shock, the nature of which your little wife should not suspect.

DONALD: No—she mustn't know.

HUGO: My presence at your meeting may enable you to dissemble better. Permit me to hold the door.

(Door opens.)

DONALD: Thank you. Wait!

HUGO: Yes?

DONALD: In the shadow of those trees—up in the street—that shrouded figure! It is like the one who disappeared into the woods last night at the chateau. The one I saw with Claude.

HUGO: *(Chuckles)* You are beginning to believe with the violation of his tomb, that your brother died from a vampire's kiss? *(Pause)* In that case the original menace would be still at large, of course.

DONALD: I—I don't know what I believe.

HUGO: It's rather a shame to shatter a growing faith in the marvelous but as your shrouded figure emerges more fully from those shadows, I recognize him as a village character. I—I can see him plainly now. He's—

DONALD: An—an old man. A monk.

HUGO: No, that monastic habit he wears is purely an affectation—in the distance, it does look like a shroud. But come—I am still holding the door for you.

DONALD: Excuse me—I am sorry.

(Door closes.)

HUGO: Not at all.

DONALD: Our room is one flight up, Doctor.

HUGO: The stairs are back here. I probably know this hotel better than you do.

DONALD: Who is that man you say is a village character?

HUGO: His name is de Moreive. He has lived here many years. How he occupies his time nobody knows, for he is seen only occasionally, and then always at night. That fact is bound to confirm your growing suspicion—as the conventional vampire must keep to his tomb by day. *(Laughs kindly.)* Forget it, my son—you have had a harrowing experience, and a strange one; but we live in a natural—not a supernatural—world.

DONALD: I am very grateful for your common sense, Dr. Hugo. There is my door—down the hall. What we found at the cemetery—

AGNES: *(Distant) (Scream)*

DONALD: Agnes!

AGNES: *(Distant)* Donald! Donald! Help—help!!

(Continue, ad lib.)

DONALD: Coming, Dear! Coming!

(Door knob rattled.)

HUGO: Locked!

DONALD: I'll break it!

(Flimsy door burst open.)

            Agnes! Darling!!

AGNES: Donald! Oh—Donald!!

DONALD: What is it, dear? What's the matter?

AGNES: Hold me tight, dear! Put on those lights—I can't be here in the dark!

HUGO: Permit me.

(Click of light switch.)

DONALD: Why did you scream? Tell me—quick!

AGNES: I fell asleep waiting for you—Such a horrible dream!

DONALD: Oh—a nightmare!

AGNES: But frightful—awful! Something came in that open window—a shrouded figure like we saw last night. I was powerless to move. It came and kissed me on the throat—a kiss as cold as death.

DONALD: Doctor Hugo! It was not a dream! On her throat is a small blue mark!

(Music)

SCENE V

HUGO: Here in my house, Madame, I am sure there will be no recurrence of your most unpleasant nightmare.

AGNES: I know you're right, Doctor—it was just a dream. I think you've even convinced Donald now that a blue mark on one's throat is more likely to be a simple bruise than—

DONALD: Yes, dear—yes! Of course that's all it is.

AGNES: But I couldn't have remained in that hotel.

HUGO: And you are doing me a favor by coming here—it will be good for a lonely old man to have youthful faces around his house. But it is very late—I shall leave you to yourselves. Goodnight.

AGNES: Goodnight, Doctor—and thank you again.

DONALD: We are more than grateful, Dr. Hugo.

HUGO: Tut tut. Oh—lest I forget! I am retired from active practice, as Daignault may have told you, and am engaged upon a work of medicine which confines me to my study during the day. We shall meet tomorrow evening. Goodnight.

BOTH: Goodnight.

(Door closed.)

AGNES: Dear, you won't worry about my silly dream any more? Our common sense tells us Dr. Hugo is right.

DONALD: He must be right. Of course he's right. I'm going to close these windows.

(Windows closed.)

AGNES: You're not sure something did not come in the room at that hotel.

DONALD: Of course I am, dear, but—it's chilly—I feel more comfortable with the windows closed.

AGNES: What are you looking for in your suitcase?

DONALD: A book I have in here—I want something to read. Here it is.

AGNES: What else are you taking out?

DONALD: Nothing. Go to bed, dear.

AGNES: It's your revolver. Why are you putting that in your pocket?

DONALD: Merely because it's a dangerous thing to leave in a suitcase.

AGNES: You are afraid—you've been fibbing to me to kill my fear.

DONALD: No, no—what could I be afraid of? Vampires—dead creatures out of folklore, who live by sucking blood from human veins? It's too preposterous—too awful! Such things couldn't be!

AGNES: No—they couldn't!

(Tap at window.)

Donald—that face at the window!! Your pistol!!

DONALD: Here!

AGNES: Quick! It's going away!

DONALD: Let me get this window up! It's gone to the side where I can't see!

(Window thrown up during speech.)

AGNES: There—it's going down the wall!

(Three shots.)

Donald—it's the thing in the shroud!!

DONALD: No—that's the habit of a monk! It's disappeared around the house—I'm going after him!!

(Door thrown open.)

AGNES: Donald, come back! Bullets can't harm the dead alive! Come back, Donald! Don't leave me—I'm afraid!! *(Gasp. Shriek.)* Donald —it's in this room with me! Keep away! Keep away! Donald!!! *(Scream)*

(Music)

SCENE VI

DONALD: When I reached the grounds, the thing—I have told you of, had disappeared. It was then I heard my wife scream.

BREAUX: And when you return at once?

DONALD: Dr. Hugo here was with her, sheriff. She was unconscious, and on her throat the blue mark had grown.

HUGO: *(Impatiently)* You forget the overwrought condition of Madame's nerves, Monsieur. She may have stumbled—fallen—

DONALD: Dr. Hugo, I know you are trying to calm my fear; but you know as well as I, that mark is not a bruise.

DAIG: Fear no more, Monsieur—in the convent where we have just left Madame, no evil thing may enter.

BREAUX: This face at the window, you are sure, my son?

DONALD: Yes, sheriff. It was the man I saw on the street last night with Dr. Hugo.

DAIG: De Moreive—we shall soon know.

BREAUX: Forty years ago, he was seen first within this village—about that time, the dead alive begin to kill.

DAIG: And who has ever seen him between dawn and sunset? When the vampire must sleep within its tomb.

BREAUX: Here is his house—the tomb may lie within.

DAIG: And now the sun is in its sky, we shall find him helpless. And I have brought the sword and sharpened stake.

HUGO: This is ridiculous—you talk like children.

DAIG: That we shall see.

(Tries door.)

The door is locked. Come—burst it open!

BREAUX: Together!

DONALD: Wait! A key is turning from the other side!

(Heavy door opens.)

DAIG: Sacre!

BREAUX: Sainte Vierge! De Moreive!

DONALD: He!

MOREIVE: Good morning, gentlemen. You seen surprised at finding me at home.

(Music)

SCENE VII

MOREIVE: It was good of you gentlemen to humor me in my desire to tell my story here in Dr. Hugo's house.

HUGO: Now that you are here—proceed.

DONALD: Yes—your explanation!

MOREIVE: Very well, Monsieur Grahame. To begin—it was I who last night appeared outside your window.

DONALD: I knew it!

MOREIVE: Wait! Had you allowed me then to give the warning, which was my purpose, madame, your wife, would have been spared a second frightful terror.

DONALD: You came to warn?

MOREIVE: By the only way I could—the trellis clinging to the wall. In my zeal, I did not consider you might have a pistol. But thanks to your poor marksmanship, I can give my warning now.

DAIG: You speak strange, Monsieur de Moreive.

MOREIVE: And I shall speak more strangely still. Monsieur Breaux, will you see that no one leave this group until I finish?

HUGO: You are in my house, Monsieur. What is your meaning?

MOREIVE: That, Dr. Hugo, you are about to learn. Attendez! For forty year, you have know Guy de Moreive in this village as "the man who walk at night." You do not know why. It is because I lose my only son by the kiss of the dead alive. It was then I become "the man who walk by night"; for at night the undead hunt—and I hunt them. It is I who open tombs. I, who rid this village of its curse— almost—for there is ever one I hunt and cannot find—until, from a curtained window in this house, I see a shrouded figure creep at sunset and return at dawn.

(General murmur.)

HUGO: This house? You lie! The man is mad!

MOREIVE: Am I, Dr. Hugo? Then tell me in which graveyard lies the body of— your wife?

(Question & murmur.)

HUGO: I won't listen to such ravings! Get out of my house! Put him out, someone. I can't stay here—*(Going away.)* I have work to do— work in my study.

MOREIVE: After him! Up those stairs! It is there her tomb is hid!!

(Running upstairs.)
(Murmur)

HUGO: *(Slightly distant.)* Keep back! Keep back! I won't let you take her from me!

DAIG: He has a pistol!

DONALD: Mine! I dropped it in the hall last night.

HUGO: I'll shoot the first who makes a step! You shall not take her from me! For fifty years I've kept her here—my wife—I love her! What if she is of those you call the dead alive? What if she does kill that she may live undead forever? It is her curse. I love her, I tell you. No, you'll never touch her heart with your sharpened stake! For the first to move shall die!

MOREIVE: After him. The demon must be destroyed!

HUGO: Wait. Keep back!

DONALD: He's—there's only one unexploded cartridge in that pistol. For my brother and my wife, I'll take the chance.

HUGO: Keep back, Grahame! Keep back!

DONALD: No!

(Single shot.)

DAIG: He turned it on himself!

BREAUX: Through his own heart!

DONALD: Dead!

MOREIVE: Never mind. Break down that study door!

DONALD: Together!

(Bodies crash against door on cue. At third crash it opens.)

DAIG: Once more!

MOREIVE: Again!

(Door crashes open.)

DONALD: A coffin!

BREAUX: A woman! In a shroud!

DAIG: Young as when she died!

MOREIVE: With blood upon her lips!

DONALD: *(Murmurs)* Agnes.

MOREIVE: At last—the fiend—the dead alive—helpless in the light of day! Monsieur Daignault, give me that sword and sharpened stake!

(Music)

EPILOGUE

NANCY: He he he...*(CAT...)* That's th' end of our romantick story, Satan *(CAT...)* Ye'll havt' go hum now. Pleasant dreams. He he he he...

(Music)

Alonzo Deen Cole

Snake House
Monday, April 4, 1932

(Musical theme.)

ANNOUNCER: And now, seated before the huge stone fireplace in their weird little house of eery sounds and shadows, old Nancy and her black cat, Satan, again await us with another ghostly tale of fear and mystery.

(Music swells...wind whistles...)

PROLOGUE

NANCY: He he he...(CAT) Hunner an eight yeer ole, I be t'day—yes'r, hunner an eight yeer ole. Much bleeged fer th' burthday presint ye brung us. These here chocluts with th' soft insides iz fine. Have 'nuther, Satan? (CAT) Choclut creems iz th' best kine o' candy there be w'en ye ain't got no teeth left—hunner and twen'y tew yeer ole, I be t'day—yes'r, hunner an twen'y tew—(CAT *interrupts.*) What say, Satan? (CAT) Did I already tell em? He he...what ye know! (CAT) Huh? (CAT) (*Angry*) Whose mem'ries gitten' bad?? (CAT) Weel!! Shet up! No cat o' mine's gonna set thar on his hine legs an' tell a body a hunner an sixteen yeer ole she dunt know whut she's sayin'!! (*Snorts*) Huh!! (CAT) Hmm-yew better 'pologise! My mem'ry's gittin—(*Hastily*) Dunt go 'way, Satan! Cum back here—I ain't reely mad at ye—I 'pologise tew!! (CAT *purrs*) He he...nice Satan—perty Satan. Whut in th' worl's gittin' inta us, talkin' back at one 'nuther like this? (CAT) I shud say not we wunt do it agin! Well, douse that candle, yew young know nuthin's! Whut ye keepin' us waitin' fer when we're gonna tell a stury? Ah—now it's nice an' cozy heer—good an' dark like it oughta be fer a cheerful leetle yarn like this. Now draw upta th' fire and gaze inta th' embers. T' Noo Yawk City I'ma takin' ye t'night—t' th' perty paths o' Central Park we're goin' fust...he he! And then I'm takin' ye t' Snake House—SNAKE HOUSE! He he he he he...

(Music)

SCENE I

DOT: *(Exasperated)* Garry, you must have picked up the germs of insanity during the three years you've spent in Europe. I've never been asked to do such a ridiculous thing as this.

GARRET: Please Dot. I know how crazy it must seem to you—but stick along—just a few minutes more.

DOT: No—I've been the helpful obedient sister long enough. If you insist on spending the remainder of our first morning back in New York following a strange woman through Central Park, you can do it alone.

GARRET: Please don't leave me. Wait! I can't follow her alone—she or a policeman might mistake me for a masher. And I must keep her in sight—I must!

DOT: Honestly, Garry—

GARRET: Please humor me. I can't explain this feeling I have—it's the strangest I've ever experienced. You know I don't claim to be psychic, but from the moment we saw that girl at the park entrance, something has absolutely impelled me not to let her get out of sight.

DOT: Well! I thought I knew you, but—You're sure that impelling "something" isn't merely the fact that she's a very pretty blonde.

GARRET: Don't talk nonsense. If I had any idea of flirtation, you don't suppose I'd want you along?

DOT: No—your best beloved sister might cramp your bachelor style. But when you begin to get psychic and have "hunches"—

GARRET: I haven't a hunch—it's a certainty. That girl ahead is going to need me—and if I lost sight of her now, I'd never forgive myself. Come on—while you've argued we've fallen behind.

DOT: Alright. How is she going to need you? And for what?

GARRET: I don't know. Hurry up.

DOT: *(Musingly)* She has acted strangely since you first noticed her. Why do you suppose she's doubled around this same path so many times?

GARRET: It looks as though she has some definite objective, yet can't make up her mind to go there. She seems dazed—frightened. She's stopped again! Every time she's approached that huge rock, she's hesitated the same way.

DOT: Hmm. This time, though—she's going over to the rock.

GARRET: Yes. Look at her—she's mortally afraid of something, Dot!

DOT: But who is there in sight to be afraid of—you, I, those nursemaids with their children or—?? What are you going to do now? You can't follow her when she's sitting still!

GARRET: Walk slowly past—we'll find a bench where we—I can't let her out of my sight—I can't. I must stay close to her now—very close. A voice keeps whispering that inside my head. Don't laugh, Dot—I'm in deadly earnest. It's the most uncanny sensation I've ever known.

DOT: Garry—

GARRET: Wait. I've never known anything like this before—it's as though another voice was talking within my mind. It's uncanny.

DOT: Well—if you weren't my own brother—

GARRET: Look! What's she holding out her arms to? Now she's trying to get away from something! But there's nothing there, Dot!

VIDA: *(Distant scream.)*

GARRET: She screamed. Help her—quick!

VIDA: *(Distant)* No, no—I can't! I'm afraid! *(Scream)*

GARRET: Hurry—she's fallen!

DOT: A fit of some kind!

GARRET: Miss! Miss! It's alright.

DOT: She's fainted!

GARRET: Do something for her, Dot! I'll pick up a taxi—get her to a doctor—

DOT: Wait! She's opening her eyes!

VIDA: *(Moans)*

DOT: She's only a child. What is it, dear—what's the matter?

VIDA: *(Dazed murmur.)* He—he did come to me here—and I was afraid again.

DOT: Who came to you, child?

GARRET: Not a soul came near you here!

VIDA: Yes—my brother was here—my brother who's been dead two years.

(Music)

SCENE II

DOT: *(Comforting)* There—there. Feel better now?

GARRET: Another cup of hot tea. *(Calls)* Harmon!

SERVANT: Yes, sir.

VIDA: No, thanks—I'm alright now. It—it was so good of you to take me away from that crowd that collected and—and bring me here to your home.

GARRET: Not at all.

VIDA: I've acted so foolishly.

DOT: Don't talk about it—don't think about it—your nerves are all unstrung.

VIDA: I—if you don't mind listening, I'd like to talk about it. You've been so wonderful and—I must tell someone! I can't know all by myself any longer!!

DOT: Dear—dear—

GARRET: Lie back comfortably in that chair and talk all you want to. Oh—you may go, Harmon.

SERVANT: Yes sir.

VIDA: *(Pause)* Naturally, you think I've just experienced an hallucination of some kind. I didn't believe in ghosts, either—two years ago. But back there in the park—in broad daylight—my dead brother came to me.

DOT: But, my dear—

VIDA: I know you didn't see anyone. Neither did I—except—depressions made in the grass by invisible footsteps—then I felt this presence—and, inside my brain, I heard his voice.

DOT: Purely imagination—

GARRET: Wait, Dot—don't interrupt her!

VIDA: You—you don't think I've just been dreaming—you can realize that one may hear a silent voice?

GARRET: Yes—

VIDA: We—we were very close, my brother and I; although he was much older—there was twelve years between us. He used to take me to that rock in the park to play when we were children. Right after he was killed—three years ago—I went there and felt his presence as I did today. I—I knew then he wanted to tell me something—but I was afraid and fainted. Because he loved me and didn't want to frighten me he never came again until last night.

GARRET: You had the same experience last night.

VIDA:	Yes—last night he came to our home—in darkness. I wonder if you can understand. I love my brother—just the same as when he was alive—but his presence is so cold—so—I'm afraid—afraid—*(Cries)*
DOT:	Dear—dear!
GARRET:	Please go on.
VIDA:	Well, because I was such a coward last night, he went away again. Then, I wanted to have him near me—to have him talk to me—I thought if I came to our rock, where I had seen—felt—him with me first, he might return. So this morning I drove in alone—I live on Long Island with my aunt—I was afraid to go to the rock then—and when I finally did—Oh, I hope he understands—I hope he forgives me for being such a coward! But he's so cold—so cold! I'm terrified!! *(Hysteria)*
DOT:	Garry—call Dr. Mason! Her nerves are in frightful shape!
GARRET:	Yes—at once!
VIDA:	No—please don't! I'm alright now—and I've put you to so much trouble—I must go.
DOT:	Nonsense! Do you think we'd allow you to leave—in the condition you're in?
VIDA:	But—
DOT:	Here—sit down again. We'll talk of something else—get your mind off this—this—Oh, my dear, your own common sense must tell you it couldn't have happened!
GARRET:	Excuse me, Dot. I believe it did happen—and I believe we should talk about it.
DOT:	Garry, you can't seriously—
GARRET:	Yes. I told you I was impelled by something to follow this young lady through the park. You thought my imagination was being imposed upon. You know better now.
VIDA:	You followed me?
GARRET:	Yes. Normally, I'm a very practical minded individual, as my sister here will admit—I think. But something very strange has occurred to you and me. Only—if the dead have the power of communication—your brother would naturally come to you. But why should the force we both felt be exercised on me—a stranger?
DOT:	Everything has happened so suddenly—we're still strangers. It might be more convenient if we knew each others names. I am Dorothy Conrad—this is my brother Garret.
VIDA:	Conrad? Garret Conrad? It seems I've heard your name from my

brother. I am Vida Hathaway.

GARRET: Your brother was Victor Hath—

VIDA: Yes. You were with him in Europe.

GARRET: Yes—three years ago. It—it was his voice that spoke inside my brain. I didn't know he was dead—I thought his letters just stopped coming because—Well, you know how the friends are we meet abroad—Americans in a strange land—one comes home and forgets. We only knew each other six months, but—

VIDA: He never forgot. He spoke of you a lot—he said you and Dr. Zander were the finest men he'd ever known.

GARRET: Dr. Zander—he was your brother's assistant—the chap who worked with Victor on his snake serums.

VIDA: Yes—they built Snake House together—that was Victor's name for his laboratory, you know. Oh, to think you are—were—my brother's friend.

GARRET: How did he die?

VIDA: A snake.

GARRET: Careless, I suppose—he knew them too well. You never met Victor Hathaway, Dot—he was, perhaps, the world authority on reptile poisons. But the anti toxins which he discovered to save others, should have—

VIDA: He was not killed by a venomous snake—he was crushed to death.

GARRET: Crushed?

VIDA: By a boa constrictor—one Dr. Zander imported from South America for some experiments. No one ever knew how it happened. Victor was alone—they just found him there. I—they wouldn't let me see him—at all.

DOT: Garry, don't make her talk about it anymore. Poor child, she's— Miss Hathaway—I'm going to call you, Vida—let me take you to my room, where you can lie down awhile. You simply must pull yourself together after your shock and—

VIDA: Thank you, but—

DOT: Please. We're not altogether strangers, as we first thought. Come—

VIDA: I must be going home—

DOT: Later. Garry will drive you home.

GARRET: Do as my sister asks, you, please.

VIDA: Will—will you stay with me, Miss Conrad? I—Oh, I want Victor to come to me—but I'm afraid—afraid!

DOT: I'll stay with you. Come, dear.

GARRET: Just one moment! Then I shan't bring up the subject again.
DOT: Garry—
GARRET: Do you mind, Miss Hathaway?
VIDA: No, I want to talk to you—I feel that you will help me.
GARRET: You say you believe Victor tried to tell you something shortly after—he was killed.
VIDA: Yes—after.
GARRET: But because you were afraid, he never came again until last night?
VIDA: No. Oh, I must know what he's trying to tell me—I must find courage to listen to him!
GARRET: Two years elapsed between his—his visitations. Did anything occur yesterday—concerning your happiness—that would make him risk frightening you again?
VIDA: Why—
DOT: Garry—please!
GARRET: Dot, I happen to know how much Victor Hathaway loved his sister. Aside from what she has told us, some force I cannot understand tells me his spirit wishes to protect her from some danger. I don't care how crazy this sounds—I know it—I believe it! He wouldn't frighten her as he did last night and again today unless there was a reason that made him careless of her terror. Did anything occur yesterday, Miss Hathaway, which might concern your happiness?
VIDA: Why—why, no—except—but I did that because of Victor—because he would have wished it.
GARRET: What did you do? *(Pause)* Do you mind telling me?
VIDA: No—o—last evening I promised Dr. Zander, Victor's dearest friend, that I would be his wife.

(Music)

SCENE III

(Door softly closes.)
DOT: *(Quietly)* She's fallen asleep.
GARRET: Oh—I didn't hear you come back, Dot.
DOT: Poor little thing—perhaps I shouldn't have left her even now. She held on to my hand until—
GARRET: I want you to keep her here until I come back.
DOT: You're going out?

GARRET: Yes. Dutley is bringing the car—I'm driving out to the Hathaway laboratory—the Snake House. I want to meet Dr. Zander.

DOT: Garry—you weren't talking merely to humor her hysterical notions—you really believe her brother—

GARRET: Yes. Don't you?

DOT: No—it's too uncanny—too preposterous!

GARRET: Dot, as you took Miss Hathaway from this room, I saw invisible footsteps sink into this carpet—something took me by the hand and pressed it—something cold—cold as death. I saw no form—I heard no voice—yet I was not alone—and I knew what I must do.

DOT: You've gone insane! From the moment you laid eyes on that girl you haven't been yourself! *(Pause)* Why must you go to that laboratory—to meet this Dr. Zander?

GARRET: I must make his acquaintance—I must see the place where Hathaway was killed—I must find out why Victor doesn't want her to marry his dearest friend.

(Music)

SCENE IV

ZANDER: *(Very hearty manner.)* This is a pleasure—a pleasure, Mr. Conrad! Any friend of Victor's couldn't help but be welcome here.

GARRET: I was afraid I might be intruding, Dr. Zander.

ZANDER: My dear fellow, it's a privilege to know you. His friends are my friends. We were very close, he and I—closer than brothers. And you've just learned of his death?

GARRET: Yes.

ZANDER: A great tragedy—a terrific tragedy! And what a loss to science! Had that man lived twenty years longer, Mr. Conrad, I truly believe there wouldn't be a reptile poison left in the world without its antidote.

GARRET: Fortunately, Doctor, you are left to carry on in his place.

ZANDER: Yes, yes—in my poor way. But with all my consuming love for our work—our labors for mankind—I'm not the scientist Victor was. Oh, I admit it—you'll find no jealousy or false ego in my nature, Mr. Conrad! Besides, since his passing, I've had too much outside business to attend to—I'm Victor's executor, you know—he left quite an estate.

GARRET: I knew he was fairly wealthy.

ZANDER: Yes—and the entire administration has fallen on my shoulders—not that I'm not glad to do it for his sake! But you natural business men have no idea how difficult it is for us retort and microscope chaps to suddenly have to dip our noses into stocks, bonds and real estate. But I've learned my way around during the past year, and I'm making his sister a wealthier woman every day. You haven't met his sister?

GARRET: I knew he had a sister.

ZANDER: I must have you meet her some of these days—charming girl. My fiance, incidentally.

GARRET: You are to be congratulated.

ZANDER: Thank you. We'd have been married long ago—but you know how it is when a poor man marries a rich woman—people talk. But—ha ha—anyone who knows me well would tell you I haven't the practical sense to be mercenary. My soul is in science, Mr. Conrad—money doesn't mean a thing to me. But you business men don't understand us dreamers. Say, that's a beautiful stone you have on your finger—must be worth twenty thousand!

GARRET: You guessed rather accurately, Doctor. You are wearing some nice diamonds yourself.

ZANDER: These? No bad, are they? Presents from Victor—tokens of our friendship. I never wore them until after his death—no one knew I had them. Now, I feel I owe it to his memory to show them off. Have a cigar? Don't be afraid—they're the very best.

GARRET: No thank you. I seem to have caught you on a holiday—I understood from Victor that you and he employed about thirty men on your staff.

ZANDER: I've cut all that down since I've been alone—useless expense for the results secured. I do all the laboratory work now, and merely keep two snake men to handle my pets. Say—perhaps you'd like to see some of our little wrigglers!

GARRET: If it wouldn't be too much trouble.

ZANDER: Trouble—for a friend of my friend?? My dear chap, come this way. Victor and I built this place ourselves. That is—I planned it and he paid for it...ha ha—just pure science for me We have a snake house here that any first class zoo might envy. Here's the door—it's the only way in.

(Heavy door opens.)

ZANDER: Isn't this a palace for the little darlings? But they deserve it.
           People are afraid of snakes—I like em. Cost fifty thousand alone,
           this room—that skylight up there set us back fifteen—ha ha, I
           mean Victor—back fifteen. No side windows at all—all light
           from the top—snakes must have sun.

GARRET: What a lot of specimens you keep—you must have twenty sepa-
           rate dens.

ZANDER: Twenty three around these walls—full of little beauties—cobras,
           rattlers, copperheads, adders—ha ha—Nice place to be left alone;
           if that plate glass didn't keep them from us. With that door closed
           back there, there's no way out but the skylight twenty feet above.
           But don't waste time looking at those little fellows—over here's
           "Baby"!

GARRET: I didn't see—that isn't the same boa that—killed Vic—

ZANDER: Yes—that's the one. You wonder why I keep him, I suppose.
           Victor would have wanted me to. It wasn't the constrictor's fault—
           it's his nature to crush. And anyway, Victor was the sort who
           forgave his enemies. Wonderful chap—wonderful chap!

GARRET: Yes. Somewhere I've read, Doctor, that constrictors crush only
           when they're hungry.

ZANDER: That's approximately correct—after they've had a meal they're
           too logy to move until digestion is completed—particularly in
           confinement. Yes, yes—you could go in Baby's cage now and
           walk all over him—he'd never move. Ha ha—he had a lamb—a
           live lamb for his breakfast this morning—and how he enjoyed it!
           I never miss his feeding time—it's marvelous to watch.

GARRET: I imagine.

ZANDER: In the interest of science—of investigation.

GARRET: Of course. Dr. Zander, knowing snakes as he did, how do you
           suppose Victor ever put himself in that monster's power?

ZANDER: I've often wondered. Became careless, I suppose—we get to know
           these fellows so well we forget their danger.

GARRET: That might be reasonable enough in handling the smaller, venom-
           ous reptiles, who are equally deadly at all times—but with a boa
           constrictor, there seems only one cardinal point to remember.
           How could Victor have been so foolish as to go into that snake's
           den, unless he was helpless in the state we now see him?

ZANDER: Victor didn't go into the den that anyone knows of. He and the
           boa were out here when we found them.

GARRET: Out here?

ZANDER: Yes—in this rotunda. You see, when we built this place, we never planned on having a constrictor for a tenant—when we got him, our dens were too small to permit him proper digestion of anything larger than a rabbit.

GARRET: I don't understand.

ZANDER: Big snakes like this swallow their prey whole after crushing the bones. This fellow's nearly twenty feet long. Ha ha—considerable distance from his throat to his stomach—and anything large can't go down easily when he's coiled. So we put his live food out here and open his den. I watch from that balcony up there—it's marvelous—marvelous to see!

GARRET: How do you open his den?

ZANDER: You see that lock on the framework—the plate glass slides up on rollers. Plenty of time to get out that door or up to the balcony while he uncoils. Besides, if there's an animal in sight, he won't attack man.

GARRET: Yet he killed Victor.

ZANDER: It's a mystery, Mr. Conrad—a great mystery. But so long as the police investigators and the coroner's jury couldn't fathom it, I hardly think we'll be able to.

GARRET: No—I suppose not.

ZANDER: Nobody but the snake and Victor's spirit knows what happened— I scarcely think either one will ever tell us.

GARRET: I wonder—I wonder. Do you believe spirits of the dead ever communicate with those left on earth, Dr. Zander?

ZANDER: The dead communicate with the living?? Ha ha ha!

GARRET: Ridiculous idea, isn't it. I've just noticed something strange here— this concrete floor is quite damp. Doctor, where do you suppose those footprints are coming from?

ZANDER: Footprints? God—something's walking I can't see!!

GARRET: They're leading someplace—let's see where.

ZANDER: No, no—get out of here!

GARRET: Take your hands off me! They're going to that ladder—to the balcony!

ZANDER: Get out of here! Get out of here! Stop—I have a pistol! You go up that ladder and I shoot!

(Music)

SCENE V

(Automobile motor.)

GARRET: Well—what is one to do when there's a pistol at his head? I accompanied Dr. Zander out of the snake room. When we reached his office, he blustered awhile, then tried to laugh the whole thing off—and I left him.

DOT: Why didn't you tell me all this when you returned that night, instead of waiting until now—a whole month later? Why, he might have shot you, Garry.

GARRET: Hardly—when you shoot a man, his death can't very well be blamed on a snake. And there was no use of telling anyone until I was prepared to act.

DOT: Darn these sharp curves. Please drive slower, Garry. You think he is responsible for the death of Vida's brother.

GARRET: I'm just as certain of it as I am that he has gambled away most of her fortune on Wall Street—only I can prove his peculations now, and have yet to prove him guilty of murder.

DOT: And you believe there's something on that balcony which will prove it?

GARRET: Yes.

DOT: But if there was any evidence there that night, he's had a month to remove it.

GARRET: I know he hasn't.

DOT: How do you know?

GARRET: As I knew I must follow Vida in the park that day. And this afternoon I mean to find it. We'll soon be at Vida's house. Don't say anything of what I've told you. It will be a good hour before Zander arrives—I asked her to invite him at four o'clock—then, in his presence, I mean to tell her about his administration of her estate and show her the proofs I've collected. I have arranged for the police to be there then. When he is in jail, I shall investigate that balcony.

DOT: What if he suspects you've discovered his operations in Wall Street? He may know you're laying a trap for him?

GARRET: He doesn't suspect! I know Dot!

(Motor sounds.)

DOT: Garry—you almost wrecked us stopping short like that. What's the matter? What are you turning the car around for?

GARRET: We won't find Vida at her home—Zander does suspect—she's on her way to Snake House!

DOT: Garry! Garry?

GARRET: I know. Her brother's hand is on this wheel with mine—and she's in danger.

(Music)

SCENE VI

(Motor car.)

DOT: You were right, Garry. Vida's car is standing at the Snake House door.

(Car halts...car door opens.)

GARRET: But she's not in it. She's inside that Snake House with—wait here!

DOT: No—I'm going with you! *(Surprise)* Garry—there she is—coming out of the house!

GARRET: Vida! Vida! Thank God you're safe!

VIDA: Garret—Mr. Conrad—what's the matter?

GARRET: How long have you been here?

VIDA: I just arrived.

GARRET: What made you come here when you were expecting us at your home? I told you how important—

VIDA: But you wanted me to be sure and have Dr. Zander there. He telephoned that he had been detained in the city and was coming back by train because his car had broken down. He asked me to come here and drive him back to the house for the meeting you wished. He should be along any moment.

GARRET: He's not in the house now?

VIDA: No.

GARRET: But we saw you come out of his laboratory door—But, of course, one of the snake men was on duty to let you in.

VIDA: No—there's no one about at all. When I rang the bell and there was no answer, I tried the door and found it open. I went in because—well, after all this was my brother's house.

GARRET: And it's deserted—Dot, the chance I've wanted! Vida, can we get into that snake room before Dr. Zander get's here?

VIDA: The snake room?

GARRET: Don't ask questions now. I want to go up in that little balcony in there.

VIDA: I have Victor's key to the snake room if the door is locked.

GARRET:	Good! Dot, you stay here in the car—if you see Dr. Zander coming, sound the horn three times!
DOT:	I wish you wouldn't do this Garry. If he should discover you there, after, after threatening you with a gun before—
VIDA:	Threatening? Who?
GARRET:	Never mind. It's up to you to see he doesn't discover us, Dot. Come Vida—let me in that snake room.
VIDA:	You don't like Dr. Zander—There's something you know about him you haven't told me!
GARRET:	Yes—I know many things about him—one of them is, he's never going to marry you.
VIDA:	Why—
GARRET:	Because you're going to marry me.
VIDA:	Garret—Mr. Conrad??
GARRET:	I'll explain that later too—at length.

(Door opened.)

	We won't need your key—the door's unlocked.
VIDA:	I've never been in this room since—
GARRET:	I forgot. Go back outside with Dot and wait.
VIDA:	No—I'd rather stay with you.

(Door slams shut.)

GARRET:	What was that?
VIDA:	The door closed behind us.
GARRET:	Oh. I'll open it and wedge it so it stays open—rather uncomfortable among all these snakes with a closed door behind us.

(Tries door.)

	It's locked!
VIDA:	Locked?
GARRET:	Spring catch, I suppose. Give me that key of yours.
ZANDER:	*(Distant)* I don't think you will find that key of much service—and that door is the only way out of a rather uncomfortable room.
VIDA:	Eric—Dr. Zander?
ZANDER:	Good afternoon, my love—and Mr. Conrad. You had never mentioned that you were acquainted with each other.
GARRET:	Come down from that balcony and unlock this door.
ZANDER:	Why don't you join me up here on the balcony? It's very safe—and you were so anxious to investigate this little perch.
GARRET:	Why have you drawn up the ladder that was here?
ZANDER:	For reasons of privacy. You see, I was expecting this little call.

VIDA: You expected—but you—

ZANDER: I made that telephone call to get you here. And I knew you'd follow her—you meddling fool. Do you think while you've been prying into my affairs, I haven't pried in yours? Well, now we'll see what good all your precious evidence will do you—the evidence that would send me to jail.

VIDA: Send him to jail, Garret?

ZANDER: So he hasn't told you yet? He was going to make a grand stand play when I came to your house this afternoon? Too bad I've spoiled your show. Of course I took her money, the little fool—that's why I was going to marry her—to cover it up. Now that won't be necessary, for by her brother's will, if she should die, everything comes to me.

GARRET: Her death? What are you going to do?

ZANDER: Show you what you wanted to find on this balcony—the things which Victor found out about too late—the secret controls by which the boa's den is opened while I sit here safe above and watch him feed. Watch!

VIDA: *(Screams)* The boa's den is opening!

GARRET: God!

ZANDER: And he's hungry and free to reach his living prey!

VIDA: Garret! Garret—save me!

(Pounding on door...snake slithers.)

GARRET: Open this door!

ZANDER: Watch him uncoil—he's slow but sure.

GARRET: Dot! Dot! Get help—help!

ZANDER: She can't hear you from here. And when she sends someone to look for you, I'll be miles away with an alibi to prove I was never here. Ha ha...uncoil, Baby—here's your living prey—live animals to crush!

VIDA: It's coming—coming toward us!!

ZANDER: Come, Baby—come and crush!

GARRET: Help—Help—for God's sake open this door!!

VIDA: Garret, the door is opening!

ZANDER: What?

GARRET: Quick—outside!

ZANDER: Let me go—what are you—hands cold as death. *(Screams)*

VIDA: Something has lifted him in the air!

GARRET: Something he can't see!

ZANDER:	*(Screams)*
(A thud.)	
GARRET:	It's thrown him from the balcony.
VIDA:	Into the path of the snake.
GARRET:	And it's got him—its coils are winding round him.
VIDA:	It's crushing—crushing—
ZANDER:	*(Screams)*
GARRET:	God—come away!
VIDA:	That's how my brother died.
GARRET:	Yes. Look, dear—on the balcony.
VIDA:	Victor! At last. I see him!
GARRET:	For the last time—he's waving goodbye—his work is finished here.
(Music)	

EPILOGUE

NANCY: He he he...and that's th' stury o' Snake House—nice, cheerful leetle yarn. Well, we got bizness t' tend tew now, Satan—neer midnight Satan...He he he he he...

Hangman's Roost
Monday July 4, 1932

(Musical theme.)

ANNOUNCER: Now up the familiar weed-grown path we travel which leads to the weather-beaten door of old Nancy and her black cat, Satan. Again we enter their little house of eery shadows—again we gather about the huge stone fireplace there and prepare for another story of ghostly mystery.

(Music swells...wind whistles...)

PROLOGUE

NANCY: He he he...(CAT) Weel, here they be, Satan—cum t' yew an' me fer anuther ov our leetle bedtime sturies. Bet they've missed us while we been vactionin'...he he. Lan' sakes—me an' Satan haz rested s' hard in th' las' tew weeks we're jest all tuckered out. Yes'r—we're 'absulootly tew tired t' even hav a buthday. Much 'bleeged for th' Fourth o' July presint ye brung us though! He he...on holidays a body dunt reely hav t' let herself git older. Hunner an' thutty tew yeer ole I be nex' week, though—dunt fergit t' bring us a presint for that. Weel—douse that candle now, an' we'll be gittin' down t' bizness. Tha's right—good an' dark now—dark, like hit oughter be t' heer our plessunt leetle yarns! Now draw upter th' fire an' gaze inter th' embers—gaze inter em deep an' soon ye'll be with us in England. Gaze inter em deep, an' soon ye'll be in "Hangman's Roost"! He he—that's th' yarn we're tellin' ye t'night—th' yarn ov "HANGMAN'S ROOST"!! He he he he he he.....

(Music)

SCENE I

ELLA: *(A middle aged Texas woman. Very enthusiastic.)* Oh, it's jest the most wonderful ole house I've ever seen! Look at that staircase Walter!

WALTER: *(Her husband. Slow, easy going.)* Doggone! When yew say this place was built, Mr. Adams?

ADAMS: *(An Englishman. Stiff and precise.)* In 1653, according to the records, Mr. Reynolds.

ELLA: Look at them carved balusters an' hand rails of that staircase—an' that balcony that leads from it above! Oh, I gotta have this house, if only fer that staircase alone!!

WALTER: Reckon you're gonna have 'bout anything you want, honey—now we've got th' money t' pay for it. Mrs. Reynolds an' me lived in tents, shacks, an' cheap lodgin' houses for a good many years 'till I brought in them oil wells I told ye 'bout, Mr. Adams—an' now we're gonna make up fer it by havin' mansions in Noo Yawk, San Antone, an' over here in England.

ELLA: *(Delightedly)* An' we're gonna commute between! My grandmother was English, is the reason I want a place over here—an' I've jest about decided this house is gonna be it.

WALTER: Ye know we made up our minds t' insist on sump'n else b'sides jest carved woodwork an' fancy staircases.

ELLA: But Walter—that real estate man up in Lundon sent us down here 'cause he said this house had jest what we're lookin' fer!

WALTER: I know—but I've heard them real estate fellers don't always tell the eggsact truth. *(Chuckles)* No, sir—when I fork over th' money this place is gonna cost, I aim to have a positive guarantee from the owner. Mr. Adams, when my wife an' I settle down to English country life, we want everything that goes with it—so we've made up our minds not t' buy anything but a real, certified haunted house with a genuine, eighteen karat ghost.

ELLA: *(Giggles)* I gave my husband that idear, Mr. Adams—I got it from readin' them stories in the Sunday magazine sections.

WALTER: *(Laughs)* 'Bout all them Dooks, an' Earls an' Lords over here that has em. Ella an' me are gonna be real aristocrats.

ELLA: *(Giggles happily.)*

ADAMS: *(Gravely)* My London agent informed me of your desire, Mr. Reynolds—that is the only reason I consented to show you this place, which has been unoccupied and off the market for over fifty years. As to a guarantee of its evil reputation, that is—

unfortunately—written rather large in the death records of this county.

ELLA: *(Triumphantly)* That's what the London man told us, Walter!

WALTER: Been some suicides here, I understand.

ADAMS: Yes—"suicides," according to the coroners' verdicts. Since 1792, until my father closed this house against further occupancy, eleven people have been found hanging by a rope from that balcony which Mrs. Reynolds has so much admired.

WALTER: Eleven? *(Whistles)*

ELLA: *(Awed)* From that balcony there, Walter!

WALTER: So that's why the place is called "Hangman's Roost"?

ADAMS: No. It was called that before the first death occurred.

WALTER: Before? What fer?

ADAMS: *(Uneasily)* If—Unless you wish to look over the house further—do you mind if we continue our conversation outside?

ELLA: I guess we've seen everything, Walter.

ADAMS: Then, permit me to open the door a little wider for you, Mrs. Reynolds.

(Heavy, creaking door opened.)

ELLA: Thanks.

WALTER: *(Chuckles)* Doggone, honey—Mr. Adams has been fidgetin' t' get outa here ever since we came in.

ADAMS: This is but my second visit to this house in the thirty years I have owned it—I hope it shall be my last. After you, sir.

WALTER: Much 'bliged.

(Heavy door closed.)

(Calls) Hey, Bob! Gettin' tired waitin'? We won't be much longer!

BOB: *(Distant)* I'm alright, Mr. Reynolds!

WALTER: That kid chauffeur we brought over from the States is jest like a son to us, Mr. Adams.

ELLA: Bob's an awful nice boy. Now tell us why this house is called "Hangman's Roost."

WALTER: Yeah—let's have it.

ADAMS: In 1760, this property came into the possession of a Justice Merrick—a judge of the Court of Common Pleas. Even in the age in which he lived, his name was notorious for the harshness and cruelty of his verdicts. He delighted to impose—and see carried out—sentence of death. How many men and women he sent to the gallows I have never learned, but he was a beast—a monster.

He become known as "The Hangman"—and this, his house, as "Hangman's Roost."

WALTER: Doggone!

ELLA: I swan!

ADAMS: When public opinion finally compelled the authorities to bring charges against him, rather than face certain punishment, he took his own life by means of the rope to which he had condemned so many others. His dead body was the first of the eleven to be found hanging from that balcony in there.

ELLA: Is it him that's supposed to haunt the place?

ADAMS: It is locally believed that the influence of his malignant spirit is responsible for the subsequent tragedies which have occurred here. And it is an undeniable fact that, since his time, ten occupants of this house have been found "hanged by the neck until dead."

WALTER: Doggone, honey! Ain't that a story t' write the folks in San Antone about?

ELLA: It's got everything beat I ever heard of!

WALTER: C'm on, Mr. Adams! We'll drive ye back to yer office—you fix up the deed—and I'll give you a check in full!

ELLA: Then we'll go right back up t' London an' buy all the furniture in sight!

WALTER: An' a couple inteerior decorators t' fix th' place up first class! We'll take the train—it'll get us there quicker. And Bob can stay here t' look after the things we send.

ADAMS: (Constrained) Mr. Reynolds—wait just a moment.

WALTER: Huh?

ADAMS: (Hesitantly) Despite your expressed desired to acquire a—a "haunted house," I gather you have no actual faith in the supernatural.

WALTER: Actual faith?? Good gravy, Mr. Adams, you didn't think we believed in sech things?

ELLA: (Laughing) Lan' sakes—no! We just wanta place with a reputation—an old house with a romantic hist'ry like this one, which'll make some o' them snooty folks back home sit up an' take notice when they hear 'bout us ownin' it.

WALTER: Pertickler them San Antone s'ciety women, whose gran'paws made money 'stead o' their husbands.

ADAMS: I am afraid this is not the house you want. Mr. Reynolds, this property is a white elephant to me—you can have it at your own

	price. But I advise you not to buy it—I warn you not to live in it.
ELLA:	Walter—I think Mr. Adams believes his own story!
WALTER:	That's right, Ella. An' if that caretaker of his can live in there without ghosts botherin' him, I guess we'll make out.
ADAMS:	Caretaker? There's no caretaker in there.
ELLA:	Then who's that old feller we saw upstairs?
WALTER:	Mr. Adams wasn't up there with us, honey.
ADAMS:	You saw a man upstairs?
WALTER:	Yeah—walked up the hall ahead of us an' into a room.
ADAMS:	The—the fourth door from the left of the staircase?
ELLA:	Yes—we thought it was his room, so didn't go in.
ADAMS:	What did he look like?
WALTER:	We only saw his back, but he was a fat old fellow—
ELLA:	Wearin' a kind of old fashioned bathrobe—
WALTER:	An sorta carried his head on one side—like this.
ADAMS:	Gad!
WALTER:	If he ain't yer caretaker, must be a tramp who's made himself a home in this empty house.
ELLA:	Mr. Adams—you're white as a sheet!
ADAMS:	*(Slowly)* The door you mention has been sealed and locked for a hundred years—and a man's head would droop to one side whose neck had been broken by a hangman's noose.
ELLA:	*(Frightened)* Walter!
WALTER:	Huh? *(Pause)* Aw, shucks, Mr. Adams—quit yer kiddin'. *(Laughs)* I'm gonna buy yer ghost, but I'll be darned if I'm gonna believe in it! C'm on, honey.
ELLA:	Yeah. C'm on, Mr. Adams—we're jest rarin' t' go!
(Music)	

SCENE II

(A powerful motor car.)

WALTER:	Next turn an' we'll be at our new home, honey.
ELLA:	I'm so excited! Look out, Walter—you're drivin' on the right side of the road again!
WALTER:	Doggone! Why has these Englishmen gotta have traffic laws jest the opposite t' us civilized Americans? I'll sure be glad when Bob is drivin' this here big car again—a flivver's what I'm usta.
ELLA:	But ain't it grand—all th' things we got now that we've never been

usta? Specially our new house. I'm jest dyin' to get there an' see what the decorators have done to it.

WALTER: They shoulda done plenty in the two weeks time we've give em—an' with all the truck they persuaded me to buy.

ELLA: I never dreamed of ownin' sech furniture as we've been sendin' down from London. Ain't you jest all hot to see it in place? If ye hadn't insisted we wait till everything was finished, I'd been down here with a apron an' dustcap pitchin' in myself.

WALTER: Apron an' dustcap—for a lady aristocrat whose husband has just bought her a guaranteed haunted house!

ELLA: *(Giggles)* Oh, I'm so happy! *(Suddenly)* Look out, Walter—you're drivin' to the right again!

WALTER: Doggone! Sech a country!

ELLA: *(Seriously)* Walter, what do you suppose made all them people hang theirselves from that staircase? You've found out everything Mr. Adams told you 'bout that was true.

WALTER: What makes people commit suicide anywhere? It's just a crazy English idea to mix ghosts up with it. Look how many people has jumped off the Brooklyn Bridge—and no American ever said it was haunted.

ELLA: Bob's an American, an' when he called last night to say the decorators was gone—

WALTER: I'm gonna kid the pants off him 'bout that! A feller his size wantin' us t' jump in the car an' drive right down 'cause he didn't wanta be left alone.

ELLA: He talked awful funny over the phone. After all, he's jest a kid and—well, he's prob'ly listened t' all them stories 'bout the place an'—he ain't parctical an' hard headed like you an' me. Here's the turn, Walter! Oh, I can see our house from here! Ain't it perty, back among them trees? Honk yer horn an' get Bob out t' help ye with these gripsacks.

(Auto horn.)

WALTER: Yeah. Hope all them servants we hired get down here first thing tomorrow like they promised.

(Motor stops.)

Where on earth is that kid? *(Calls)* Hey Bob!

ELLA: He's prob'ly still in bed—You know how he likes his sleep mornin's.

(Prolonged blast of horn.)

WALTER: This oughta rouse him. Here—I'll open the door fer you, honey.

(Car door opened.)

ELLA: Say, Walter—did you tell Bob to give that old tramp we saw in the bathrobe upstairs a couple of dollars before he cleared him out?

WALTER: Doggone—I fergot to tell Bob anything 'bout that tramp at all fer we left. He prob'ly took care of him, though.

ELLA: *(Laughs)* Wasn't it jest too ridic'lous—Mr. Adams sayin' that door we saw the old fellow go inta was locked up an' sealed when, a minute before, he'd told us he'd only been in the house twice in thirty years?

WALTER: Yeah—as though he'd know whether it was locked or not! *(Laughs)* And he tried to make out he was the spook o' one o' them fellers who'd hanged theirselves.

ELLA: Crazy.

WALTER: I'll say! *(Calls)* Hey, Bob!! Doggone that kid!

ELLA: Let him sleep. C'm on, let's go in, Walter—I'm jest dyin' t' see the place fixed up.

WALTER: Alright—c'm on.

(Door latch...door opened.)

                  The door's unlocked! *(Theatrically)* Welcome, me lady, to yer new palatial castle!

ELLA: *(Same tone.)* Thank you, me Lord—I accept yer invitation t' "Hangman's Roost"! *(Laughs)*

(Door closes.)

                  Walter—look how they've fixed things! Oh, I'm so happy!

WALTER: Doggone!

ELLA: *(Screams)* Walter! Walter! Hangin' from that balcony!

WALTER: Good God—BOB!!

ELLA: *(Shrieks)* He's dead!!

(Music)

                                    SCENE III

WALTER: *(Wearily)* Aw, what's the use of askin' me, honey? There wasn't no reason in God's world fer that kid t' do away with himself.

ELLA: *(Her voice breaking.)* He was like our own son—we was gonna give him everything—

WALTER: There, there, honey—no use carryin' on any more. The—the boy's gone. I—I ain't shed no tears since I was a baby, but—When I saw that spadeful of earth fall on his coffin this afternoon—

ELLA: Don't, Walter! I—I shouldn't started talkin' 'bout him again, only—Oh, Walter, do ye think this house had anything t' do with it?

WALTER: No—it couldn't have. I don't care what folks say 'round here—I don't care if them servants all did go back t' London soon's they heard 'bout it! It don't stand t' reason—sech a thing ain't possible!

ELLA: It don't seem so, only—He's the twelfth. An'—an' the night before—he didn't wanta stay here alone.

WALTER: I've thought of that till I'm near crazy. If we'd only driven in—if he'd only given some reason for askin' us to—But there ain't nothin' in this house that coulda made him do it! We been here three days now—it's jest a ordinary house! If there is sech a thing as a evil sperrit, it couldn't hang a man!

ELLA: No—we can't b'lieve a thing like that, but—Walter, we found that door upstairs is locked an' sealed.

WALTER: That old tramp prob'ly left it that way when he cleared out—I'm gonna break it open t'morrow. But a locked door couldn't take Bob's life!

ELLA: No—an' like you say, it's jest a ordinary house—with nothin' here to be ascared of.

(Upstairs a door slams.)

What's that??

WALTER: Door slammed shut upstairs, I guess.

ELLA: Oh. I—I left a couple windows open. *(Pause)* I hope we get some new servants down tomorrow, Walter, It's lonesome-like with just us in this big house.

WALTER: Yeah—two people's kinda little in a great big place like this.

(Distant, flopping footsteps.)

ELLA: Walter—there's someone upstairs!

WALTER: What you talkin' 'bout?

ELLA: Listen!

WALTER: *(Pause)* Hmm—that's funny.

ELLA: Them's footsteps, Walter—sure's yer born!

WALTER: Doggone! Lemme get that big poker here!

ELLA: You're not goin' up there??

WALTER: You bet I am! If there is any funny business goin' on round this house, I'm gonna know jest what it is! *(Going away.)* You stay there.

ELLA: No! I'm goin' with you!! It's up in the hall there!

(Footsteps closer...going away.)

WALTER: I hear it! Switch on them bright lights!

(Light switch.)

ELLA: I got em!

WALTER: There ain't no one here!

ELLA: But there's gotta be! Listen!

WALTER: It's in that locked room! I ain't gonna wait till tomorrow to open that door!

(Forces door with poker.)

ELLA: Walter, keep away from there—I'm scared!

WALTER: 'Salright, honey—stay back where ye are! With this big poker, I'll have it open in a jiffy!

ELLA: No, Walter—NO!

(Door crashes open.)

WALTER: I got it—there she busts!

ELLA: Don't go in, Walter—don't go in!! *(Pause)* Why—the room's empty.

WALTER: Yeah—jest four walls.

ELLA: I'd swore I heard footsteps in here.

WALTER: So would I. Wait a minute! There's an old curtain hangin' here— maybe someone hidin' behind it.

(Curtain torn aside.)

ELLA: No—it was just coverin' a big picture! Walter—the man in the picture! He's wearin' a funny bathrobe jest like that old tramp we seen!

WALTER: *(Slowly)* Yeah. Only, I guess that ain't no bathrobe, Ella—that's what English judges wear.

ELLA: Judges?

WALTER: Yeah—I've seen pictures of em before. An' that black cap he's holdin' in his hand is somp'n they put on when they sentence a man to hang.

ELLA: *(Awed...frightened.)* This—this must be the picture of the judge who—Mr. Adams told us 'bout.

WALTER: I—I kinda reckon it is.

ELLA: What funny eyes he's got—they're so mean lookin', but they— *(Dazed)* Why, I—I can't hardly pull mine away from em.

WALTER: *(Bewildered)* They seem to hold ye, somehow. *(Pause, then abruptly.)* Let's get outa here! Quit gazin' at that picture, Ella! Ella! Come away!!

ELLA: *(Dazed)* Huh? What? Oh. Why, Walter—for a moment I don't think I knew where I was!

WALTER: Let's get outa this room!

ELLA: Yeah—right away! I'm scared in here!

(The flopping footsteps...near by.)

                 Walter!! There's them footsteps again—they're in here with us!!

WALTER: They can't be—there ain't nothin' here!!

ELLA: But they got t' be—I can hear em!!

WALTER: So can I, but—I see it! Lemme get it!!

(Poker strikes bare floor.)

ELLA: *(Screams)* A RAT!!

WALTER: Missed him!

ELLA: Kill him, Walter! Oh, he's big as a kitten!!

WALTER: Where did he go?

ELLA: There he is! Oh—he jumped right inta that picture!

WALTER: There's a hole there—I can see his eyes ashinin'!

ELLA: Get him with yer poker, Walter! Get him—get him!!

WALTER: I—I can't. Somp'n holds me from goin' after him. The eyes of
                 that rat—they're jest like those of the picture!!

ELLA: Yeah—they seem t'—t' fasten on ye. *(Terror)* Come away from
                 here, Walter! Let's get outa this room—outa this room!!

WALTER: Yeah—fer God's sake! Come on, Ella! Come on!!

(A low chuckling laugh.)

SCENE IV

WALTER: You gotta pull yerself together, honey—you gotta! Why you an'
                 me has been carryin' on like a couple children—over a rat that
                 threw himself around so he sounded like footsteps, an' a old,
                 dusty picture of a man dead a hundred years! There ain't nothin'
                 gonna hurt ye, honey—go on t' sleep an' ferget about what dumb
                 fools we been.

ELLA: I can't go t' sleep. Every time I try, I seem t' see them eyes
                 alookin' at me—the eyes of that picture—an' the rat—jest as we
                 actually saw em couple hours ago.

WALTER: I don't know what got inta us back in that room. A rat's eyes an' a
                 picture couldn't look alike! An' if they did, what's that t' make us
                 act so crazy? Aw—go t' sleep, honey—it must be after midnight.

ELLA: I'll try again. *(Pause)* It's awful dark here—kinda wish we'd left a
                 light burnin'.

WALTER: I'll get up an' turn one on, if ye want.

ELLA: *(Hastily)* No, no! Don't leave me—even t' go jest that little distance!

WALTER: *(Gently)* You're jest all shot t' pieces, ain't ye? But there's nothin' t' be afeared of—nothing's gonna hurt ye.

ELLA: *(Pause)* Walter—do you still think it was a tramp we saw goin' inta that room that day?

WALTER: What else could it have been?

ELLA: With his head all crooked—an' wearin' what we thought was a bathrobe, an' was really a judge's gown.

WALTER: That—that tramp didn't have on no judge's gown, honey—The—the picture jest made us think that.

ELLA: But you had to break in the door that we saw him open that day.

WALTER: The—that door coulda been sealed up since.

ELLA: You—you don't think the old judge in that picture had anything to do with—Bob?

WALTER: No—NO! That old judge is dead—an' harmless! The dead has got t' be harmless! There's nothin' t' be afeared of, honey—nothin's gonna hurt ye!!

(Flopping footsteps...approaching.)

ELLA: Walter—listen! *(Pause)* them footsteps again!

WALTER: Yeah—I hear em. But we know it's jest a rat.

ELLA: It's comin' down the hall—towards our door!

WALTER: It's only a rat, honey—only a rat!

ELLA: Did ye lock the door?

WALTER: Yeah. But it's only a rat—a rat!

ELLA: It's comin' closer!

WALTER: Only a rat!

ELLA: It's in this room—I can see its eyes!!!!

WALTER: I'm gonna kill it—'fore it drives us crazy!!

ELLA: NO—don't leave me!! Walter—a funny light is growin' round it!

WALTER: I see it!

ELLA: Somethin's shapin' in the light! *(Shrieks)* Walter—the rat's growin' bigger—it's becomin' the old judge of the picture!!

WALTER: And he's grinnin' at us—he's movin'—Ella—he's puttin' on his back cap!!!

ELLA: Make him take his eyes off me, Walter—make him take his eyes off me!!!

WALTER: I can't move—I can't do nothin'—he's got em on me, too! His lips are workin'—he's sayin' somethin'!

ELLA: Yes—to us!!

WALTER: I can't hear—but I know what he's sayin'!!

ELLA: So do I! That's why he put on his black cap!!!! *(Screams)* No! NO!! NO!!!'

(Music)

SCENE V

ELLA: We didn't hear a sound, Doctor—but, jest as plain as I'm talkin' to you, we know he said: "I sentence you to be hanged by the neck until you are dead, dead, dead."

WALTER: Then he disappeared—the room went black again—an' I heard that rat go out an' down th' hall.

ELLA: I—I guess I'd fainted then.

WALTER: Mebee I had, too—mebee we'd both fainted, an' dreamed everything that happened. We musta dreamed it!

ELLA: Anyway, my husband—carried me outa the house; an', half dressed like we are, we came to you.

WALTER: Doctor, is there any cure for folks who imagine crazy things like we just told you?

DOCTOR: It is "Hangman's Roost" which requires cure rather than yourselves, Mr. Reynolds.

WALTER: You ain't gonna be like everyone else in this town, an' say it's haunted—that there's a evil sperrit there??

DOCTOR: Your experience tonight should render my opinion valueless as to that.

WALTER: But I don't believe it—it ain't possible!

ELLA: I don't care whether it's possible or not—I believe it, Walter. And I'll never go back into that house again.

DOCTOR: The savage who has never seen an aeroplane will tell you it is impossible for man to fly, Mr. Reynolds. Possibilities are purely matters of human experience. Ghosts and evil spirits are written too large in human records to be dismissed by a mere denial of their existence.

WALTER: Then you think we really—

DOCTOR: Yes. The malignant force which once inhabited the body of Justice Merrick still lives within "Hangman's Roost." Tonight it passed upon you a sentence of death.

ELLA: But we'll never go back there where it can hurt us! We're never goin' back there!!

DOCTOR: I'm afraid you can't escape it so easily as that. I know the history of "Hangman's Roost"—when the hour of your execution arrives, I am afraid you will be unable to remain away.

(Music)

SCENE VI

ELLA: Walter—what are we gonna do? That old doctor was right—we have come back here.

WALTER: What made us do it. What kept pullin' at us, Ella—forcin' us t' come?

ELLA: I dunno. Every hour it seemed t' pull a little harder—stronger—till t'night we couldn't fight it—we couldn't stay away.

WALTER: It's the same thing that's in the eyes of the rat an' the man in the picture—when they fastened themselves on us, we couldn't do a thing.

ELLA: That's what happened to Bob that night—when he wanted us to come to him 'cause he couldn't come to us.

WALTER: But if we had come, we couldn't of saved him—no more'n anyone can save us now.

(The flopping footsteps.)

ELLA: There's them footsteps, Walter! The rat is comin'—the rat with the eyes of the judge!!

WALTER: An' we can't do nothin'—we're helpless!

ELLA: There it is—up on the balcony! Its eyes are fixed upon us! Hold me back, Walter—hold me back—it's drawin' me up there!!

WALTER: I can't—I can't! It's pullin' me like you!

ELLA: There's that funny light again! It's gettin' bigger—the rat is growin' inta the judge—jest like the time before! An' he's grinnin' at us—grinnin'!

WALTER: An' he's holdin' a rope in his hand—a rope with a hangman's noose!

ELLA: An' we're walkin' up the stairs—walkin' toward him on that balcony! Hold me back, Walter—hold me back!!

WALTER: I can't—I'm helpless—I gotta go along!!

ELLA: He's holdin' the noose out fer our necks!

WALTER: We'll reach him in a second!

ELLA: Then he'll draw it round our throats! We're gettin' closer—closer—CLOSER—*(Screams)*

(A single shot.)

WALTER: Ella—honey—somethin's happened! He's disappeared—we're free!

ELLA: I heard a shot!

WALTER: That can't be the reason—no bullet could stop the dead!

DOCTOR: A silver bullet can—and has.

WALTER: Doctor??

DOCTOR: Come.

ELLA: Where you leadin' us? No—not inta that room with the picture!

DOCTOR: It's just a picture now. Come. Look.

ELLA: The eyes have lost their shiny gleam—There's a bullet hole through th' picture!

DOCTOR: But the bullet is in the body of the rat.

WALTER: It lies there dead! I've heard of silver bullets destroyin'—

DOCTOR: In man's age long struggle with the supernatural there is a record of victory as well as of defeat...I have been a student of that record and knew the power of silver to destroy unholy things.

ELLA: *(Sobs)* But why didn't you tell us you could save us? Why did you let us suffer so?

DOCTOR: *(Gently)* The malignant spirit that compelled you here was master of your minds as well as your bodies; your knowledge was his knowledge. Had I told you of my plan, he would have known. I have waited many years for the opportunity that came tonight. Isn't your wait—and suffering—justified when you know that the last helpless victim has met his death on the stairway of "Hangman's Roost"?

(Music)

EPILOGUE

NANCY: He he he...(CAT) Weel, that's th' end o' that un, Satan! Yew folks come see old Nancy nex' week on her buthday and she'll have another perty yarn t' spin ye. He he he he he he....(CAT)....

Editor's note: Horror writers draw their ideas from many different sources. If this story reminds the reader of Bram Stoker's "The Judge's House" (though it has different elements), the reader may also be reminded that Stoker "borrowed" the idea for "Dracula" from earlier sources.

La Mannequinne

Monday, September 11, 1933

(Musical theme.)

ANNOUNCER: Again, we bring you The Witch's Tale, written by Alonzo Deen Cole. And now old Nancy and Satan, her black cat, await us with another eery story of supernatural mystery.

(Music swells...wind whistles...)

PROLOGUE

NANCY: He he he...(CAT) Hunner an twel' yeer ole, I be t'day—yes'r, hunner an twel' yeer ole! Weel, Satan—heer 'tis time fer us t' go t' work agin an spin these folks a yarn what'll keep em from sleepin' t'night. Ye know, 'long ez manyfackterers use this heer noo fangled raddio thingumbob t'advertize things they wants ter sell, we cud edvertize red flannel underwear t'keep folks warm w'ile we send cole shivers down their spines! *(Chuckles)* He he. Weel, we gotter be gittin on our job now, so douse that candle. Tha's right—make hit good an dark! Now draw upter th' fire an gaze inter th' embers w'ile we takes ye crost th' seas t' gay Paree. "Paree" iz th' name us eddicated peepul has fere th' town ordynary folks calls "Paris." Gaze inter th' embers deep, an soon ye'll see inside a leetle shop thar—a curiosity shop hit is—an soon, he he...ye'll see th' thing our yarn's erbout t'night: Th' Mannequinne...he he! TH' MANNEQUINNE!! He he he he he he...(CAT)....

(Music)

SCENE I

HENRI: *(A voluble Parisian shopkeeper.)* Regardez ici, Monsieur—de veree shaveeng mirror of Napoleon—le grand Napoleon, Messieurs—

NANETTE:	*(His wife, and a first class salesman also.)* Of such a beautee, Messieurs!
HENRI:	Of such a cheapness!
NANETTE:	But tree t'ousand francs.
HENRI:	De shaveeng mirror of Napoleon!
MONTY:	*(A young American.)* No, thanks. If I needed a shaving mirror, I would buy a very serviceable one—not used by Napoleon—for only ten francs.
HENRI:	*(Desolated)* Monsieur do not desire de shaveeng mirror of Napoleon, Nanette!
NANETTE:	*(Tragic)* Ahh—he does not desire dee shaveeng mirror of Napoleon!
PAUL:	There's nothing you want among this assortment of junk, Monty.
MONTY:	Guess not—most of these antiques are fakes, and the prices are ridiculously high.
PAUL:	What did you expect in a curiosity shop of this type? I don't know why you insisted on coming in here!
MONTY:	I told you my reason. It was because—
HENRI:	*(Slight distance.)* Regardez ici, Monsieur!
NANETTE:	*(Slight distance.)* Monsieur, regardez ici!!
PAUL:	*(Low)* Quick—let's get out before they start another selling talk on something else.
HENRI:	*(Coming up.)* Dees so beauteeful powdair box, Messieurs!
NANETTE:	*(Abetting him.)* De powdair box of Marie Antoinette—Of such a cheapness!
MONTY:	I'm frightfully sorry, really—but I'm afraid I've just been wasting your time.
HENRI:	*(Despair)* Monsieur do not desire dee powdair box of Marie Antoinette????
NANETTE:	*(Unbelieving)* For but two tousand francs?????
MONTY:	No. Thanks for all the trouble you've taken, but I find nothing here that—
HENRI:	*(Quickly)* Nanette! Show Monsieur dee pistol of Maximilien Robespierre!!
NANETTE:	Immediatement! Regardez, Messieurs—dee pistol of—!
MONTY:	I haven't the slightest use for it!
NANETTE:	Henri—queek! Dee sword of La Fayette!!!
HENRI:	Oui! Monsieur est American—Regarde—dee sword of La Fayette!!!
MONTY:	*(Who has been trying to get in a word.)* No, no, no—I don't want that either!!
PAUL:	All Monsieur wants is to get out of here!

MONTY:	Wait, Paul—I really owe some sort of explanation after looking at everything in their place. Madame—Monsieur—I came into your excellent shop in search of something I have not found.
NANETTE:	Quesque il dit?
HENRI:	W'at ees eet Monsieur seeks he has not find?
MONTY:	I don't know.
NANETTE:	Quesque il dit?
HENRI:	*(Tragic again.)* Je ne comprehends pas!
MONTY:	I'll try and explain! The first time I passed your curiosity shop, by chance about a month ago, I felt a definite, compelling urge to come in—why, I don't know, as I'm not particularly interested in the sort of things you sell. Every time I've passed here since, the urge has been stronger—it seemed as though something in here was calling to me in some telepathic way to come and purchase it. This morning, as my friend and I strolled by, I was unable to resist that call any longer—and now, I have established to my satisfaction that my psychic summons was just a fake.
PAUL:	I told you it was the most ridiculous thing I ever heard of!
MONTY:	As a medical student, you would be skeptical of anything so spiritual as a hunch! But don't forget that time you bet the limit on a bluff pat hand, and a hunch made me call you with a single pair of deuces! There was two hundred dollars of your money in that pot, thank you.
PAUL:	Ha—and because of some of your hunches since, I've gotten back that hundred ten times over!
MONTY:	Why bring that up?
NANETTE:	*(Helplessly)* Je ne comprehends pas.
HENRI:	*(Bewildered)* Je ne comprehends pas!!
PAUL:	*(Laughing)* We've bewildered em, Monty—let's make our escape while they're still in a daze.
MONTY:	*(Laughing)* I haven't the nerve to go without buying something. Here—this will do! Madame, Monsieur—I'll take this little blue vase.
NANETTE:	*(Again the saleslady.)* Ahh!
HENRI:	*(Himself once more.)* La petite vase bleu!
NANETTE:	Of such beautee!
HENRI:	Of such cheapness!!
NANETTE:	De petite vase of—!!
MONTY:	*(Laughing)* Wait! Wait!! If you tell me it belonged to Charlemagne or Louis the umpteenth, I don't want it! Besides, I see "Made in

Czechoslovakia" stamped on the bottom, which guarantees it's strictly post war. And fifty francs is top price.

HENRI: *(Mortally wounded.)* Cinquante francs??

NANETTE: *(Aghast)* Cinquante francs???

MONTY: That's my limit.

HENRI: No, no, no!

NANETTE: We are poor people!

HENRI: To sell at such price we cannot live!

MONTY: Take it or leave it.

NANETTE: Nevair!

HENRI: Nevair!

MONTY: Sorry. Good day.

HENRI: Monsieur—WAIT!!

NANETTE: Wait—WAIT, Monsieur!!!!

HENRI: Pour cinquante francs dee vase ees yours.

MONTY: *(Laughing)* I was afraid it would be. Wrap it up.

NANETTE: *(Going away...delighted.)* Oui, oui—immediatement, Monsieur!

MONTY: I shall place it in a prominent place in my studio, Paul—as a reminder of the hunch that failed.

PAUL: *(Laughing)* If it prevents similar hunches in future, it'll be fifty francs well spent.

MONTY: *(Seriously)* I can't understand it—You have no idea how strongly I've been drawn to this shop. I was sure I'd find something here that—well, crazy as it may sound: something that wanted me to have it.

PAUL: I always knew a man had to be insane before he'd choose art as a career—but that notion proves you're even crazier than the average artist! *(Scornfully)* "Something that wanted you to have it."—Bah!

HENRI: *(With suppressed excitement.)* Pardon! Do I on'erstan' Monsieur ees un artist??

MONTY: Eh? Why yes.

HENRI: An artist who paint??

MONTY: Guilty. But don't worry—I'll pay you for that vase in cash.

HENRI: *(Calling excitedly.)* Nanette—Nanette!! Monsieur ees un artist!!

NANETTE: *(Distant)* Un artist???

HENRI: Oui! Oui!!

NANETTE: *(Excitedly...coming up.)* Mon Dieu—Il fut envoye a Ciel!

HENRI: Dieu Merci! Il soit notre saveur!!

MONTY: Hey—what's all the excitement about??

HENRI:	Monsieur—Monsieur! Come queek dees way!
MONTY:	What for?
HENRI:	*(Going away.)* I have someteeng you weel buy!
NANETTE:	Someteeng only for un artist!

(Locks and bolts are drawn on door.)

HENRI:	*(Slight distance.)* Come queek!
MONTY:	What—??
PAUL:	Must be something darn precious if he keeps it back of all those locks!

(The last bolt is drawn and the door opened.)

HENRI:	Enfin! Entree, Messieurs!
PAUL:	You want us to go down in that cellar?
HENRI:	Oui, oui—follow me! I turn on de light!

(A light switch clicks...he goes down stairs.)

MONTY:	What in the world—?
NANETTE:	Come, Monsieur—please come!
PAUL:	There's nothing down there but a lot of crates and broken junk!

(More locks and bolts are drawn on another door.)

MONTY:	He's unlocking another door!
NANETTE:	Please come, Messieurs—please come!
MONTY:	Come on, Paul!

(They descend the stairs toward the door.)

PAUL:	What the deuce does he want to show you??
MONTY:	*(Excitedly)* I think it's the thing I came here looking for! I feel it calling me again—whatever wants me to have it lies behind that door!
PAUL:	Rot! And you won't be able to afford anything he keeps behind two triple locked doors!
MONTY:	We'll soon find out—he's drawing the last bolt.
NANETTE:	*(Fearfully)* Henri—prenez garde à ce que vous faites! Je crains!
PAUL:	*(Wonderingly)* She says she's afraid!
MONTY:	And now the door's unlocked he doesn't open it! What's the matter with them??
HENRI:	*(Fearfully)* Ne craignez rien, Nanette. *(With an effort.)* Regardez, Messieurs, I—I open dee door!
MONTY:	But you haven't opened it! What's wrong with you two??
PAUL:	You're trembling like a pair of frightened children! What are you afraid of?
MONTY:	What's behind that door??

HENRI:	I—I—
NANETTE:	*(Frightened)* Henri—!
HENRI:	*(Mastering himself.)* I open de door! Regarde!!

(Door thrown open.)

PAUL:	What—???
MONTY:	Good god! There's a woman in that closest—hanging by the neck!!!
PAUL:	Her hands and feet are bound!! These people are cutthroats! They—
MONTY:	Call the police!
NANETTE:	No, no, no, no!!!
HENRI:	She ees not a woman, Messieurs!
NANETTE:	She ees une mannequinne!!
HENRI:	Une mannequinne for artist!!
MONTY:	Oh—good Lord—!! *(Starts to laugh.)*
PAUL:	What—??
MONTY:	It's only a mannequinne, Paul—a lay figure!
PAUL:	You mean—a dummy??
MONTY:	*(Still laughing.)* Yes—every artist has one in his studio. You've seen mine—I drape costumes upon it instead of using a living model.
PAUL:	The figure in your studio isn't anything like that!
MONTY:	I should say it isn't! This is a work of art—it's positively life-like.
PAUL:	*(Slightly awed.)* I'll say it is.
MONTY:	Why have you got it trussed up like some dangerous animal? Take that rope from around its neck and bring it under this light where I can have a good look at it.
HENRI:	*(Fearfully)* Oui, Monsieur.
MONTY:	*(Pause)* Well—what are you hesitating about?
PAUL:	They're frightened to death of that thing.
HENRI:	No, no, no, Monsieur!
NANETTE:	*(Fearfully)* Dere ees not'ing to fear, Monsieur—
MONTY:	Certainly not—it's just a figure made of wood and cloth and cotton stuffing! Bring it out!
HENRI:	Oui—oui, Monsieur.
MONTY:	That's right—cut that rope from the neck. Hurry—it's not going to bite you! Here—now lay it down under this light.
HENRI:	Oui, Monsieur.
MONTY:	Aren't you going to cut these cords that bind its hands and feet? I want to see how the joints work. *(Impatiently)* Here—give me that knife; I'll do it!
HENRI:	*(Thankfully)* Oui—oui, Monsieur!

PAUL: *(Awed)* The—the thing is incredible, Monty—even now, when I can see it's only made of stuffed cloth, it seems positively human.

MONTY: It's the finest mannequinne I've ever seen. The outer skin is of silk—and look how it's padded: every muscle is brought out to perfection!

PAUL: The face is beautiful.

MONTY: Worthy of a master sculptor! He was a crackerjack mechanic, too—listen as I move these joints about; you don't hear the slightest squeak.

PAUL: How is her hair fastened on? It actually seems to be growing from her head.

MONTY: Golly! How did anyone do a job like that?? It isn't an ordinary wig—that hair has been worked into whatever substance forms the head—wood most likely.

PAUL: *(With a shudder.)* Those unblinking eyes stare at us as though she understood every word we're saying.

MONTY: They do give an illusion of intelligence. Whatever possessed her maker to give her glass eyes and that human hair?

HENRI: *(Timidly)* Monsieur finds dee mannequinne good?

MONTY: Good? She's perfect!

NANETTE: Oui—Monsieur weel take her away?

MONTY: I certainly want to—but I know I can't afford her.

HENRI: Mais, oui, Monsieur—dee price ees veree low!

NANETTE: Of such a cheapness, Monsieur!

MONTY: I've already heard samples of your cheap prices. How much?

HENRI: Trois mille francs, Monsieur!

MONTY: Three thousand francs?

NANETTE: Deux mille francs, Monsieur!!

MONTY: Two thousand—??

HENRI: Une mille francs!

MONTY: One thousand—???

NANETTE: Oui, Monsieur! *(Pleading almost.)* You weel buy—you weel take her away??

MONTY: A thousand francs is only forty dollars.

PAUL: Even I can see it's worth far more than that!

HENRI: Eet ees no matter! Say you weel buy, and take her away!

MONTY: At a price like that I certainly will!

PAUL: Wait, Monty! There's something funny about that figure—they're too anxious to get rid of it!

MONTY: It wasn't stolen, was it?

NANETTE: No, no, no!!!

HENRI: We are hones' people! We buy from Lyons—a lot of teeng togehair—dees mannequinne, she come weeth lot. We buy cheap— we sell cheap to you!

NANETTE: *(Pleading)* You weel buy, Monsieur—you weel take away?—

MONTY: I don't know what this mystery is, but she's sold. Pack her up— I'll tell you where to send her!

HENRI: *(Eagerly)* Oui, oui! Here ees de box een w'ich she came, Monsieur!

(A heavy box dragged across bare floor.)

PAUL: It looks like a coffin! You want to have her delivered in that to your door?? It'd frighten Fleurette to death!

MONTY: Not if I tell her what to expect. But better than that—we'll take it home with us on top of a cab! Will you call us a cab, Madame?

NANETTE: *(Delighted)* Oui, oui—immediatement!

MONTY: Wait! First take your thousand francs. Monsieur will help us with the packing.

NANETTE: Merci, Monsieur—*(Going away...up the stairs.)* I weel call you cab— you weel take her away immediatement!

MONTY: Well, Monsieur—aren't you going to place my purchase in its box?

HENRI: *(Timidly)* Would—would Monsieur mind himself—?

MONTY: *(Laughing)* I forgot—I forgot—I removed the cords you had her bound with! With her hands free, she might throttle you or some- thing. Well, I'm not afraid of her—

PAUL: *(Together, in alarm.)* Monty!!

HENRI: *(And terror.)* MONSIEUR!!!

MONTY: What—??

PAUL: That figure!! As you stooped to pick it up, I'll swear its arms stretched out for you——as though it were a living woman!!

MONTY: You're mad!

PAUL: I'm not! Ask him—he saw it, too!

HENRI: No, no—I saw no'teeng!!

PAUL: You're lying! You want to get rid of that mannequinne because you know something about it you won't tell us!

HENRI: No—I swear to you—!!

PAUL: Monty—don't take it home with you! Leave that figure where it is!

MONTY: You're talking like a chump! *(Laughing)* Time to prescribe spec- tacles for yourself, Mr. Medical Student, when you see a dummy's arms move.

PAUL: I did see them move, and so did he! These people have some real
               reason for their fear—leave that figure where it is!!

MONTY: What in the world's got into you?? I wouldn't leave her now for
               anything! She's what I came here to look for—the thing that drew
               me to this shop.

PAUL: And that very hunch of yours proves there's something wrong!
               There's something uncanny about this whole business!

MONTY: Rats! I'm just winning another big pot on a pair of little deuces:
               this lovely work of art for only forty dollars.

NANETTE: *(Coming down the stairs.)* Monsieur—Monsieur! Your cab ees
               waiteeng at dee door!

MONTY: Good! Well, since you and my friend don't like this lady, Mon-
               sieur, I'll have to lift her into the box myself. Come sweetheart—
               let me take you up and—

PAUL: *(Together)* Monty—!!!

HENRI: *(In alarm.)* Mon Dieu—!!!!

NANETTE: *(And terror.)* Sacre Vierge—!!!

MONTY: *(Hesitant...awed.)* I—I know what you saw this time—I—I felt this
               figure's arms curl around my shoulders. It feels now as—as though
               she were—embracing me.

(Music)

                                    SCENE II

(Taxicab effect.)

MONTY: There's the house—cette maison blanc, chauffeur—la!

DRIVER: Oui, Monsieur.

MONTY: Now that we're nearly home, Paul—wipe that look of supersti-
               tious gloom off your face. Aren't you convinced yet that my new
               mannequinne is just a mannequinne?

PAUL: *(Glumly...convincing himself.)* Oh, naturally, your explanation of the
               thing's weird movements is the only reasonable one.

MONTY: Of course! Hanging in that damp cellar, it's wooden framework has
               become warped and out of adjustment—and that's what made its
               limbs perform those eery contortions. *(Laughs)* I'll confess I was
               plenty startled, though, when it's arms wrapped themselves so
               lovingly around my neck! I mustn't tell Fleurette I've purchased
               such an amorous dummy—you know how jealous she is. Ah—

(The cab draws up to the curb.)

MONTY: Here we are!

(Cab door opened.)

PAUL: Just the same, in spite of your obviously natural explanation of that thing's actions—I don't like its looks. And with its coffin-like box above us on this cab, I've felt as though I was riding with a corpse.

MONTY: *(Laughs)* There's Fleurette at the window—I'd better hurry and assure her that's not what we're bringing home!

PAUL: Raymond's with her.

MONTY: By Jove! Thank heaven I'll have a brother artist to help me gloat over my new purchase—he won't share your dislike of her.

PAUL: *(Grunts)* Um. They've left the window—must be coming to the door.

MONTY: Take down that box, cabby—I mean: ôtez cette boite.

DRIVER: Oui, monsieur.

(A heavy box is slid from top of cab.)

MONTY: I'll send Potter out to help him.

FLEUR: *(Distant...She is a young French girl...his model...questioning)* Montee—??

MONTY: Hello, Fleurette!

RAY: *(Distant, coming up...A young Englishman.)* I say, old man—what have you got in that beastly looking box?

MONTY: Wait'll you see her, Raymond!

FLEUR: *(Coming up.)* "Her"?

MONTY: *(Gaily)* Yes, darling—I'm bringing home my new sweetheart.

FLEUR: Your new—??

MONTY: *(Calling)* Potter! Potter!!

POTTER: *(A cockney servant...distant...coming up.)* Yes, Mr. Montague?

MONTY: Help the cabby with that box! Never mind—Mr. Steele is giving him a hand.

FLEUR: Montee, what ees een dat box?? What are dey bringing een our house???

MONTY: You'll soon find out! Just lay it down anywhere, you fellows.

PAUL: Ici, chauffeur.

DRIVER: Voila!

(The box is set down.)

MONTY: Get me a hammer, Potter—there's one in my studio. I want to remove this lid and show my prize. Will you pay the cabby, Paul?

FLEUR: Montee, take off dat leed immediatement—show us w'at you 'ave eenside!!

RAY: We're dying of curiosity!!

POTTER: *(Coming up.)* 'Ere's th' 'ammer, sir. Shall I—?

MONTY:	I'll do it—there's only a nail at each end holding the boards. Now, everybody—open your mouth and shut your eyes!

(A nail is drawn and boards thrown off.)

	Behold!!!
FLEUR:	*(Screams with fright.)*
RAY:	*(Startled)* Good Lord—!!
POTTER:	*(Frightened)* Mr. Montague—!!!!
MONTY:	*(Laughs)* I always did love a good dramatic effect!
FLEUR:	*(Terrified)* Take 'er away! Eet ees a corpse!!!
RAY:	Don't be silly, Fleurette—it's just a wax figure!
MONTY:	You're both wrong—it's my new mannequinne.
RAY:	Mannequinne?
MONTY:	Wait'll I lift her out and show you!
FLEUR:	*(Screams)* Ahh—she puts 'er arms aroun' your neck!!
MONTY:	*(Laughing)* You explain that, Paul—while I place her in this chair.
PAUL:	The framework inside is warped, Fleurette—so the limbs spring into queer positions. *(Glumly)* At least, that's what Monty says.
RAY:	The thing's an absolute work of art, Monty!
MONTY:	I knew you'd appreciate her!
RAY:	But those joints aren't warped in any way—they move in my hands without the slightest effort!
MONTY:	I can't quite figure that out.
FLEUR:	*(Vehemently)* Because warpeeng ees not de raisen 'er arms moved just like life! She ees not good—I do not like 'er! Take 'er away!!
MONTY:	*(Laughing)* You're jealous, Fleurette—jealous of my new sweetheart!

(We hear a deep contented sigh.)

FLEUR:	*(Awe and terror.)* W'at was dat???
RAY:	I heard it, too!
MONTY:	What?
FLEUR:	Dat—dat feegure sighed!
MONTY:	You're crazy!
PAUL:	She's not—three of us distinctly heard it!
POTTER:	Four, sir—I 'eard hit, too!
FLEUR:	*(Hysterically)* Take 'er away—out of dees 'ouse! I weel not 'ave 'er 'ere!!
MONTY:	Fleurette—darling—!!
FLEUR:	Take 'er away—I am afraid!!
MONTY:	Dearest—precious—You're not going to become hysterical over a stuffed mannequinne?? Here—let me hold you in my arms, and—

(A malevolent, threatening hiss.)

FLEUR:	*(Gasps)*
PAUL:	Monty—that figure made a hissing sound!
RAY:	It did—no mistake!!
FLEUR:	An' look at 'er eyes! Dey stare at me weet hate!!
MONTY:	*(Angrily)* Have you all become raving lunatics??
FLEUR:	She or I mus' leave dees house—I weel not stay here weet 'er!!
POTTER:	Nor I sir—I give notice!
MONTY:	This is ridiculous!
RAY:	Monty's right—this is ridiculous! That figure is so extremely life-like, it's making us subject to delusions!
PAUL:	*(Awed)* That—that must be the natural explanation.
MONTY:	Of course it is! Potter, stop trembling like a fool, and mix us all a cocktail—yourself included! Maybe that will steady your flighty nerves.
POTTER:	Yes sir.
MONTY:	Let's go in the next room.
RAY:	Come Paul, old man. *(Going)*
MONTY:	Wait, Fleurette—before we go, I want you to take a good look at this mannequinne and convince yourself it's merely cloth and cotton stuffing.
FLEUR:	*(Low...fearful.)* Eet's eyes steel stare at me weet hate.
MONTY:	*(Impatiently)* How can glass eyes show any emotion?? *(Laughs fondly.)* Oh, what a silly little goose you are! Come on—let's get that drink.
FLEUR:	I am afraid to turn my back on 'er—she do not like me.
MONTY:	She will when she knows you as well as I do. Come dear.
FLEUR:	*(Shaking off her fears.)* Oh, of course I am seely to be afraid of such a foolishness—she ees just a great beeg doll!
MONTY:	That's the idea!
FLEUR:	I am not afraid of 'er! Look—I slap 'er face!
MONTY:	*(Hastily)* No, no—don't do that! You might knock her off that chair and break her!!
FLEUR:	Alright. *(Laughs)* But because I meant to slap 'er face, you see I am not afraid from 'er no more! *(Both laugh.)*
MONTY:	Come on!
FLEUR:	Wait! Before we go to de othairs, firs' kees me, mon petit—you deed not kees me w'en you arrive.
MONTY:	I guess I was too excited. Here—now I'll make up for lost time!

FLEUR: *(A short hurt cry.)*
(A dull thud.)
MONTY: Fleurette, what's the matter?? Paul—Raymond—Help!
PAUL: *(Together)* What's wrong?? Fleurette—!!
RAY: Monty, what—?? Fleurette—!
MONTY: She suddenly collapsed in my arms—as though she'd been struck by something!!
PAUL: She has been—there's blood oozing through her hair!
MONTY: She's not badly hurt—??
PAUL: No! Nasty gash—but just a flesh wound! What did it?
RAY: There's a hammer on the carpet—somebody threw this hammer!
MONTY: But we were alone—there was no one—!!
PAUL: You were not alone! And you left this hammer laying on the box beside that figure.

(Music)

SCENE III

FLEUR: He fines a natural explanation for ever'teeng, Raymond—he even say she deed not t'row dat hammer at me!
MONTY: *(Exasperated)* Ray, will you talk to this poor deluded child??
RAY: My dear Fleurette—Monty is perfectly right to find a natural explanation! How in the world could that inanimate figure throw hammers at anyone?
FLEUR: But she deed! You weel not admeet eet because de worl', you teenk, would laugh at you! She tried to cause my deat' because she hates me—because she ees jealous—because she, herself, love Monty!!
MONTY: Did you ever hear anything so asinine?? That's the sort of stuff I hear all day from her and Potter! First they threatened to leave the house unless I kept the figure locked in the studio—and then they said they heard it prowling around in there at night, so I had to put a lock on its box and keep it in there when I wasn't using it! Now—it's in love with me!! Next thing—Fleurette will say I'm in love with it!
FLEUR: No, not yet—but, een time, who knows what may happen.
RAY: My dear child—if you really believe such nonsense as that, you'll find yourself in an asylum.
FLEUR: Raymond, leesten—I mus' make someone un'erstan' for Monty weel not! Since dat feegure came here, he have change.

MONTY: I haven't!

FLEUR: You 'ave! I am steel your sweetheart—but I also was your model. Now—no more you let me pose for you! You paint onlee from de mannequinne!

MONTY: Raymond, you know I'm working on a canvas depicting Abelard and Heloise—Fleurette posed for Heloise—the face is finished— now, I'm simply painting in the costume, which I drape upon the mannequinne.

RAY: Most every artist does that, Fleurette.

FLEUR: But he ees not only painting een de costume—he has retouched de face for w'ich I posed teel now eet look like de mannequinne!

MONTY: (Uncomfortably) Well—I—I—

RAY: (Curiously) Why have you done that? I thought Fleurette a fine model for Heloise.

FLEUR: I weel tell you! Heloise' face should be all love! I love Monty, but I am jus' a woman—dat feegure love heem more dan me!

MONTY: (Hesitantly) I—I did catch an expression of absolute adoration from that mannequinne's painted face that—

FLEUR: Because she adores you! You said she called to you before you even saw her!

MONTY: Oh, I'm sick of this whole business! I know she's nothing but a jointed image, but I'll never have a moment's peace while she remains here! You win, Fleurette.

FLEUR: You mean—??

MONTY: Yes. You've admired her, Ray—you'll take care of her.

RAY: You're going to give me—??

MONTY: If you want the figure, take it away.

RAY: (Delighted) If I want it! I'll take it this minute—before you change your mind!

FLEUR: Oh Montee—I'm so happy!!

RAY: (Calls excitedly.) Potter! Potter!! Get me a cab—at once!!!

POTTER: (Coming up.) Yes, sir—yes, sir!

FLEUR: (Happily) Potter—dat feegure leave dees house!

POTTER: No??

MONTY: Yes—your worries are over. And I'll have a little peace—thank God!

POTTER: Oh, sir—I'm so glad!

RAY: (Slightly distant.) Cab! Cab! I've got one, Potter! (Coming up.) You help me get that figure!

MONTY: It's in its box—in the studio. I—I won't go in with you. *(Low)* Somehow, I don't want her to know I'm sending her away.

RAY: What say?

MONTY: Nothing. Potter'll show you where to find it.

(A heavy box is dragged toward us.)

POTTER: *(Coming up.)* I'm already bringing hit hout, sir—I'm that glad to 'ave hit leave th' place!

RAY: I'll help you! Mind if I take Potter with me to assist in getting it in at home?

MONTY: No—not at all.

FLEUR: I weel open de door for you!

(Door opened.)

RAY: Thanks. Easy through the doorway, Potter. *(Going away.)* I'll take good care of her, old man—and thanks a thousand times!

FLEUR: *(Exultantly)* She ees gone out dees door now—gone! Merci Dieu— she has left dees 'ouse forever!!

WOMAN: *(A thin ghostly voice.)* No, no—I will return!

FLEUR: *(Screams)*

(Distant crash as the box is dropped.)

MONTY: That voice—????

POTTER: *(Distant)* Lord 'elp us—hit spoke inside this box!!

(Music)

SCENE IV

RAY: *(Impatiently)* I've heard enough of your silly talk about a voice inside this box, Potter—pour yourself another drink and be quiet!

POTTER: *(Fearful throughout.)* Yes'r—but there was a voice. Miss Fleurette 'eard hit, an Mr. Montague—standin' way back there in th' doorway.

RAY: And you let your end of the box fall to the pavement! If I find the figure broken I'll strangle you! Where's something I can use to pry this lid open? Monty forgot to give me the key.

POTTER: You're not going to tike th' figger hout, sir??

RAY: Naturally—now she's mine, I'm going to enjoy her possession! The lock doesn't look very strong—this heavy hunting knife will pry it off, I think.

(He pries at lock with knife.)

POTTER: If you're going to take 'er out, I've got to go, sir—I can't stand th' look of 'er!

RAY: Potter, I'm disgusted with you—you should be ashamed to call
            yourself an Englishman!
POTTER: *(Mastering his fears.)* I—I'll stay, sir.
(The lock falls off.)
RAY: There! I thought this knife would manage the lock!
(Lid of box thrown open.)
            And now I'll lift the fair cause of so much unreasoning terror
            from her most uncomfortable bed! Out you come, pretty one—
            I'm not afraid of you! And you're going to live with me now—I'll
            never let you go back to Monty any more!
POTTER: *(Screams)* Look out—her hand!!
RAY: Eh??
POTTER: Hit's grabbed that knife!!
RAY: *(In terror.)* Good God! And she's holding me—! Potter, get that
            knife—Help—help—!! *(Screams)*
POTTER: She's stabbed 'im—killed 'im! *(Going away.)* 'Elp! 'Elp! 'Elp!!
(Music)

SCENE V

MONTY: Fleurette, will you stop pacing the floor like a caged animal??
            Raymond has the figure safely at this studio by this time—and it's
            not coming back here!
FLEUR: *(Hysterical)* She said she would return—you, also, heard de voice
            from een dat box!
MONTY: I—I heard something that sounded like a voice—But it's impos-
            sible—everything you fear about that mannequinne is impossible!
            I was a fool to give it away—I'm going to miss her—I—Oh, what
            is the matter with me?? What has that big doll done to us all that—
(The door bell rings.)
FLEUR: *(A little startled cry.)*
MONTY: Get hold of yourself, dear—that's merely the doorbell!
FLEUR: Eet might be her—she said she would come back.
MONTY: Rot! It's probably Potter returning—I'll let him in.
(Door opened.)
PAUL: *(Coming in.)* Hello, Monty. *(His manner is grave.)*
            Good evening, Fleurette.
FLEUR: Oh Paul—I am glad to see you! You, alone, do not call me a
            fool—when I say I fear dat mannequinne.

MONTY:	You've been away, Paul.
PAUL:	Yes—in Lyons, where your mannequinne came from.
MONTY:	What do you mean?
PAUL:	I've discovered some interesting things about that figure—which I've come to tell you. I want to show you a photograph—but first let me cover half of it with this paper. Look.
MONTY:	A picture of the figure!
PAUL:	No—of a woman. Now let me show you the other half.
FLEUR:	A man stans beside her—Eet ees Monty!!!
MONTY:	It is of me! But I never had such a photograph taken! And those clothes—
PAUL:	The costumes are those of a hundred and twenty years ago. The people in the picture are long since dead.
MONTY:	What is that picture—where did you get it??
PAUL:	I had it photographed from a painting in the Lyons Museum, dated 1813.
FLEUR:	But Monty an dees man in de picture who both look so much alike—?
PAUL:	I can't explain the resemblance—I think it just one of nature's duplications. But let me tell you all I've learned.
FLEUR:	Yes, yes!
PAUL:	The painting is of a sculptor named Marcel Valmont, and his wife. They were greatly in love with each other—so much so that, when she died, he lost his reason. He was reputed to have made a life sized figure that resembled her, which he kept always at his side until his death.
MONTY:	My mannequinne!
PAUL:	I'm sure of it.
FLEUR:	Dat ees why she love my Montee den—because he ees like her husband!
MONTY:	The mannequinne is only a copy of the woman Paul is speaking of.
PAUL:	From what we have seen, I think it something more.
MONTY:	Something "more"?
PAUL:	Monty, I want to examine that mannequinne—carefully.
MONTY:	It's gone.
PAUL:	Gone, where??
MONTY:	I gave it to Raymond, not two hours ago.
PAUL:	It's alright then—he'll keep it safe.

(The doorbell rings.)

FLEUR: What's that???

MONTY: Only the door—!

(The door thrown open.)

POTTER: *(Coming up.)* Mr. Montague! Oh, Mr. Montague!!

MONTY: Potter??

PAUL: He's handcuffed!

FLEUR: Who ees dees man weet you???

GROSJ: Pardonnez moi, Madame-Messieurs. I am Sergeant Grosjean of de Surete.

FLEUR: Police!!!

MONTY: Why—??

GROSJ: Because dere hafe been attempt at murder!

POTTER: I didn't do hit! When 'e's able t' talk, 'e'll tell ye 'ow hit 'appened! She stabbed 'im with a knife—I saw 'er do hit!!

MONTY: Who stabbed who???

POTTER: Mr. Raymond! Th' figger did hit—an then she got away!

FLEUR: *(Cries)* Ahh!

MONTY: You're lying—that's impossible!

GROSJ: Hees story ees eensane, Messieurs—dat ees w'y we breeng heem 'ere for question in your presence! De wounded man cannot yet talk.

FLEUR: Hees story ees not eensane! She try to keel Raymon' because he take 'er away from you, Montee!!

MONTY: Fleurette—!

FLEUR: An she weel come back here jus' like she said!

MONTY: I won't believe that—I believe nothing anyone has said about her!!

PAUL: Quiet, everyone! Listen!!

(The footsteps of a woman...distant.)

GROSJ: Queek-dat door!!

MONTY: Here!

(Door thrown open.)

FLEUR: *(Cries in fright.)* Ahh!!

PAUL: God! In that moonlight—!!

FLEUR: De mannequinne!!

MONTY: A bloody knife is in her hand!!

POTTER: Th' same she used on Mr. Raymond!!!

FLEUR: She ees coming for me!! *(Screams)* Montee—save me!

GROSJ: Queek—queek!!!

PAUL: I have the knife—I knocked her down!

MONTY: She's just a padded figure! She couldn't walk—she couldn't try to kill anyone! We're all of us mad, and seeing things!!

PAUL: We won't see things any more!!

MONTY: Don't! Don't slash her with that knife!!

PAUL: I'm going to find the infernal mechanism that makes her run!

MONTY: Ahh—you've ripped her open! Spoiled a thing of beauty! Are you satisfied now?? Now when you see she's nothing but cloth and wadded stuffing on a wooden frame???

PAUL: *(Pause...awed.)* The framework isn't wooden—it's a human skeleton.

FLEUR: *(Gasps)*

MONTY: God!

GROSJ: *(Awed)* An dee head, eet ees a skull—dees hair ees growing from a human scalp.

FLEUR: *(Moans)*

MONTY: Valmont's wife, Paul—he put her skeleton inside that figure that he made?

PAUL: So it seems.

FLEUR: *(Pityingly)* Her bones denied rest een de grave have wandered. She loved you Montee—because you look like heem she loved in life.

PAUL: I think that's the explanation.

MONTY: Where—where is her husband's grave, Paul?

PAUL: In the Cemetaire de Loyusse.

MONTY: As soon as you police have finished, Sergeant, I—I'd like to see that these poor bones are buried at his side.

(Music)

EPILOGUE

NANCY: He he he...(CAT) Weel, that's th' end o' that un, Satan! You an me haz bizness t' tend tew now—pertant bizness, Satan—neer midnight, Satan. He he he.

(Musical theme.)

Alan Devitt (left) and Mark Smith (right)

The Altar
Wednesday, November 8, 1933

(Musical theme.)

ANNOUNCER: Again we bring you The Witch's Tale, written by Alonzo Deen Cole. And now let us join old Nancy and Satan her big black cat.

(Music swells...wind whistles...)

PROLOGUE

NANCY: He he he...(CAT) Hunner and twen'y one yeer ole, I be t'day—yes'r, hunner and twen'y one yeer ole I be even ef this iz Wensday 'stead o' m' regular Monday buthday! (CAT) Yer' right, Satan—we iz suttingly glad this heer 'lekshun bizness is over fer awhile, 'cause with them pollyticians cussin' one another over th' raddio all hours o' day an night yew an me never knowed when we'd git a chanct t' tell these folks their weekly bedtime stury. But here we be at last—an if ye'll jest douse that candle we'll be gittin down t' bizness. Tha's right—make hit nice an dark an cheery-like. Now draw up t' th' fire an gaze inter th' embers. We're takin' ye t' France t'night—th' France o' days gone by—th' France o' Revolootion.

(Music..."Marseillaise"...very softly under dialogue.)

NANCY: *(Continues)* He he...t' th' land o' Brittany we're goin', whar—In th' city o' Nantes, a man named Carrier iz the law—Jean Baptiste Carrier, who hist'ry calls "Th' Butcher." He he...hit ain't a perty stury we're gonna tell ye—but hit weren't a perty time. Gaze inter th' embers deep w'ile we spins ye our yarn o' Th' Altar...he he! TH' ALTAR! He he he he...(CAT)

(Music..."Marseillaise" full volume.)

SCENE I

(As Nancy fades out and the music swells, the voice of a mob fades in and continues as background to the scene...Close at hand we hear a battering ram at work upon a door, which creaks and gradually splinters under the impact...Music fades out...)

MOB: Break down that door! Break down that door!! Death to the aristocrats who try to hide from us! To the guillotine with all Chouans!

BRISSAC: The cursed door is giving on its hinges, Citizen Carrier—in a moment we shall be inside.

CARRIER: *(He is the personification of cruelty...quiet, suave.)* Drive this mob away, Citizen Brissac—when we gain entrance, their enthusiasm for the cause of brotherhood might bring death too quickly for those who hide within.

BRISSAC: *(He is a boisterous bully.)* Aye, the people are stupid in their hatred— It is you who know how to serve the aristocrats properly! *(Bawls out.)* Sergeant Pedron—drive back these good people—keep them at a distance!

SERG: At once, Citizen Captain. *(Goes away, calling.)* Back, citizen people— back! You heard Captain Brissac's order. Citizen Carrier wishes to enter this rat's nest alone!

MOB: *(Backing away...ad lib.)* Back! Back! The Citizen Carrier knows how to treat such vermin.

CARRIER: *(Chuckling)* How these excellent citizens trust me, Brissac.

BRISSAC: They have reason for their faith! *(Laughs brutally.)* Ha ha—no patriot in France has better served Madame la Guillotine than you! By your noble work, bodies of the dead so fill our River Loire it almost overflows its banks.

CARRIER: Yes—I have taught these good citizens of Nantes the proper way to Freedom. The yonder door proves stubborn.

BRISSAC: The dogs built it stoutly, but—

(The door crashes in...We hear shouts of triumph from nearby soldiers and the distant mob, who now push forward.)

BRISSAC: Ah—there it goes now!

SERG: *(Cries)* Stand back—stand back, good people! Citizen Carrier will go in alone!!

CARRIER: Not quite alone, Sergeant—the rats within may still have teeth. You go first, Brissac—I will follow.

BRISSAC: Yes, Citizen Carrier. *(Bawls)* Citizen soldiers: come with me!

SERG:	Citizen soldiers—forward—in the name of Liberty!
SOLDIERS:	*(Going away.)* Aye—in the name of Liberty!
CARRIER:	*(Calling)* I am right behind you, Citizen soldiers. Brissac—call me when you seize the traitors.
BRISSAC:	*(Distant)* There they are—all three together!
SERG:	Take them, Citizen soldiers!! *(Distant)*
SOLDIERS:	*(Distant...ad lib.)* We have them! The aristocrats are our prisoners!
BRISSAC:	They are ours, Citizen Carrier—the two old ones and their cub! Come quick—they make no show of fight!
CARRIER:	I'm coming! *(Pause...He pronounces the following titles ironically.)* Well, Monsieur le Comte and Comtesse des Lauriennes, and Monsieur le Chevalier des Lauriennes—you are run to bay at last.
COMTE:	*(A middle aged aristocrat...proudly, quietly.)* We are your prisoners. There is no need to ask what you will do to us—
(Over-blend.)	
	Call your tumbrils, I expect no mercy from such an enemy as you.
CARRIER:	And you will not even ask for it—not even for your wife and son?
MADAME:	*(Proudly)* My husband will not plead for our lives, and neither will I.
CHARLES:	*(A boy of sixteen.)* Nor, I, Monsieur—I, like my parents am ready to die.
MADAME:	*(Suddenly weakens.)* Oh, my son—my Charles—! *(Sobs)*
CARRIER:	Ah—she weakens!
COMTE:	*(Sternly)* Helene!
CHARLES:	Mother—don't!
MADAME:	*(Sobbing)* I cannot help myself—I am a mother. Oh, Monsieur—I know I am speaking to a man without a heart, yet speak I must!! If bearing a noble name, if loving France, if hating the reign of blood such men as you have brought about are crimes—then Monsieur le Comte and I deserve the death you mean to bring us. But my son is but a boy—a child—! You can't kill him.
COMTE:	Helene, be still!
CHARLES:	Mother, I beg—!!
CARRIER:	*(Suavely)* Go on, Madame.
MADAME:	*(Hopefully)* You bid me speak. Oh, perhaps you are not the butcher I have thought—perhaps you have a grain of pity in your heart—!
COMTE:	Helene—do not lower thyself by pleading with this brute!
CHARLES:	Don't, Mother—I am not afraid to die—!
CARRIER:	Let her go on! Madame—I assure you of my deep attention to your plea, and you will find me a most sympathetic man.

MADAME: Then spare my son! He is but sixteen—a child—even you cannot kill children—!!

CARRIER: Madame, you have touched me deeply—I will grant your plea.

MADAME: You—???!!!

BRISSAC: *(Angrily)* Citizen Carrier—you do not mean to spare this—??

SOLDIERS: No! They are aristocrats! Young as well as old! All three must die!

CARRIER: Silence! I command here—I will spare your son.

BRISSAC: No!

SOLDIERS: No! You shall not!! *(Continue until silenced.)*

CARRIER: Quiet! Quiet—Your son will be spared, Madame—on one condition.

MADAME: Anything!

COMTE: Yes—anything to save our son!

CARRIER: Ah—now the father is not to proud to beg!

CHARLES: I will not let them! Father, Mother—I will die with thee!

MADAME: No, no, Charles—thou are the last of our line. Thou shalt carry on our name! My son must live!

COMTE: Your condition, Monsieur—

MADAME: Name it—we will meet it!

CARRIER: Your son will be spared, Madame, Monsieur, if he will be—your executioner.

COMTE: *(Gasps)* What—??

MADAME: *(Gasps)* Monsieur—??

CHARLES: You—??

CARRIER: Your son shall live—if he will operate the knife that drops your heads into the basket.

CHARLES: NO!

MADAME: You monster!!

COMTE: You are worse than the butcher they call you—you are a fiend from hell!

BRISSAC: *(Laughs boisterously, in which he is joined by soldiers.)* Ha ha...a stroke of genius, Citizen Carrier!

CARRIER: *(Chuckling)* You thought I had forgotten my duty, Brissac.

BRISSAC: Ha ha...only you could have thought of that! Let the puppy kill the dogs who sired it!

SOLDIERS: What a jest! What a stroke of genius!

CARRIER: Your answer, Citizens?

CHARLES: *(Enraged)* The answer is NO—No. Do you think I would buy my life at such a cost? Send for your tumbrils—take us to your

	guillotine and see how aristocrats, both young and old, can die!!
COMTE:	*(Softly)* My son, thou dost make me very proud—but I am head of my house, I answer for it. *(Decisively)* Butcher Carrier—my son submits to your condition.
MADAME:	Henri—??
CHARLES:	Thou art not in earnest, Father! Thou dost only mean to test my love!
MADAME:	No, Charles—thy father is in earnest, and I know his reasons. I add my voice to his—thou art our son, thou wilt obey us.
CHARLES:	No—if God commanded, I would not obey!
COMTE:	Charles—thou, my only son, must live. Monsieur Carrier, we cannot escape. Will you withdraw your men outside this room a moment?
CARRIER:	That you may persuade the young man privately? With pleasure. You will withdraw Citizen soldiers—out of hearing, but not out of sight.
CHARLES:	You are wasting time—we three die together!
CARRIER:	I am counting much on the persuasive powers of your parents, young man. I think they understand my motives as I understand theirs—and they know I will keep my promise that you be allowed to live.
COMTE:	Please leave us.
CARRIER:	*(Chuckling)* Come citizens. *(Going away.)* We shall watch from just outside this open door.
CHARLES:	*(Low...hopeful.)* Father—Mother, thou hast some plan for escape—that is why thou hast persuaded them to withdraw?
COMTE:	*(Sadly)* No—there is no escape except for thee, my Charles.
MADAME:	Thou must accept that fiend's condition.
CHARLES:	How canst thou even bid me think of such a crime against all nature?? Dost think I am a coward—that I love my life so much—
COMTE:	Thou dost not understand, my son. The name you bear has been an honored one in France since the days of Hugh Capet—
MADAME:	Thou are the last of thy line, and that name must not die.
CHARLES:	Dost think I would preserve it by depriving thee of life??
COMTE:	We are already doomed to die—by thy hand or another's.
MADAME:	A cause is more important than the individual.
CHARLES:	I will not live at such a cost!
COMTE:	Then thou art a coward, unfit to be our son!
CHARLES:	Father—?

MADAME:	He is right—for thou wouldst take the easy way!
CHARLES:	Mother—??
COMTE:	To die is not difficult, for death sometime must come to all— Thou art afraid to live!
CHARLES:	The executioner of my parents—yes!
COMTE:	There is no other choice. And that beast out there will keep his word to spare thee, for thou wilt be an aristocrat at whom all such scum as he may point and say: "There goes a coward, who bought his life by a crime against all nature!"
MADAME:	Thou wouldst be the bravest of the brave—my Charles—for thou wouldst bear men's scorn so thou couldst hate and punish!
CHARLES:	No, no—I cannot—will not! *(Calls)* You, wait at that door—take us to your guillotine, we three will die together!
MADAME:	No—for I have a final argument at my command!
CHARLES:	Mother—that knife—??
BRISSAC:	*(Distant)* The she-wolf has a dagger!!
CARRIER:	*(Coming up.)* Wrest it from her hand!!
COMTE:	Helene—!
MADAME:	*(Gasps)* Too late.
BRISSAC:	She's thrust it in her breast!
CHARLES:	Mother—Mother—!
CARRIER:	She's cheated me!
MADAME:	*(Gasping...dying.)* No—I am granting your desire. It was too much to ask, my son, that thine should be the hand to bring thy mother's death—but now, that death accomplished, thou wilt fulfill her final wish—and live.
COMTE:	Yes—thou wilt fulfill this man's condition on thy father. Carrier, do you swear to keep your bargain?
CARRIER:	It will not make so good a show to see him drop but one head in the basket—still *(Chuckling)* the other will have died by his hand, indirectly. The terms yet stand, aristocrat.
MADAME:	*(Very weak.)* Thou wilt fulfill them, Charles—it is my dying wish.
COMTE:	And thy father's last command.
MADAME:	*(Dying)* Promise, my son—to live—
COMTE:	Promise, Charles!
CHARLES:	*(Sobbing)* Mother—Father—Mother—
MADAME:	Prom—*(Gasps and dies.)*
CHARLES:	Ahh—she's dead—my mother's dead! My mother!! And you who call yourselves the "Government of France" have killed her! You

have killed her! Yes, I will keep my life. I promise, Mother, to fulfill thy dying wish—Thou art dead, but thou wilt hear my promise. I will be thy executioner, Father, that I may live to serve a holy hate—to punish and avenge a hundredfold! Do you hear me, murderers, beasts—you fiends of hell? I will live to serve a holy hate—to punish and avenge a hundredfold!!!

CARRIER: *(Laughs)* Call the tumbril, Brissac. And inform the citizens outside that Madame la Guillotine will be well served tonight.

BRISSAC: *(Laughs)* Ha ha...an aristocrat for victim, and one for executioner—Citizen Carrier, you are a genius!

CHARLES: *(Sobbing...low.)* Dost hear me, Mother? I will punish and avenge a hundredfold.

(Music continues softly under dialogue.)

INTERLUDE

NANCY: He he he...we warned ye hit warn't a perty stury—but, ef yo've read yer hist'ry, ye know hit wern't a perty time. Weel, Charles lived by fulfillin th' condition set upon him. Now, when we find him onct agin, thutty yeer haz passed—th' Revolootion's over—Butcher Carrier, hisself, has died upon th' guillotine—in France, a Bourbon king iz on th' throne onct more—an th' boy we left sobbin' b' th' body ov hiz mother is now a man near fifty; an ole man neer fifty, who's lyin' on hiz death bed. *(Fading out.)* Gaze inter th' embers deep an see him thar. He he he...

(Music dies away as scene blends in.)

SCENE II

CHARLES: *(A prematurely aged man...weak, irritable.)* I know I have but a few moments left upon this earth, Monsieur le Curé—but, with no disrespect to your church, I long ago found a creed much better suited to my needs. I have no wish for your communion.

CURÉ: I know the creed of which you speak, Monsieur le Comte—it is a religion of hate which you have set up in your heart.

CHARLES: Yes—a hatred that is holy.

CURÉ: No hatred is holy—none is justified in Heaven's eyes. Come back to the faith of forgiveness and of love—confess your sins and—

CHARLES:	*(Impatiently)* That which you priests call sin I regard as virtue. Bother me no more—go and call my son.
CURÉ:	*(Pleading)* Monsieur le Comte—
CHARLES:	Call my son, I say! He will be my confessor—the only one I either wish or need!
CURÉ:	*(Sadly)* Very well.
CHARLES:	Call him quickly! I have very little time, the doctors said—and I must speak with him before I go.
CURÉ:	*(Going)* I left him waiting in the hall outside.

(A door is opened.)

CURÉ:	*(Distant...calls softly.)* Henri—thy father calls for thee.
HENRI:	*(A young man of twenty...coming in.)* I am here, Monsieur le Curé. Father—
CHARLES:	Come in—come in, Henri! Come close to the bed, so I will not have to raise my voice.
HENRI:	Yes father.
CHARLES:	I have very little strength. Leave us alone, Monsieur le Curé.
CURÉ:	You will not change your mind?
CHARLES:	No, no! Leave us alone.
CURÉ:	*(Going away...sadly.)* Very well.

(The door is closed.)

HENRI:	Thou wouldst not accept his priestly rites?
CHARLES:	Priestly rites for me? Thou, like all of France, doth know I was my father's executioner.
HENRI:	But like all of France I know the reasons for thy deed.
CHARLES:	But one living man besides myself knows the true reason for my deed—but no living man besides myself knows how I have kept my promise.
HENRI:	Thy promise?
CHARLES:	To my dead mother—and the scum who killed her. Ring the bell—call old Guinard to my beside.
HENRI:	Yes, father.

(A very distant call bell tinkles.)

CHARLES:	As thou knowest, Guinard served my parents and he has ever been my confidant and trusted friend.
HENRI:	I know—and I have envied him that privilege. I never knew my mother, so thou wert all I had to love—I had wished to be thy confidant, thy trusted friend.
CHARLES:	And so thou shalt be now, my son—for thou must carry on the

work I have no time to finish.

HENRI: I will not believe that thou wilt leave me!

CHARLES: I shall be dead when I tell thee what I have to say—my will shall make me live till then.

HENRI: Father—

(A knock at the door...softly.)

CHARLES: Guinard is at the door—let him in.

HENRI: Yes.

(Door opened.)

GUINARD: *(An old servant...coming in.)* Monsieur le Comte—thou wishest something from thy servant?

CHARLES: Yes, old friend: a last wish which thou wilt grant—a last command: that thou shalt serve my son as for over thirty years thou hast served me.

GUINARD: He bears thy honored name—I was born a servant of des Lauriennes.

CHARLES: I, too, have served that name. Close the door—and lock it, Guinard.

GUINARD: Yes, Monsieur le Comte.

(Door closed and locked.)

CHARLES: Henri, I have said thou must carry on my work. Ah, did I not know thee for a faithful son, I even now would stay the hand of death that tightens on my burned out heart—but thou, I know, will fulfill my uncompleted promise.

HENRI: I do not understand thee.

CHARLES: No—thou hast believed I dropped the knife upon my father's head that I might live to perpetuate our line—that a noble name might not perish from the earth. But that was only half my reason—the greater half was that I punish and avenge, that I serve a new religion hate had fostered in my soul. Guinard—open the secret panel of our holy shrine.

GUINARD: Yes, Monsieur le Comte.

(A panel slides open.)

HENRI: *(Gasps)* Ahh!

CHARLES: Look, my son—at the altar of my hate!

HENRI: An altar built of human skulls!!

CHARLES: Yes—the skulls of those who, in the name of Liberty, defiled the natural rights of all created men! The skulls of those who served Madame la Guillotine! The skulls of those who made my life a loathsome horror! An executioner they made me—I have persisted in that calling! Before that sacred shrine thou canst see a

	headman's block—and upon it leans a bloody axe.
HENRI:	Close that panel—I can look no more!!
CHARLES:	Thou must do more than look—thou shalt fulfill my uncompleted promise! I vowed to repay a hundredfold—two skulls are missing from that altar.
HENRI:	Thou meanest I—??
CHARLES:	Thou art my son. Ninety eight heads adorn that shrine—thou shalt make see a hundred rest there! And thine own hands must wield the axe.
HENRI:	I cannot—will not!
CHARLES:	Thou must—thou wilt!
HENRI:	No, no, NO!
CHARLES:	I am thy father—I command thee as mine commanded me! Thou shalt obey.
HENRI:	I beg thee—!
CHARLES:	Promise, or I curse thee with my dying breath!
HENRI:	Father—
CHARLES:	Promise!!
HENRI:	I—I—
CHARLES:	Promise!!!!
HENRI:	*(Murmurs)* I promise.
CHARLES:	Swear! Swear! Ah—now I know thou art my son, fit to bear our honored name—
HENRI:	Father—
CHARLES:	*(Dying)* I die content. I will have punished and avenged a hundredfold—*(Sighs)*
HENRI:	No! Father, I cannot let thee die deceived! I lied to thee—I will not do thy awful bidding—I withdraw my promise! Father, answer me! Dost thou not hear me?? I tell thee I withdraw my promise!
GUINARD:	Thy father has ceased to breathe—and one cannot withdraw a promise from the dead.

(Music)

SCENE III

HENRI:	I tell you I shall keep my promise, Guinard—but I must have more time—just a little more time.
GUINARD:	Six months have passed since your father breathed his last. Has not that been time enough?
HENRI:	Oh, will you never leave me alone? Every day it is the same—

morning, noon and night, you speak of nothing but that awful promise!

GUINARD: It is my duty. Your father rests uneasy in his grave because you make no move to keep your plighted word—the word of a des Lauriennes. His spirit comes to me at night and bids me tell you that he cannot rest.

HENRI: *(Awed, fearful.)* You dream he comes to you.

GUINARD: Nay, I do not dream. His spectre stalks these halls from dusk till dawn, bitter and accusing because of a broken faith.

HENRI: *(Nervously)* Be still! Don't say such things—I will not believe you!

GUINARD: Gaze upon his portrait hanging there—then tell me that you doubt.

HENRI: *(Fearfully)* The—the eyes do look at me as though—*(Slight hysteria.)* But that's just imagination! It's only a painted figure standing in that frame! You have hounded me so much my mind is being weakened by your ghoulish chatter! Leave me alone! I shall keep my promise—but I must have more time!!

GUINARD: How much more time?

HENRI: How can I tell you that? A man does not set forth to do cold blooded murder as he takes an evening stroll!

GUINARD: Just vengeance is not murder.

HENRI: *(Vehemently)* Such vengeance is not just!! Oh, I know the awful cause my father had for hatred—but no cause on earth can make such hatred right or good! Or—or excuse the dreadful altar that lies behind that panel!

GUINARD: That altar is a holy shrine to Heaven.

HENRI: It's not—it's a monument of Hell! One man alone was responsible for all my father's misery—one man alone. Yet the head of Butcher Carrier did not fall by my father's hand—his head is not included in that edifice of skulls! No—the heads of innocents compose my father's holy shrine!!

GUINARD: They were followers of Butcher Carrier—they were dogs who shared his guilt.

HENRI: You've told me that altar has claimed victims who, like me, were not yet born when the Reign of Terror ended!

GUINARD: They were of the blood of those who reveled in that Reign of Terror—of the vile blood of those who cry to you for hate!

HENRI: But how can I hate beings whom I have never seen? For a thing that happened before I came upon this earth?? I won't hate!! I saw hatred burn my father's life away—I saw him die of old age at fifty, a time when other men are in the prime of life! I will not hate! I will not?

GUINARD: Then you have been lying from the first—you never meant to fulfill your plighted word—the word of a des Lauriennes?

HENRI: I—I—Guinard, two heads are needed to complete that altar. Bring—bring me two of Butcher Carrier's blood and—and I will keep my promise.

GUINARD: You renew your promise to the dead before that portrait of your father?

HENRI: I—Yes, I renew my promise to the dead—on the conditions I have said.

GUINARD: Good! I am content—for within this hour your father's shade will be at peace.

HENRI: Within this hour?

GUINARD: Then our holy altar shall have its hundred skulls.

HENRI: What do you mean??

GUINARD: That I have foreseen your conditions. Last night I went upon the hunt—this morning I came back with game. It lies waiting behind that panel. Look?

(Panel slides back.)

HENRI: Ahh-two bodies lie there by the headman's block!!

GUINARD: Live bodies, bound and gagged—ready for the axe which you will wield!

HENRI: Your prisoners are women!!!

GUINARD: My prisoners are enemies—they are the sister and the niece of Butcher Carrier!

HENRI: You devil! Cut these cords that bind them as I tear away these gags!

GUINARD: Stop!

HENRI: No!

MARG: *(Groans)*

HENRI: Oh, you beast—this one is just a girl!

GUINARD: *(Enraged)* You are setting them free—you mean to spare the breed of Butcher Carrier!

HENRI: Yes! And I withdraw my promise now for evermore! I shall not kill—I shall not kill!

GUINARD: You cannot withdraw a promise to the dead! Gaze upon your father's portrait—look into its eyes! They are telling you, Monsieur le Comte: BEWARE!

SCENE IV

HENRI: Marguerite, you truly forgive me for Guinard's dreadful treatment of you?

MARG: My mother and I remain here in your house as guests. Does that not prove forgiveness? And—and we know the wrong my uncle brought upon your name—it is for us to beg forgiveness, not for you.

HENRI: "Forgiveness." What a blessed word that is to one who has only known of hate and vengeance. Even love must lack such wondrous meaning.

MARG: I—I don't know. I have never been in love—that is, except the love I bear my mother.

HENRI: Neither have I. I think I loved my father—but he never let me know him very well.

MARG: How old are you, Monsieur le Comte?

HENRI: On my next birthday I'll be 19.

MARG: I'm 16.

HENRI: That's a nice age.

MARG: Nineteen is a nice age, too. I suppose we're really too young to know much about love.

HENRI: I suppose so—we're just country people. But I've heard that, in the city, girls and men much younger than we know all about it—some are even married.

MARG: I have never been in the city.

HENRI: Neither have I.

MARG: It must be nice.

HENRI: To know about love?

MARG: Yes—and to live in the city.

HENRI: I—I suppose so. I wonder what it's like.

MARG: To live in the city?

HENRI: And to know about love.

MARG: It must be wonderful.

HENRI: Very wonderful.

MARG: Yes, Monsieur le Comte.

HENRI: I—I wish you wouldn't call me that any more—my name is Henri.

MARG: But you are a noble—a des Lauriennes! And I am only—a niece of Butcher Carrier.

HENRI: Oh, what difference does that make! We've known each other now for two whole weeks—two wonderful weeks—the most wonderful I've ever known! And—and I—

MARG: *(Pause)* Why do you stop? What were you going to say?

HENRI: I think I meant to say I love you.

MARG: Henri?

HENRI: Marguerite! That is what I meant to say! I've found what love is now—and I love thee!

MARG: And I love thee!

HENRI: I want thee for my wife!

MARG: And I want thee for my husband!

HENRI: Dear one!

(A huge portrait crashes to the floor.)

MARG: What was that??

HENRI: My father's portrait!

MARG: It has fallen to the floor!

HENRI: Its eyes—they gleam at me with hate!

(Music)

SCENE V

MARG: Goodnight, Mother.

BLANCHE: Goodnight, my little Marguerite—and bless thee.

HENRI: May I also call thee Mother now, Madame, since thy daughter is my wife? I would like to—I never knew my mother.

BLANCHE: Thou poor starved boy—I am thy mother now. Take my daughter with my blessing—she is thine—I know thou wilt be good to her.

MARG: Of course he will—he loves me, Mamma. Goodnight, Monsieur le Curé.

CURÉ: Goodnight, Madame la Comtesse—Goodnight Monsieur le Comte—and God's blessing on you both.

HENRI: Thank you, Monsieur le Curé. *(Hesitantly)* Guinard, old servant— I once knew you as my second father—won't you cease to look at me with loathing—won't you also bless our wedding?

GUINARD: When you took this woman for your wife tonight, you lost all claim upon my service. You are no longer a des Lauriennes, but of the breed of Butcher Carrier.

CURÉ: Guinard!

GUINARD: Don't interfere, Monsieur le Curé! Upon this bridal pair I lay my curse—the dead has laid another, and a more weighty one upon them.

MARG: *(Frightened)* Henri—!

HENRI: Don't be afraid, Marguerite, my wife—we who love have naught to fear from hate. Come into the house.

(Door opened.)

MARG: *(Going)* Goodnight, Mama—Monsieur le Curé.

(Door closed.)

GUINARD: Go—go to your wedding bed, cursed spawn of Butcher Carrier!

BLANCHE: Marguerite—Henri! Come back—I am afraid!!

CURÉ: Madame—!

GUINARD: You cannot call them back! The dead has summoned them—the dead await their coming.

BLANCHE: Don't let him say such things!!

CURÉ: *(Angrily)* Guinard, cease your superstitious lies! The dead are dead, and harmless in their graves! And if they were not, the boy was right—love has naught to fear from hate!

GUINARD: So says your religion—the dead and I hold another, different faith.

HEN & MAR: *(Distant screams of terror.)*

BLANCHE: *(Gasps)* Ahh!!

CURÉ: Those screams??

BLANCHE: Open that door!

(Door thrown open.)

CURÉ: Come!

BLANCHE: *(Terrified)* Marguerite—my baby Marguerite!!

CURÉ: Monsieur le Comte—Monsieur le Comte!! Where are you?

BLANCHE: They do not answer—

GUINARD: You will find them in this room, I think.

CURÉ: His father's room!

BLANCHE: Marguerite, my baby—answer me—*(A frightful scream of anguish and horror.)* AHHH!!!

CURÉ: That opening in the wall—that pile of grinning skulls!

GUINARD: Look close—two freshly severed heads now lie upon it!

BLANCHE: *(Screams)* My baby's!

CURÉ: Monsieur le Comte's!!

GUINARD: Now the altar is complete! Not even the grave could keep my master from fulfillment of his vow—he has repaid a hundredfold! And hate has triumphed!

CURÉ: No—for love lives on and hate, as ever, has defeated its own ends. Your master's hate was born that a name might not perish; with hate fulfilled, that name is ended on the earth.

(Music)

EPILOGUE

NANCY: He he he...We warned ye this warn't a perty stury—but in hit, mebee, ye'll find a leetle food for thought. Goodnight. He he he he he...

The Roll Call

Friday, August 10, 1934

(Musical theme.)

ANNOUNCER: Again we bring you The Witch's Tale, written and produced by Alonzo Deen Cole. And now let us join old Nancy and Satan, her wise black cat.

(Music swells...wind whistles...)

PROLOGUE

NANCY: He he he...(CAT) Hunner and ten yeer ole, I be t'day—yes'r, hunner an ten yeer ole! Weel, Satan—'cordin' to all me an yew has been readin' in th' noospapers, them furrin countries over in Europe air tryin' hard ez they kin t' bring erbout anuther war. (CAT) Now, ef ye'll douse out them lights, we'll spin ye a leetle yarn 'bout a war—th' las' war we wuz in. Draw up t' th' fire an gaze inter th' embers—gaze inter em deep, an soon ye'll be across th' seas in France in th' yeer ov 1918—soon ye'll heer a boomin' ov th' distant guns o' battle...*(Effect of distant artillery.)* ...soon ye'll heer a sergeant callin' off th' names o' soljers—

BLISS: *(A hard boiled U.S. Army sergeant...He is calling the roll...distant.)* Riley!

RILEY: *(Distant)* Here!

BLISS: Robins!

ROBINS: Here!

BLISS: Silverstein!

SILVER: *(Jewish accent.)* Here!

NANCY: Soon ye'll heer our stury ov Th' Roll Call...he he!

BLISS: Smith-Lewis!

LEWIS S: Here!

NANCY:	He he he he he *(CAT) (Fades out.)*
BLISS:	Smith-William!
WM. S:	Here!

(Bliss and answering voices now take Nancy's place at mike...The guns, while still distant, acquire a sharper and more ominous quality.)

BLISS:	Tessatori!
TESSA:	*(Italian)* Here!
BLISS:	Vurowski!
VUR:	*(Russian)* Here!
BLISS:	Watrus!
WATRUS:	Here!
BLISS:	Wurtz!
WURTZ:	*(German)* Jah!
BLISS:	Hey, Dutchman—how many times do I hafta tell he not t' say "yah"—but "here"??
WURTZ:	*(Hastily)* Jah—here!
BLISS:	Try t' remember it this time! *(Calls)* Yong!
YONG:	*(Chinese)* Me heah!
BLISS:	*(Irritated)* And just plain "here" is all th' answer I want form you, Chinaman!!
YONG:	*(Pleasantly)* Yes'm—me plesant *(General laugh.)*
BLISS:	Attention! ATTENTION!!!...*(Laugh subsides.)* You cut out that "yes'm" stuff, Private Yong—an' if th' rest o' youse guys wanta get some breakfast can th' laughin' an lemme get this roll called! *(Grumbles)* Nex' time I enlist I'm gonna join a army where all th' soljers is just one nationality...*(A titter from ranks.)* 'Tenshun!—I said!! *(Resumes calling.)* Youritzan!
YOURITZ:	Here!
BLISS:	Yost!
YOST:	Here!
BLISS:	Zeigler!
ZEIGLER:	Here.
BLISS:	*(With relief.)* Well—you greaseballs are all present or accounted for after th' pleasant little hike we finished las' night. Alri'—go get yer breakfast. Comp'ny—disMISSED!! *(There is an ad lib shout as the men break ranks of: "Chow! Wow! At last we eat!"...etc...)* Hey—!" 'Tenshun!! 'TENSHUN!!! *(Shouts are hushed.) (Disgusted)* Don't you birds know no better'n t' set up a holler th' minute I turn ye loose? We ain't in trainin' camp no longer—we're—just twen'y

keelometers b'hind th' front line trenches from a fine big war—an', if y' don't b'lieve me, lissesn t' them guns. T'morra we'll be right up in th' war—but until we are, an ye can't do nothin' t' keep from bein' bumped off, use a little sense an' don't go yellin' t' 'tract some Boche aeroplane who might lay an egg on all of us. That's all...disMISSED!

(There is a low murmur as the men break ranks...The distant guns sound ominously close for a moment.)

ARKW: *(A captain...coming up.)* Sergeant Bliss.

BLISS: *(Snapping to attention.)* Yes, Captain!

ARKW: Sergeant Turner is sorting a bag of mail that was waiting for us here—I know the men will be very anxious to receive it. Will you see it's distributed as soon as they finish their breakfast?

BLISS: Yes, sir.

ARKW: You'll have to work fast—we may receive orders to proceed to the front at any moment. Better get your own breakfast, Sergeant—God only knows when any of us will get another. *(Moving off.)* That's all.

BLISS: Yes, sir.

ZEIGLER: *(He is neither young nor old, cultured or uncultured, intelligent nor unintelligent—He, in civilian life, was the "average man"—diffidently.)* Sergeant Bliss.

BLISS: Huh?? *(Irritably)* What d' you want, Zeigler?

ZEIGLER: I—I just heard what Captain Arkwright said about there being mail for us. My name is always called at the last—beginning with a Z, you know. I hate to ask favors, but I'm so worried about my wife, I—I wondered if you—

BLISS: *(Truculently)* Y' mean if there's a letter for ye—will I let y' have it ahead o' th' others??

ZEIGLER: *(Miserably)* I—I know what a nerve I have to ask it, but—Well, it's been weeks since I've heard from home, and—*(Half hysterically.)* I—I'm nearly desp'rate, Sergeant!! *(He stifles a sob!)*

BLISS: Hey—hang on t' yerself, soljer! *(Kindly)*

ZEIGLER: Y'will??

BLISS: We'll walk over an get it from Turner now.

ZEIGLER: Oh, gee, Sarge—I'll never forget this!

BLISS: Can it!

ZEIGLER: You—you think there'll be a letter for me?

BLISS: *(Comfortingly)* Sure there will! *(Pause)* Y' still havin' them funny

	dreams about yer wife—th' ones ye've told th' guys about?
ZEIGLER:	*(Low)* Yes. But they're not dreams, Sarge—they're visions. I have them when I'm awake, as well as when I'm sleeping.
BLISS:	*(Uncomfortably)* I oughta send you t' th' Doc an' have your brain examined.
ZEIGLER:	I'm not crazy or imagining things—honest I'm not! *(Low again.)* My wife and I've known each other ever since we were kids—we—we've been in love with one another all that time. Don't gimme the laugh for saying I'm in love, Sarge.
BLISS:	I ain't laughin', guy—I gotta wife an a couple kids back home m'self.
ZEIGLER:	What I'm getting at is—that Jennie and I are very close; closer than folks usually are, I think—so when I began to get those visions a month ago—
BLISS:	They're always th' same—them visions y' talk about?
ZEIGLER:	Yes—I—I see Jennie lying in a pool of blood in the office where she works. And there's a big dark man standin' b'side her with a pistol. His face is photographed on my brain—with the picture of Jennie lying on the floor. *(Desperately)* Sarge—if I don't get a letter from her sayin' she's alright—if I don't learn for sure my visions are just imagination—I—I will go crazy!!
BLISS:	Easy buddy! Here we are—an I'll just bet Turner has a letter for ye. *(Calls)* Oh, Sarge—!
TURNER:	*(Slightly distant.)* 'Lo, Top.
BLISS:	C'm in, Zeigler. Say, Turner—you got any mail for this guy?
TURNER:	*(Approaching mike...uncomfortably.)* Oh—'lo, Zeigler. Yeah—there is a letter fer ye. Uh—Captain Arkwright has it.
ZEIGLER:	The Captain has my letter?
TURNER:	You know—comp'ny commander has t' censor mail. *(Going slightly away.)* He's in th' nex' room with a motorcycle guy that just rode up—I'll call him.
ZEIGLER:	Why should he have my letter? Why—?
TURNER:	*(Slightly distant.)* Cap'n Arkwright, sir—!
ARKW:	*(From next room.)* Yes, Sergeant?
TURNER:	Private Zeigler's here, sir.
ARKW:	*(Approaching)* Be right with you, Sergeant.
ZEIGLER:	Why should the Captain have my letter—?
BLISS:	'Tenshun! Here he comes.
ARKW:	*(Coming in.)* At ease. Sergeant will you leave me alone with Private Zeigler for a moment?

BL & TUR:	Yes, sir.
ZEIGLER:	Why—? Why—? Captain—you have a letter for me.
ARKW:	*(Sympathetically)* Yes, Zeigler—a letter I've just read.
ZEIGLER:	Captain—???
ARKW:	You must prepare yourself for bad news, old man.
ZEIGLER:	Bad—news?
ARKW:	I read your letter because I've heard of the worry you've undergone during the past month—and because it bore the return address of the New York Police Department.
ZEIGLER:	The—police—?
ARKW:	*(Softly)* Zeigler—your wife is dead.
ZEIGLER:	*(Groans...then a low murmur.)* My vision was true—Jennie has been murdered.
ARKW:	Yes. God only knows how that vision, as you call it, came to you. Your wife was shot down by a hold-up man in the place where she worked—the police describe her killing as you've seen it in your dream.
ZEIGLER:	*(Low)* A—a big man shot her. Did the—police arrest him?
ARKW:	The murderer got away. Your wife was alone—no living witness saw him.
ZEIGLER:	I saw him. *(Going...his voice rising in furious decision.)* And he won't get away from me!!
ARKW:	Zeigler—come back here!! Sergeant Bliss—Turner!! Get that poor devil!!
ZEIGLER:	*(Slightly distant...struggling.)* Lemme go! Lemme go!!
BLISS:	We got him, sir!
ZEIGLER:	Lemme go!! He killed my Jennie and he got away! But he won't get away from me—he won't get away from me!!!
ARKW:	Zeigler, man—pull yourself together! I know it's hard, but you've got to do it. You're in the Army. Nothing personal has any meaning here: wife, parents, children, love, or hate or revenge—we've got to forget all that when there's a war on! I've just had orders to take this company to the front—you're part of the company—where it goes, you must go—your place is with your outfit!
ZEIGLER:	You're going to take me into the trenches—to make me kill men I've got no cause to hate while the man who killed my Jennie lives?? Oh, no!!
ARKW:	It's my job—Sergeant Bliss—get the men together—we march at once.
BLISS:	*(Going)* Yes, sir.

ZEIGLER: I won't march—I'm going home! There's just one man I've got to
            kill! I'm the only one who knows him—no one but me can make
            him pay!

(Sergeant's whistle.)

ARKW: Hold him, Sergeant.

BLISS: *(Distant)* You guys! Get yer stuff an' be ready t' fall in—we're
            goin' up!

(Murmur of men outside.)

ZEIGLER: I'm not going up—I'm going back!!

ARKW: *(Going)* Take charge of him, Sergeant—I've got to get ready.

TURNER: I got him, sir. C'm on, Zeigler.

ZEIGLER: No! If I go to the trenches, I may be killed—I can't die until I find
            that tall dark man!!

TURNER: *(Calls)* Hey, Corp'ral—this guy's in your squad—see he gets in line!

CORP: *(Coming up.)* Get yer pack an' rifle, Zeigler!

ZEIGLER: No!

BLISS: *(Outside...bawls.)* Packs an' rifles! Get ready t' fall in!!

(Voices, rattle of accoutrements, etc...)

ZEIGLER: I won't go up—I'm goin' back!!

TURNER: You fool—Y' gotta go with yer outfit— if we let ye loose an' y'
            started back, y'd be shot as a deserter! If y' really wanta live t' get
            th' guy who killed yer wife, come on with us and pray no German
            bullet's got yer number on it!!

ZEIGLER: *(Pause...quietly.)* Yes—all I can do is pray. I pray to be spared, oh
            Lord—not for selfish vengeance, but as Thy instrument of Justice.

BLISS: *(Outside)* Fall in!!

CORP: C'm on, Zeigler—y' gotta go with th' outfit!

ZEIGLER: I'm coming. *(Going)* I pray Thee let me live, oh God, until I do
            Thy Justice—then give me unto Death—I'll be ready.

CORP: What's happened t' th' guy?

TURNER: I'll tell y' later. Th' outfit's in line—I gotta get my own stuff.

CORP: Step on it, Sarge—th' old man's gettin' ready t' take over. *(Going)*

BLISS: Company—'tenSHUN!! Sir—all present or accounted for.

ARKW: Company—left by squads—Route Step—'ARCH!!

(The company moves in broken step...The distant guns grow louder.)

ZEIGLER: *(A prayerful murmur rising above the marching feet.)* I pray Thee let me
            live, oh God—let me live to bring Thy Justice.

(The distant guns.)

(Music)

SCENE II

(Now the guns are very close...We hear an occasional "whizz-bang" and the rattle of rifle and machine gun fire.)

ZEIGLER: *(Slightly distant.)* I pray Thee let me live, oh God—let me live to bring Thy Justice. *(Low...half hysterical.)*

CORP: Gawd—ain't it bad enough we gotta go over th' top in a minute without havin' t' lissen t' that guy prayin'!

BLISS: Shut up! Zeigler kin pray if he wants t'.

ZEIGLER: *(Slightly distant.)* —not for selfish vengeance, Lord—but as Thy instrument of Justice.

CORP: He's been mutterin' that same stuff over and over ever since we started up here. If he don't stop now my nerves is gonna snap!

ZEIGLER: —let me live until I do Thy Justice—then give me unto death and I'll be ready.

CORP: That guy is yella! He's gotta be yella—prayin' for his life like that!!

BLISS: He ain't yella—he's just got a purpose. Your knees is shakin', soljer—his'r steady as a rock. Better do a little prayin' yerself—when we get th' whistle t' climb outa this trench a lot of us are goin' on a long, long trip.

CORP: If a bullet's got yer number on it, no prayer is gonna stop it.

BLISS: I dunno 'bout that. Faith can move mountains, they say—an' Zeigler seems t' have th' kind o' faith that takes.

CORP: I ain't got no faith, at all.

BLISS: I have—I just ain't got enough. I wish I had.

ZEIGLER: I pray Thee let me live, oh Lord—let me live to bring Thy Justice.

(A whistle from down the trench.)

ARKW: There's th' whistle! *(Shouts)* Over we go—c'm on!!

(An answering shout from men...A burst of machine gun rifles and a trench mortar from German trench...Cries of wounded men.)

CORP: Th' Boche see us—an' they're ready for us!

BLISS: God—they've started Hell t' poppin'! We'll never make it, but come on!!

CORP: Guys are droppin' all around us!

BLISS: We can't stop! Come on!!

ZEIGLER: I pray Thee let me live, oh Lord—I pray Thee let me—Ahh-! *(A choking cry.)*

CORP: Zeigler's struck! There's a big hole in his chest!

BLISS: He's done—we gotta go with th' outfit! C'm on!!

CORP: *(Hysterical)* Ha ha...I said no prayer would stop a bullet that had yer number on it—! *(Cries)* Ahh—I'm hit!! *(Choking)* Sarge—!

BLISS: *(Groans)* They got me, too—in th' stomick—oh, God—!

CORP: *(Gasping)* Ha ha...th' three of us'll die t'gether; me who ain't got any faith—you who didn't have enough—an' Zeigler, who had th' kind it take t' move a—mountain. *(A final gasp.)*

ZEIGLER: *(Weakly)* Thou wilt not let me die, oh Lord—Thou knowest I must—live—to—bring—Thy—Justice.

(The sounds of battle drown his voice.)

(Music)

SCENE III

(Desultory rifle and machine gun fire in the foreground and big guns in the rear...The sector is not "quiet.")

1ST MAN: *(A stretcher bearer.)* There's nothin' but dead ones here, soljer.

2ND MAN: *(A stretcher bearer.)* Yeah—stiffs, every one of em.

1ST MAN: Just a waste of time—them Boche was sure ready for our bunch when they went over last night.

2ND MAN: Sure were. B Company, who went first, was completely wiped out, I hear.

1ST MAN: So was F, further down th' line. But th' Heinie trench was fin'ly taken, so I s'pose them Gen'rals back at Headquarters'll say it was a great vict'ry.

2ND MAN: *(Morosely)* Yeah—them Gen'rals safe in G.H.Q. has a lotta fun outa this war.

1ST MAN: *(Blithely)* Th' papers say this'll be th' last war, though.

2ND MAN: Uh huh—an' it'll make th' world safe fer th' Democrats. That means us, prob'ly—I think them Gen'rals is all R'publicans.

(A shriek of a shell.)

1ST MAN: Duck!!

2ND MAN: Gawd!! *(The shell burst slightly distant.)*

1ST MAN: A whizz-bang!!

2ND MAN: An it landed damn close! Le's beat it back t' th' dressin' station 'fore th' next one gets us!

1ST MAN: Yeah—we ain't doin' no good out here—these poor guys lyin' around us all got theirs for keeps last night.

ZEIGLER: *(Distant...weakly.)* Thou wilt not let me die, oh Lord—

2ND MAN: Wha's that???

ZEIGLER: —Thou knowest I must live to bring Thy justice.

1ST MAN: One o' these stiffs is speakin'!

2ND MAN: It's th' guy lyin' here.

1ST MAN: This fella??

2ND MAN: Yeah—

1ST MAN: Yer' crazy—there's a hole in his chest big enough t' drive a truck through!

2ND MAN: It's th' guy who spoke I tell ye! Look—his lips is movin' now.

ZEIGLER: —then give me unto Death—I will be ready.

1ST MAN: Gawd! He is alive!!

2ND MAN: You take his feet—we'll roll him on th' stretcher.

1ST MAN: What's th' use? He'll croak b'fore we get him in.

2ND MAN: Don't argue—help me roll him on! Them shells is fallin' too thick around here for comfort.

1ST MAN: Alright—but takin' this guy is just a waste o' time: he's dead right now an' won't admit it. Okay my end.

2ND MAN: Okay here. Lift!

1ST MAN: Alley oop! C'm on.

ZEIGLER: —not for vengeance, Lord—but for Thy justice.

(The distant guns for a moment.)

SCENE IV

COLONEL: *(A medical officer.)* You say he's still alive, Sister?

SISTER: *(A French nun.)* Yes, Colonel Docteur. An' he ees growing strongeer— he ees going to remain alive.

COLONEL: I can't understand it. With that hole in his chest, he shouldn't have survived ten minutes after he was struck. How he lasted the trip from dressing station to field hospital, and then here to the Base, I don't know. Now—I've done my best for him as a surgeon; but my best shouldn't have been enough. It's a positive miracle.

SISTER: Yes—God must 'ave a purpose in preserving thees man's life.

COLONEL: *(Skeptically)* Hmm—I'm not a very religious man, Sister—so excuse me for asking why God should preserve this chap out of an entire company. Except for him, his entire outfit was destroyed.

SISTER: I cannot presume to guess God's purpose, Colonel Docteur. *(Low)* We mus' be quiet—thee pauvre soldat ees waking.

COLONEL: *(Hushed...rather awed.)* It's unbelievable that he should wake. I feel as though I'm in the presence of something unnatural—a living dead man.

SISTER: Shh—his lips are moving—he ees saying something.

ZEIGLER: —let me live to bring Thy justice, Lord—then I'll go with the outfit.

(Music)

SCENE V

CASEY: *(A police inspector.)* Come in, Mr. Zeigler—sit down. Sorry I was away yesterday when you called.

(Door closed.)

ZEIGLER: I suppose your assistant, Captain Evers, told you who I am and why I'm here, Inspector Casey.

CASEY: Yes. You just got back from France yesterday, eh? I suppose little old New York looks pretty good to you ex-doughboys.

ZEIGLER: I am very glad to be back here.

CASEY: And you have extra reason to be glad, Evers tell me—said you'd been in the hospital for a year after being all shot up in the trenches.

ZEIGLER: I am the only man of my company who still lives. Inspector—you have never found a clue to the man who killed my wife?

CASEY: No—we haven't. Don't think the Police Department has laid down on its job—we've simply had no lead to follow. Your wife was alone when the burglar shot her. The murderer left no evidence behind him, and your dead wife was the only one who saw him.

ZEIGLER: No. I saw him.

CASEY: You saw him?? You were three thousand miles away!

ZEIGLER: Still—I saw him.

CASEY: How—??

ZEIGLER: If I told you, you wouldn't understand. Yesterday, Captain Evers allowed me to look through your rogues gallery. The picture of my wife's murderer is not there. Inspector, I don't know anything about police work so I'm here today for your advice. How shall I begin searching for a man whose face nobody knows but me?

CASEY: If you really have some way of recognizing the killer, and if he's still in New York—it'd be like looking for a needle in a haystack.

ZEIGLER: A needle can be found in a haystack if a man is willing to pull it apart one straw at a time. I'm willing to do that, Inspector.

CASEY: *(With growing discomfort.)* There's an—an old saying that if you stand long enough on the corner of 42nd Street and Broadway, you'll see most of the world pass by. But I don't think there's a living man with the patience to try that very long.

ZEIGLER: I'm not a living man, Inspector.

CASEY: *(Startled)* Huh??

ZEIGLER: *(Quietly)* I'm merely an instrument of Justice. *(Going)* Thanks for your advice. Good day, Inspector.

(Door opened and quietly closed.)

CASEY: *(To himself...awed.)* Well, I'll be—!

SCENE VI

(A key is turned in lock and a door opened.)

ANNA: *(A young chambermaid...stridently.)* 312 is next, Mamie—Th' party just checked out, and th' housekeeper says t' clean th' room thorough.

MAMIE: *(An old chambermaid, and a rather grouchy one.)* Whew—I'll say they needs cleanin'! *(Fussily)* Cigar butts an' bottles all over th' floor— we'll be in here half a hour, at least.

ANNA: *(Blithely)* I don' mind. I like t' woik in 312 'cause y' get such a good view of Broadway an' Foity-secont from th' winda. I always say chambermaid woik is real educational if yer' in a hotel near Times Square an can watch th' people passin'.

MAMIE: Y' sure see some funny ones.

ANNA: I'll say. Well Crazy Zeigler is holdin' down his usual spot this mornin'.

MAMIE: "Crazy Zeigler"?

ANNA: Don't tell me you ain't never noticed him! He's th' guy who's allus standin' on th' northeast corner—y—know: th' fella who looks like sumthin' th' undertaker forgot t' call fer.

MAMIE: Oh—him! Sure—ev'ry mornin' fer a year, I've seen him on that corner when I came t' work; an' he's still there when I leave at night.

ANNA: I don't think he ever leaves it even long enough t' eat.

MAMIE: "Crazy Zeigler," they call him, eh?

ANNA: Uh huh.

MAMIE: What's his racket?

ANNA: I dunno. He never seems t' do nuthin' 'cept watch th' crowds pass by.

MAMIE: 'S a wonder th' cops don't chase him—they don't usually allow fellas t' hang out in one spot like he does.

ANNA: They got orders t' leave him alone—I got that straight from Mike Donlin. Y' r'member Mike—he usta be th' traffic officeh on S'vent Av'na an' ferty-t'ooid who was s'wild about me.

MAMIE: Well, we can't bother about nutty guys who stand all day on corners—we gotta get at this mess. I'll pick up th' bottles an you start in with th' broom.

ANNA: (*Excitedly*) Wait! Mamie—come back t' th' winda! I'll show y' a guy that's woith botherin' about!

MAMIE: What d'ye mean?

ANNA: Lookut that big dark fella comin' down Ferty-secunt! He's Black Nick Fozzi!!

MAMIE: (*Excitedly*) Black Nick Fozzi??

ANNA: Yeah—th' big gangster!

ANNA: Gee—Lemme take a look!!

ANNA: Take a good look, Mamie, while y' gotta chanct—Nick don't come t' Times Square often; his hang-out's in th' Bronx. An y'd never know him if a goil like me, who knows her onions, wasn't here t' pernt him out—he's too wise t' let th' papers get his pitchurs; an' th' cops have never mugged him, though he's been a crook fer years!

MAMIE: Yeah—but just a little crook 'til afta th' war.

ANNA: He ain't little now—he runs the Bronx! (*In surprise.*) Mamie—lookut Crazy Zeigler!

MAMIE: (*Incredulous*) He's leavin' his corner.

ANNA: Yeah—What'n th' woild—?? Say—I think he's follyin' Black Nick Fozzi!

(*Music*)

SCENE VII

NICK: (*An Italian-American gangster...He is a little more than half drunk.*) Louie, quit talkin' lika fool—y' gimme a pain!

LOUIE: (*A ratty gunman from the ghetto...His speech is excited and rapid.*) But it's fer yer own good, I'm talkin', Nick! I'm tellin' y' yer takin chances lettin' this crazy Zeigler guy hang around y' all th' time! Who is he—what d' ye know about him, 'ceptin' dat he had d'noive t' brace y' on th' street one day?

NICK: I told y' t'ousand times he's justa nut dat wants t' be my frien' b'cause I'ma big shot! (*Laughs*) Ha ha...he's lika leetla boy who wants t' shake da hand ova General Pershing—he'sa geev me lotta laughs.

LOUIE: If he should be a dick, mebbe—y' wouldn't find s'much t' laugh at.

NICK:	A dick?? Dat leetla guy all skin an' bone, dat I could pull apart weet jus' two finger! *(Laughs uproariously.)*
LOUIE:	Alright—alright! I edmit he dunt look like no cop—but—fellas dat do look like cops has been hangin' 'round dis joint aplenty lately—dis Crazy Zeigler may be stoolin' fer em.
NICK:	Aw, ferget it! I'va checked on heem—an' he'sa justa harmless nut dat usta stan' all da time on Forty-second Street an Broadway. He'sa fonny to me—I like t' have him 'round.
LOUIE:	Yeah—y' like him round 'cause he tells y' what a great big guy y' are!
NICK:	*(Truculently)* Well?? Ain't I a biga guy??
LOUIE:	*(Hastily)* Sure! Sure y'are, boss!! Gee—I didn't mean dat I dunt t'ink so!!
NICK:	*(Mollified)* Huh—you'da better...

(Knock at door.)

	Who'sa dere?
BUTCH:	*(A gangster...outside.)* Me, boss—th' crazy guy is here t' see y'.
NICK:	Send him in—an' bring another bottle whisky, Butch!
BUTCH:	*(Going)* Okay.
LOUIE:	I'm goin'—if yer' gonna sit here with yer' notty fren an' tell him bedtime sturies!
NICK:	*(Laughs drunkenly.)* Better stick aroun', Louie—ye'll maybe hear a lotta teengs y' never knew b'fore.
LOUIE:	I already heard y' spillin' t'ings t' dat guy y' shoulda kept under yer hat—'spechly when y' been drinkin', like t'night.
NICK:	*(Angrily)* What d'y' mean???
LOUIE:	*(Hastily)* Nuthin'—nuthin'!! Gee, boss—dunt get hot 'bout ever'thin' I say! I'm only warnin' y' on account of I'm yer friend!
NICK:	My frien'—ha! You wouldn't steeck weet me one minute if I wasn't in da dough! Da only guy who don't take nothin' from me is th' guy y'r always knockin'! You an' da rest ofa dese rods who hang around me are justa buncha rats—dat Crazy Zeigler is da only frien' I got!!
LOUIE:	You been drinkin', boss—y' dunt know what yer sayin'!

(Door thrown open.)

NICK:	Get outa here, ye rat—GET OUT!!
LOUIE:	*(Going away...fearfully.)* Okay, boss! Okay! Okay!
NICK:	*(Bawls)* Zeigler—where are y'?
ZEIGLER:	*(Distant)* Here, Nick.
NICK:	I thought y' was comin' in t' see me! What y' stallin' fer??

ZEIGLER:	*(Coming up.)* Butch said you wanted another bottle, so I went after it myself—you know how I like to do things for you, Nick.
NICK:	*(Drunkenly)* Yeah—'cause y'r my frien'! Da only frien' I got, Zeigler.
ZEIGLER:	It's nice to hear you say that, Nick—I've wanted to be close to you.
NICK:	You teenk Nick isa one great guy.
ZEIGLER:	You're the most important guy in the world to me.
NICK:	*(Laughs delightedly.)* Open dat bottle—you anda me weel have a dreenk!
ZEIGLER:	*(Simply...quietly.)* Then will you tell me some more about yourself, about the big jobs you've pulled that made fools of the police?
NICK:	*(Lowering his voice in drunken caution.)* Shut dat door—I don't want d' other guys t' hear us talk.
(Door closed.)	
	I don' trust dem like I do you. *(Chuckles)* Y' like Nick t' tell y' 'bout himself, huh—you teenk he's bigger guy dan Jesse James?
ZEIGLER:	I don't think Jesse James had so many notches on his gun as you have, Nick.
NICK:	*(Laughs heartily.)* Ha ha...you maka me laugh! I betcha you're more old dan I am, but you talka lika leetla boy! What a funny craziness you got!
ZEIGLER:	*(Quietly)* I'm not crazy.
NICK:	Not crazy?? *(Nearly bursts with laughter.)* When I hear you say dat, eets da funniest teeng of all!!
ZEIGLER:	Can I see your gun again, Nick—with all the notches on it?
NICK:	Sure! Here, look good—da same gun I've always carry since I hold up dat groc'ry store I tole y' 'bout when I was justa punk. *(Quickly)* No, no—don't touch! Nick never let nobody lay dey're hand upon his gun!
ZEIGLER:	I thought you trusted me.
NICK:	I don't trus' no one dat much. Come on—we have a dreenk!
ZEIGLER:	None for me, thanks.
NICK:	You won't dreenk wit me? Ha ha...you are mad at Nick! *(Laughing)* You are like da leetla boy whose modder say he cannot have da ice cream! Here, my frien'—look! I place da pistol on da table to show I really trus' you—you may look, but do not touch. Is dat alright now?
ZEIGLER:	Yes—for I know you wouldn't do that for anyone but me.
NICK:	Nobody else is such a harmless fool like you...ha ha!
ZEIGLER:	There's five notches on the grip—and each one stands for a man

	you've killed.
NICK:	Yeah—when people get funny weeth Nick, they fin' he's one bad guy t' monkey weeth.
ZEIGLER:	You've told me about each notch: the first for the grocer who didn't put up his hands when you told him—
NICK:	*(Chuckles)* Ha ha...he looked so funny when I plug heem!
ZEIGLER:	The second is for the paymaster; the third for that policeman; and the other two for men who tried to double-cross you.
NICK:	You know dem notches now so well as me.
ZEIGLER:	And the law never got you for a single one.
NICK:	Not me—Black Nick's too smart. No one knows but you—if you told, nobody would believe a crazy man who usta stand all day on a corner.
ZEIGLER:	I'm not going to tell, Nick. Are five all the people that this gun has killed?
NICK:	Ain't dat enough?? *(Laughs)* Oh, so like a leetla boy you are!
ZEIGLER:	I'm so interested in you, Nick, I don't want to think there's anything I haven't learned about you. There's no one in this world who means so much to me as you do. Isn't there something you haven't told me about—someone so unimportant, maybe, that you didn't bother to cut a notch for them upon this gun? Or maybe it's someone you don't want to remember—someone you were ashamed of killing.
NICK:	Ashame??
ZEIGLER:	Yes—perhaps a woman.
NICK:	*(Pause...low and tensed.)* What make you say dat???
ZEIGLER:	Why—I was only talking.
NICK:	*(Dangerously)* You talk too much!
ZEIGLER:	Nick—don't put the gun away!
NICK:	*(Pause...his good nature showing.)* Alright. Pah—I am crazy to t'ink for one minute dat you mean anyt'ing! Pour me 'nother dreenk.
ZEIGLER:	Sure, Nick—sure! Then will you tell me about the woman?
NICK:	I did not say there was a woman.
(Drink poured.)	
ZEIGLER:	You're not afraid to tell me about her, Nick? You like to tell me things—and you know how much I love to hear about your life. This may be more interesting than anything you've ever told me—I know it will be! Here's your drink, Nick.
NICK:	Eet ees not wort' while to talk about. But you guess right! One

time I keel a woman—an' I cut no notch because I was ashame. You keel a man an', even eef you got da hot seat, you are still beeg guy—but a woman: ever'body say you dirty dog.

ZEIGLER: What was the name of the woman you killed?

NICK: *(Carelessly)* I dunno. Eet was in da paper—but I do not bother to remember. She was cashier in beeg office—I watch da joint, an' when I know she was alone I go een an' say I want da dough een cash drawer. She start t' scream an' run for help, so I geev her quick da heat.

ZEIGLER: *(Tensely)* Then, before you ran away—you stood over her a moment with your smoking pistol.

NICK: Yeah, lookin' at her face—I t'ink she kinda perty—*(Suddenly realizing.)* Say—how you know I stand an' look at her?? *(Alarmed)* Zeig, you crazy fool—put down my gun!!

ZEIGLER: Stay where you are—and put your hands up high!

NICK: *(Cries)* Butch—Louie—HELP!!

ZEIGLER: Scream, Nick—SCREAM! Your cries won't save you any more than her cries saved my wife!!

NICK: Your wife???

ZEIGLER: She was the woman you killed, Nick. The love we had called out across the ocean and stamped her dying message and your picture on my brain! I knew you were the man God brought me back from death to punish when you passed me on the street long months ago—but I wanted to be sure! You've made me sure, at last—and now, as you killed her, I'm going to kill you!!

NICK: *(Terrified)* No, no—don't shoot! Don't press dat trigger!! DON'T!!! *(Pause)* You—you are not going to shoot me.

ZEIGLER: I—I can't! God let me live for Justice—not for vengeance.

NICK: Ha ha! You are yellow! Geev me dat gun!!

ZEIGLER: No! Keep back—!! *(Groans)*

NICK: Now eet ees you who weel die—an' Black Nick's gun weel have another notch cut een its handle!!

(The window crashes in.)

CASEY: You'll never cut it, Nick!

NICK: Cops!!

(Door broken open.)

CASEY: Drop that gun! Your joint's surrounded, and we've got your hoods where they can't help you! If you try to make a fight, we'll burn you down!

NICK: I—I ain't gonna fight.

(Gun dropped to floor.)

CASEY: Pick up that gun he dropped, Martin!

MARTIN: Got it.

NICK: What d' y' mean breakin' in here? You cops got nothin' on me, 'cept takin' a gun from a crazy guy who tried t' shoot me.

CASEY: We heard everything you told this crazy guy tonight before he tried to shoot you.

NICK: Dat won't stand in court! I was only kiddin'—you can't prove a t'ing I said!

CASEY: Your pistol will prove plenty, Nick.

NICK: What d' y' mean?

CASEY: No two guns leave the same ridges on the slugs they fire—we've saved the bullet that killed Zeigler's wife.

NICK: *(Desperately)* Gimme dat pistol!!

MARTIN: Try an get it!

CASEY: It's going to send you to the hot seat, Nick! Take him away!

POLICE: C'm on! *(A struggle.)* C'm on we said!!

NICK: *(Goes screaming.)* No, no, no—y' can't burn me! Y' can't send me t' th' hot seat!! No—no—no—!!

(Fades out.)

CASEY: Well, Zeigler—I guess we got here just in time. I've had men watching you ever since you took that stand on 42nd Street—I was sure you were crazy till I learned you'd left your corner to become a pal of Nick's. We didn't know what you were up to with him, but tonight I thought we'd better take a chance and crash the place. *(Puzzled)* Hey, Zeigler—aren't you listening to me?

MARTIN: Inspector—there's somethin' wrong with th' guy—he just sits there starin' at us!

CASEY: Zeigler—!! Get some water, Martin—I think he's fainted! No—wait! He's coming to—his lips are moving!

ZEIGLER: *(Murmurs)* Let me live to bring Thy justice, Lord—then I'll go with the outfit.

BLISS: *(Distant...ghostly.)* Tessatori!

TESSA: *(Distant...ghostly, as are all the voices.)* Here.

BLISS: Vurowski!

VUR: Here!

BLISS: Watrus!

WATRUS: Here!

BLISS: Wurtz!

MARTIN: Inspector—this guy ain't just fainted—he's hardly breathin'!

CASEY: Get to that phone, Martin—call a doctor! Quick!!

MARTIN: *(Going)* Yes'r!

BLISS: Youritzan!

YOURITZ: Here!

BLISS: Yost!

YOST: Here!

BLISS: Zeigler!

ZEIGLER: *(Ghostly like the others.)* Here!

CASEY: Martin—don't bother about the doctor. Zeigler's heart has stopped.

BLISS: Company all present or accounted for, Captain.

(A ghostly bugle sounds taps.)

(Music)

EPILOGUE

NANCY: Weel—that's th' end o' that un, Satan. He he he he...

(Musical theme.)

Devil Hands

Friday, September 14, 1934

(Musical theme.)

ANNOUNCER: We bring you the one hundred and sixty fourth weekly presentation of the famous dramatic feature, The Witch's Tale, written and produced by Alonzo Deen Cole and starring Mr. Cole and Miss Marie O'Flynn. The Witch's Tale. And now let us join old Nancy and Satan, her wise black cat.

(Music swells...wind whistles...)

PROLOGUE

NANCY: He he he...(CAT) Hunner and ten yeer ole, I be t'day—yes'r, hunner an ten yeer ole! Weel, Satan—'fore we gits down t' our yarn spinnin', we got a leetle dooty t' perform. (CAT) Tha's right...me an' you haz been gittin' a lotta letters lately askin' why we ain't been tellin' more o' our magic charms—pertickler our love charms. So t'night we're gonna tell th' young folks—an' th' ole folks, too—how t' gain th' girl or feller they've set their eyes on. All ye gotta do is git seven common beans, w'ich ye place in a circle on th' road whar th' pusson ye got a hank'rin fer is bound t' pass...then, if th' loved one steps over th' beans or on em, he or she'll be drawn to ye t' declar' his or her affection. But—if they steps 'round th' magic circle, th' charm has failed. An' now that we got that off our chests, Satan, tell ever'one t' douse their lights. (CAT) Tha's hit...Make hit nice an' dark an' cheerful when ye hears our bedtime sturies. Draw up t' th' fire an' gaze inter th' embers...gaze inter em deep, and soon ye'll heer a clock astrikin' *(As clock strikes ten...)* Soon ye'll see a nervous, worried man apacin' up an' down a fine big room—soon ye'll hear our yarn o' "Devil Hands"...he he...DEVIL HANDS.

SCENE I

(At tenth stroke of clock dialogue begins.)

TERRY: *(Nerve wracked...half hysterical.)* Dr. Shelton—Laine, dear—it's ten o'clock. In an hour, Ivan Turgoff will be strapped in the electric chair. His last request is that I visit him before he dies! Don't try to dissuade me from going any longer.

LAINE: *(His wife.)* Terrance, darling—you're in no condition to visit that prison tonight! You've been ill for a week—on the verge of a nervous breakdown.

TERRY: *(Bitterly)* What does that matter when another man is going to his death—a death to which I've sent him?

SHELTON: *(A middle aged physician...impatiently.)* Son—for the love of Heaven, try to think and think sensibly! Six months ago the people of this town elected you their District Attorney. As the defender of decent society, you've sent a degenerate murderer to the just punishment he deserves. Why should you have any qualms about it?

LAINE: You know he killed that woman, dear—you proved it to the hilt.

TERRY: *(Wearily)* Oh yes—I know he killed the woman.

SHELTON: Then why should you have any sympathy for him?

TERRY: Oh, you don't understand.

SHELTON: Your wife and I understand a great deal better than you do! You're a sick man. You ought to be in bed—and, as your physician, I want you to go back there without any more argument.

TERRY: Dr. Shelton, I must talk to Turgoff again before he dies. I'm going to put on my clothes and have Nicholas drive me to the prison!

SHELTON: *(Belligerently)* Those pajamas and that dressing gown are the only clothes you're going to wear tonight, young fellow—and you're not stirring from this house!

TERRY: Oh, yes I am!

SHELTON: Oh, no you're not!

LAINE: Terry—please—!

TERRY: Let me go—both of you!

SHELTON: Not a chance! Now you sit down in that chair and act rational!

LAINE: There isn't the slightest reason for the way you're acting—you've just admitted that you have no doubt that Ivan Turgoff strangled his sweetheart—! You can't have any doubt—it was proven, he admitted it!

TERRY: That's not the point.

SHELTON: No—the point, in your overworked, half hysterical, condition is that your mind has been dwelling upon the man's absurd defense!

LAINE: *(Incredulously)* Doctor—Terry couldn't believe the mad story Turgoff told in court!

SHELTON: This was your husband's first murder case, Mrs. Burke—and he's Irish. Temperamentally, he's apt to believe any fairy tale.

TERRY: Turgoff's story may not have been a fairy tale.

LAINE: Darling—Turgoff's story was one which only a lunatic would tell.

TERRY: That's what I thought at the time. But the psychiatrists found him sane—they helped me send him to the chair.

SHELTON: *(Impatiently)* The specialists who testified at his trial found him to be a congenital liar with a perverted mentality, but capable of distinguishing between right and wrong—which is all the law requires in determining criminal liability.

TERRY: I know all that, but—You're really convinced there would be no basis in his claim that—?

SHELTON: That his hands strangled his victim without connivance of his brain? Of all the arrant nonsense!

TERRY: He said they were not his hands, but the Devil's—Devil Hands, he called them.

LAINE: Terry—Only people who lived in the dark ages would credit that ridiculous story of witchcraft! Turgoff's own lawyers were apologetic when he told it on the witness stand, and the jury frankly laughed! It was by ridiculing his asinine testimony that you made the jury bring in a verdict of guilty on the first ballot!

TERRY: Yes—I know I ridiculed it. But who was I to say it was just a childish lie? How can anyone deny the Devil exists simply because they've never seen him?? For thousands of years tales have been told of the compacts he has made with men. Who are we to say those tales were never based on truth?? Turgoff was a great painter, a fine sculptor—yet he had had no schooling in the arts— he displayed no talent for them until he was a grown man. He said he gained that talent by a Satanic compact—that the Devil gave him his clever hands.

LAINE: Oh, Terry—!

SHELTON: *(Disgusted)* For the love of Heaven—!

TERRY: I had no right to say he told a lie. You have no right to laugh at his story now!! It was shown in court that strange ceremonies were often held in his studio—that he belonged to a cult of Satanists. His story may be true—the hands that strangled his sweetheart

	may have been not his, but the Devil's.
SHELTON:	If they were, it's an additional reason why he should go to the chair without any sympathy from anyone.
TERRY:	No. No matter how bad a man is, the law should not condemn him for a crime that's not his own!
SHELTON:	I've heard enough of this nonsense! When your brain was functioning normally you realized the man was merely aiming at an insanity verdict when he told that story. Now you're going back to bed!
TERRY:	No! He's asked to see me—it's his last request!
LAINE:	You're going to do as the doctor says, Terry!
TERRY:	Let me go—don't take me to my room!
SHELTON:	*(Firmly)* Come on.
TERRY:	Doctor—Laine—in an hour the man will die. I know I can't save him, but I must talk to him again.
SHELTON:	In this room with you, son.
TERRY:	No. Oh, I haven't strength enough to fight you, but—Doctor, please—Call the garage, Laine—tell Nicholas to bring the car.
LAINE:	Go to bed, Terry—!
TERRY:	I've got to see Turgoff! I've got to hear him tell me that not Devil Hands, but his were guilty of the crime for which I've sent him to his death!
SHELTON:	Help me pull off his dressing gown, Mrs. Burke.
TERRY:	Doctor, I beg—!
SHELTON:	Alright, Mrs. Burke—now I'll lift him into bed.
TERRY:	*(Weakly)* Laine, make him let me go—
LAINE:	Go to sleep, dear—rest, for my sake.
SHELTON:	He will. Come on, Mrs. Burke—I'll turn out the lights.
(Light switch.)	
TERRY:	No—please—Laine—*(Going away.)*
LAINE:	Goodnight, dear.
TERRY:	*(Growing distant...weakly.)* He may not have meant to do it—he may have told the truth of Devil Hands—
SHELTON:	*(Softly)* Let me close this door.
(Door closed.)	
LAINE:	Doctor—you're certain we dare leave him alone?
SHELTON:	I'm going to lock him in.
(Door locked.)	
	He'll be alright—he's exhausted himself with those outbursts—

	he'll be sound asleep in five minutes.
LAINE:	You're sure his mind is alright? When I heard him say he believed that mad story of—
SHELTON:	That's just the result of his brain fatigue and frayed nerves. A good long rest will soon put him on his feet, mentally and physically.
TERRY:	*(Inside...muffled.)* Devil Hands...Devil Hands...
LAINE:	*(Hushed)* Listen—He's talking to himself in there.
SHELTON:	He won't talk long—he's too tired. Come back to the other room. *(Going away.)* I want to write a prescription for you to give him when he wakes.
TERRY:	*(Inside...muffled.)* Devil Hands...Devil Hands...Devil Hands...

(Music)

SCENE II

(Soft clicking of a telephone hook.)

TERRY: *(Low)* Operator—Operator, won't you hurry, please and get that number? Hello. That you, Nicholas? This is Mr. Burke—I can't talk any louder—I don't want anyone to know I'm calling you. Nicholas, I want you to take the car out the back way and wait for me on Elm Street, a block from the house—Oh, I know I'm supposed to be sick—but there's nothing wrong with me. Listen: you mustn't let Mrs. Burke know you're meeting me—she and Dr. Shelton have me locked in my room and they think I'm asleep. I'm leaving by way of the window—don't argue! If you don't do as I say, I'll fire you! Alright. I'll be dressed in five minutes—you meet me, and be prepared to drive fast. Where are we going? We're going to the State Prison.

(Music)

SCENE III

(Steel door unlocked and opened.)

WARDEN: *(Low)* Turgoff's cell is at the end of the block, on the right, Mr. Burke. You won't have long to talk to him, for everything's ready in there.

TERRY: *(Hushed)* In there—the electric chair?

WARDEN: Yes—just beyond that little door.

TERRY: *(Murmurs)* God—and I'm sending him there. If he'll only tell me he is guilty—not his hands.

WARDEN: Thompson.
GUARD: *(Coming up...low.)* Yes, Warden?
WARDEN: This is District Attorney Burke—he will talk to Turgoff without the usual precautions.
GUARD: Yes sir.
TERRY: Thank you, Warden. I—I'll go to him.
WARDEN: *(Receding)* You and I will remain here, Thompson.
GUARD: *(Distant)* Yes, sir.
TERRY: Hello, Turgoff.
TURGOFF: *(With a light accent...insolently.)* Good evening, Mr. Burke. It is nice of you to grant a soon to be dead man's last request.
TERRY: Why did you wish to see me, Turgoff?
TURGOFF: Because you are the man who sent me here.
TERRY: You're a murderer—it was my duty to see that you are punished.
TURGOFF: You are not sure I am a murderer. You mocked at the story I told in my defense—but you are not sure it was a lie.
TERRY: You still swear—?
TURGOFF: *(Low, but vehement.)* Yes! The mad story that I told was true. These hands of mine are not like other men's—their actions are not directed by my brain; they have intelligence of their own: the intelligence of Hell, from where they came. It was not I who was Ivan Turgoff, the great artist, the great sculptor—it was my Devil Hands. They wielded the brush—they plied the chisel! It was not I who was a murderer—these hands, it was, that curled themselves about the woman's throat and pressed upon it till she died! You, of all the world, are unsure that story is a lie.
TERRY: I—God hear me, I'm not sure! And now there's nothing I can do.
TURGOFF: No—but there is something I can do.
TERRY: What do you mean?
TURGOFF: In a moment I meet the death to which you've sent me. In that moment shall begin my vengeance on you!
TERRY: Vengeance?
TURGOFF: *(Chuckles softly...maliciously.)* Ha ha...in a moment, you think I will be helpless—dead. In a moment, they will lead me through that little door and pull a switch to send searing fire throughout my body. But my hands are not a part of my body—my hands are the Devil's—and you shall have them!
TERRY: You're talking madness!
TURGOFF: I am talking truth—In court, people told of strange rites that were

held within my studio—they said those rites were degenerate orgies. But they weren't—they were ceremonies which have been practiced since the world began by men who wished the powers only Hell can give! I gained those powers—I still retain them, although my body goes to death! I shall use those powers to give you my Devil Hands!

TERRY: That's impossible! You can't frighten me that way!

TURGOFF: Wait and see!

WARDEN: *(Coming up.)* Sorry, Mr. Burke—time's up.

TURGOFF: Which means it's time for me to go in there.

WARDEN: Yes, Turgoff.

(Cell door unlocked and opened.)

TURGOFF: I'm ready. But send that sniveling priest away—I've already told him I want none of his religion!

PRIEST: *(Gently)* My son—at your final hour, repent and seek Divine forgiveness—

TURGOFF: In my final hour, I die as I have lived—in a faith of Evil, Fear and Hate! Come on, Warden.

TERRY: Turgoff—!

TURGOFF: Goodbye, Mr. Burke. *(Going)* I am willing you my Devil Hands...ha ha—I am willing you my Devil Hands!

(Fades off laughing.)

(Music)

SCENE IV

LAINE: Terry, darling—you shouldn't be working at that desk tonight. You know Dr. Shelton's orders are that you remain in bed.

TERRY: *(Testily)* I'm not sick—and I have work to do.

LAINE: You are sick. You might have been completely well by this time if you hadn't sneaked out through the bedroom window last week—and driven to the prison. The exposure and whatever that murderer said to you before his execution has made you worse than before.

TERRY: I—I'm alright, I tell you.

LAINE: No—your nerves are in a dreadful state. *(Pause)* Dear, why won't you tell me what Turgoff said to you that night?

TERRY: Because it's of no consequence. You and Shelton were right—I was a fool to have gone—to have doubted Turgoff's guilt. He only talked a lot of nonsense—made impossible threats. He's dead now—let's not speak of him anymore.

LAINE: Alright. But I wish you'd go to bed, dear.

TERRY: *(Mutters)* Impossible threats. Uh—what did you say?

LAINE: That I want you to go to bed.

TERRY: Not now—I have too much work to do.

LAINE: But you're not working—you're only making idle pencil marks upon that paper.

TERRY: I'm making notes for a court address next week.

LAINE: You haven't been writing dear. What have you been doing with that pencil?

TERRY: I tell you I—God—!!

LAINE: What's the matter??

TERRY: I've drawn a picture here!

LAINE: You can't draw a straight line!

TERRY: I never could before—but look what I've done now!

LAINE: A perfect portrait of a man. It's Turgoff!!!

TERRY: Yes—Turgoff! And I've signed his name to it...in his writing! Only I didn't do it...my hands did it!

LAINE: Terry—what do you mean???

TERRY: *(Wildly)* Turgoff's kept his promise! He's cursed me with his hands—his Devil Hands that can draw and paint and strangle!!

(Music)

SCENE V

TERRY: *(Hysterically)* That picture was only the beginning, Doctor. I haven't told Laine—I haven't told anyone of the things that have happened since. But today I had to come to you—to beg your help.

SHELTON: *(Comforting)* Take it easy, son—and tell me.

TERRY: Well, as I say, I—my hands—drew that portrait six days ago—

SHELTON: And you immediately concluded Turgoff's impossible threat had come true.

TERRY: It has come true! And that picture was only the beginning, I tell you! That night, if my mind had allowed me to sleep, rest would have been impossible. The hands pinched my body—scratched my flesh until the blood came—tortured me until I almost screamed! Every night since they've done the same.

SHELTON: Your hands??

TERRY: They're not my hands any longer—they have an intelligence of their own—a guiding force beyond control of my muscles or my mind!

SHELTON: Terry, you're—

TERRY: Wait! Don't tell me I'm mad until you look at these notes.

SHELTON: Notes?

TERRY: Yes—in Turgoff's writing. Turgoff's dead—but his hands wrote them—his Devil Hands that now are mine!

SHELTON: There, there, now—! Let's have a look at these mysterious notes.

TERRY: Read them. I know you think me crazy—but read them.

SHELTON: Hmm—this one says: "I have kept my promise."

TERRY: That's the first—there's been one every day. The second reads: "Hands that will not die, I will to you."

SHELTON: That's what Turgoff told you in the Death House.

TERRY: Yes. The next note says: "Devil Hands for the Devil's business."

SHELTON: I see. And the next: "Hands that hurt and hands that wound."

TERRY: The day I—these fingers—wrote that, I made this gash in my cheek while shaving. But the razor didn't slip. My hand—this hand—slashed it deliberately into my flesh.

SHELTON: *(Noncommittally)* Hmm.

TERRY: The next note reads: "Hands that strangle, hands that kill."

SHELTON: They didn't strangle or kill anyone the day you wrote it, did they?

TERRY: Don't make fun of me, Doctor. Impossible as this seems, try to believe—and help me!

SHELTON: I'm going to try to help you—but, above all, you must try to help yourself. *(Impatiently...vehemently.)* Good Lord, Terry—you're a man of brains, with a position in this community! Can't you realize all this is merely a delusion born of a weakened body? You've got to pull yourself together! And I'm going to see that you do it with the rest your body needs! I'm going to give you a hypodermic that'll put you to sleep for a week!

TERRY: That won't do any good. There's only one thing that will do any good, Doctor.

SHELTON: What's that?

TERRY: Cut off these hands.

SHELTON: Cut off your hands???

TERRY: Yes—I'm deadly serious. There's a note you haven't read yet— the last. It says: "Devil Hands that lead to death." And that's where they will lead—to my death or another's if you don't do the thing I ask.

SHELTON: *(Angrily)* Do you think for one minute that I'd amputate two healthy members of anyone's body for such a crazy reason as you have given me?? These ridiculous notes—that you wrote in a script resembling Turgoff's don't mean a thing! In preparing his prosecution, you poured over letters of his for weeks—in your present state of mind, it's a natural thing for you to imitate his writing. If I didn't know the man you are when well, I'd take steps to have you put in a sanitarium for mental cases—as it is, I'm going to call an ambulance and send you to a hospital where they'll make you take the rest you need!

TERRY: *(Laughs)*

SHELTON: What are you laughing about??

TERRY: *(Hysterically)* While you were telling me I suffer from delusions, look what my Devil Hands have done!!

SHELTON: Another note?

TERRY: Yes—a note which says: "Tonight these hands will kill!" Look at it—read it!! It says: "Tonight these hands will kill!!"

SHELTON: What are you doing with that pencil now??

TERRY: I'm doing nothing! These Devil Hands are writing again! They write—*(Screams)* No, NO!

SHELTON: You've written: "You're wife!"

TERRY: "Tonight these hands will kill your wife," it says! *(Going...wildly.)* No, no, NO!

(Door thrown open.)

SHELTON: Terry, come back!! Where are you going???

TERRY: *(Going)* I'm taking these Devil Hands away where they can do no harm—away from my wife, from Laine!!

SHELTON: Terry—TERRY!!! Someone stop that madman!!

TERRY: *(Distant)* They shan't harm Laine—they shan't harm Laine!! These hands shan't harm my wife!

(Music)

SCENE VI

(Approaching taxi...street effects.)

TERRY: Taxi—taxi! Taxi!!

DRIVER: *(Coming up.)* Right here, boss!

(Cab stops with squeaking brakes...Door opened.)

TERRY: Drive me to the railway station—fast as you can!

DRIVER: Yes'r! Which one?

(Car door slammed shut...Car starts.)

TERRY: The Western! Ha ha...that's where trains leave for the farthest points away from here! I'll beat you, Turgoff—I'll beat your Devil Hands!

DRIVER: *(From box.)* What say, boss?

TERRY: Never mind! Drive—drive—get me to that station!

DRIVER: Okay.

TERRY: I'm going to beat you, Turgoff—I'm going to beat your Devil—

(His fists beat on glass of windows.)

DRIVER: Hey—what y' doin' back there?? Stop poundin' on them windows!!

TERRY: The hands are doing it—not me!!

DRIVER: Cut it out before y' break th' glass!!!

TERRY: I can't stop them—I can't stop them!!!

DRIVER: *(Furious)* I'll see about that!!

(Car stops quick.)

TERRY: Don't stop your cab—get me to that station!!

DRIVER: I ain't drivin' no crazy lunatic who thinks it's fun to pound on windows!!

(Car door thrown open.)

Get outa here!

TERRY: *(Desperately)* You don't understand! I'm not beating on your window—it's these hands that want to keep me here—they took this way to make you stop your cab!

(Beating stops.)

No! Don't pull me out of here!! Drive me to that station!!

DRIVER: Out ye come, nut—there!!! *(Slams door.)* I—

TERRY: Wait—wait! I'll give you fifty dollars if you'll—

DRIVER: I wouldn't drive you anywheres for all the money in the mint!

(Car starts off.)

TERRY: *(Calls)* Come back! Come back!!!

DRIVER: *(Going away.)* You walk to where you're goin', bug!

TERRY: Yes—walk, walk! But I'll beat you, Turgoff—I'll beat your Devil Hands!!

(Music)

SCENE VII

(A railway terminal...Voices of passengers, porters, announcers, etc.)

MAN: *(A train announcer...distant.)* Trains for all points West on Track 7! Chicago, Kansas City, etc. etc...

TERRY: Give me a ticket, please—to the farthest point out West!

AGENT:	Seattle, Portland or Frisco?
TERRY:	Seattle will do.
AGENT:	Round trip?
TERRY:	No—one way. Quick, please—quick!!
AGENT:	Train doesn't leave for half an hour—no hurry.
TERRY:	No hurry? You don't know! But I'm going to beat you Turgoff—I'm going to beat these Devil Hands!
AGENT:	Here's yer ticket—Fare is sixty three dollars an twenty seven cents.
TERRY:	Thank you. I—The hands won't take the money from my pocket!!!
AGENT:	Huh??
TERRY:	Come outside your office—you take the money for that ticket from my pocket!!
AGENT:	What's the idea??
TERRY:	Don't question—get the money! Then you can have a hundred for yourself if you'll give the conductor my ticket and put me on that train! I'll beat you, Turgoff—!
AGENT:	I think you're crazy!
TERRY:	For God's sake, do as I ask you! I've got to leave this town before tonight! Porter—PORTER!! You do it!!
PORTER:	*(A negro...coming up.)* Yas, suh—yas, suh! What you want me do, suh?
TERRY:	Put your hand in my inside pocket and take out the wallet there!
PORTER:	Tha's kinda unusual, but ah'll do it, suh.
AGENT:	I wouldn't George—the guy's goofy, if ye ask me.
TERRY:	Hurry, hurry!! I'm going to beat you, Turgoff—!!
PORTER:	*(A choking scream.)*
AGENT:	Let go that man's throat!!
PORTER:	*(Gasping)* He's chokin' me t' death—!!
TERRY:	The Devil Hands—I can't let go!!
(Crowd gathers.)	
VOICES:	*(Coming up...ad lib.)* Help—help!! Police! A madman!!
AGENT:	*(Shouts)* Someone stop that maniac before he kills the porter!! Ryan!! Ryan!!!
RYAN:	*(Coming up.)* Make way—make way!! I got th' murderin' thug—Good Lord save us!!—District Attorney Burke!!!
TERRY:	*(Sobbing)* Take me to jail, Ryan—lock me in a cell! There, these Devil Hands can do no harm!!
RYAN:	*(Aghast)* I don't understand, sir.

TERRY: You don't have to—just see if that man is hurt, then lock me up!
AGENT: The porter's okay—he's comin' to.
TERRY: Thank God!
RYAN: Take care of th' porter, Becker. All you people clear away—there ain't no circus goin' on here!

(Crowd moves away muttering.)

            (Low) Now you come with me, Mr. Burke—I'll get you outa this without anyone even guessin' who yez are. I've heard what a sick man ye've been—just take it easy now—ye're not yerself.
TERRY: No, I'm not myself...ha ha! Part of me is a man who's dead. But you're going to help me beat him—you're going to lock me in a cell.
RYAN: Hardly that, ser—a cell would be no place for this town's District Attorney.
TERRY: You're not taking me to jail??
RYAN: Certainly not, ser—I'm takin' ye home t' yer wife.
TERRY: No—no—NO!!!
(Music)

SCENE VIII

RYAN: *(With relief.)* Sure, Mrs. Burke—bringin' yer poor husband t' this house is th' hardest work I ever did in my life! He fought me every step ov th' way.
LAINE: Thank heaven you did find him and bring him home, Officer Ryan!
SHELTON: I say "amen to that!" When he ran out of my office this afternoon I didn't know what he meant to do with himself. Now that he's safely in his room—in bed—Well, I can breathe easily again.
RYAN: It's sure a queer notion he has in his head about his hands, ser.
SHELTON: It's merely an hallucination caused by his illness.
LAINE: Please don't say anything about it. If the papers should learn—
RYAN: I wouldn't breathe no scandal about a big shot like your husband, ma'am! *(Thoughtfully)* But it's doggone queer—He fought me when I brought him here in a cab. But he did his fightin' with his feet an' head an' body. Looked almost as if he was right about them hands wantin' t' come home, while th' rest ov him wanted t' stay away.
SHELTON: He'll forget it after this night has passed and that silly note is proved a lie.
RYAN: Guess them hands of his won't strangle Mrs. Burke or anyone

else when they're fastened to his bed with handcuffs.

LAINE: I'm so glad you suggested putting those handcuffs on him, Mr. Ryan—when you locked them on his wrists he went to sleep like a baby.

SHELTON: Yes—poor devil felt you were safe then. And he's going to have a good long sleep this time that will put him on his feet—I gave him a hypodermic that will attend to that.

RYAN: *(Thoughtfully)* I was glad t' see you give him that shot, Doc—cause it'll keep him outa trouble if th' handcuffs fail.

SHELTON: What do you mean: "If the handcuffs fail"?

RYAN: Well—if there was any truth in that sick idea he's got about th' Devil Hands, I just remembered that Turgoff was a regular Houdini.

LAINE: Houdini??

RYAN: Yes'm. When we had him in th' city jail here, he usta amuse th' boys by slippin' outa any handcuff they wanted t' put on him.

(Distant door thrown open.)

SHELTON: What's that???

LAINE: Terry!

RYAN: He's comin' from his room!

SHELTON: His hands are free!!

RYAN: They clutch th' wall, an pull his body along behind em!!

SHELTON: I stupefied the man with drugs! How—??

LAINE: *(Going)* Terry—Terry, darling—!

RYAN: Mrs. Burke—!!

SHELTON: Come back here—Don't go near him!!

RYAN: Only Devil Hands like Turgoff's coulda slipped them handcuffs! Keep away!!

LAINE: *(Slightly distant...going.)* I'm going to help him back to bed. Terry—

(A choking scream.)

RYAN: He has her by the throat!!!

SHELTON: Ryan—help me get him!!!

RYAN: I'm with ye! Pry his fingers from her neck—force him away!!

(Struggle)

SHELTON: I can't—he has her in a grip of steel!

RYAN: I'll hit him with my blackjack!

SHELTON: That won't help! Those hands have a life of their own—I see that now!

RYAN: Ahh—we've got him loose—he's let her go!!

SHELTON: Hold him, Ryan—while I see to her!

RYAN: He didn't kill her, Doc—he didn't—?

SHELTON: *(Pause...slowly.)* Yes. God help him now—his wife is dead.

RYAN: *(Pitying)* Holy Mother. *(Pause)* He's shakin off th' drug, Doc—his eyes have opened.

TERRY: *(Murmurs)* I'm going to beat you, Turgoff—going to beat your Devil Hands—

SHELTON: *(Low... quickly.)* Lead him away, Ryan—don't let him see her now.

TERRY: *(Screams)*

RYAN: Too late!

TERRY: Laine—! Laine's dead! The Devil Hands! The Devil Hands!! The Devil Hands!!!

(Music...Very short cue.)

SCENE IX

TERRY: *(As at end of scene.)* The Devil Hands! The Devil Hands!! The Devil Hands!!!

SHELTON: *(Coming in...hurriedly.)* Terry—Terry! Snap out of it, son!

LAINE: *(Coming in.)* Dear—you'll awaken the entire neighborhood!

TERRY: Eh—? Laine? Laine—!

LAINE: *(Laughing)* Don't look at me as though I were a ghost.

TERRY: Laine, you're—

SHELTON: What on earth were you dreaming of, Terry? Your screams were enough to wake the dead!

TERRY: Dreaming?

LAINE: I don't think he's entirely awake yet.

TERRY: Laine—come close to me! Oh, my dear—let me touch you— make sure it's really you—alive—No! I mustn't touch you with the Devil Hands!

SHELTON: Oh—so that's what the nightmare was about!

LAINE: If it was, there need be no more—about that subject. We just had a telephone call from the prison.

TERRY: From the—prison!

SHELTON: The warden phoned to give you Turgoff's last message.

TERRY: Turgoff's last—? What was it?? It may be my dream come true!!

LAINE: It seems Turgoff had an idea his execution would prey upon your conscience, dear...so he asked the warden to assure you that his punishment was just. He made a full confession that he planned the murder long before it was committed...and he went to the chair on the arm of a priest praying to Heaven for forgiveness.

TERRY: *(Murmurs)* The Devil Hands were all a lie?

LAINE: Of course. You never seriously believed a power of evil could control the life of a man?

SHELTON: Certainly, he didn't...Terry realizes that man, thank God, is a free agent who can choose between good and evil.

TERRY: *(Low)* Yes, thank God. *(Pause)* Thank God.

(Musical conclusion.)

EPILOGUE

NANCY: He he he...(CAT) Weel, that's th' end o' that un, Satan! G'night, everyone—an' pleasant nightmares. He he he he (CAT)...

(Musical theme.)

The Alchemist
Friday, October 5, 1934

(Musical theme.)

ANNOUNCER: Again we bring you The Witch's Tale, written and produced by Alonzo Deen Cole. And now let us join old Nancy and Satan, her wise black cat.

(Music swells...wind whistles...)

PROLOGUE

NANCY: He he he...(CAT) Hunner and four yeer ole, I be t'day—yes'r, hunner an four yeer ole! Have these folks douse out them lights now so's we'll have hit dark an cheerful. Draw up t' th' fire and gaze inter th' embers—gaze inter em deep, an soon ye'll be in Lunnon, England, back in th' yeer o' 1796. Thar, at a auction sale ov queer ole books, b'gins our stury o' Th' Alchemist...he he. TH' ALCHEMIST!! He he he he he...(CAT)....

(Music)

SCENE I

AUCTION: *(Somewhat distant...booming.)* And now, gentlemen, I am putting on the block the final treasure of this great auction sale. Gentlemen—it is an alchemical treatise written and inscribed by the hand of that great master of metaphysics, Roger Bacon! Written by Roger Bacon, gentlemen—in his own hand!! What a treasure for the collector! What a treasure for the student!! What a treasure is this volume for one who delves into the mysteries of Nature and the secrets of Black Magic! In short, gentlemen—this work before you is—a treasure!

RICHARD:	*(Wearily...calls.)* Come, Mr. Price—get on with the sale!
VOICES:	*(Ad lib.)* Yes, yes—get on! Waste no more time—it's growing late! Call for bids and let's have done!
AUCTION:	Very well, gentlemen—very well! This priceless manuscript is now upon the block. *(Gavel rapped.)* What am I offered—who'll start with a bid of thirty guineas?
MAN:	*(Slightly distant.)* One guinea!
AUCTION:	One guinea?? That's an insult, sir! Who'll offer twenty for this priceless treasure?
2ND MAN:	*(Distant)* Two guineas!
AUCTION:	Two?? Gentlemen, cease jesting and let's proceed to business. Two guineas I am bid—someone say ten!
3RD MAN:	Four guineas!
AUCTION:	Four! Mr. Kendall—you recognize the value of this priceless work, and you are also one who worships at the shrine of Knowledge. I appeal to you, sir—an alchemical treatise by the hand of a master of Alchemy!
RICHARD:	Ten guineas.
AUCTION:	Ah—I knew I could depend on you, sir!!
ERIC:	*(Low)* Ten guineas for that sheaf of parchment, Richard?
RICHARD:	*(Low)* I'll never get it for that—it's the gem of the sale.
ERIC:	"Gem?" You mean the treasure.
AUCTION:	Ten guineas, Mr. Kendall bid—Who will say fifteen?
ROD:	*(A surly Italian.)* Eleven guineas.
AUCTION:	Eleven! Now we're getting somewhere!!
ERIC:	The Italian is bidding against you again.
RICHARD:	I expected he would.
AUCTION:	Signor Tarsi bids eleven guineas! Who'll say twelve?
RICHARD:	Twenty five!
AUCTION:	Twenty five!!! Ah, Mr. Kendall—!!!
ROD:	Twen'y seex!
AUCTION:	Twenty six from Signor Tarsi!
RICHARD:	Thirty!
AUCTION:	*(Delighted)* Thirty—thirty, Mr. Kendall bids! Signor, you're not stopping now!
ROD:	T'irty one!
AUCTION:	Thirty one from the Signor! You'll go higher, Mr. Kendall!
RICHARD:	Forty!
AUCTION:	Forty!!

ROD:	Forty one!
AUCTION:	Forty one!
RICHARD:	Fifty!
ROD:	Fifty one!
RICHARD:	Sixty!
AUCTION:	Sixty—sixty, I'm bid, Signor! Do you say sixty one? Wait Signor—don't turn away! Are you going to let Mr. Kendall deprive you of this treasure as he's taken every other book you've bid on at this sale? Quick, Signor—the work is going to Mr. Kendall at sixty guineas...*(Rap of gavel.)* It's going, Signor...*(Rap)*...going—going—
ROD:	No—WAIT! I say seexty one!
AUCTION:	Sixty one!
RICHARD:	I say seventy five!
AUCTION:	Seventy five!!
ROD:	*(Screams with rage.)* Ahh—take eet, an' weeth eet take my curse!! *(Going away.)* I curse you—curse you—curse you—!!

(A distant door slams behind him.)

AUCTION:	*(Laughing)* Well, Mr. Kendall—it seems you've gained an enemy and I've lost a customer.

(Laugh from crowd.)

ERIC:	That chap looked as though he'd like to stick a knife between your ribs, Richard.
RICHARD:	Poor devil—he's been keeping a strangle hold on his temper all day. I've bought everything he wanted.
AUCTION:	Now gentlemen—unless I hear any more bids, this priceless treasure is going to Mr. Kendall here for seventy five guineas...*(Rap of gavel.)*... going...*(Rap)*...going at seventy five...*(Rap)*....going at seventy five...*(Rap)*...going—going—gone! *(Final rap.)* And that, gentlemen, completes this sale of priceless treasures—Thank you one, and thank you all.

(Crowd goes out amid a confused babble.)

ERIC:	*(Grumbles)* Thank Heaven, it's over! If I had to hear that fellow say "treasure" again, I think I'd scream.
AUCTION:	*(Distant...calling.)* Mr. Kendall—will you take your treasures with you?
ERIC:	AWKK!!
RICHARD:	*(Laughs)*
AUCTION:	*(Distant...solicitously.)* Is your friend ill, Mr. Kendall?

RICHARD: *(Laughing)* He'll be alright soon, Mr. Price. I'll send my coachman in for the volumes I've purchased—I believe the deposit I have with you more than covers their cost.

AUCTION: It is more than sufficient, sir. Thank you very much, sir. Good day to you, sir.

RICHARD: Good day.

ERIC: *(Decidedly)* Goodbye. *(Grumbles)* This is the last time you'll ever get me in a place of this sort, Richard.

RICHARD: I thought you'd enjoy the novelty of such a sale—you would if you realized the value of the works I've purchased.

ERIC: "Value?" I've seen you spend over five hundred guineas for a dozen dog-eared manuscripts which a sensible man wouldn't consider worth a penny.

RICHARD: You've never thought me a "sensible man," Eric.

ERIC: No—I think a chap with your wealth, and the opportunities it affords for enjoyment, is a perfect madman who lives as you do! Why this auction is the only thing that has drawn you outside the four walls of your laboratory for a month.

RICHARD: I am very busy—

ERIC: At what?

RICHARD: I—I'd rather not tell you until my experiments are more successful.

ERIC: You needn't bother telling me—I know. And I also know that such mad experiments as yours will never be successful.

RICHARD: What do you mean? You can have no idea of my work!

ERIC: You forget we have been friends since we were babies. I know your impractical nature, I know your love of the marvelous—and now I see you buying volumes concerning alchemy and magic. What are you searching for—the Elixir of Life?

RICHARD: *(Hotly)* If I am, who are you to call it a mad experiment that cannot be successful??

ERIC: Hmm—it seems I guessed right. No one has ever yet found that legendary cure-all, have they?

RICHARD: Some men, if they didn't actually find it, came very close to its discovery! Some of them may have left hints that will help me in my search. In the ancient manuscripts that I have bought today, there may be—

ERIC: *(Irritably)* Stuff and nonsense! As though your house weren't already filled with the worthless scribblings of charlatans and fools! *(Gently)* Richard—I don't want to see you throw your life away like this. Forget that laboratory and your studies—for just a month, let's say. We'll go to France and have some fun.

RICHARD: I'm alright. Besides, I went to France with you last year.

ERIC: That's why I suggest you go again—because there, for awhile, I saw you forget your crazy labors and become altogether human.

RICHARD: I tell you, I—

ERIC: Richard, you might find that girl once more in Paris.

RICHARD: *(Pause)* What girl?

ERIC: You know very well! The girl who walked in the Parc Monceau each afternoon—the girl to whom you never had the nerve to speak. I mean the girl with whom you fell in love.

RICHARD: I—you're mad.

ERIC: Am I? When she ceased to come to the Parc—when you realized you'd lost her without ever having met her, you took to your bed in fever! You were in love with her, alright.

RICHARD: I—I—If I went with you to France, I wouldn't find her! I'll never find her! But if I ever do, I swear she won't disappear from me again! Don't talk about her any more! Let's get out of here—I have work to do at home.

ERIC: "Work!"—seeking the Elixir of Life! Bah—if you found it, you wouldn't know what to do with it.

(Door opened and closed.)

RICHARD: There's the carriage—get in and stop talking. Simon!

SIMON: *(A coachman.)* Yes, sir.

RICHARD: You'd best go with him, Adam.

ADAM: *(A footman.)* Aye, sir.

ROD: *(Slightly distant...bitterly.)* A carriage, a coachman and a footman in fine liveries! Eet ees no wonder you can purchase volumes w'ich my small purse denies me.

RICHARD: I beg your pardon?

ERIC: Well—it's the unsuccessful bidder who so roundly cursed you, Richard!

ROD: *(Coming up.)* I 'ave waited to apologize mos' humbly for dat deesplay of temper, gentlemen. Mr. Kendall, weel you say dat you forgeev me?

RICHARD: Why—of course.

ROD: *(Maliciously)* Dat ees mos' generous of you. Now permit me to introduce myself—I am Roderigo Tarsi, at your service.

RICHARD: I am pleased to make your acquaintance, Signor Tarsi. This is my friend, Mr. Waverly.

ROD: I am mos' charm, sir.

ERIC: *(Coldly)* A pleasure, I'm sure.

ROD: And now, Mr. Kendall, I would make you a proposal.

RICHARD: A proposal?

ROD: Yes. Dose manuscripts you bought in dere for more than I could pay—I assume you did not buy dem jus' to gratify a whim; I assume you are a seeker for de truths de Masters knew.

RICHARD: I have a laboratory in my home, Signor, where I am conducting—er—certain experiments.

ROD: *(Eagerly)* Do you seek de Universal Panacea—de Elixir of Life??

RICHARD: Why, I—

ROD: Do not be afraid to speak! Dere ees no Holy Office here in London—no Inquisition dat weel torture you because you search for truths dat fools deny!

ERIC: *(Laughs)* Tell this gentleman your secret, Richard—he seems to be a kindred soul.

RICHARD: I do not hesitate! You have guessed correctly, Signor—I do seek a means to prolong the life of man.

ROD: Then our paths run side by side! I am older than you—perhaps I am closer to our mutual goal! Today you 'ave acquired writings of the Masters w'ich may contain the hint I need to crown my life-long work weeth triumph! Two can read those works as well as one—two may succeed where one might fail. My proposal ees that weeth me you share dose books—w'ile, een return, I share weeth you my experience an' knowledge.

RICHARD: Really, I—

ROD: I can speedily conveence you of my talents een a laboratory! Be generous, Signor—say, at least, dat you weel try me—dat you weel let me read dose books!

RICHARD: *(Coldly)* I am sorry—but I am accustomed to working alone.

ROD: *(Pleading)* Mister Kendall, I beg—!

RICHARD: I prefer to conduct my research alone, Signor Tarsi. Good day.

ROD: Dat ees your last word?

RICHARD: It is.

ROD: *(Furious)* A curse upon you, den! A curse upon you for a stupeed English dog!!

ERIC: *(Angrily)* This fellow needs a horse-whipping—and, by the Lord, he's going to get it!!

ROD: No—don't dare to touch me! *(Going)* Do not dare! A curse upon you—oh, a curse upon you! *(Fades out.)*

RICHARD: Come back, Eric—don't go after him.

ERIC: *(Coming back...laughs.)* Look at him flying up the street as though the Devil himself was after him.

RICHARD: He's a lunatic—I saw that the moment he spoke to us. That's why I refused his proposal.

ERIC: Humph—fine one you are to talk of lunatics!

RICHARD: Get up on your box, Simon. You, Adam—put those manuscripts inside the carriage.

SIMON: Yes, sir. The foreign gentleman seemed werry angry with you, sir.

ADAM: I'll siy 'e did! An' a mur'drous lookin' bloke 'e is.

RICHARD: I fancy we've seen the last of him now. Drive home, Simon.

SIMON: *(From box.)* Yes, sir. Gee up, nags!

(Horses start.)

RICHARD: Simon—stop the horses!! WAIT!!

SIMON: *(Startled)* Whoa!

(Horses pulled up.)

ERIC: What's the matter with you??

RICHARD: Eric—look! The girl who just came out that doorway up the street—It's the girl of the Parc Monceau?

ERIC: Good Lord, it is!

RICHARD: She's here in London! I've found her again—I've found her!!

ERIC: Richard—she's joined that mad Italian!

RICHARD: Tarsi knows her—he can introduce me to her!! Simon—drive after the foreign gentleman and that young lady and when you reach them, stop the carriage!

SIMON: *(From box.)* Yes, sir! Gee up!

(Horses trot with carriage.)

ERIC: You crazy fool—do you think Tarsi will do you a favor now??

RICHARD: He's got to! Now I've found that girl once more, I can't ever lose her again! *(Calls)* Signor Tarsi—wait!

ERIC: He thinks we're after him with the whip—he's going to run!

RICHARD: Signor Tarsi—wait! I come in friendship! Simon—stop the carriage!

SIMON: Whoa!

(Horses stop.)

ROD: *(Distant...fearful.)* Why 'ave you follow me??

RICHARD: To apologize, as you awhile ago apologized. And I have reconsidered our conversation about a partnership—if you permit, I would discuss the matter further. But I intrude, perhaps—you are talk-

	ing with this young lady?
ROD:	*(Distrustfully)* Thees young lady ees my ward.
RICHARD:	Your ward??
ROD:	Yes. Mees Harley, thees ees Mister Kendall.
RICHARD:	Miss Harley, I am honored.
BERNICE:	*(Bashfully)* How do you do, Mr. Kendall. I—I believe I have seen you before—somewhere.
RICHARD:	I–I believe I have seen you somewhere—before.
ROD:	*(Sharply)* Where you two meet before?
BERNICE:	Oh, we've never met!
RICHARD:	We've only seen each other. I—I think it was in Paris.
BERNICE:	I—I think it was in the Parc Monceau.
ROD:	Hmm. Mees Harley's uncle, an old friend of mine, died not long ago—He appointed me her guardian. She now makes her home with me.
RICHARD:	She lives with you?
ROD:	With her chaperone, of course. Now, Mister Kendall, you say you 'ave reconsidered your rejection of my services.
RICHARD:	Yes, Yes! It will give me great pleasure to have you share my laboratory, Signor Tarsi! And you will wish to live near the scene of our research. My house is very large—you and Mistress Harley will stay with me as my guests.
ROD:	You are veree kind—we accept your invitations.
RICHARD:	Good! Good!! And your chaperone, Mistress Harley—there will be accommodations for her, too, of course.
ROD:	Your kindness overwhelms us, sir. But de chaperone weel not be necessary long—for, een two months time, Mistress Harley 'ave promise to become my wife.
RICHARD:	Your—your wife?
ROD:	Yes. Now let us shake hands upon our future partnership in science. You forgeev my curses, and I forgeev you for outbidding me on de manuscripts I wished—Onlee—*(Lowered tone....sinister.)* I hope, Mister Kendall, that you weel never again overbid me for a t'ing which I deesire.

(Music)

SCENE II

ROD:	*(Angrily)* Bah—we 'ave failed again! De mixture weel not amalgamate.

RICHARD: *(Listlessly)* What did you say?

ROD: What did I—?? *(Disgusted)* What ees de matter weeth you? In de month since I came to help you een dis laboratory you 'ave shown no more interest een our work dan would a dead feesh! Pah! I t'ought you said you was an alchemist.

RICHARD: I—I haven't been feeling very well lately. The elements didn't fuse in the tube?

ROD: No. Look at dem.

RICHARD: Perhaps we didn't read the manuscript right, or maybe we failed to follow its directions.

ROD: We read correctly—and we did exactly as de writing says. Dese ancient parchments lie! De masters who wrote dem—dey did not put down in writing de great secret dat we search.

RICHARD: Perhaps they didn't really know it—perhaps the Elixir of Life is but a myth.

ROD: No!—If you believed it, you would not 'ave bought dese manuscripts! Dere ees a means by which man can prolong life—a means which men have found an which men weel find again—a means which we must find! If de masters' writings weel not help us learn for ourselves de secret—and, eef by experiment we cannot learn, dere ees yet another way.

RICHARD: What other way can there be to—?

ROD: Eet ees a way I once attempted, but which I weel not try again—at least not now. Eet ees too dangerous.

RICHARD: No means we could employ would be too dangerous if it revealed the secret of prolonging life forever.

ROD: Yes. I do not want immortality eef it cost me somet'ing I want more dan life.

RICHARD: I don't understand you.

ROD: Do not try. Come—back to work! We weel try de mixture again—een different proportions.

RICHARD: I—It's stuffy—I think I'll take a walk in the open air.

ROD: Hmm. You 'ave required many walks seence I came here, my friend. Yet I 'ave been told dat, formerly, you scarcely ever left dees room.

RICHARD: I—

ROD: *(Angrily)* Go and take your walk! Only, eef eet leads you to de garden where Meestress Harley spends each afternoon, you weel remember she ees soon to be my wife.

RICHARD: I don't like your tone or your insinuation, Signor Tarsi!

ROD:　　　Den do not geev me reason for dem! I 'ave seen de way you look at de girl who ees to marry me—an I warn you once again: do not overbid me twice for a somet'ing I desire!

RICHARD:　I accept warnings and threats from no man, Signor Tarsi.

ROD:　　　*(Pause...in dismissal.)* Bah—I cannot spare time to argue. An' I do not fear you as a rival, anyway—eef you are een love weeth Mistress Harley, you 'ave not de nerve to let her know eet—you are de kind of fool who can onlee make calf eyes.

RICHARD:　I—!

ROD:　　　*(Impatiently)* Go away and take your walk—I weesh to begin a new experiment an' you distract me!

RICHARD:　*(Pause)* I'll rejoin you in an hour.

(Door opened.)

ROD:　　　*(Distant)* Alright! Get out.

(Door closed.)

RICHARD:　*(Mutters)* God—he's right! I haven't the nerve.

BERNICE:　*(Distant)* Good afternoon, Mr. Kendall.

RICHARD:　Mistress Harley—! I—I thought you'd be in the garden.

BERNICE:　*(Coming up.)* I was. Mrs. Shelton is sewing out there, and I came in to fetch a spool of thread. Won't you come out and sit with us awhile?

RICHARD:　Yes—I'd like to—No! Wait. Since your chaperone is in the garden, I'd like to talk with you a moment here—here, where we can be alone!!

BERNICE:　Alone?

RICHARD:　I'll show that sneering Italian that I have the nerve to speak! And I can't keep silent any longer!

BERNICE:　Mr. Kendall—?

RICHARD:　For a month I've had you near me in this house—as from the first time I saw you in the Parc Monceau I dreamed and prayed that I might have you close some day. For a month, I've tried to remember that you are promised to another man—now I can't remember anything except I love you! I've said it at last! I love you, do you hear? I love you!!

BERNICE:　*(Quietly)* You have only put something into words that I have known a long, long time.

RICHARD:　You—you knew?

BERNICE:　Of course—I am a woman. If you were not just a man you would know that I love you.

RICHARD:　You—love me?

BERNICE:	Ever since I saw you in the Parc Monceau.
RICHARD:	But—but you have said you'll marry Tarsi??
BERNICE:	My uncle, on his death bed, made me promise that against my will. He was my only relative; he loved me—he thought Signor Tarsi would protect me when I was left alone. He didn't know I feared him.
RICHARD:	You fear Tarsi?
BERNICE:	I have reason!
RICHARD:	Then—then you'll marry me??
BERNICE:	*(Simply)* I've told you that I love you.
RICHARD:	*(Letting himself go at last.)* Oh, my dear one—my dear one!! Oh, my darling—!!
ROD:	*(Slightly distant.)* A veree pretty scene.
BERNICE:	*(In alarm.)* Roderigo!!
ROD:	*(Coming up.)* Yes. I see that I misjudged you as a rival, Mister Kendall.
RICHARD:	As you were spying from behind that doorway, you have heard what has passed between us.
ROD:	Yes—I heard. A second time you have overbid me, Mister Kendall—remember that I warned you. Now I leave you two lovers to your—happiness.

(Music)

SCENE III

BERNICE:	Richard, has this first year of our marriage seemed as wonderful to you as it has to me?
RICHARD:	It has passed like a lovely dream—and my love for you has grown each day, each hour.
BERNICE:	But now its growth is from a distance—whilst only a few short months ago you wished me near you every moment.
RICHARD:	Dearest—you're not growing jealous of my work?
BERNICE:	I shouldn't be, should I? Especially since it never takes you from this house. Only—when you enter that laboratory of yours, in thought we might be the whole wide world apart.
RICHARD:	I suppose, at times, I do become so absorbed in my experiments that you imagine I'm neglecting you. But I'm not, really—in my heart.
BERNICE:	Are you making any progress—in your experiments?
RICHARD:	No—my goal is as far away as ever.

BERNICE: Dear—why don't you give up this impossible dream of yours?

RICHARD: *(Piqued)* Because it's not impossible! The secret of prolonging life exists somewhere in Nature—and that which exists in Nature, man can find and harness to his will. Don't you be like the fools who say a thing can't be because it hasn't been in their experience! Man can learn to live forever!

BERNICE: You wish to live—forever?

RICHARD: Yes—not because I fear death, but for the wisdom the centuries would bring me. I would be the benefactor of mankind! And we should have forever in this world to love each other instead of but a few brief years.

BERNICE: *(Quietly)* I believe there is a better world than this where, if we really love on earth, we shall know a far, far greater happiness.

RICHARD: And I believe that "better world" is but a churchman's lie, concocted by the great to make the small contented with their bitter, hard existence!

RICHARD: Richard—??

RICHARD: You know my views, dear—I'm sorry our opinions differ as to life beyond the grave. Now kiss me, sweet—I must be returning to my work.

BERNICE: Richard—before you go back to your laboratory, there's something I wish to tell you.

RICHARD: What is it dear?

BERNICE: This morning your coachman saw Roderigo Tarsi.

RICHARD: Where?

BERNICE: On the street.

RICHARD: Hmm. The fellow's back in London, then—we heard he'd left the country. But that doesn't concern us.

BERNICE: His return may concern us very much. He threatened us, Richard—and he doesn't forget.

RICHARD: *(Laughs)* Darling, you can't be afraid of that harmless coward! One has only to crack a horsewhip at his back to see him run. I've seen that happen.

BERNICE: I know him better than you do—and I have cause to fear him.

RICHARD: But, darling, the cause you've given me is so very, very silly.

BERNICE: *(Hurt)* Do you think so?

RICHARD: Of course! You blame Tarsi for something in which your uncle was equally at fault—and neither meant you any harm; they merely made you subject of a chemical experiment.

BERNICE: Yes, an experiment that filled my soul with horror—

RICHARD: *(Indulgently)* You exaggerate. All that was done, according to your own story, was that Tarsi and your uncle brought you to their laboratory one day and had you inhale a gas or vapor that made you lose consciousness for a few minutes.

BERNICE: But in those few minutes it seemed as though I lived through centuries of pain—as though I lived a life-time in each single second—hundreds of life-times filled with misery and anguish before they brought me to myself again. And if they hadn't wakened me so quickly, I know I should have died.

RICHARD: *(Consoling)* It will never happen again, my dear. Tarsi will come here with no vapors that will give you horrid dreams. *(Chuckles)* As a matter of fact, if we ever see him again, he'll probably cringe and apologize as he always has before. Now I must go to work.

BERNICE: *(Dispirited)* I'll walk with you to the laboratory door.

RICHARD: Good! I'm sorry it's so near when you walk with me and hold my hand. Here we are already. Kiss me now and say au revoir.

BERNICE: Oh, Richard—you do love me?

RICHARD: Do you doubt it, dear? I love you better than my life.

BERNICE: *(Sadly)* But not better than the secret of life you hope to find. *(Going)* Au revoir.

RICHARD: Bernice—?

BERNICE: *(Distant...a sob in her voice.)* Au revoir.

RICHARD: Hmnm. *(Mutters)* Women are a little mad, I sometimes think.

(Door is opened and closed.)

ROD: *(Slightly distant.)* 'Ave you closed de door tightly, Mr. Kendall?

RICHARD: *(Startled)* Tarsi!!

ROD: *(Coming up.)* Don't be alarmed—your humble servant is not here in anger.

RICHARD: How did you get in this laboratory??

ROD: By climbing through dat open window.

RICHARD: Why are you here?

ROD: For a double reason. First: at our last meeting I said some angry words to you—I weesh to apologize.

RICHARD: Apologize?

ROD: Most humbly. Knowing my nature as you do, you perhaps expected such a t'ing of me. Secondly: I wesh to show you de way to learn de secret we both seek.

RICHARD: You show me the way??

ROD: Once I told you there was another means than by experiment or study to solve de riddle dat has baffled us. I would not take dat method then, an' now I cannot—but you can.

RICHARD: What do you mean?

ROD: Has Mistress Harley—I mean your wife—ever told you of a vapor dat she once inhaled weeth strange effect?

RICHARD: Yes. But what has that to do with—

ROD: Everyt'ing. My friend, your wife ees one of does rare human beings who are clairvoyant.

RICHARD: Clairvoyant?

ROD: Yes. Not een her conscious state—but under de influence of a vapor I, by chance, descovered she can be made to read all secrets of de present an de past.

RICHARD: That is impossible!

ROD: (Vehemently) Ha—you say a t'ing ees impossible? You who seek de Elixir of Life! Listen: dere are wise men in de East who say each man an woman lives a t'ousand times on earth. In de memories of most of us dose former lives have no existence. But sometimes one ees born in whose brain a faint impression of de past ees traced. If such as dey inhale de vapor from de liquid in dees tiny flask one second, dat memory comes to life and dere tongues can tell of all de wisdom dat mankind has ever known! Dey can tell de secrets of de masters who left no written word to guide!

RICHARD: If that were so, you would already know those secrets!

ROD: No—because I feared to use de power een my hands. I loved de woman who, of all de world perhaps, could tell me what I wished to know—de woman who ees now your wife! Dees vapor can be deadly—I would not trifle weet her life!

RICHARD: But you did trifle with it! She has told me how you—!

ROD: A single drop of dees liquid cast upon a spirit lamp was all dat she inhaled—no more; I took no chances! For a single minute she spoke de wisdom of de dead forgotten ages!

RICHARD: What, in that minute, did she tell you?

ROD: You 'ave seen me work weeth crucible an test tube. Do you know another man weeth the knowledge dat ees mine?

RICHARD: (Slowly) No. You taught me things I never knew before—and I have been a student of the Masters.

ROD: Your wife an a drop from dees flask weel teach you more.

RICHARD: But there is danger.

ROD: Yes. I would not risk it a second time when I dreamed dat she would someday be my wife. Now—de choice ees yours to make.

RICHARD: And I say NO! *(Pause)* Yet—you say a single drop is harmless.

ROD: Eet proved to leave no ill effects de only time I tried eet.

RICHARD: Except a nightmare memory.

ROD: De choice ees yours, my friend. *(Pause)* A choice dat may teach you de secret of life.

RICHARD: I—I—Prepare your vapor. I—I will call Bernice.

(Music)

SCENE IV

RICHARD: Bernice, darling—there's nothing to fear. Tarsi knows if you are harmed he'd never leave this room alive.

ROD: Of course! Dat knife upon de table would find eets way into my heart. But I do not deceive. We weel use but a single drop—an', before, a single drop left no bad effects behind.

BERNICE: *(Low...bitterly.)* No—none but a haunting fear, a nightmare memory that never leaves me. Richard, how can you ask that I submit to this ordeal a second time?

RICHARD: Do you think I would if I thought it would bring you any hurt?? But it won't! It may make you the greatest of the heroines of science! Through you the race of men may be as gods—may live forever! And you and I, my dear, may never lose each other—we may love forever!

BERNICE: *(Low)* Our opinions differ as to life and love beyond the grave. Prepare your vapor—I am ready.

RICHARD: You'll submit to the experiment!

BERNICE: Prepare your vapor.

ROD: Eet ees ready. Your husband weel take de flask himself, and let fall into dees spirit lamp one single drop.

RICHARD: Yes, yes—then I will be sure no harm will fall!

ROD: When you drop de liquid een de lamp before her chair, you and I must queek retire to de far corner of de room—eet ees not for us to inhale de fumes, eet ees for us to listen an remember!

RICHARD: Yes, yes! Kiss me, darling, ere the experiment begins.

BERNICE: *(Low)* Not now—wait until the experiment is over.

RICHARD: Darling—you don't wish to kiss me??

ROD: Come, come—begin! Here ees de flask.

RICHARD: One single drop.

ROD: Into de flame.

RICHARD: One single drop, no more. It's done!

ROD: *(Distant)* Run queekly to dees corner now! De vapor rises quickly— you must not inhale de fumes!

RICHARD: No—I join you! It is for me to listen and remember!

ROD: *(Madly)* Eet ees also for you to see, my friend...ha ha—to see and to remember! *(Laughs)*

RICHARD: Why are you laughing?? What—??

ROD: Ha ha! LOOK!!

(A body falls.)

RICHARD: Ahh! Bernice has fallen to the floor!!

ROD: *(Laughs)*

RICHARD: *(Panic stricken.)* Bernice! Bernice!! Her heart's not beating—she's not breathing! You swore a single drop would do no harm!

ROD: I said eet did no harm before—I also said I would not use it once again!!

RICHARD: But you knew, this time, it carried death! You've killed her!

ROD: No—you have killed her!! You would find de Elixir of Life...ha ha—you killed her whom you would love forever! You killed her an she knew eet! She accepted death despising you!!

RICHARD: *(Shrieks)* You devil!! You fiend of hell—!!

ROD: *(Groans)* Ahh—Ahh—! You 'ave thrust a knife eento my breast— but still I laugh! *(He laughs feebly.)* Ha ha—laughing I weel die, for until you are hanged upon de gallows for my murder, you weel 'ave memories to live weeth...memories—ha ha—of how she died despising you...an you weel have thoughts...ha ha—thoughts of how, eef dere ees a life beyond de grave, you—*(Gasps)* You weel never find her. *(He dies.)*

RICHARD: *(Moans)* Oh, God have pity—God have pity.

(Music)

EPILOGUE

NANCY: He he he...(CAT) Weel, that's th' end o' that un, Satan. Yew folks cum see us nex' time I haz a buthday. He he he he he...(CAT)...

(Musical theme.)

Mrs. Hawker's Will

Thursday, June 20, 1935

(Musical theme.)

ANNOUNCER: ...again brings you its famous weekly series, The Witch's Tale, written and produced by Alonzo Deen Cole and featuring Mr. Cole and Miss Marie O'Flynn. THE WITCH'S TALE! And now let us join old Nancy and Satan, her wise black cat.

(Music swells...wind whistles...)

PROLOGUE

NANCY: He he he...(CAT) Hunner an' one yeer ole, I be t'day—yes'r, hunner an' one yeer ole! Weel, Satan—I reckon th' fust thing we better tell these folks t'night iz that nex' week they gotter come an' see us a day earlier. Yep—nex' week ole Nancy iz gonner change her wisitin' hours t' Wensday night at ha'f pas' ten o'clock, Eastren Daylight Savin' Time. Fer yew folks who lives out Wes' that means ye'll heer me an' Satan jest a hour an' a quarter later'n ye do t'night an' a day sooner. I'll be havin' a buthday then...he he— hunner an' six yeer ole I be nex' Wensday night at ha'f pas' ten!— Now, Satan—ef ye'll tell everone t' douse their lights we'll be gittin' down t' bizness. (CAT) Tha's hit! He he...we wants hit nice an' dark fer our leetle bedtime sturies. Draw up t' th' fire an' gaze inter th' embers—gaze inter em deep, an' soon ye'll see four peepul outside th' door ov a fine big house...(*As key is inserted in lock*)...Heer that key arattlin– in th' lock? W'en hit opens th' door we starts our yarn 'bout Mrs. Hawker's Will...he he MRS. HAWKER'S WILL!! He he he he he...(CAT)

(As Nancy and the cat fade out, the door is unlocked and thrown open.)

WEEKS: *(A jovial, middle aged attorney...slightly distant.)* There—I've got it open at last! *(Coming in.)* Now just a moment, you folks, till I find the light switch.

BABS: *(A girl of twenty...excitedly from outside.)* Do hurry, Mr. Weeks!

RODNEY: *(A boy of fifteen...excitedly from outside.)* Gosh, yes!—we can't wait another secunt!

MAGGIE: *(A middle aged spinster...excitedly from outside.)* We're so excited, we're all on pins an' needles!

WEEKS: *(Laughs indulgently.)* I have it—there!...*(As the light switch clicks.)*...Now you can see the inside of your new home!

BABS: *(Gasps delightedly.)* Ohh—

RODNEY: *(In admiration.)* Gee whiz!

MAGGIE: *(Almost speechless.)* Barbara, it's just—Oh, it's just—!

WEEKS: Like it?

BABS: *(Coming in.)* It's heavenly!

RODNEY: *(Coming in.)* A reg'lar mansion!!

MAGGIE: *(Coming in.)* Perfectly scrumptious!!!

WEEKS: *(Chuckling)* You're merely looking at the reception hall now— *(Going slightly away.)* Come into the living room and have a real thrill...

(As a second light switch clicks.)

There we are!...

(A chorus of excited gasps from Babs, Rodney and Maggie.)

And this is all yours, Miss Turner, house, grounds and furnishings—if you'll carry out the conditions of Mrs. Hawker's will and live here continuously for one year, beginning tonight.

RODNEY: "If she'll live here?" Just try an' get ye t' go away, eh Babs?

BABS: I'll say so—after you and Aunt Maggie and I have had to live in two rooms and a kitchenette all our lives! Oh—doesn't it just seem as though we're dreaming??

MAGGIE: *(Murmurs)* My, my—I can scarcely believe it's true.

WEEKS: *(Laughing)* It is.

RODNEY: *(Slightly distant...He is exploring.)* Look, Babs—Mr. Weeks has even had a telephone put in for us!

WEEKS: Yes—I've had the place set in order as though I was moving in myself. Doesn't look like a house that's been closed and tenantless for five years, does it?

BABS: It's just perfect—thanks to you.

MAGGIE: Perfectly scrumptious!

RODNEY: I'm goin' out an' get our baggage from th' car so's we can start t' get settled—*(Going)* then I'm gonna explore this house from cellar to attic!

MAGGIE: *(Calls)* Rodney—don't fergit t' bring in my hatbox an' umbrelly!

RODNEY: *(Outside now.)* I won't, Aunt Maggie!

BABS: *(Slightly distant.)* Aunt Maggie, just look at these gorgeous window curtains—real lace!

MAGGIE: *(Admiringly)* My, my! But the kitchen is what I want to see—that's my special bailiwick!

WEEKS: *(Going slightly away.)* You'll find it at the end of this hall, Miss Carpenter.

MAGGIE: *(Going)* I'll find it. I've got to have a look at that kitchen 'fore I do another thing!

BABS: Oh, we're all so terribly excited, Mr. Weeks! And we'll never forget that our good fortune is entirely due to you.

WEEKS: *(Coming back.)* Nonsense! I've only acted as any attorney would to serve his clients' interest.

BABS: But other attorneys kept this place away from us for five whole years.

WEEKS: They had no legal ground for their action, as the courts have finally decided. The terms of Mrs. Hawker's will were specific and clear, in spite of certain rather strange provisions. Your sister, Helen, was named as sole heir—and, in the event of her demise, it was provided that the estate should pass to her nearest female kin—which happened to be you. At your sister's untimely death, the executors should have placed you in immediate possession.

BABS: Now—to continue in possession—I simply have to fulfill the terms originally imposed upon my sister?

WEEKS: That's all. You are to reside in this house for a period of one year, during which time you will sleep in the master bedroom upstairs which was formerly occupied by Mrs. Hawker. You are not to pass so much as a single night away from here, and you must spend at least three hours in that bedroom from every midnight to sunrise—alone.

BABS: *(Thoughtfully)* Funny conditions, aren't they?

WEEKS: But very simple ones.

BABS: Very. *(Pause)* If poor Helen hadn't been killed in that auto accident the day of Mrs. Hawker's funeral, she would have found them as easy to fulfill as I shall—then she would have enjoyed this wonderful good luck.

WEEKS: *(Gently)* She would have shared it with you. And if the dead know what transpires among the living, she will enjoy it now—in your happiness.

BABS: *(Softly)* Yes—that's true.

WEEKS: *(Musingly)* Your sister must have been a very sweet and lovable character—Mrs. Hawker had known her scarcely two weeks when she executed that will in her favor.

BABS: And Helen was only her paid companion—a trained nurse, like myself. Wasn't it extraordinary?

WEEKS: Hmm—most.

BABS: What sort of woman was Mrs. Hawker? Helen used to write that she was very—peculiar.

WEEKS: That's amply proven by her will.

BABS: But, despite her eccentricities, Helen implied that she was a highly intelligent old person who spent most of her time in scientific research.

WEEKS: *(Chuckling)* I've heard that—but I hardly think her studies were very scientific. You'll find some mighty queer stuff in the library she left—works on magic, alchemy and such outlandish things.

BABS: Is that what she studied?

WEEKS: They're the only books on the shelves with English titles—I don't know what the volumes treat of that are written in Chinese.

BABS: Chinese?

WEEKS: Yes—you've inherited quite a collection of oriental literature. You see, Mrs. Hawker had spent much of her life in the Far East—mostly in Tibet as the wife of a missionary, I believe. And that's all I, or anyone else in this town really knows about her. From the time she came here fifteen years ago and built this house, she rarely left it—in fact she scarcely ever left that room upstairs which you will occupy in accordance with her will.

BABS: *(Thoughtfully)* She must have been very eccentric—that provision isn't the only strange one that she made.

WEEKS: You don't have to worry about the others—the executors have seen to their fulfillment.

BABS: I know. But why do you suppose she wrote those other funny clauses about—?

RODNEY: *(Distant)* Hey—help me, someone!!

BABS: Rod?? Why didn't you make two trips with that luggage instead of loading yourself like a packhorse?

WEEKS:	I'll unload you.
RODNEY:	*(Comes up puffing from exertion.)* Much 'bliged.

(As bags and suitcases are placed on floor.)

	I wanted t' get ever'thing in at once, Babs, so's I'll have nothin' t' do but look over our new residence. 'Sides, it's Mr. Weeks' car we had cluttered with this stuff—an' he may wanta drive it home some time t'night.
WEEKS:	Say—it's nearly midnight! I must be running along right now!
BABS:	It was awfully good of you to meet us at the train and bring us out here.
WEEKS:	I wanted to enjoy your first excitement over the place.
MAGGIE:	*(Distant...ecstatically.)* Barbara—Barbara, just wait till ye see my kitchen!
BABS:	*(Laughing)* That excitement hasn't ended yet, Mr. Weeks.
MAGGIE:	*(Coming in.)* That kitchen is simply scrumptious, Barbara! There's copper pots an' pans—real silverware—china dishes—an' a stove that's just too—! *(Abruptly)* Rodney—did you bring in my hat box an' umbrelly?
RODNEY:	Here they are, Aunt Maggie.
MAGGIE:	*(In relief.)* Oh—thank Goodness.
WEEKS:	*(Laughing)* Well, I'll run along.
MAGGIE:	You goin', Mr. Weeks?
WEEKS:	I must. Goodnight.
RODNEY:	Wait—I'll take you to yer car! *(Going)*
BABS:	*(Going)* We'll all take you!
MAGGIE:	Indeed we will—anyone who's been so nice ez you! My stars!—Th' moon has come out!
BABS:	Isn't it nice outside now? It was dark as pitch when we drove up here.
RODNEY:	Mr. Weeks, what's that little white building b'hind th' house—our garage?
WEEKS:	No, son—that's Mrs. Hawker's tomb.
BABS:	So that's the mausoleum you told me she had built?
WEEKS:	That's it.
MAGGIE:	*(Glumly)* It's one thing I ain't goin' t' like about this place—that tomb.
BABS:	We'll have to get used to it—one of the will's provisions is that it never be removed.
WEEKS:	That's right.

(As car door is opened and closed.)

WEEKS: Well—Goodnight, all.

BABS: Goodnight, Mr. Weeks.

(Motor is started.)

RODNEY: G'night, sir!

MAGGIE: Goodnight—an' thanks a thousand times.

BABS: From all of us.

(Car starts off.)

RODNEY: You bet!

WEEKS: *(Calling back.)* It's been a pleasure. Good luck!

(Motor fades away in distance.)

RODNEY: *(Excitedly)* Now let's go back in, Babs—you an' me'll explore that house from top to bottom!

BABS: You bet we will! *(Going away.)* Come on, Aunt Maggie! *(Stops)* Aunt Maggie—what are you looking at?

MAGGIE: *(Glumly)* At that tomb in th' back yard. I don't like it.

BABS: You knew it was there before we came here!

MAGGIE: *(Unhappily)* I didn't know it was so near th' house. It ain't right fer th' dead an' livin' t' be so clost t' one another.

BABS: Don't be so silly! Come inside and stop gazing at it.

MAGGIE: Alright. *(Pause)* Now shut that door, Rodney—an' lock it tight.

RODNEY: *(As he shuts and locks the door.)* Gee whiz, Aunt Maggie!—you ain't afraid Mrs. Hawker'll get lonesome out there an' try t' pay us a visit?

MAGGIE: If she wanted to, locks an' bolts wouldn't stop her—ghosts kin git in anywheres.

BABS: *(Irritably)* Don't be so ridiculous!

MAGGIE: *(Apologetically)* Guess I am talkin' old fool's nonsense—but seein' graves at night allus gave me a turn. Like ye say, I'll soon git used t' havin' that mauseyleum there.

BABS: Of course you will. Now, Rod—before we do anything else, let's take this luggage up to our bedrooms.

MAGGIE: *(Mistress of herself again.)* You two keep away from them bedrooms until I look em over!

RODNEY: Why?

MAGGIE: "Why?"!!! Ain't I been keepin' house for you orphans almos' all yer lives? I'm goin' up an' see th' beds're made up proper with clean sheets an' all—an' when I've fixed things up I'll call ye!

BABS: *(Laughing)* Alright, Aunt Maggie—But I must sleep in the east wing room, you know.

MAGGIE: I ain't fergittin' that or anything else in that crazy will. Here—I'll take my hat box an' umbrelly. *(Going upstairs.)* You kin bring th' rest o' that truck up later.

RODNEY: Okay, Aunt Maggie! Now, c'm on, Babs—let's explore!!

BABS: *(Low)* Wait a moment—till she finds the lights up there. With the mausoleum in her mind, she may be timid of the dark.

RODNEY: *(Low)* Then why didn't she let us go with her? Gosh, she's allus gotta fix things—like we were still just kids.

BABS: *(Low)* You still are.

RODNEY: *(Low)* Who is? You're only twenty, which ain't so doggone old!

BABS: *(Low)* But you're only fifteen—and don't say "ain't."

RODNEY: *(Mutters)* Humph—sisters are a awful pain in th' neck sometimes.

BABS: *(Calls)* Aunt Maggie—have you found the bedroom lights alright?

MAGGIE: *(From upstairs.)* Yep. An', Barbara—this here east room o' your'n is jest scrumptious!

BABS: *(Calls)* I knew it would be. *(Normal tone.)* Oh, Rod—isn't it wonderful to know all this belongs to us—that we're going to live in this wonderful house??

RODNEY: You gotta live here for a year.

BABS: As though that could be anything but pleasure!

RODNEY: C'm on now—let's explore!

BABS: Alright. Oh—tonight I'm just the happiest girl in all the world!!

MAGGIE: *(From upstairs...A piercing scream of terror.)*

RODNEY: What was that???

BABS: Aunt Maggie!!

RODNEY: Come upstairs—sump'ns wrong!!

BABS: *(As they run upstairs...calls frantically.)* Aunt Maggie—why did you scream??

RODNEY: *(Calls)* Aunt Maggie—what's th' matter???

BABS: She don't answer! *(Cries)* Oh!!

RODNEY: *(In terror.)* The lights have gone out!!

BABS: What made them go out?? Aunt Maggie—where are you? We can't find you in the dark!

RODNEY: Gimme your hand, Babs! The east room'll be in this direction—that's where she was before she yelled!

BABS: *(Frantic)* What made her scream—why don't she answer us?? Aunt Maggie! Aunt—Ohh!!

RODNEY: Th' lights have come on again!!

BABS: There she is—in that room!

RODNEY: She's lyin' on th' floor!

BABS: Aunt Maggie, dear—What happened—??

RODNEY: She doesn't move—she musta fainted!

BABS: She hasn't fainted, Rod—look at her eyes.

RODNEY: They're starin' at th' ceilin'—like she was scared o' somethin'! What made her—?

BABS: I don't know. But her heart's not beating—she isn't breathing— *(Sobbing)* Rod—she's dead.

(Music)

SCENE II

CRANE: *(A lieutenant of police...skeptically.)* You still insist, Doc, that this woman was frightened to death?

DOCTOR: I do, Lieutenant. Until an autopsy shows me some chronic organic weakness that isn't apparent now, I'll say she died of paralysis of the heart muscles brought about by sudden shock—and the expression of her face and eyes indicate that shock was caused by sheer, stark terror.

BABS: *(Sobbing)* But what could have frightened her! There was nothing here to do it!

CRANE: You two entered this room almost immediately after she screamed?

RODNEY: *(Choking back his tears.)* Yeah—an' the room was just like ye see it now.

CRANE: *(Thoughtfully)* She couldn't have been frightened by anything seen through those windows—shutters are closed and shades drawn. Ryan.

RYAN: *(A young detective...drawls.)* Yes, sir.

CRANE: You're positive that you've checked every door and window in this house?

RYAN: Yes, sir—and I'm positive that every one is locked from inside, just like I told ye.

CRANE: Yet you found no one hiding in the place?

RYAN: No, sir—or sign of anyone, and I searched in every corner.

CRANE: Son—you're sure that neither you or your sister touched anything after you found your aunt?

RODNEY: Not even th' front door, which we left locked until you got here.

BABS: We—we just phoned for you police—and then sat downstairs until you came.

CRANE: If this woman died of fright then she must have been scared by her own imagination.

BABS: That's impossible—she wasn't that kind!

CRANE: *(Kindly)* It's the only explanation that is possible, Miss. When the doctor here first gave us his theory of her death I suspected a tramp or burglar had surprised her—but we've proved that no one could have gotten in or out of the place, and that no one's here now except ourselves.

BABS: Someone must have turned out those lights!

RODNEY: Yeah—and turned em on again!

CRANE: That was probably caused by defective wiring—I'll have the electric company check on that. Well, boys—this is a coroner's case, not a police matter—let's go.

MEN: *(Mutter)* Yes'r.

RYAN: Lieutenant Crane, sir—

CRANE: Yes, Ryan?

RYAN: Do ye mind putting me on duty inside this house fer a couple days, mebbe?

CRANE: What for? The case is closed.

RYAN: *(Drawls)* I kinda gotta notion that it ain't.

CRANE: *(Sharply)* What d' ye mean?

RYAN: Oh—I just kinda gotta notion.

CRANE: You're always gettin' crazy notions—c'on! *(Starts to go, then stops suddenly.)* Wait a minute! *(Laughs)* I've got his idea, boys! Detective Ryan is an authority on spooks—and they're an explanation for us! A ghost could frighten a woman to death—and it couldn't be stopped by locked windows or doors.

RYAN: *(Calmly)* I'm not suspectin' any ghost of bein' in this house t'night, sir—for I've just found somethin' that no ghost could leave behind.

CRANE: *(Sharply)* What have you found?

RYAN: This, sir—it was snagged on the back of that chair.

CRANE: A hair!

RYAN: Two hairs—two white human hairs.

CRANE: Anyone might have shed a few hairs here—at any time. They may have been on that chair for days—or years.

RYAN: Maybe, sir—but I don't think so, for they're a little too unusual—look.

CRANE: Say—!!!

RYAN: Uh huh—I'm six feet tall, and these hairs are almost as long as I am.
(Music)

SCENE III

RODNEY: *(Wearily)* It's almost one o'clock, Mr. Ryan—how much longer do we have to sit here in th' dark?

RYAN: Hmm—it was a little after twelve you heard yer aunt scream in this room last night.

BABS: Yes, Mr. Ryan.

RYAN: I kinda had a notion that hist'ry might repeat itself, but it begins t' look like I was wrong. *(Gently)* You're all in, aren't ye, Miss Turner?

RODNEY: *(Irritably)* Of course she's all in—she hasn't had a wink of sleep since—

BABS: *(Low...depressed.)* That doesn't matter, Rod—if there's anything to be gained by watching here.

RYAN: I'd like t' sit it out a little longer, if ye don't mind.

BABS: You still think those hairs you found had something to do with Aunt Maggie's—death?

RYAN: Well—I've kinda gotta notion.

RODNEY: But what could have hair like that—almost six feet long?

RYAN: To tell ye th' honest truth, that sorta has me stumped.

BABS: You say the—the autopsy—this afternoon strengthened the police surgeon's conviction that my aunt was frightened to death?

RYAN: Yes, Miss.

BABS: But you are positive no human being could have been in this place or left it. Mr. Ryan—do you believe in ghosts, as the Lieutenant said last night?

RYAN: Well—I keep a sort of open mind on things of that kind. Ye know—most folks are apt to say that certain things can't be, just because those things have never been a part of their personal experience. I read a lot of funny old books the boys at headquarters kid me about an—Well, they've gimme a kinda notion that strange things sometimes happen ye can't explain away by simply sayin' they couldn't happen.

BABS: You're Irish, aren't you, Mr. Ryan?

RYAN: *(Chuckles)* Ryan ain't exactly a Polish name. You mean mebbe I come by my funny notions 'cause my father was born in County Mayo?

BABS:	Belief in the supernatural is common to all races—but the Irish seem to have a greater flair for the mystic than others, and—Well, only the Scotch can compete with them when it comes to—er—having notions.
RYAN:	Yes'm. My mother was Scotch.
BABS:	Is that so? I'm Scotch-Irish, too.
RYAN:	You are?? Say—I kinda had a notion! Yes'r—the minute I first looked at you, I said t' myself: now, there's too nice a girl to be anything but Scotch an'—
RODNEY:	*(Impatiently)* Say—if anything's gonna happen in this room, when is it gonna begin?
RYAN:	Eh? Just wait a little longer, son. Yes'r, Miss Turner—you're just the type of girl who I always wanted t'—Say—you're not engaged or goin' with anybody steady, are ye?
BABS:	Why, Mr. Ryan—what—??
RODNEY:	Ye know, 'cordin' to Mrs. Hawker's will, my sister has to stay in this room at least three hours every night alone!
BABS:	Oh, I don't care anything about that, Rod—after what's happened I hate this house and everything about it!
RODNEY:	Gee, Babs—I don't care anything about the money, either. I didn't mean—
RYAN:	Hmm—funny conditions in that will you told me 'bout—awful funny. *(Abruptly)* Son—let's you and me leave yer sister alone in here!
RODNEY:	Not if you think somethin' gonna happen.
RYAN:	I don't anymore—that was just a bum notion! Here—I'll switch on these lights.

(Click of switch.)

	Leave em burnin' the rest of the night, Miss—I think ye'll sleep better.
BABS:	But—
RYAN:	Leave em burnin' and don't lock yer door—that's a police order.
BABS:	That's alright—but I'd rather you and Rod would stay here with me. I'm not afraid, but I'm too upset to sleep—
RYAN:	*(Brusquely)* I'm not—an' I'm goin' to bed!
BABS:	*(Hurt)* Mr. Ryan—??
RYAN:	C'm on, son—out this door!
RODNEY:	*(Angrily)* Say—if my sister don't want to be left alone here, I'm—!!
RYAN:	She'll like it when she gets used to it—c'm on!
RODNEY:	*(Going)* Hey—leggo my arm!

(Door opened.)

BABS: What on earth—???
RYAN: Goodnight!

(Door slammed shut.)

RODNEY: Have you suddenly gone crazy??
RYAN: *(Low)* Shut up!
RODNEY: *(Belligerently)* I will no—! Ugh——*(His words are smothered.)*
RODNEY: *(Low)* Now I'm gonna keep my hand over your mouth till ye nod yer head ye'll keep yer face closed! We ain't gonna leave your sister in there unprotected, for we ain't gonna budge two feet from outside her door. Now will ye keep quiet? Alright.
RODNEY: *(Hushed)* What's the idea?
RYAN: I just gotta notion that things might happen in that room a lot quicker if so many people weren't hangin' around.
RODNEY: Ye mean—?
RYAN: Come back here—watch that crack of light under th' door. If it goes out or your sister yells, we throw ourselves inta that room double quick!

(A distant clock strikes one.)

     Hmm—one o'clock.

RODNEY: But, My Ryan—what's yer reason for all this??
RYAN: There ain't no reason—I've just kinda gotta notion.

(Music.)

SCENE IV

(The clock strikes two.)

RYAN: Two o'clock.

(Scene played in whispers.)

RODNEY: *(Plaintively)* We've stood here like statues fer a solid hour—my legs are cramped.
RYAN: Rub em. *(Pause)* Yer sister's asleep in there now—I can hear her breathin'. She breathes nice—kinda soft an' perty-like.
RODNEY: Huh?
RYAN: I wasn't talkin' t' you.
RODNEY: Then who were ye talkin' to?
RYAN: Mind yer own business.
RODNEY: *(Unhappily)* Gee, Mr. Ryan—you say and do the craziest things. *(Pause)* You're not still expectin' a ghost t' walk, are ye? Ghosts don't come around after midnight.

RYAN:	I never expected a ghost—ghosts don't leave their hair behind.
RODNEY:	I think that hair, and us waitin' here, is all bunk. Nothin' was in that room last night but poor Aunt Maggie—and nothin' could get in there now with us guardin' the only door—*(Suddenly cries.)* Ah—the crack of light's gone out!
RYAN:	You keep back—I'm goin' in!
BABS:	*(From inside...screams in terror.)*
RYAN:	*(As he crashes against the door, which slams open.)* I'm comin', Miss Turner!
RODNEY:	*(Cries in terror.)* Look—by the bed!!
RYAN:	Good Lord!
RODNEY:	It's covered with hair!!
RYAN:	A hairy monster!!
BABS:	*(Frantic)* Don't let it touch me again—don't let it—!!
RYAN:	I won't!
(Two shots.)	
RODNEY:	Shoot again! *(Screams)* Now it's comin' toward us!!!
RYAN:	*(As he empties his gun.)* I hit it—I hit it each time, but it doesn't drop!!
BABS:	Bullets won't kill it—it's something unnatural—awful—dead!!!
RODNEY:	Shoot again!
RYAN:	My gun's empty—I'll have t' grab it!!
BABS:	No—don't touch it—don't let it touch you!!!!
RODNEY:	It's goin' through that wall!!
RYAN:	There's a false panel—a secret passage there! *(Going)* I'm goin' after it!! Boy—stay with yer sister!
BABS:	No, no—don't go into that darkness alone!!!
RODNEY:	He's already gone—down these stairs inside the wall!
BABS:	Come on—after him!
RODNEY:	We can't see, Babs—he has the only flashlight!
BABS:	We'll follow it! *(Going)* quick—the thing'll kill him!
RODNEY:	Babs, come back—that thing'll kill us all!!
BABS:	*(Going away.)* Mr. Ryan—Mr. Ryan—!!!
RODNEY:	*(Frantic)* Babs, I'm coming with ye—wait! Where are ye?
BABS:	*(Distant)* At the foot of the stairs! *(Closer)* I see his flashlight up ahead—come on!
RODNEY:	I'm with ye!
BABS:	Hurry!
RODNEY:	His light ain't movin' any more—he's stopped!

BABS: *(In thankful hysteria.)* That means he's safe! The hairy thing has got away—it hasn't hurt him!

RODNEY: Look out, Babs—there's more steps goin' up here!

BABS: Yes, yes—I've found them! *(Calls)* Mr. Ryan—you're safe? That monster didn't hurt you?

RYAN: *(Coming up.)* No, praise God. I lost th' thing—it disappeared 'fore I could reach it.

BABS: What was it?? It wasn't human, covered with that awful matted hair! *(Hysterical)* It wasn't human—it smelled of mold and earth and death! *(Sobbing)* I woke up to find it standing by my bed—its hands upon my mouth—it tried to smother me as I slept!!!

RYAN: Here, here, Miss Turner—ye gotta pull yerself t'gether! I don't know what it was we saw and followed, but it won't harm ye again! I'll find it here, right where I lost it—an' I'll destroy it here, at th' end o' this passage!!

RODNEY: This is the end of th' passage.

BABS: Where—where are we?

RYAN: I gotta kinda notion that we're in—Mrs. Hawker's tomb.

(Music)

SCENE V

BABS: But, Mr. Ryan—that frightful thing we saw last night couldn't have been Mrs. Hawker! She's been dead five years—and you say yourself it wasn't a ghost.

RYAN: Nope—ghosts don't leave hair behind, nor little things like this.

BABS: What's that??

RYAN: A human finger nail—five inches long. I found it by th' panel that leads inside that passage, an' I've read that nails grow out about an inch each year—but they don't grow after death—ordinary death, that is.

BABS: What do you mean—?

RYAN: I think last night we saw th' dead alive.

BABS: A—a vampire?

RYAN: No. A vampire drains yer blood—Mrs. Hawker came last night t' steal yer body as, when she was placed in this tomb, she had everything arranged t' steal yer sister's.

BABS: I don't know what you're talking about!

RYAN: I've done some funny readin', as I told ye, Miss Turner—an' I've read that in Tibet, where Mrs. Hawker usta live, there's magicians who know how t' suspend all animation of their organs an' t' live like th' dead fer almost any time they want. They also know how t' kill another human bein' by smotherin' their breath—an' then they can set up their own spirits inside th' flesh whose soul is gone. Mrs. Hawker was very old—she wanted another body in which t' live another lifetime, and—she knew all about th' magicians of Tibet.

BABS: If—if this incredible thing can be true—it explains the conditions of her will.

RYAN: Uh huh—that her heir occupy that room, from which a secret passage led t' this mausoleum. An accident cheated her of yer sister, an' she'd waited five years when you came t' the house— she was overanxious t' claim your life that she might live again, so she entered that room without caution an' yer aunt saw her awful figure in th' moonlight. Last night she waited—careful, as she thought.

RODNEY: But the lights—what made them go out?

RYAN: A master switch inside th' passageway—she built this house herself, ye know. And among the queer conditions in her will was one that th' slab above her tomb should be made so it might be lifted by a lever inside her coffin. Another stipulation was that she shouldn't be embalmed.

BABS: I—I thought that was because of an old woman's fear of burial alive.

RODNEY: So did the executors who saw her wishes were fulfilled—but she had an altogether different notion.

RODNEY: But why didn't your bullets kill her if she's really living? They say you're a champion pistol shot—yet we didn't find a drop of blood.

RYAN: She hasn't any blood—her body is just a dried up husk held t'gether by her evil spirit that bullets can't destroy. But when th' husk is gone entirely, she'll have nothin' av earth on which t' fasten—that's why I'm havin' them lamps put up inside her tomb.

BABS: Those huge sun-ray lamps?

RYAN: Yeah. Th' sun that preserves life is a destroyer of th' dead—that's why she can only leave her tomb in darkness.

BABS: It's night now—there may be danger if you lift that slab! Why don't you wait till morning—when the natural sun comes out??

RYAN: 'Cause I can't have her in th' same world with you another hour.

Ye know, Miss Turner—you're th' type o' girl I've always—

MAN: *(Distant...calls.)* Everything set now, Ryan!

RYAN: Huh? Oh yeah. You an' yer brother wait outside here, Miss—just in case anything goes wrong.

BABS: No! If there's any danger, I'm going with you!

RYAN: Miss Turner, you're absolutely th' type of girl who—! Say—you're not engaged or goin' with anybody steady, are ye?

BABS: I—

MAN: *(Distant...calls.)* C'm on, Ryan—we're ready, if you are!

RYAN: Uh—alright! Lamps set an' lever placed?

MAN: *(Closer)* Everything!

RYAN: Turn yer lamps on, then—'fore we put pressure on th' lever!

MAN: Here they go!

(The hum of powerful arc lamps.)

RYAN: Alright, boys—heave that slab off!

(The creaking of stone and steel.)

2ND MAN: It's liftin' easy—there she goes!

RYAN: Keep away from here, Miss Turner!

(A heavy stone and lever falls.)

RODNEY: The slab is off!

BABS: You were right—in Mrs. Hawker's coffin is the hairy monster!!

RODNEY: *(In terror.)* An' she is alive—she's gettin' up!!

RYAN: *(Cries)* Keep back, you two! Turn those rays there—on that coffin!!

MAN: I've got em focused now—LORD!!!

BABS: *(Screams)*

(Hum of arc lamps stop.)

RYAN: Those lamps went out! What's wrong???

MAN: *(Wildly)* Connection came apart! I'll fix it!!

BABS: Ahh—she's rising from her tomb!

RODNEY: All covered with that awful hair!!!

RYAN: Keep back, Miss Turner—keep away, I'll stop her!! Ahh—!!

RODNEY: She's got her hands on Mr. Ryan's throat!!

BABS: With those long nails—like knives!!!

RYAN: *(Choking)* Those lamps—fer Good Lord's sake, th' lamps!!

BABS: Help, someone—she's tearing him to ribbons!

RODNEY: Babs—you can't help him, keep away!

MAN: *(As the arc lamps resume their hum...cries.)* I've fixed the connection— th' lamps are on again!

2ND MAN: An' the rays are workin'! Look!!!

BABS:	She's let him go!
RODNEY:	She's fallen on th' ground!!
BABS:	*(Hysterically)* She's becoming just dust and bones—and hair!!
MAN:	She's gone!
BABS:	Destroyed forever! *(Sobbing)* Mr. Ryan—are you alright? Are you alright???
RYAN:	*(Weakly)* I—I kinda got a notion.
RODNEY:	He's covered with blood!
MAN:	She's slashed his face and throat!
2ND MAN:	I'll get a doctor!
BABS:	First get me iodine and bandages! Oh, thank goodness, I'm a nurse!
RYAN:	*(Weakly)* Ye're a nurse?
BABS:	Yes, lie quiet!
RYAN:	Well—now I know ye're just th' type of girl who—
RODNEY:	Mr. Ryan—you gotta lie still!
RYAN:	Son, you've butted in enough—shut up!
BABS:	Mr. Ryan—!
RYAN:	My first name is Michael—Say, Miss Turner, are ye engaged or goin' with anybody steady?
BABS:	Please—! You're weak and losing blood.
RYAN:	But are ye?
BABS:	No—not yet.
RYAN:	*(Sighs contently.)*
BABS:	Why do you keep asking me that—Michael?
RYAN:	Oh—I just kinda gotta notion.
(Music)	

EPILOGUE

| NANCY: | He he he...(CAT) Weel, that's th' end o' that un, Satan! Yew folks come see me nex' Wensday on m' buthday, an' me an' Satan'll have anuther cheerful yarn t' spin ye! Dunt fergit—nex' Wensday night at Noo York time ov ha'f pas' ten o'clock! He he he he he he...(CAT) |

(Musical theme.)

Editor's note: In the preceding script, Miriam Wolff, who at age thirteen played Old Nancy, the Wtich, also "doubled" by portraying Rodney, the heroine's fifteen year old brother.

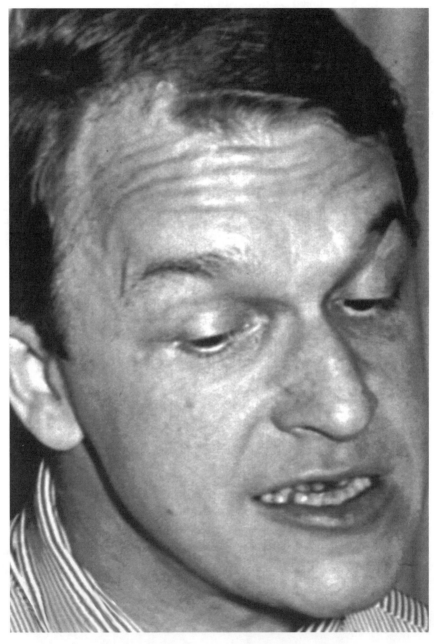

Satan, the wise black cat, as portrayed (with clear relish)
by the program's creator Alonzo Deen Cole.

The Mirror
Tuesday, October 22, 1935

(Musical theme.)

ANNOUNCER: We bring you the two hundred and seventeenth broadcast of the famous weekly series The Witch's Tale, written and produced by Alonzo Deen Cole, featuring Mr. Cole and Miss Marie O'Flynn, and sponsored by Martinson's Coffee.

(Music fades out for commercial.)

COMMERCIAL

(Music fades in at end of commercial.)

And now let us join old Nancy, witch of Salem, and Satan, her wise black cat.

(Music swells...wind whistles...)

PROLOGUE

NANCY: He he he...(CAT) Hunner an' nine yeer ole, I be t'day—yes'r, hunner an' nine yeer ole! Weel, Satan—we got a scientifick bedtime stury t' tell these folks t'night. (CAT) Yew, said it, Satan—when it comes ter science me an' yew knows more than them who makes a livin' at hit. Douse out them lights—an we'll git right t' bizness. Now draw up t' th' fire an' gaze inter th' embers—gaze inter em deep, an' soon ye'll see a fine big office in a fine tall buildin' down in Noo York City. An' thar b'gins our yarn erbout "Th' Mirror"...he he! TH' MIRROR!! He he he he he...(CAT)...

(Music)

SCENE I

FOSTER: *(An elderly attorney.)* So, Mr. Clements—you will not even make partial restitution of the money you received from those investors?

CLEM: *(Youthful, suave.)* Mr. Foster, Ace High Mining stock as offered by me was a purely speculative venture, and those who bought it did so at their own risk. In no way can I be held responsible for the project's collapse.

FOSTER: I know that you covered yourself from every legal angle. In coming to your office this morning, my intent has been to appeal to you on moral grounds. Those who bought your Ace High stock are poor people, Mr. Clements. Since it became apparent that the security was worthless, two shareholders have committed suicide and over a hundred have been compelled to appeal to the city for relief funds. Do you want more suicides and paupers on your conscience?

CLEM: *(Easily)* My conscience is not burdened with matters for which I am not to blame. Since an association of investors has engaged you as their attorney, you can earn your retainer by brining suit against me, if you wish—a suit that will get you nothing. That is all I can say to you, Mr. Foster.

FOSTER: Clements, you're the type of thief who operates always under cover of the law—but man's law isn't always the protection that you think. Something will trip you eventually—and then, no matter how you squirm and dodge, it'll hold you down. This world isn't big enough for your kind and decent people—someday you'll find there isn't room for you here. Good day.

(Door opened.)

CLEM: *(Mockingly)* Thanks for the sermon—so glad you called.

(Distant door slams behind him.)

(Chuckles) Miss Austin, will you come in? I have some letters to dictate.

IRENE: *(A young stenographer....She is morose, irritable...coming up.)* Alright.

(Door closes behind her.)

Foster seemed in bad humor as he went out.

CLEM: Yes—I don't think he likes me very well.

IRENE: Strange—so many people are crazy about you.

CLEM: *(Sharply)* Is that meant as a dirty crack?

IRENE: Take it any way you like.

CLEM:	Say—you're forgetting yourself, aren't you?
IRENE:	I don't think so. I'm not merely your stenographer when we're alone, you know.
CLEM:	Irene, what's the matter with you this morning? You've been carrying a chip on your shoulder ever since you came to work.
IRENE:	*(Shortly)* We'll discuss that later—after business hours.
CLEM:	My dear—
IRENE:	Take your hands off me—I don't feel like being pawed.
CLEM:	*(Shrugs)* Just as you wish.

(Telephone rings.)

	Will you answer that phone?
IRENE:	*(Lifting receiver.)* Mr. Clements' office—his secretary speaking...Just a moment. *(To Clements.)* Ingram calling.
CLEM:	I'll speak to him.
IRENE:	He's not on the phone—it's his secretary. She wants to know if you'll be here during the next quarter hour—Ingram's coming over.
CLEM:	He's coming here?
IRENE:	Yes.
CLEM:	Tell her I'll be in.
IRENE:	*(At phone.)* Hello...Mr. Clements will wait here for Mr. Ingram....You're welcome. Goodbye. *(Hangs up receiver.)*
CLEM:	*(Thoughtfully)* Wonder what he's coming here for.
IRENE:	You ought to have a pretty good idea.
CLEM:	You think he's wise?
IRENE:	About you overselling his authorized stock issue? If he wasn't such an Honest John he'd have suspected that months ago.
CLEM:	*(Half to himself.)* Well, if he's come for a showdown, I'm ready for him.
IRENE:	*(Bitterly)* I suppose you've played well inside the law, as usual.
CLEM:	*(Shortly)* I always play inside the law.

(Phone rings.)

	Answer that.
IRENE:	*(Lifting receiver.)* Mr. Clements' office...I'll tell him. *(To Clements.)* That German inventor, Morris Bloch, is outside and wants to see you.
CLEM:	I can't be annoyed with him—say I'm not in.
IRENE:	Miss Miller says he claims to have important news for you. Maybe you'd better see him—that rubberizing process he discovered made you sixty thousand dollars.

CLEM:	That was a lucky accident—the fool was trying to discover some impractical thing he calls "The Fourth Dimension" when he stumbled onto that cheap rubber formula. He'll probably never produce anything commercial again as long as he lives. But tell him to wait—I'll see him after I get rid of Ingram.
IRENE:	*(At phone.)* Hello...Have Mr. Bloch wait. *(Hangs up.)* I don't see why he comes to you with his schemes after the trimming you gave him on that other deal.
CLEM:	*(Chuckling)* He doesn't know what I made out of it. The chump was tickled silly for the fifteen hundred I paid him—thinks I did him a big favor. *(Sighs)* Wish all my business was with saps like him.
IRENE:	Be a great world then, wouldn't it? *(Pause)* You've looked a little worried since that call from Ingram. Afraid your foot has slipped somewhere?
CLEM:	Of course not. He hasn't got a leg to stand on—legally, but—he's a fool, and fools are dangerous.
IRENE:	What're you going to do if he gets tough?
CLEM:	Buy him off.
IRENE:	What with? I happen to know how much money you've lost at the race track lately. *(Bitterly)* Talk about saps—you're as big a chump for the bookmakers as the small investors are for your racket.
CLEM:	*(Shortly)* If I want to bet on the horses, that's my business. Besides, I'm far from broke—I raised a hundred thousand yesterday.
IRENE:	Where?
CLEM:	That doesn't matter. But you see I don't have to worry about Ingram.
IRENE:	Maybe not—but you'll have to worry about me.
CLEM:	What do you mean?
IRENE:	Now that you have a hundred thousand in your hands, you and I are going to have a showdown.
CLEM:	Irene—??
IRENE:	*(Bitterly)* A moment ago you asked why I carried a chip on my shoulder. Well, today I merely showed what I feel every morning when I come to work while your wife has her breakfast served in bed.
CLEM:	My dear, you know—
IRENE:	Oh yes—I know she's your wife "in name only," but you know I want that name myself! I'm entitled to it—I'm entitled to the respectability she has—and now you're going to give it to me!

CLEM:	I've told you I'll divorce my wife and marry you when I can, Irene—but I can't do it now—she'd fight me every step I made, and she has money of her own to do it with.
IRENE:	With a hundred thousand dollars you can beat her. Your excuse for putting me off has always been that you couldn't afford to fight. You couldn't "afford" it...ha!—when I've seen money flow through your hands like water! Now you can't put me off any longer—you're going to start things moving to give me what I want!!
CLEM:	Even if I—I can't use this money for what you want.
IRENE:	Why?
CLEM:	Because I got it from my wife.
IRENE:	You got it from—? She wouldn't give you a penny!
CLEM:	She doesn't know I have it. I—I got it on her diamonds. She and I still share a safety deposit vault, you know.
IRENE:	You—you stole her diamonds to—??
CLEM:	*(Easily)* My dear—man and wife are one person at law, and neither can be accused of "stealing" from the other. If Mrs. Clements should learn her jewelry is missing before I can redeem it, she might create a great deal of unpleasant mess, but I would be quite safe from criminal action. You see, however, how impossible it is for me to start proceedings now that might cause her to look for weapons that could be turned against me.
IRENE:	*(Low)* What a slimy little crook you are. *(Sobbing)* I don't know why I stay with you—I don't know why I don't shout from the housetops everything I know about you—I don't know why—!
CLEM:	Yes, you do—it's because you love me.
IRENE:	*(Her sobs gradually ceasing.)* Yes—God help me. But you can't get away with the things you do forever—not even with me—this world isn't big enough to hold your kind and decent people too—something will catch up with you someday and, when it does, you'll be finished.
CLEM:	*(Chuckles)* I heard a similar prophecy from Foster awhile ago.
(Phone rings.)	
	Answer that phone, and leave me to worry about my future.
IRENE:	*(Wearily...lifting receiver.)* Mr. Clements' office...One moment. *(To Clements.)* Ingram's out there.
CLEM:	Have him come in.
IRENE:	*(At phone.)* Send Mr. Ingram in. *(Hangs up.)*

CLEM: You wait outside while I talk to him.

(Door opens.)

Well—come in, John—Will you close the door as you go out, Miss Austin?

(Door closed.)

John—old man—shake hands and have a chair!

INGRAM: *(A middle-aged business man...quiet, bitter.)* I don't shake hands with thieves.

CLEM: Why, John—??

INGRAM: Don't play the hypocrite with me—you know why I'm here.

CLEM: *(Insolently)* No—suppose you tell me.

INGRAM: Alright. A year ago I authorized you to sell a new issue of Ingram Company stock.

CLEM: Well—I sold it, and you've received the money for five thousand shares minus my commission.

INGRAM: I learned yesterday that you sold ten thousand shares—twice the issue which I authorized.

CLEM: So? Have you looked at our contact recently?

INGRAM: Yes—and this morning I found the joker in it which makes your crooked action within the law. I can't even prosecute you for not turning over the money you received from the sale of the extra issue unless you fail to do so now when I demand it.

CLEM: You'll receive that money according to the terms of our contract, "thirty days from date of demand for all stock of the issue then outstanding." Large blocks of the stock have reverted back to me—they'll be turned over to you in thirty days together with about twenty thousand dollars representing the outstanding value.

INGRAM: *(Quietly)* No—tomorrow you will pay me par value for every certificate of your overissue—the sum of half a million dollars.

CLEM: You're crazy!

INGRAM: You don't yet know how crazy an honest man can be. Clements, you unloaded every share of that second five thousand shares in secret—then you forced the market quotation of Ingram Products down to less than a third of what you had received, after which you systematically bought back, at the reduced price, almost all of what you'd sold. Now you're going to give me every cent of the money you took from investors in my name, so that I can return it to them dollar for dollar.

CLEM: *(Insolently)* That's a very noble idea—but it isn't in our contract.

INGRAM: I have something here that's better than a contract.

CLEM: What are you doing with that gun???

INGRAM: I'm only showing it to you now—but in twenty four hours, if you don't meet the terms I've just laid down, I'll use it.

CLEM: You idiot! Do you want to go to the chair for murder??

INGRAM: If that's the only way I can wipe out my mistake in helping you to cheat poor people of their savings through use of my name, I'm willing to risk the chair. You see, honest men don't fear the law as your kind does.

CLEM: Now, look here, John—we can fix things up. What do you care for a lot of saps who don't know enough to come in out of the rain? You and I will split the profits I made—that's what I've intended all along. John, I'll give you a check for fifty thousand dollars now—!

INGRAM: *(Quietly)* In twenty four hours you'll pay me half a million.

CLEM: Be sensible man! I'll give you a hundred thousand—that's every cent I've got!

INGRAM: Twenty four hours, Clements—and then, if you don't make good, no matter where you hide in this world, I'll find and kill you.

(He moves away at end of speech.)

CLEM: John—!

(Door opened.)

INGRAM: *(Slightly distant.)* That's all.

(Door closed.)

CLEM: For God's sake, man—

(Throws open door.)

            John—!!

(Distant door closes.)

            Miss Miller—Irene—go after Mr. Ingram—bring him back here!!

I & M   *(Going)* Yes, sir!

(Distant door opened and closed.)

BLOCH: *(An excitable German scientist...distant, coming up.)* Ah—Mr. Clements!! At last you come out from dot office!!

CLEM: I can't be bothered with you now, Bloch!

BLOCH: *(Arriving)* But someding pig I godt to tell you! All diss time I wait, undt now—!

CLEM: Let me go!

BLOCH: No—to Morris Bloch you godt to listen! I haf found idt—I haf found idt!!

CLEM: Take your hands from me, or I'll knock you down!
(Distant door opens.)
             Irene—did you stop Ingram! Did you—??
IRENE: *(Coming in.)* He wouldn't come back—said you'd heard his last
             word.
CLEM: God! And I know him—he means it.
BLOCH: Mr. Clements, will you listen now? You gotta hear aboudt my
             greadt disscovery!!
CLEM: *(Angrily)* You idiot—I've got to raise four hundred thousand dol-
             lars by tomorrow noon to save my life! Do you think anything you
             can tell me will take my mind off that??
BLOCH: Vhat I haf come to tell you 'boudt iss vort four hundred billion!!
CLEM: Four hundred bil—
BLOCH: Come vit me insidt your office vhere we can pe alone! Diss vill pe
             our secret—yours undt mine!
(Door closes behind them.)
             Now I tell you! Mr. Clements, in my laboratory, I haf found
             anudder vorldt!!
CLEM: Another world??
BLOCH: Jah—a vorldt unknown, a vorldt dot's part of diss vun, yet is
             furder dan de sun or moon—a vorldt vich you undt me can enter
             in vun minute, yet vhere no vun can ever find us!
CLEM: Where no one can ever find—??
BLOCH: Come to my laboratory—you shall see! I haf discovered anudder
             vorldt, I tell you—I have discovered anudder vorldt!!
(Music)

                              SCENE II

BLOCH: *(Excitedly)* Come into my laboratory!
(Door opened.)
             You t'ink old Morris Bloch iss mad...ha ha—but soon you shall
             see he toldt de truth!
CLEM: It's not you who's mad—I'm the idiot for coming here. What do
             you mean by all your gibberish about another world?
BLOCH: *(Slightly distant.)* Look at dis from vhich I draw aside de curtain!
CLEM: That big mirror?
BLOCH: Jah...ha ha—dis mirror!
CLEM: It's just a distorted looking-glass, such as they have at Coney

	Island. *(Angrily)* Is that what you've brought me here to see??
BLOCH:	Standt in front of it vit me! Like you say, idt iss a distorted looking-glass, but does idt reflect us fat or t'in like dose at Coney Island??
CLEM:	It doesn't reflect us at all.
BLOCH:	No—for insteadt of reflecting, idt absorbs!
CLEM:	Absorbs??
BLOCH:	Dot mirror iss nodt a looking-glass, my friend, idt iss a door—a door to de Fourth Dimension!
CLEM:	Fourth Dimension?
BLOCH:	Jah! I, Morris Bloch, haf discovered dot vhich science so long hass sought in vain! T'ree dimensions haff ve always know; length, breadth und t'ickness. De fourth, vhich ve could never see or feel, iss Time.
CLEM:	Time is a dimension??
BLOCH:	Jah—for if ve say anyt'ing has a certain length und breath und t'ickness, dose dimensions must be constant; they must have duration insteadt of being like a block of ice dot melts beneat' de sun. Und only in time do t'ings exist forever as dey are!
CLEM:	I don't know what you're talking about!
BLOCH:	Dos iss no matter—de absorption iss beginning—in a moment you vill see!
CLEM:	What's happening in that mirror?? It's becoming like a window!
BLOCH:	Idt iss a door!
CLEM:	I see a dark landscape—valley, mountains—! *(Cries)* Ahh—the mountains are all about us now!! We're standing on a peak—on the edge of a chasm!!!
BLOCH:	Don't pe afraid—but be careful nodt to fall! Now you are standing in de land of time—in de Space Dimension where not'ing changes, vhere everyt'ing endures! De mirror hass absorbed us.
CLEM:	You've practiced some illusion on me—this can't be true!
BLOCH:	Feel de rocky vall behindt you. Iss idt illusion?
CLEM:	*(Awed)* Lord! It—it is another land. How do we leave here—how can we go back??
BLOCH:	Ha ha...don't voorry—ve go back much quicker dan ve came, for de t'ree dimensional vorldt iss our natural element vile diss iss nodt. Vatch me now, as I take diss liddle lens undt holdt it pefore my eyes.
CLEM:	*(Screams in terror.)* Bloch—you've left me!! Where have you gone??

For God's sake, man—come back!! If you leave me in this desolation I'll go mad!! Bloch—Bloch—BLOCH—!

BLOCH: *(Chuckles)* Ha ha...vas you afraidt, mein friendt?

CLEM: You're beside me again! You disappeared and reappeared before my eyes!!

BLOCH: I vent back to my laboratory undt returned again. Just py looking t'rough diss lens.

CLEM: By looking through that lens?

BLOCH: Dot iss all. Diss small glass iss de exact opposite of de big absorbing mirror—idt iss a reverser—I exblain idt's principal to you—

CLEM: Never mind—I wouldn't understand. Only tell me—is it possible to leave this place without that lens?

BLOCH: No—never.

CLEM: Without the lens anyone absorbed by that mirror would be imprisoned here?

BLOCH: Now anyvun vouldt pe imprisoned but vhen my discovery iss made known, to diss landt vill people come undt go as now dey travel to dere next door neighbor's.

CLEM: But, thus far, you have told no one of this discovery but myself?

BLOCH: Nein! You are my friendt. To show my gratitude for the fifteen hundred dollars you vonce gave me I told you first of all—undt you shall share my triumph!

CLEM: I shall reciprocate your generosity. May I see that lens?

BLOCH: Take idt in your handt! You vish to see how you can return to de laboratory undt come back again?

CLEM: *(Slowly)* Not exactly. I was told today that the other world wasn't big enough for me—I wish to be sure this world is—*(Savagely)* mine alone!!

BLOCH: *(In terror)* Vhat you doing?? Let me go!! *(He screams.)*

CLEM: When you body lands at the bottom of this chasm, I will be sure!!

(A feeble, distant scream from Bloch...A thud.)

Ha ha...you wouldn't have known how to take advantage of your discovery, Morris Bloch—but I know how to use your mirror and I know what to do with a world that's mine alone! Ha ha...I know what to do with a world that's mine alone!!!

(Music)

SCENE III

CLEM: *(Suavely)* Come in, John—come in and sit down.

INGRAM: *(Stiffly)* I prefer to stand during the few minutes I shall be here. You telephoned me that if I came to your home this evening you'd give me a certified check for the money I've demanded.

CLEM: Yes—I mean to settle with you well within the twenty four hour period which you allowed me. By the way, have you brought that ugly little pistol with you?

INGRAM: You needn't worry about the pistol if you have the check ready.

CLEM: Oh, I'm not worrying—and I have everything ready. I wonder if you wouldn't be interested in the freakish mirror I've installed here—it's new, the moving men set it up only half an hour ago.

INGRAM: *(Shortly)* I'm interested in nothing but your check.

CLEM: But you must look at my new mirror. Here—I'll remove its covering.

INGRAM: *(Angrily)* Clements, if you're stalling for time it won't do you any good!

CLEM: "Stalling?" Why, my dear fellow—I'm in greater haste than you are to have our business ended. But I wish you'd look in my mirror—just to humor me. Look at it closely—you'll find it most absorbing.

INGRAM: *(Wonderingly)* It doesn't reflect our images. A—a picture is growing in that glass—a landscape!

CLEM: Yes—of bare mountains and bleak valleys!

INGRAM: *(Cries)* Ahh—we're standing on a mountain peak! We're no longer in your house—we're in another world!!

CLEM: A world where you are going to stay!!

INGRAM: *(Cries in terror.)* Clements—where are you?? You were here beside me—now you've gone! Clements, come back!! Don't leave me here alone or I'll go mad!! Clements, come back—come back— COME BACK!!!!

(Music)

SCENE IV

CLEM: It's nice to have you in my home tonight, Irene. Before Mrs. Clements' mysterious disappearance, this was a pleasure we could not enjoy.

IRENE: *(Miserably)* I'm not enjoying it now—I wouldn't have come here if you hadn't insisted.

CLEM: I must say you're very hard to please. Two months ago, the height of your ambition was to be mistress of my house.

IRENE: Two months ago a lot of strange things hadn't happened. Two months ago I wasn't afraid of you.

CLEM: You're afraid of me now?

IRENE: Yes. Bob, you can fool the police—you have fooled them; but you can't deceive me. What happened to Ingram the night after he told you you'd have to make that stock good? What happened to your wife after she learned you'd taken her diamonds? What happened to Morris Bloch? What's happened to a dozen other people whom you had cause to fear or hate? In every case, except Bloch's, this house was the last place where they were known to be—alive.

CLEM: (Easily) You know the police have practically torn this house apart—Do you think I have a number of corpses buried in my cellar or between these floors that they couldn't find?

IRENE: Oh—I don't know what to think.

CLEM: But you are thinking a little too much for your own good. That's why I insisted you come here tonight—I want you to see a funny mirror I've acquired.

IRENE: A mirror?

CLEM: Women are always interested in mirrors. I keep this one draped usually with a curtain—look.

IRENE: That's a distorting glass—like I've seen at Coney Island.

CLEM: Is it?

IRENE: (Wonderingly) No! It doesn't reflect at all.

CLEM: Look into it closely—I'll stand here, out of its focus.

IRENE: Why—?

CLEM: Just stand there—and soon many questions you've been asking will be answered. You've asked a lot of questions lately.

IRENE: But what has this wavy sheet of glass to do with—?

CLEM: You'll learn very soon.

IRENE: A picture is forming in the glass!

CLEM: A landscape?

IRENE: A dark—horrible landscape! And I see people!

CLEM: Can you see who they are?

IRENE: Bob—your wife is there—and Ingram! Everybody's there who— (She screams....A scream that fades out abruptly.)

CLEM: And now you have joined them! (Chuckles) Goodbye, Irene—you asked too many questions, and you knew too much about me.

(Music)

SCENE V

CLEM: *(Wearily)* Sergeant Rourke, aren't you policemen ever going to give me a moment's peace?

ROURKE: *(A detective sergeant...angrily.)* We're gonna find out what you've done with Irene Austin!!

CLEM: I've told you a hundred times that I've done nothing with her.

ROURKE: And when ye say that ye lie! Though we're mortally certain the dozen others who've disappeared were last seen alive in this house, we can't prove it—BUT, when ye brought yer secretary here last night, six of my men were trailin' ye—they saw her come in with ye, but they didn't see her come out! What have ye done with her??

CLEM: If you can prove that she was here and never left, what does that get you, Sergeant? I know law, and you can't substantiate a case of either abduction or murder unless you can produce the body, dead or living, of the missing person. Tear this house apart—again—splinter by splinter, if you wish—and still you won't have anything on me.

ROURKE: You're mighty sure o' that, aren't ye??

CLEM: I'm absolutely sure.

ROURKE: *(Pause...dropping his bullying manner.)* Ye're a perty smart guy, Mr. Clements.

CLEM: Thank you.

ROURKE: *(Admiringly)* Yes'r, you're as smart a feller as I've ever met up with. Boys—there ain't no use of us pulling any more cheap third degree stuff on this gentleman—you clear out and leave him and me alone.

MEN: *(Ad lib.)* Okay. Alright, Sarge.

ROURKE: Close th' door an' don't come back until I call ye.

MAN: Okay.

(Door closed.)

CLEM: I'm glad you've finally got rid of your gorillas.

ROURKE: Me and them has been ridin' ye perty hard for th' last couple hours, haven't we?

CLEM: It hasn't got you anywhere.

ROURKE: No—and I kin see now that it never will with a smart guy like you.

CLEM: You may as well drop that—I'm no more susceptible to flattery than I am to browbeating. You see, I'm thoroughly familiar with your police methods, Sergeant.

ROURKE:	*(Good naturedly.)* Oh, come off yer high-horse! If you was an ordinary run-o-th' mill gangster or crook, I might try t' con ye inta a confession after everything else has failed—but I ain't fool enough to try such a dodge on you. To prove I'm on the level, I'll talk straight. I'm still dead sure that you're responsible for the disappearance of Irene Austin an' all them other people—but I'm convinced th' law will never get you for it.
CLEM:	If I'm the wholesale murderer you think, there must be something wrong with the law that can't touch me for my "crimes."
ROURKE:	There's plenty wrong with th' law. Why, it's so screwy, Clements, that if I should disappear like all of them others while alone in this room with you—even though th' house is surrounded by my men, no court would ever try ye. Yes'r—th' law is downright goofy.
CLEM:	Isn't it, though?
ROURKE:	*(Chuckles)* Lord—if you was th' ordinary vain crook, how you could prove it—if ye have some secret means of gettin' rid of people?
CLEM:	*(Musingly)* Yes. *(Chuckles softly.)* It would be a very good joke, Sergeant—if I had a secret means of getting rid of people. Are you interested in curios?
ROURKE:	Curios?
CLEM:	I have a mirror here that is very rare—
ROURKE:	A mirror?
CLEM:	Here. You and your men lifted the curtain which covers it many times—in order to make sure no bodies were concealed beneath— but you never exposed the mirror long enough. Stand in front of it—with me.
ROURKE:	Th' thing don't reflect us!
CLEM:	But soon it will reflect something else.
ROURKE:	Holy Mother!—a picture's growing in th' glass!!
CLEM:	Yes—a picture of mountains and dark chasms!
ROURKE:	I see people there! They're comin' closer!
CLEM:	They're the people you've been searching for—the fools you're going to join!!
ROURKE:	What's happenin' here?? You an' me is in th' picture now.
CLEM:	*(Laughs)* And I've played my biggest joke upon the law! Don't draw that pistol, Sergeant!
ROURKE:	I've got it pointed at yer heart! I don't know where I am or how ye brought me here—but it's what I played ye for, an' ye fell for my

connin' like th' cheap dumb crook ye are! Now, Clements, ye're gonna take me an' those others outa here—if ye don't I'll blow ye apart!

CLEM: *(Calmly)* You won't use that pistol, Sergeant, any more than these others have attempted to harm me on my visits to their land of exile. Ingram, you were the first I brought here, and you have an automatic in your pocket now. Tell him why you haven't used it.

INGRAM: You tell him, Clements.

CLEM: *(Puzzled)* Very well—but what's wrong with all of you today? You usually have a lot to say when I appear. You see, Sergeant—if you or any of your future companions should kill me here, your hope of possible escape from this world of the Fourth Dimension would be gone forever.

ROURKE: Th' Fourth Dimension?

CLEM: Yes. Put down your pistol if you ever hope to leave here—in my continued life lies all your hope, for I, in all the universe, possess the secret of escape.

BLOCH: *(Slightly distant.)* No! Eh? I know de secret, too.

CLEM: Bloch????!

BLOCH: *(Coming up.)* Jah—Bloch.

CLEM: You fell a thousand feet—you're dead—you're—!!!

BLOCH: No. When you tried to kill me, you forgodt dot I hadt toldt you dis vas de land vhere everyt'ing endures forever! You cannot kill or be killed in de vorldt of Time. Seize him!!

CLEM: Let me go! Ahh! *(He struggles.)*

INGRAM: Now you see why we didn't plead with you today!

BLOCH: I found my vay dis morning to de odders an' toldt dem how ve'd beat you!

IRENE: Give us the lens!

VOICES: The lens! The lens!!

CLEM: *(Struggling)* Let me go—let me go!

IRENE: I have it!!

BLOCH: Holdt it up before your eyes—all you who've suffered here!!

VOICES: Yes, yes—all of us must look together!

CLEM: Don't push me away! What do you mean to do??

BLOCH: Ve return to life, you wander here forever—vhere misery iss endless, vhere death does not come!!

CLEM: No—NO!!!

BLOCH: Wander here alone t'rough all eternity, for vhen I reach de world

I break de mirror!!

CLEM: Irene—!

IRENE: The world isn't big enough for you and decent people.

BLOCH: Look in de lens—now!

CLEM: *(Screams)* Ahh—you've all gone!! Gone forever! *(Sobs)* A world of my own—a world of my own.

(Music)

EPILOGUE

NANCY: He he he...(CAT) Weel, that's th' end o' that un, Satan! An nex' week, we'll have a Halloween yarn ter spin ye. He he he he he...(CAT)...

ANNOUNCER...DIRECTLY INTO COMMERCIAL...AFTER WHICH...

(Musical theme.)

The Tenant
Thursday, May 6, 1937

(Musical theme.)

ANNOUNCER: We bring you the two hundred and eightieth weekly broad-cast of the famous dramatic feature, The Witch's Tale,writ-ten and produced by Alonzo Deen Cole and starring Mr. Cole and Miss Marie O'Flynn. THE WITCH'S TALE! And now let us join Nancy and Satan, her wise black cat.

(Music swells...wind whistles...)

PROLOGUE

NANCY: He he he...(CAT) Hunner an' ten year ole I be t'day—yes'r, hunner an' ten year ole! Weel, Satan—we gotta perty cute leetle bedtime stury p'pared fer folks this evenin'—he he...one that'll give em pleasant nightmares when they goes t' bed. (CAT) Tha's right, Satan—me an' you is allus thinkin' o' people's happiness an' comfurt. Tell ever'one t' douse their lights an' we'll git right down t' bizness! (CAT) Tha's hit—make hit nice an' dark an' cheerful. Now draw up t' th' fire an' gaze inter th' embers—gaze inter em deep, an' soon ye'll see a ole fashioned two stury house on a ole fashioned street in a ole New England town. Downstairs in that house, ye'll see a perty girl p'arin' supper fer her father an' her sister—th' upstairs floor is rented to a man who lives alone. An' now b'gins our tale erbout "Th' Tenant...he he. TH' TENANT! He he he he he...(CAT)...

(A slight rattle of pots and pans....Scene blends directly from prologue without musical interlude.)

GERT: *(A young school teacher...calls.)* Dad—I have supper almost ready! Will you come and set the table?

TOM: *(A middle aged mechanic...distant...grumbles.)* I suppose so.

GERT: I hate to ask you—but if I leave my cooking now, something's sure to burn.

TOM: *(Coming up...sourly.)* That sister of yours is going to get a good talking to from me when she comes in—she knows she's supposed to be home in time to help you with this supper job, yet this is the third time this week I've had to leave off reading my paper to do her work.

GERT: *(With slight irritation.)* She's probably been kept late again at the store.

(Rattle of cutlery.)

TOM: That store closes at six o'clock, don't it?

GERT: Jane says they're taking stock in her department now.

TOM: Humph—and last week she had a different explanation! Tonight I'm gonna make her tell me the real reason for these late hours she's keeping.

GERT: Dad, please—

(Cutlery slammed on table.)

TOM: *(Thoroughly angered now.)* No daughter of mine's gonna pull the wool over my eyes!! You remember that, too!

GERT: *(Calmly)* Have I ever attempted to "pull the wool over your eyes"?

TOM: *(Grumbles)* I haven't caught you at it yet.

GERT: *(Worried)* What on earth has come over you lately, Dad? You've changed terribly in the last several months.

TOM: What d' ye mean?

GERT: That you used to be a very pleasant person to live with. You're not any more.

TOM: Is that so?

GERT: *(Angrily)* Yes, that's so! You've become grouchy, picky, and downright mean! I have a pretty good idea of why Jane stays away from home as much as she possibly can—for when I finish teaching school in the afternoon, I hate to come back to this house myself—knowing I'll find you with a good sized chip on your shoulder!

TOM: *(Roars)* You two girls'd like to get out and leave me, I suppose! Because I've been out of work for the past year, you figure you'll have to support me for the rest of my life and you want to get out from under!

GERT: Dad—!

TOM: I know that's what's eatin' you! But so long as I own this house and have a tenant in those two rooms upstairs who pays his rent, I'm not dependent on you and Jane for a single moment!!

GERT: *(Pause...quietly.)* Aren't you just a little bit ashamed of yourself?

TOM: I—! *(Subsiding)* Well—I guess you're not the sort of kids who think much of the money end of things. *(Apologetically)* I—I don't really think what I said, Gertie.

GERT: *(Gently)* I know you don't, Dad.

TOM: *(Unhappily)* I wonder what has got into me lately—I'm always flyin' off the handle. I don't know why you don't marry that lawyer feller of yours and get as far away from me as ye can. He's got himself a good job as Assistant D.A. now—there's no reason for you to put off marryin' him any longer.

GERT: There's the reason that I don't want to leave you—until things are different here—like they used to be again.

TOM: I'll be alright soon as I find a job—a man who's worked hard all his life, like me, can't just stop and not have it affect his disposition.

GERT: *(Thoughtfully)* It isn't only you who's changed—Jane and I aren't the same anymore. It's as though something nasty had come into this house during the last six months that—that's changed our natures.

TOM: Yeah. *(Pause)* Funny thing, Gert—ye know, when I'm away from here I ain't a sorehead.

GERT: Neither am I—neither is Jane.

TOM: The old place gets on our nerves, I guess.

GERT: I guess so. But, as we've lived in it for almost twenty years, I don't see why it should at this late date.

TOM: When I get money comin' in again, I'll have some new paint and wallpaper spread around—to sort of brighten things up. Maybe that'll help.

GERT: *(Sighs)* I don't think so. There's nothing wrong with the house, Dad—it's just us. Better set that table—things are almost done.

TOM: Alright.

(He starts to lay the table...Cutlery and dishes...Upstairs we hear the nervous footsteps of a man pacing the floor....Pause for effects.)

That feller upstairs is home—I hear him walking around.

GERT: Yes. *(Pauses while she lifts a pot lid and replaces it.)* I wish he wouldn't pace the floor like that—he kept it up nearly all last night directly over my bedroom.

TOM: I've spoken to him about it, but he says he's gotta walk when he's thinkin'.

GERT: Let's hope he'll soon finish that book he's writing—so he can stop thinking and give us a little peace.

TOM: Yeah. He ever tell you what kind of book he's working on? He always changes the subject when I ask him.

GERT: He's never said anything to me except "good morning" or "good evening"—which is just as well, for I can't stand the sight of him.

TOM: He isn't a very good lookin' feller.

GERT: He's the ugliest, most repulsive looking man I've ever seen. It makes me almost physically sick to look at him.

TOM: I'd never rented them rooms to him if I hadn't needed the money. But, in the six months he's been here, he's paid his rent regular, so we shouldn't kick.

GERT: I suppose not.

TOM: *(Sniffing)* Say—you burning something?

GERT: I don't think so. *(Pot lids removed and replaced.)* No—everything's alright.

TOM: Something's burnin' somewhere! Can't ye smell it?

GERT: *(Sniffs)* Yes. I've noticed that odor several times before—I think it's something that man upstairs cooks.

TOM: He takes his meals outside.

GERT: I know—but I always smell it strongest near that door which leads to the stairway.

TOM: *(Going away.)* That so? *(Slightly distant.)* Guess you're right—I get an awful whiff of it here. *(In disgust.)* Whew—it's worse than rotten eggs! Better open that window and air the place out.

GERT: *(Irritably)* Open it yourself— I can't leave this stove.

TOM: *(Angrily)* When there's something to do, you and Jane always have some excuse!

(Door opens and closes.)

JANE: *(A young shop girl...coming in...belligerently.)* What's this about Jane?

TOM: *(Unpleasantly)* Oh—so you're home at last!

JANE: Looks like it, don't it? This place smells like a pig pen—better open a window.

TOM: Instead of givin' orders, suppose you tell me why you weren't here an hour ago!

GERT: Dad, for Heaven's sake, don't start grouching again! I thought you had it out of your system for the evening.

JANE: He'd better have it out of his system—for I haven't come home to be browbeaten!

TOM:	*(Roars)* Don't you dare talk to me like that—either of you!! You girls aren't so grown up that you can treat your father like a child!
JANE:	Then don't act like one!
GERT:	Jane—stop it!!
TOM:	She'd better stop it!
JANE:	You won't make me!
TOM:	We'll see about that!!
GERT:	Dad—don't—!!

(A slap.)

JANE:	*(Cries)* Ohh—!!
GERT:	*(Incensed)* You nasty brute!!
JANE:	*(Furious)* He'll never have a chance to strike me again!!
TOM:	Come back here!!
JANE:	*(Going)* I'm leaving you and this rotten house forever!!
TOM:	Oh no, you're not!!
GERT:	Dad—let her go!!
JANE:	*(Wildly)* If he don't let me go, I'll kill him!!
GERT:	Jane—throw down that knife!!
JANE:	You keep away from me, too!! I hate you—hate you both!!
TOM:	You little devil!!
JANE:	Don't touch me—don't you dare, or—!!!
GERT:	*(Arresting)* Dad—Jane—STOP!! Have you both turned into beasts??
TOM:	*(His anger gone...bewildered.)* I—I—Jane—!
JANE:	*(Sobbing...hysterical.)* Dad—! Oh, I'm so sorry, Dad—I didn't mean—!
TOM:	*(Brokenly)* Neither did I, kid. I—I'm sorry, too.
GERT:	*(Sobs)* What came over you both? What's happening to all of us here—what's happening??

(From upstairs...a frightful scream.)

TOM:	*(Gasps)* Good Lord!
GERT:	What was that??

(The scream again.)

JANE:	It's Mr. Black upstairs!!

(Crash of furniture above.)

TOM:	Someone's up there with him—they're fighting!

(Scream)

JANE:	Oh, those screams!
TOM:	*(Starting away.)* I'm going up there!!

GERT: No—wait! Call the police!!

JANE: Dad—come back!!

(Door thrown open...He runs upstairs.)

GERT: We can't let him go alone! *(Going)* Jane—come on!!

JANE: *(Going)* I'm coming!

(They run upstairs.)

GERT: *(Returning to microphone again.)* Dad—!!

TOM: *(Slightly distant...trying door.)* His door is locked!

JANE: The screams have stopped!

GERT: What's happened in there??

TOM: *(Cries...knocking at door.)* Black—Mr. Black—!!

JANE: He doesn't answer!

TOM: I'm going to break this lock!!

(Throws himself against door.)

GERT: No don't. Whoever fought with him is still inside—for this is the only door!

TOM: I'm big enough to handle whoever's there—I'm going in!!

(The door crashes in.)

JANE: Dad—!

GERT: There's Mr. Black upon the floor!!

JANE: *(In horror.)* His face is all purple—horrible!

TOM: He's dead.

GERT: Let's get out of here—let's get out quick!

JANE: Yes—call the police!!

TOM: You go and call. *(Starts away.)* If the murderer's still here, I'll give him no chance to get away!

GERT: *(In terror.)* Don't go in that other room—he may be hiding there with a gun!

TOM: If he had a gun, he'd have shot Black—and we heard no shot!

(Door thrown open.)

                  Come out, whoever ye are—come out!! *(Pause)* This room is empty.

JANE: *(Trembling)* So—so is the bathroom there.

TOM: *(In wonderment.)* All these windows are closed—and locked. *(Coming up.)* Let's see that other room again!

GERT: The windows are closed and locked in here.

JANE: And in the bathroom.

TOM: No one could have got out of here—yet no one's in these rooms but us and—

JANE: *(Murmurs fearfully.)* And—and that dead man.

TOM: *(Awed)* How—?
JANE: What—?
GERT: *(Low)* That—that awful odor—it permeates this place.
(Musical interlude.)

SCENE II

DWAN: *(A burly police lieutenant.)* So ye heard screams and the sound of scuffling—and, when ye got up here, this man was dead?

TOM: Yes, Lieutenant.

DWAN: Yet ye say ye touched nothin' in these rooms, that ev'ry window was closed and fastened tight as they are now, and that the only door to the flat was bolted on the inside??

TOM: Yes.

DWAN: *(Roars)* Then how d' ye explain how the murderer got away??

JANE: *(Miserably)* We can't attempt to explain it, Lieutenant.

GERT: *(Nervously)* If there was a murderer—he couldn't have got away.

DWAN: There was a murderer, alright! This room looks as if a cyclone had struck it—the dead man didn't throw this furniture all about, and then commit suicide!! You found out yet what killed him, Doc?

CHALM: *(A police surgeon...slightly distant...puzzled.)* I can't find any external wound. The congestion of blood in the face suggests strangulation—but there's no pressure marks upon the throat. I can't tell you what caused his death until after the autopsy—but off hand, I'd say it was fear.

DWAN: Fear?

CHALM: I admit that's not a very scientific diagnosis. But have you ever seen a more terrified look upon a human face?

DWAN: *(Slowly)* I never saw a more ugly face—it gives me the creeps, and I'm pretty hard-boiled. *(Sharply)* Ye mean he mighta been so scared o' something that his heart stopped?

CHALM: It's possible.

DWAN: How about poison? Some poisons'd account for that scared expression—and, also them screams these people heard.

CHALM: *(Thoughtfully)* Yes—and in the death agony induced by a few violent poisons he might have caused the wreckage in this room.

DWAN: Maybe he did commit suicide then.

CHALM: Perhaps, but—violent poisons, like carbolic or prussic acid for instance, always leave their tell-tale marks upon a body and their characteristic odor—neither is present here.

DWAN:	*(Sniffing)* There's an odor of some sort in these rooms—a rotten odor.
CHALM:	I noticed that the moment I came in—but it's not that of any poison I'm familiar with. Besides—you haven't found any bottle or glass that might have contained a drug, have you?
DWAN:	Hmm—no. Suppose you get that stiff outa here and on an autopsy table, so I can have the real dope on this as soon as possible.
CHALM:	Take him down to the wagon, boys.
MAN:	Yes'r.
CHALM:	*(Going)* I'll report to you soon as I'm finished with him, Lieutenant.
DWAN:	Okay, Doc.
GERT:	*(Miserably)* Can we go downstairs now?
JANE:	I can't stand being in this awful room much longer.
DWAN:	*(Unsympathetically)* Ye'll have to stand it a little longer, sister.
TOM:	My girls can't tell ye any more'n they have already! This thing has been a rotten shock for them. Why don't ye let em go?
DWAN:	'Cause there's still a few questions I want answered. Screwy as it looks right now, I gotta hunch this is a murder case—and; if it turns out that way, the story you've told me so far ain't so good.
TOM:	What do ye mean?
DWAN:	Ye claim ye found this dead guy alone in a room that was all locked up inside.
GERT:	We did!
DWAN:	That's what you say.
JANE:	*(Incredulous)* You don't think—??
TOM:	*(Belligerently)* Are you tryin' to accuse us of bein' in on this??
JIM:	*(Slightly distant...a young lawyer.)* That's probably his bright idea, Mr. Sharon.
DWAN:	*(Surprised)* Jim—??
TOM:	Jim McGrath!
JIM:	*(Coming in.)* Hello, Gertie—'lo Jane—how're you, Lieutenant?
JANE:	How—?
DWAN:	What're you doin' here??
JIM:	We just got word of what's happened over at the D.A.'s office— naturally, I came right over. I overhead your conversation as I came up the stairs.
DWAN:	*(Angrily)* Since when have you Assistant D.A.s been detailed to butt in on police cases??
JIM:	I detailed myself to butt in on this case—for the very good reason

that Miss Sharon and I are engaged to be married.

DWAN: Huh?? *(Cordially)* Why didn't you folks tell me Jim McGrath was that close to your family? Why, he and I vote in the same ward—and he gets a chance to do me a favor now and then! Don't ye, boy...ha ha? *(Intimately)* Jim—these girls are pretty upset by what's took place here t'night—s'pose you take them and their father downstairs so's they can pull themselves t'gether. I'll not be botherin' em any more!

JIM: Thanks, Lieutenant—but, in case they need a lawyer later on, I'd like to look about up here a bit, if you don't mind.

DWAN: Sure—help yerself!

JIM: Mr. Sharon—you take the girls downstairs.

JANE: *(Starting away.)* Come Dad—let's get away from here.

TOM: *(Going)* Lord knows I'm willing enough to go.

GERT: I'll stay here with you, Jim.

JIM: I'd like to have you, Gertie. I met Dr. Chalmers as he was leaving, Lieutenant—he let me look at the dead man.

DWAN: Pretty sight, wasn't he?

JIM: Very—but scarcely more repulsive than he was in life.

DWAN: *(Sharply)* You knew him?

JIM: I'd seen him coming in and out of the house here—I call most every evening.

DWAN: Oh, yeah—sure. None of the family seem to know much about him.

JIM: He wasn't given to confidences, I understand. Even your Dad has never been in these rooms since he rented them to the man, had he, Gert?

GERT: No. Mr. Black had a special lock put on the door—that one Dad broke—and his every action implied that he wished to be left alone.

DWAN: *(Musing)* One o' them mysterious eggs. May have been a crook using this place as a hide-away—we'll find out about that when we check his fingerprints.

JIM: I don't think he'll prove to be a criminal—not a professional, at any rate.

DWAN: Why not?

JIM: Too many books around the place—bad men, as a rule, don't go in for scholarship.

DWAN: Hmm—Black bring these books with him when he moved in,

	Miss Sharon, or did he buy em later?
GERT:	He had them when he came—several dozen big packing cases full. He told Dad that he had spent most of his life collecting them.
DWAN:	A crook on the lam don't travel around with his own personal liberry, that's certain.
JIM:	Did you look over these books?
DWAN:	No. Why should I?
JIM:	What a man reads is often a pretty good index of his character.
DWAN:	What did this guy read?
JIM:	Not very healthy stuff, apparently—this case is devoted to works on Satanism.
GERT:	Satanism?
JIM:	Devil worship.
DWAN:	You don't mean people worship—??
JIM:	Oh, yes—there's a secret, worldwide cult that practices such a faith.
DWAN:	Saints preserve us!
GERT:	Jim—the volumes here deal with witchcraft and magic.
JIM:	(Interested) And some of them very rare. I've done quite a little research on this sort of thing, as a hobby—
DWAN:	Are all these books about such screwy stuff?
JIM:	Yes—it's all concerned with demonology of one sort of another. (Going slightly away.) Let's have a look at this big case over here.
DWAN:	(Pause) I can't read most o' them titles—they're in a furrin language.
GERT:	What's here, Jim—more work on occultism?
JIM:	(Slowly) No—although these subjects are allied with its most perverted forms. (In disgust.) These shelves contain some of the vilest stuff ever written:—the Marquis de Sade's "Justine and Juliette"—the works of Restif de la Bretonne, the "Crimes of Gilles de Raiz"—every book here is concerned with torture, cruelty and downright filth. I don't see a single decent, wholesome volume in the room. That man's mind must have been more repulsive than his face, since this is what he fed it with.
DWAN:	(Practically) Knowin' that won't help me find who murdered him—if he was murdered.
JIM:	No, I suppose not. Doc Chalmers said he might have taken poison.

DWAN:	There's nothin' here he coulda took it from. And suicides usually leave farewell notes behind. He didn't—there ain't a scrap of writin' in the place.
JIM:	No writing?
GERT:	They haven't even found the book he told us he was writing.
JIM:	*(Thoughtfully)* That book's what I was thinking of. It might give you a line on him, Lieutenant Dwan.
DWAN:	He may have it locked up in this little safe here—I'm having it cracked open in the morning.
JIM:	How about those scraps of paper in the fireplace?
DWAN:	We looked them over—no leads there. It's evidently just some waste he touched a match to.
JIM:	*(Pause)* Funny—all four margins are left on these charred sheets— only the center, where writing may have been, is burned away.
DWAN:	*(Puzzled)* I thought that was screwy myself—fire don't usually stop at the edges of a piece o' paper. *(In dismissal.)* But that don't tell us nothin', either!
JIM:	No—it doesn't! *(Sniffs)* What a peculiar odor.
DWAN:	You just notice that?
GERT:	It's very weak now, Jim—but it filled these rooms when—when we found the tenant dead.
DWAN:	*(Impatiently)* That's another thing that don't mean nothin'—only I'm sick of inhalin' it. It reminds me of—uh—a slaughter house! Let's get outa here.
JIM:	We may as well. Come dear.
GERT:	I'll be glad to go.

(They descend the stairs.)

JIM:	You're returning to headquarters, Lieutenant?
DWAN:	Yes—to wait for Doc Chalmers report on the autopsy findings.
GERT:	Jim—did the police surgeon tell you his idea that—Mr. Black may have died from fear?
JIM:	*(In surprise.)* No—he didn't.
DWAN:	That's another screwy thing that don't mean nothin'! *(Calls)* Brooks—!
BROOKS:	*(A detective...distant.)* Yes, sir?
DWAN:	I want you and Dolan to go upstairs and stay in them rooms until relieved.
BROOKS:	*(Coming up.)* Yes, sir.
DOLAN:	*(A detective...coming up.)* Any special orders, sir?

DWAN:	No—there's no more investigatin' to be done until I get a man here to open that safe; we've already covered everything else. Just stay on the job and keep your eyes open.
DOLAN:	*(Going)* Okay.
BROOKS:	*(Going)* Yes, sir.

(They ascend the stairs.)

GERT:	Those two detectives will remain up there—all night?
DWAN:	*(Chuckles)* And what a soft snap I've given em—them lads love to play pinochle together, an' they'll have nothin' else to do 'till mornin'. They're great buddies, Jim.
JIM:	*(Casually)* I've heard they're the Damon and Pythias of your department.
GERT:	*(Half to herself.)* I—I'd hate to have to stay in those rooms—with that frightful odor.
DWAN:	*(Laughs)* A nasty smell won't do a couple of tough cops any harm.
GERT:	*(Murmurs)* I hope not. *(Pause)* I hope not.
JIM:	What do you mean, dear?
GERT:	*(Slowly)* I don't know.

(Musical interlude.)

SCENE III

JANE:	*(Irritably)* Please, Dad—sit down and stop walking the floor!
TOM:	*(Pacing back and forth...angrily.)* Why shouldn't I walk the floor? You heard what Jim McGrath told us!
JIM:	*(Uncomfortably)* Perhaps I shouldn't have said what I did—but I didn't want you to be fooled by the change in Lieutenant Dwan's attitude when he learned I was engaged to Gertie. He'll kid me along for political reasons—but he's a bull-headed cop who sticks fast to an idea when he gets one no matter whom it hits.
TOM:	Yeah, and he has an idea that we had someth' to do with the death of that tenant!
GERT:	No matter what he thinks, Dad—he can't prove us guilty when we're innocent.
TOM:	No, but he can make us feel like a bunch of criminals—an' he's doin' it! He's got them two detectives spendin' the night upstairs, and a couple others prowlin' around outside my house!
JANE:	I know how Dad feels—it isn't very pleasant to be treated like a murderer.
GERT:	*(In angry spite.)* Why be so thin-skinned? Only a few hours ago, you

and Dad were murderers at heart—you wanted to kill one another!

TOM: *(Hurt)* Gert—?

GERT: *(In quick contrition.)* I'm sorry—I didn't mean to remind you of that foolishness! *(With a sob.)* Oh, what's the matter with us all—what makes us say and do such awful things.

TOM: *(Helplessly)* I don't know.

JANE: *(Morosely)* We've all gone crazy, I think.

JIM: *(Pacifically)* The three of you are terribly upset tonight—with good reason. You're not accountable for your jumpy nerves.

GERT: *(Wanly)* It isn't only tonight, Jim—I haven't told you, but this has been going on for months.

JIM: What has?

JANE: I'll tell you! We've got to the point where Gert hates Dad and me, he hates us, and I hate them!

GERT: Jane—!

JANE: It's true! Why lie about it?

TOM: *(Mutters)* God help us all.

GERT: *(Low...miserably.)* Yes—God help us.

JIM: Hmm—you're not your normal selves, that's certain.

GERT: *(In tearful hysteria.)* If you lived here, you wouldn't be normal, either! There's something horrible about this house—a ghastly curse of some kind! That was proved tonight when that man upstairs was killed!

JIM: Gertie, darling—

GERT: *(Wildly)* Go away—don't touch me—leave me alone!!

JANE: *(Laughs bitterly.)* You're having an opportunity this evening to learn what a nice family we really are, Mr. McGrath.

TOM: *(Angrily)* Shut up, Jane!!

JANE: Shut up, yourself!!

GERT: Both of you be still! Be still!! Be still!!!

TOM: *(A pause...sighs.)* I'll say no more.

JANE: *(Helplessly)* I'm finished.

GERT: *(Sobs)*

JIM: Hmm...

(Telephone rings.)

That'll be for me, I think—Dr. Chalmers promised to call me about his autopsy findings.

TOM: You answer it, then.

(Receiver lifted.)

JIM: *(At phone.)* Hello...McGrath speaking, Doctor...What? That's very peculiar...You've already reported to Lieutenant Dwan, of course?...What'd he say??...That sounds like him...Thanks very much for letting me know. Goodnight. *(Hangs up.)*

GERT: What—what did he find?

JIM: You won't have to worry about any further police investigation.

TOM: Black wasn't murdered?

JIM: No.

JANE: Then what killed him?

JIM: Dr. Chalmers doesn't know.

ALL: Doesn't know??

JIM: Here's what he told me: Black's lungs and other inner organs appear to have been seared by flame—

TOM: Flame??

JIM: Yes. But there is no mark of a burn on his body, or in such external passages as the mouth or nostrils.

GERT: Then how—?

JIM: Let me finish—what I've just told you is the least puzzling part. Black has been dead not quite three hours, yet decomposition of his body has advanced to the state normally found in cadavers exposed to the air three weeks.

JANE: What—?

GERT: I don't understand.

TOM: It don't make sense.

JIM: *(Dryly)* I'm informed Lieutenant Dwan said it was "screwy" when the doctor told him.

GERT: Jim—what do you think?

JIM: *(Slowly)* I'm trying to think—but I don't know where to begin.

BROOKS: *(Upstairs, distant...screams with rage and pain.)*

TOM: Good Lord!

GERT: What's that??

(Upstairs...six heavy pistol shots.)

JIM: Pistol shots!!

JANE: Upstairs!

TOM: Them two cops is up there!

JIM: *(Starting away.)* Mr. Sharon—come on!!

GERT: *(Hysterically)* I'm afraid—afraid—!!

BROOKS: *(Closer, but still distant...laughs madly.)*

GERT: Oh, that crazy laughter—??

JIM: *(Slightly distant.)* There's a madman up there!

TOM: *(Slightly distant.)* The door is open!

JIM: *(Closer)* What's happened in there?? What—??

BROOKS: *(Coming up.)* Ha ha...I killed him! Killed him!!

JIM: Brooks??

BROOKS: *(Gasping, dying, but still laughing madly.)* I killed him like he wanted to kill me...ha ha! It was swell to see him die as I pumped six bullets in his head...ha ha—*(Gasps)*—swell to see him die—*(He falls.)*

JANE: He's fallen!

GERT: *(Cries)* There's a knife stuck in his chest!

TOM: These two cops have killed each other!

JIM: Dolan stabbed Brooks with that knife—and Brooks emptied his service gun in Dolan! These men were partners—friends—Why—?

JANE: Why—?

TOM: Why—?

GERT: *(Murmurs)* That—that odor—it permeates these rooms again.

(Musical interlude.)

SCENE IV

(An ambulance siren...A speeding motor.)

INTERN: Slow down and cut the siren, Bill—this ambulance'll never make the hospital on time.

JIM: Brooks is dying, Doctor?

(Siren out...motor slows.)

INTERN: Almost gone, Mr. McGrath—when that other cop stuck a knife into his chest he did a thorough job. I told you it was hopeless when we put him in this bus.

JIM: But he's got to tell me what happened in those rooms! The man he shot was dead before you got there—I've got to know what made them fight! They weren't enemies, but friends.

INTERN: *(Thoughtfully)* There's one chance in a million of making him talk—and it can't hurt him now.

JIM: What are you doing?

INTERN: Injecting glonoin directly into his heart muscles—if anything'll make him rally for a moment, this is it.

JIM: *(Pause)* He's opened his eyes. Brooks—can you hear me?

BROOKS: *(Weak...bewildered.)* Huh? Hello—
JIM: You just killed your partner, Dolan. Why—??
BROOKS: I remember—I wanted to kill.
JIM: Wanted to kill?
BROOKS: And so did he. Something got into us both—as we sat b'side that safe—and sniffed that rotten smell.
JIM: Safe? Smell??
BROOKS: *(Gasping)* We didn't quarrel—he was always a right guy, Dolan—he just—stabbed me and—I shot him. As we sat b'side that safe and breathed that smell—I wanted to hurt someone—anyone—to see em in pain—to watch em die—and so did he. *(Dying)* As we sat b'side that safe and breathed—that rotten odor—*(A last sigh.)*
INTERN: *(Quietly)* He's gone, Mr. McGrath.
JIM: Yes. *(Murmurs thoughtfully.)* "That safe—that rotten odor."
(Musical interlude.)

SCENE V

DWAN: *(Irritably)* Now look here, Jim—you and I vote in the same ward and can do each other favors, but I don't like the idea of all this monkey business in a place where two of my boys have made murderers of themselves!
JIM: Please take a chance on me, Lieutenant—it's only a wild idea that I have, but it may prevent further tragedies in this house. And you haven't a better idea.
DWAN: *(Glumly)* I have none at all. Last night the Sharon's tenant is found dead in these rooms, from Lord only knows what screwy cause—and then Brooks and Dolan—*(Helplessly)* Go ahead—do anything you want.
JIM: Thanks. How are you coming along with that safe, Berner?
BERNER: *(A German...slightly distant.)* Idt iss an easy vun—oldt style—I haf idt oben in a minute.
JIM: Don't open it when you get the actual combination—leave that to me!
BERNER: Jah, jah—I remember.
JIM: Touch a match to that kindling in the fireplace now, Malloy—I want a good strong blaze there.
MALLOY: *(A policeman.)* Okay.
DWAN: What's the idea o' that—on such a hot day??
JIM: It's just an idea. Will you call the Sharons up now?

DWAN: *(Grumbles)* Oh, alright.
(Door opens.)

     (He calls sarcastically.) You folks can come up—Dr. Sherlock Holmes has got his stage all set!

TOM: *(From below.)* Come on, girls.
(They ascend stairs.)

BERNER: De lasdt tumbler I chust hear fall! You can oben de safe door now.

JIM: That's fine, Berner.

TOM: *(Coming up.)* What ye gonna do in these rooms, Jim?

JIM: I'm not sure yet, Mr. Sharon—but I want all of you here. Gertie—have you and Jane those little crucifixes I asked you to bring?

GERT: Yes—but why did you want us to—?

JANE: *(Sourly)* That's what I'd like to know!

DWAN: *(Irritably)* It's all part of the myst'ry our friend is buildin' up! Now it's time to start yer show. What's it all about?

JIM: I'll tell you—and if it proves a failure you won't have to laugh me out of town, for I'll already be gone. I have an insane theory concerning the deaths in this apartment because there is no sane explanation for them, as we understand sanity. Gertrude—it was shortly after Mr. Black become a tenant here that you and your father and Jane began to quarrel, wasn't it?

GERT: Why—I guess it was.

TOM: What's that got to do with—?

JIM: Much, I think.

JANE: I don't see how.

JIM: I believe you'll all agree that thought is the greatest force man has ever developed—for thought has been the instigator of every step in his advancement from bestial savagery to what we know as civilization. But, like all other great forces, it has power for evil as well as good—it can destroy as well as aid.

DWAN: I don't get ye.

JIM: If the books on these shelves are any clue, the man who owned them never had a thought that wasn't degenerate and vile. I think his thoughts polluted this house—I think that rotten odor we've all noticed is an emanation from his perverted mind—I think, at last, this thoughts took physical form and destroyed him. And, though he is dead—inwardly consumed by fire, and decayed as normal flesh does not decay—I think the monster his filthy brain conceived is still alive—I think, last night, its power made two good men turn into murderous beasts.

GERT: Jim—?

DWAN: You're screwy!

JIM: We'll see when I open this safe.

TOM: Do ye expect to find yer "thought monster" in there??

JIM: No—but I expect to find the thing that binds it to this earth.

JANE: What?

JIM: The book its creator wrote—a book even worse, perhaps, than those he read; for he added the sum of his own twisted imaginings to those he borrowed. A fundamental rule of the Satanism he doubtless practised is that, to receive gifts from the Devil, one must do things pleasing to the Devil—this book was his offering; one that was accepted all too well. Dark things are strongest in the dark, their natural element—I'm hoping, in the light of day, we'll be able to destroy it. *(He moves away.)* I'll open the safe.

GERT: *(In fear.)* No, no—don't! Jim—that odor pervades this room again!

JIM: That book must be destroyed.

DWAN: Wait, boy!! *(Awed)* I don't believe a word of what ye've said—but that smell is gettin' awful!

JIM: *(Going)* It mustn't stop us.

(Small safe door opened.)

TOM: *(Fearfully)* He's opened the door.

JANE: A pile of manuscript is in there!

DWAN: The book!

GERT: Don't touch it, Jim!

JIM: It must be thrown into that cleansing fire! Fire destroyed those other pages he wrote, it destroyed him—it's the only element that consumes entirely.

GERT: Don't take it in your hands!!

TOM: Jim—!

JANE: A dark shadow's forming round him!!

GERT: An awful monstrous shadow!!

DWAN: His face is changing!!

JIM: *(Laughs madly, savagely.)*

TOM: He's laughing like that cop who killed his friend!

JIM: *(Cries)* Kill—kill...ha ha!!!

GERT: He's coming after me!!

DWAN: *(Cries)* Malloy—Sharon, help me hold him!!

(A struggle.)

JIM: Let me go! I'll kill you—kill you all...ha ha! Kill—kill—!!!

TOM: Gertie—we've made him drop the book! Throw it in the fire!!

DWAN: But don't touch it with yer hands as he did—use the fire tongs!!

GERT: Yes—yes!!

JANE: It can't hurt you, Gert—you wear a crucifix!

GERT: I've got it!!

MALLOY: Throw it in the fire!!

GERT: There!

(Book thrown in fire....Small explosion.)

JANE: The flames have got it!

(Crackle of flame.)

TOM: Jim's gone limp in our arms!

GERT: Jim—!

DWAN: He'll be alright—the devil is outa him now!

JANE: *(Screams)* Look!

DWAN: A shape is forming in the flames!

TOM: Above that burnin' book!

JANE: It's the monster he said was there!

GERT: The Thought Monster of Evil.

(An eery demoniac cry of rage...diminishing.)

ALL: *(Gasps in horror.)*

DWAN: *(Pause...awed.)* It's gone now—disappeared.

TOM: *(Awed)* The odor's gone, too.

GERT: *(Slowly)* Yes—the air is fresh and clean again.

JIM: *(Weakly)* Gert—oh Gert, what did I do?

GERT: *(Gently)* Nothing you meant to, dear—nothing any of us will ever do again, for now the tenant of this house is gone—forever.

(Musical conclusion.)

EPILOGUE

NANCY: He he he...(CAT) Weel, that's th' end o' that un, Satan! You folks be keerful o' yer thoughts from now on, fer ye see th' trouble they're like t' git ye inta. Come see me an' Satan nex' week on m' buthday—hunner an' two year ole I be nex' week! He he he he he...(CAT)

(Musical signature.)

ANNOUNCER: This concludes the two hundred and eightieth weekly broadcast of The Witch's Tale, written and produced by Alonzo Deen Cole and starring Mr. Cole as Jim and Miss Marie O'Flynn as Gertie. Tom, her father, was played by Mr. Alan Devitt—Jane, her sister, by Miss Miriam Wolff—Lieutenant Dwan by Mr. Mark Smith—Dr. Chalmers by Mr. Thomas Hoier—Detective Brooks by Mr. Mark Smith—Dolan by Mr. Thomas Hoier—and old Nancy and Satan, as usual, by themselves.

Lord of the Jungle
Tuesday, November 16, 1937

(Musical theme.)

ANNOUNCER: We bring you the 305th weekly presentation of the famous dramatic feature, The Witch's Tale, written and produced by Alonzo Deen Cole and starring Mr. Cole and Miss Marie O'Flynn. THE WITCH'S TALE! And now let us join old Nancy and Satan, her wise black cat.

(Music swells...wind whistles...)

PROLOGUE

NANCY: He he he (CAT) Hunner an' twel' year ole, I be t'day—yes'r, hunner an' twel' year ole! Weel, Satan—if ye'll tell folks t' douse their lights we'll git right down t' bizness. (CAT) Tha's hit...we wants hit nice an' dark an' cheerful when we tells our bedtime sturies. Now draw up t' th' fire an' gaze inter th' embers...gaze inter em deep, an soon ye'll see a perty moonlit garden down in Yucatan whar th' mighty Maya people usta live be'fore th' white men came. Soon, almos' hidden in th' shadders o' that garden, ye'll make out a man an' woman who come from these United States...an' soon ye'll hear our tale o' th' "Lord o' th' Jungle"...he he. LORD O' TH' JUNGLE! He he he he he...(CAT)...

(Scene I blends in directly without musical interlude.)

SCENE I

BRITT: *(An American of about 35...low, ardent.)* I'm crazy about you, Janis.

JANIS: *(A young American woman, feline, savagely passionate....softly.)* Say it again—I like to hear it.

BRITT: I'm crazy about you.

JANIS: And I'm crazy about you. Kiss me again, Britt—hard.

MARIA: *(An old Spanish woman...After a pause, distant.)* Señora Dexter!

JANIS: *(Startled)* Let me go.

MARIA: *(Still distant, calling.)* Oh, Señora!

JANIS: *(Calls)* Here I am, Maria.

MARIA: *(Distant...approaching.)* Ah! All over deesa garden I have look for you
            anda Señor Carmen, Señora. Your husband say weela you come
            queek in de house, please.

JANIS: Tell Dr. Dexter we'll join him at once. *(A pause...with impatience.)*
            Go ahead—we'll follow you, Maria.

MARIA: *(Slightly distant...going.)* Si, Señora.

BRITT: *(Pause...low.)* Do you think she saw us?

JANIS: *(Softly)* No. I was startled when she called, though. *(Chuckling)*
            Don't know why I should have been—if she saw us and told
            Archie, he wouldn't do anything about it.

BRITT: *(With a low laugh of understanding.)* You're not very much afraid of
            your husband, are you?

JANIS: *(Shrugs)* One isn't afraid of a rabbit. Let's go see what he wants.

BRITT: Alright. *(Pause, then lightly.)* Why on earth did you every marry
            Archie?

JANIS: You've heard that opposites attract, haven't you? Well, he had
            money and I had none; he was a famous scientist and I was
            nobody; he was mild as milk and I—

BRITT: You knew that you could manage him.

JANIS: I hoped so.

BRITT: And you also hoped that someone would come along who wasn't
            your opposite but your counterpart, like me.

JANIS: *(Laughs lightly.)* We are counterparts, aren't we, Britt? We're both a
            little savage.

BRITT: *(Chuckles)* Primitives, eh.

JANIS: Uh huh—we have no more inhibitions than—than the monkeys
            in the jungle of this godforsaken place.

BRITT: You might compare us to something a little more lordly than
            monkeys.

JANIS: *(Laughs)* The great cats of the jungle, then—I love cats. We're like
            the jaguars who are strong and alive—and a little sneaky, I ad-
            mit—but who take what they want in spite of everything.

BRITT: *(Laughs)* Except, sometimes, another jaguar. But we must hide
            our claws and purr now or we'll frighten the rabbit.

JANIS: Wonder why he sent Maria for us.

BRITT: *(Thoughtfully)* Don't know—he's usually so preoccupied with his work that he doesn't know when we're out of the house.

JANIS: Britt, there's a car standing in the road.

BRITT: Visitors—that explains it.

JANIS: It's Dr. Henderson's car, I think.

BRITT: You mean the old chap who looks so disapprovingly at you and me whenever we meet him?

JANIS: Yes—not that it means anything. *(Pause)* Open the door and let's see what it's all about.

BRITT: Alright...

(A door opened.)

    (Calls genially.) Hello, Archie! Were you looking for us?

ARCHIE: *(A mild mannered little scientist in his early thirties...from slight distance...happily.)* Come in, Britt and Janis! *(Coming up.)* Darling, Dr. Henderson just drove in from Chitzen-Itza.

JANIS: *(Cordially)* How do you do, Doctor.

HEND: *(A grave middle aged archaeologist...coming up.)* Very well, thank you, Mrs. Dexter.

ARCHIE: And this is Mr. Carmen.

BRITT: Dr. Henderson and I have met before, Archie.

ARCHIE: *(In mild surprise.)* Have you? I'm terribly absent minded about such things.

HEND: *(Rather coldly.)* I remember Mr. Carmen very well—he seems to be rather a member of your family, Archie.

JANIS: *(Returning his coldness in kind.)* Mr. Carmen comes to see my husband whenever he is in this part of Central America, Doctor—as he is a correspondent for a newspaper syndicate back home in the States, he is naturally interested in the news value of Archie's work.

BRITT: Yes, indeed—Dr. Dexter has provided me with some very interesting material concerning his archaeological researches.

ARCHIE: *(Enthusiastically)* What Dr. Henderson has just told me may provide you with the greatest scientific story ever to come out of Yucatan, old man. Sit down—sit down and listen! That's what I had Maria call you for. Then, if you're both good children, I may even take you with me!

JANIS: Take us with you?

ARCHIE: Into the jungle—on our expedition.

BRITT: What expedition?

ARCHIE: *(Laughs delightedly.)* Tell them what you've told me, Henderson—
            then they'll understand!

HEND: Very well. I imagine you both have heard of the "Lord of the
            Jungle."

BRITT: You mean the legend of —?

ARCHIE: We may prove it isn't just a legend!

HEND: At any rate, here's the story: As you probably know, many undis-
            covered relics of the ancient Mayan civilization must lie hidden in
            the jungle that forms the greater part of Yucatan—among them,
            according to tradition, is a colossal monument to an unknown
            god. Who or what that deity is tradition doesn't say—it is simply
            called "Lord of the Jungle." Well, a week ago, I attended a dying
            man who I think had seen this fabled monument.

BRITT: Say—that does sound like a story!

ARCHIE: *(Eagerly)* Go on, Henderson—go on!

HEND: This man, a Mexican, had been shot by people of a village on the
            jungle fringe who mistook him for a prowling jaguar. When I
            happened along, he was almost gone.

ARCHIE: But he was babbling about "Lord of the Jungle."

HEND: Yes—over and over, he repeated the phrase in Spanish. It obvi-
            ously held some highly important meaning for him. And several
            times he mumbled the words, "statue" and "great steps."

ARCHIE: If the monument exists, it would naturally consist of a statue
            situated on top of a pyramid of steps—for it was Mayan custom
            to erect all their important memorials in such a fashion.

HEND: Yes—but, unfortunately, the poor fellow didn't amplify his mea-
            gre description—if that's what it was. Aside from the words I've
            mentioned, his only utterances were—well, they resembled the
            growls of an animal.

JANIS: Growls?

HEND: He was delirious—I think. *(Pause)* After he died, we identified
            him as a young aviator of the Mexican Army who was reported
            lost four months ago while on a test flight over the jungle—other
            airmen sent out to search for him spotted the wreckage of his
            plane on top of the dense bush; but, as it was impossible for them
            to land at the spot, the investigation was carried no further.

ARCHIE: Dr. Henderson has learned the exact location of the wrecked
            plane and we can use it as a guide for our expedition! A healthy

man, alone, must have traveled in a fairly straight line to have reached the point where this poor chap emerged from the bush after four months—A properly equipped expedition can traverse the same distance in that many weeks or less, and somewhere along that line we'll find the "Lord of the Jungle."

BRITT: You say a "healthy" man could have traveled the distance. Wasn't this fellow—?

HEND: Apparently, he had suffered no injury when his plane crashed; for I never saw a more splendid physical specimen—he was lean and muscular as—well, as a wild animal.

ARCHIE: I know you'll want to be in on this for your newspaper, Carmen— and you, Janis, have always wanted to go on a jungle expedition. Will you join us? You can be company for one another while Henderson and I are hard at work.

BRITT: *(Too smoothly.)* My editors wouldn't forgive me if anything comes of this and I missed it.

JANIS: *(Too sweetly.)* And I will be delighted to go—to keep you from becoming lonely, Archie.

ARCHIE: Then it's all settled!

HEND: *(Coldly)* It is only fair to warn such inexperienced explorers as your wife and Mr. Carmen that the jungle may prove far different from their expectations, Archie.

JANIS: That will add zest to our enjoyment—won't it, Mr. Carmen?

BRITT: Yes, Mrs. Dexter. Archie and Dr. Henderson want to get at their plans, I know, and we're only in the way here.

JANIS: Suppose we go back to the garden.

BRITT: If your husband will permit.

ARCHIE: Of course—of course!

JANIS: *(Going)* We shall look forward to a very pleasant holiday, Archie.

BRITT: *(Receding)* Yes, a very pleasant holiday.

(A door closes behind them.)

ARCHIE: *(Fondly)* Fine boy, that fellow—fine boy.

HEND: *(Dryly)* Boy? He's probably a year or so older than you are.

ARCHIE: Eh? *(Chuckles)* You're right, I think he is—but then I'm so much more settled than he is—more mature. That's because I'm happily married and he's just a bachelor, I suppose.

HEND: *(Keenly)* And because the civilized child usually regards the savage adult as his junior.

ARCHIE: Huh? I never thought of that. Carmen is a bit—elemental, in a nice way, isn't he?

HEND: *(Slowly)* So is your wife.

ARCHIE: Janis? *(Pause...then frankly.)* She is, come to think of it. That's probably why we're so well mated—the attraction of opposites, you know—for I'm such a stodgy, bookish sort of person.

HEND: *(Thoughtfully)* You know, that poor devil of an aviator was a fellow of your type, Archie.

ARCHIE: The man you've been telling me about, who—?

HEND: Yes. He majored at the finest universities in Mexico and in the States, I've learned—flying was just a hobby with him. Then the bottom fell out of his world and he fell sprawling into the jungle—he came out of it a growling naked beast.

ARCHIE: He really growled, Henderson, when he wasn't babbling "Lord of the Jungle"?

HEND: Like one of the big cats the people who shot him thought he was.

ARCHIE: *(Thoughtfully)* Peculiar.

HEND: I haven't yet told you the most peculiar thing about him. The Indians who mistook his naked figure in the bush for that of a jaguar weren't such fools as they sound—From what cause, God only knows, that Mexican aviator's skin was covered with queer rosette-shaped spots—spots like those of a jaguar.

(Musical interlude.)

SCENE II

(Throughout the scene we hear occasional calls of jungle birds and the chattering of monkeys.)

JANIS: A very good luncheon, Manuel.

MANUEL: *(An Indian half-breed.)* You like, Señora?

ARCHIE: We all liked it. *(Laughs)* Look what Dr. Henderson did to his second helping—and Mr. Carmen. There's one good thing about being in the jungle—the appetite improves tremendously.

HEND: That's alright when you're equipped to satisfy it, but the poor devil whose trail we're following couldn't have found the jungle any picnic.

BRITT: Hardly—chap didn't even have means to build a fire, our trackers say.

ARCHIE: No. I'm sure they're following his spoor correctly—and there's no indication that he built any fires or possessed implements other than his hands with which to penetrate the bush. *(Thought-*

fully) It's very strange—when army men fly over the jungle they are usually required to carry supplies for coping with it in case of accident.

JANIS: There were a lot of strange things about that Mexican aviator, unless Dr. Henderson imagined some of them.

HEND: *(Coldly)* I am not given to flights of fancy, Mrs. Dexter.

ARCHIE: There's some good natural explanation for those spots and everything, of course, if we knew it. Well, it's time to put our Indians back to work with their machetes.

HEND: Yes. Manuel, tell the men to start cutting trail again—luncheon hour is over.

MANUEL: Si, Señor. *(Calls in Mestizo-Spanish as he goes away.)* Back to your work, compadres!

(There is an answering murmur from Indians in the near distance, and presently we hear them hacking at bush with their machetes.)

BRITT: If you're really going to find Mr. Lord of the Jungle, we should be getting pretty close, now, shouldn't we, Archie?

ARCHIE: According to my calculations, we're within two miles of where the wrecked plane was sighted—If Henderson's aviator saw the monument it must be somewhere within that remaining distance.

JANIS: The men ought to cut through those two miles before dark.

ARCHIE: They will.

BRITT: And if you don't find your stone god?

ARCHIE: Then we've simply been on a wild-goose chase.

JANIS: *(With a tinge of regret.)* And we'll go back home.

ARCHIE: There'll be nothing else to do. *(Laughs)* I don't think this wife of mine wants to go back to civilization—she likes the wilderness.

JANIS: *(Purrs)* I merely like freedom, Archie—and you, as the perfect husband, have given me that everywhere. Shall we take a walk on the back trail, Britt?

BRITT: I'd like to.

ARCHIE: *(Rather unhappily.)* Don't you two want to be around if we find the statue?

JANIS: *(Easily)* You can call out if anything develops—we'll hear you. *(Starting away.)* Come on, Britt.

BRITT: *(Going)* See you later.

ARCHIE: Wait.

JANIS: *(Slightly distant...with annoyance.)* Yes?

ARCHIE: *(Diffidently)* Dear, we've seen a lot of jaguars in the last few days, you know—they're nasty brutes and—well, I'd feel happier if you and Carmen didn't leave the party.

BRITT: I have my revolver, Archie—

JANIS: *(Laughs)* You needn't worry when I have Britt to protect me.

ARCHIE: Uh—well—I don't worry, of course.

BRITT: *(Moving away again.)* Come on, Janis. *(With a chuckle.)* I'll take good care of your wife, Archie.

ARCHIE: Oh, I—I'm sure you will.

JANIS: *(Going)* Call when you want us—we'll hear you.

BRITT: *(Receding)* Yes, Archie, just sing out. *(Both laugh softly.)*

ARCHIE: *(A pause.)* I—I suppose I should really put my foot down, Henderson—those two don't know the jungle as we do, and shouldn't be off by themselves—it's dangerous.

HEND: *(Dryly)* Very.

ARCHIE: You think a jaguar or a boa-constrictor might harm them?

HEND: *(Shortly)* I wasn't thinking of jaguars and boas.

ARCHIE: What were you thinking of?

HEND: Nothing. Come on to the trail—we've got to keep an eye on those Indians or they'll loaf on the cutting job.

ARCHIE: You must have been thinking of something, or—

HEND: I wasn't.

MANUEL: *(Distant...excitedly.)* Señors! Señors—señors!!

HEND: Manuel! Something's happened!

MANUEL: *(Closer)* Come queek, Señors—look here!!

ARCHIE: What is it?

(The cutting stops...An excited murmur from the Mestizos.)

MANUEL: *(At mike.)* Look! Look!!

HEND: Archie!

ARCHIE: It's the uniform coat of a Mexican Army officer!

HEND: With the Aviation Corps insignia upon it!

MANUEL: De men jus' find eet by deesa tree, Señors!

ARCHIE: *(Excitedly)* It belonged to your flier, Henderson—this proves we're on the right trail!

MANUEL: Look! Look, here ees more, Señors!

HEND: A revolver, a sheath knife and a compass on the ground!

ARCHIE: He discarded them as he did the coat!

HEND: And there's a water-proof packet of matches in the coat pocket!

ARCHIE: Matches, compass, knife and—*(...as he breaks the revolver...)* fully loaded gun—necessities for a man in this wilderness! Why, in

Heaven's name, did he discard them?

HEND: He must have been stark, raving mad. *(Slight pause.)* Thank you, Manuel—tell the men to go back to their cutting.

MANUEL: Si, Señor. *(To the men, in Spanish.)* Back to your work, compadres—back to work!

(Cutting resumes.)

ARCHIE: *(Thoughtfully)* Yes, he must have been mad—and his insanity induced a reversion to savagery in keeping with his surroundings—he didn't want to be bothered with civilized things. *(Pause)* That's really not so strange—you know, Henderson, during our three weeks in the bush, I've become a little savage.

HEND: What do you mean?

ARCHIE: Well—for the past four mornings in succession, I haven't wanted to brush my teeth, and when it comes to shaving—I just hate to do it.

HEND: *(Laughs kindly.)* I hardly think that qualifies you for the role of Tarzan, Archie.

ARCHIE: No—not just that alone. Janis and Carmen will be interested to know about these things—I'll go and find them.

HEND: Wait. *(Uncomfortably)* Why don't you just—uh—call to them.

ARCHIE: Call?

HEND: They can't have gotten very far away—they'll hear you.

ARCHIE: *(Pause)* Henderson, this must be the dozenth time lately that I've started out to look for my wife and Carmen and you've either suggested that I shout for them, or that you go in my place.

HEND: *(Embarrassed)* Is that so? I—well—

ARCHIE: *(Angrily)* I'm not altogether a fool—you think there's more than friendship between Carmen and Janis and are afraid that, if I come upon them without warning, I'll see proof of it. You're trying to protect me, but I don't need your protection—and I won't have you suspecting my wife! Do you hear? I won't have you suspecting my wife!

HEND: *(Pause)* Whatever put this—ridiculous idea in your head, Archie?

ARCHIE: I—I *(His anger dies...miserably.)* Oh, it must be ridiculous—no one could doubt her. Forgive me, old man. I—I guess the crazy notion sprang from—from my own jealousy.

HEND: Your—jealousy?

ARCHIE: I'm ashamed to admit it, but lately I've been—resentful of Carmen. He seems in his natural element here, as Janis does, and I—I feel inferior. He's all that I'm not—tall, good looking, sure of himself—a splendid animal—and I'm just a little runt, not good enough for my wife.

HEND: *(Gently)* A man with your brain doesn't have to be a "splendid animal," Archie.

ARCHIE: We're all animals beneath the surface—and every rabbit, I suppose, is envious of the stronger brutes. *(Half to himself.)* Sometimes when I see Carmen and Janis together, I'm afraid he has power to take her from me—and I want to kill him, as the beasts kill—with tooth and claw. I want to—*(His voice breaks.)* Oh, I despise myself for having such nasty, unjust, bitter thoughts! There's no reason for me to be jealous—no possible reason! *(Controlled again.)* I—I'll go find them now. *(A pause.)* No, I—*(low)* Henderson, will you—call?

HEND: *(Gently)* Alright. *(Calls)* Mrs. Dexter! Carmen!

BRITT: *(Very distant.)* Hallo?

HEND: *(Shouts)* We've found something! Will you come here?

JANIS: *(Very distant.)* Alright!

ARCHIE: Of course, Henderson, you'll forget the silly confession I've just made.

HEND: Of course.

(A sudden crash of a heavy animal in the nearby bush...then it bounds away.)

ARCHIE: *(Startled)* What was that??

HEND: A jaguar! There he goes streaking through the bush—Too late to try a shot at him now—

ARCHIE: *(Calls in warning.)* Janis, we just saw one of the big cats! Keep your eyes open, Carmen.

BRITT: *(Distant)* I will!

ARCHIE: It's strange about those jaguars—every day we see several of them—I've spent months in the jungle with other expeditions and never caught a glimpse of one.

HEND: That's been my experience, too.

ARCHIE: *(Thoughtfully)* They're so thick around here. Why do you suppose that poor mad aviator wasn't killed by one? He had no weapons to stand them off with.

HEND: I don't know. Rather a grim joke—after the jungle spared him, he was killed by men like himself.

ARCHIE: And his skin was covered with spots like the markings of these big cats.

HEND:	I'd like to know the answers to a lot of things about that fellow—and, somehow, I have a feeling that we'll learn them when, and if, we find the Lord of the Jungle.
ARCHIE:	What do you mean?
HEND:	I can't explain it, Archie; it's just a—a rather uncomfortable hunch.
JANIS:	*(Slightly distant.)* Here we are, darling.
BRITT:	*(Approaching)* What's your find, Dr. Henderson?
HEND:	This coat—and these.
BRITT:	They were left here by your flier!
HEND:	Looks that way.
BRITT:	Knife, compass, gun and matches!
ARCHIE:	Apparently, he just threw them away, Janis.
JANIS:	Since he left these things behind, he must have killed the animals necessary for food with his bare hands and devoured them raw—by choice.
ARCHIE:	*(Murmurs)* I've been thinking of that.
BRITT:	Why on earth would any man—?

(Distant cutting stops.)

| MANUEL: | *(Distant...wildly excited.)* Señors! Señors! |
| HEND: | What—? |

(Distant cries of excitement from Mestizos.)

MANUEL:	Come here queek! Come queek!!
JANIS:	What's Manuel so excited about?
BRITT:	The men have thrown down their machetes!
HEND:	*(Going away.)* We're coming, Manuel!
ARCHIE:	*(Going away.)* What is it??
MANUEL:	*(Closer)* We are t'rough de bush—we have find some beeg stone step'!
ARCHIE:	Stone steps?
MANUEL:	*(At mike.)* Big pyramid! Look see!
BRITT:	Pyramid? That means—!
HEND:	Yes, for there's a colossal statue on the summit!
ARCHIE:	We've found the Lord of the Jungle! We've found it—found it!!
JANIS:	What does the statue represent?
BRITT:	It's too dark in that tangle to see anything but shapes!
ARCHIE:	*(Tremendously excited.)* This forest has been growing over and above the monument for centuries. Even the Spanish Conquistadores may not have seen this treasure of the Mayas!
HEND:	Send men up the trees to cut foliage, Manuel—we've got to let

	some daylight in there!
ARCHIE:	We'll be able to see in a moment—there's a natural opening just above the figure! Right now the sun's behind a cloud, but when it passes over there'll be all the light we need. We're wasting time—let's start up these steps in the dark and—!
BRITT:	Wait! What are those funny lights?
JANIS:	They're like points of fire—like eyes.
ARCHIE:	My word.
HEND:	They're thick about the pyramid.
ARCHIE:	Here comes the sun! Now we'll—
ALL:	*(A gasp of fear.)*
HEND:	Good Lord!
JANIS:	They are eyes!
ARCHIE:	Eyes of jaguars!
HEND:	There must be hundreds on those steps! *(Cries)* Everybody—rifles!
ARCHIE:	No, no—don't shoot! *(Awed)* Look at the statue of the god above them.
JANIS:	*(Low...fearful.)* It is a great stone—jaguar.
ARCHIE:	*(Half to himself.)* That's why legend called it "Lord of the Jungle."

(Musical interlude.)

SCENE III

(Jungle birds and monkeys more distant than in preceding scene.)

JANIS:	*(Uneasily)* You're sure it's safe to venture up those steps now, Dr. Henderson—that all of those big cats are gone?
HEND:	*(Shortly)* You saw them disappear into the jungle, Mrs. Dexter. Come on, Archie.
ARCHIE:	Wait. *(Uncomfortably)* It was so strange—after they gazed at us for a moment, they all sprang away together—as though they'd received some signal.
BRITT:	We were the signal—they were more afraid of us than we were of them. If you hadn't stopped us shooting, Archie, we'd have gotten a nice bag of em.
ARCHIE:	It didn't seem right to shoot them—here, when they made no attempt to attack us. I know it's silly, but I felt as though they were—at worship. And one doesn't want to profane a church.
BRITT:	*(Laughs derisively.)* You think that big stone cat above is god of the cats??

JANIS: *(Laughing)* If he is, he certainly protected his own by inspiring Archie with religious consideration.

HEND: *(Thoughtfully)* You two may laugh at Archie but what we saw inspired fear and a little superstitious awe in all of us.

BRITT: Suppose you only speak for yourself, Doctor—I felt nothing more than surprise.

JANIS: You have nerves of iron, Britt. Shivers ran up and down my spine for a minute or two—and, like Archie, I'm still a little timid about starting up those steps.

ARCHIE: *(Quiet, but resentful.)* I'm no more timid than Carmen, Janis.

BRITT: Come on, then—I'm anxious to see that big image close too. Let me help you, Janis—and don't worry; if any of the cats are still around I promise they won't get near enough to hurt you.

ARCHIE: *(With unaccustomed firmness.)* Pardon me, but I am capable of protecting my wife.

JANIS: Archie—?

BRITT: I only—

ARCHIE: Take my hand, Janis—these steps are steep.

JANIS: *(Coldly)* Thanks, but I can manage alone. And I think you've been a little rude to Mr. Carmen.

BRITT: *(Largely)* That's alright—all this excitement has left Dr. Dexter a bit unnerved; he didn't mean anything.

ARCHIE: *(Murmurs)* No—I suppose not.

HEND: *(Calls)* Manuel! You and your men cover us with your rifles as we go up the pyramid.

MANUEL: *(Distant...fearful.)* Si, Señor.

BRITT: *(Chuckles)* We can't rely much on those Indians, they're scared stiff.

(Jungle effects fade away to silence as they mount the great steps...and gradually, very softly at first, a deep animal purring sound fades in.)

JANIS: Look at that image, Britt—it's huge.

HEND: Must stand thirty feet above its base at the shoulders, Archie.

ARCHIE: *(Murmurs)* Yes.

HEND: I think close inspection will show it to be a very fine specimen of Mayan sculpture—its outlines are magnificent.

ARCHIE: Yes.

JANIS: How life-like it is, for its great size.

ARCHIE: Yes.

BRITT: You're not very enthusiastic, Archie—you know this is the Mr.

Lord of the Jungle you came so far to find.

ARCHIE: *(Trance-like)* Lord of the Jungle.

HEND: What's the matter with you?

ARCHIE: Nothing.

JANIS: *(A pause...constrained.)* It's so quiet here—I wonder why we don't hear any animal sounds as we do on the trail.

ARCHIE: I hear—a kind of purring.

HEND: Purring?

ARCHIE: Yes.

BRITT: I don't hear anything.

JANIS: Nor I.

ARCHIE: I noticed it the moment we started climbing—and it grows louder all the time.

HEND: There's no sound of any kind in here—you imagine it.

ARCHIE: Perhaps.

BRITT: *(Chuckles)* Maybe that boss cat up there is purring for Archie's special benefit.

JANIS: *(A little awed.)* He's so real looking, I almost fancy he could purr.

BRITT: *(Subdued)* He does look like a giant, ugly jaguar.

ARCHIE: I think he's beautiful.

HEND: I'd hardly call him that.

ARCHIE: *(His voice rising.)* You don't understand him; you've never wanted to be like him—you've never had reason to envy those who are like him!

JANIS: Archie??

HEND: Why are you leaving us??

BRITT: He's out of his head—he's running up the steps to that statue!

HEND: *(In alarm.)* You idiot! One of those cats may still be lurking in the shadows there! *(Starting away.)* After him, Carmen—come on!

BRITT: Wait—look at the fool!

JANIS: He's kneeling before that big stone cat!

HEND: What—?

JANIS: *(Gasps)* Ahh!

HEND: Lord—what's causing that??

BRITT: Henderson?

JANIS: What is it??

HEND: It—it's just—shadows cast by the sunlight through those trees.

BRITT: There were no such shadows there before.

JANIS: *(Fearfully)* They cover Archie—they make him look all spotted—

like a jaguar
(Purring louder, then...musical interlude.)

SCENE IV

(The occasional hoot of an owl and other jungle sounds of the night.)

BRITT: *(Slightly irritable.)* I tell you, for the hundredth time, Janis, that nothing happened to Archie on that pyramid this afternoon but a brainstorm. That's his own explanation, and it's the true one.

JANIS: *(Fearfully)* But he hasn't been the same person since he came back down those steps to rejoin us, Britt.

BRITT: *(Impatiently)* He's been a little crabbed and restless, and he didn't eat his dinner this evening—but when he and Henderson return from their walk over the back trail you'll see that his nerves will be calmed down.

JANIS: Neither nerves or a brainstorm explain the spotted light that surrounded him when he knelt before that statue.

BRITT: Janis—

JANIS: You know it wasn't caused by just shadows. And—and, afterwards, when he came down to us, his eyes—his eyes shown in the gloom like—like an animal's.

BRITT: *(Uncomfortably)* We—we merely imagined that. *(Pause)* Anyway, why should you worry about him? We'd both be delighted if he dropped dead.

JANIS: I'm not worried about him, but us—I'm afraid of him.

BRITT: Afraid?

JANIS: Yes. He's suddenly—different. And—and I think he's suspicious of us.

BRITT: Nonsense! *(Chuckles)* Kiss me, darling, and forget such crazy notions.

JANIS: *(Pulling away.)* Careful—someone might see us by this firelight.

BRITT: The Indians are too far away, and your husband and Henderson aren't anywhere around. We're safe.

JANIS: *(Yielding...passionate.)* I'm crazy about you, Britt—kiss me hard. *(She gasps in fear as there is a sudden angry rustle of leaves.)* What was that??

BRITT: *(Unconcerned)* Just some little animal in the bush.

JANIS: *(Relaxing)* Of course. Kiss me again.

BRITT: *(Chuckles)* I knew I could drive your uneasiness away. Believe me, dear, there's nothing to fear from Archie—he'll never be anything but a harmless little rabbit.

(The savage roar of a jaguar nearby.)

JANIS: Britt!!

BRITT: A jaguar!

JANIS: It sounded right behind us!

BRITT: It was! At the edge of the bush—there—as I turned I caught a flash of its eyes!

JANIS: It wasn't a dozen feet away!

BRITT: Don't be afraid—it's gone now.

HEND: *(Distant...excitedly.)* Mrs. Dexter! Carmen!

BRITT: There's Henderson.

HEND: *(Approaching)* Is Archie here?

BRITT: No.

JANIS: Wasn't he with you?

HEND: *(Arriving)* He deliberately gave me the slip a while ago. You just heard that big cat—jaguars only snarl like that when they're in a nasty mood, and Archie hadn't a gun with him!

JANIS: You don't think—?

HEND: I think we've got to look for him quick! Never mind your rifle, Carmen, you have a pistol—come on! *(Starts away.)*

JANIS: *(Murmurs hopefully.)* Britt—

BRITT: *(Same tone.)* Janis—

JANIS: Maybe—

HEND: *(Slightly distant.)* What are you waiting for??

BRITT: I'm coming.

ARCHIE: *(Coming up...silkily.)* And where are you going?

JANIS: Archie!

HEND: Where did you appear from??

ARCHIE: *(Purrs)* Back there—right there.

BRITT: There?

JANIS: *(Low...in fear.)* Britt—that's where we heard the jaguar.

(Musical interlude.)

SCENE V

(The crackling of a campfire.)

ARCHIE: *(He is a cat now, playing with mice.)* My dear Janis, why are you and Carmen so concerned because I happened to step out of the

	jungle at a certain point?
JANIS:	I tell you we'd just heard a—a jaguar there.
BRITT:	*(Much of his assurance is gone.)* If you were so close, we can't understand why—why he didn't go after you.
HEND:	He was in a killing mood, Archie, if that snarl we heard meant anything.
ARCHIE:	Still, the fact remains that he didn't kill me.
HEND:	*(Grunts)* You were darn lucky, is all I've got to say. Do you mind telling me why you gave me the slip back there on the trail and went prowling into that bush without a gun?
ARCHIE:	Frankly, your conversation bored me, Henderson, while the jungle promised one of interest.
JANIS:	The jungle promised—
BRITT:	A conversation?
ARCHIE:	Uh huh—and kept its promise. I heard a lot of—things in there.
JANIS:	*(Very low.)* You heard—?
ARCHIE:	*(Lightly)* The worried voice of—windblown trees, Janis. The kindly scolding of an old ape to a younger one, Henderson. And the gasp of a dying rabbit, Carmen.
BRITT:	*(Murmurs)* Rabbit?
ARCHIE:	Yes.
HEND:	*(Snorts)* If you're going to sit there and talk nonsense, I'm going to bed. *(Going away.)* Goodnight.
ARCHIE:	*(Calls)* Goodnight, Henderson.
BRITT:	*(A pause.)* I—I think I'll turn in, too.
ARCHIE:	Please don't—I feel like getting better acquainted with you tonight Carmen.
JANIS:	I—
ARCHIE:	And you stay also, Janis—I want you to get better acquainted with me.
JANIS:	What do you mean? *(A pause.)* Archie, what's come over you? *(Pause...low.)* Why do you sit and stare across the fire at us—like a cat?
ARCHIE:	You've always admired cats, haven't you, dear—big, sleek, handsome cats? And men are like cats, aren't they, Carmen?
BRITT:	I—I've never noticed.
ARCHIE:	No? There are drab, meek little house cats, like me for instance—and there are strong, masterful alley cats who sometimes steal all that the puny cat has. The jaguar, Lord of the Jungle, is the only cat in the world who has nothing to fear from another of his

kind—except a stronger one of his own species. *(Politely)* Are you the jaguar type, Mr. Carmen?

JANIS: What—what are you talking about?

BRITT: Archie is–just talking—he doesn't mean anything, Janis.

ARCHIE: Don't I?

BRITT: I mean—

ARCHIE: You mean that I don't mean anything, you've always thought.

BRITT: I—

JANIS: *(In alarm.)* Archie!

BRITT: Why did you snatch that pistol out of my holster??

ARCHIE: *(Chuckles)* Just to see if I could do it. Would you like to see if you can get it back?

JANIS: He's playing with us, like a cat plays with mice!

BRITT: He's acting like a mad man!

ARCHIE: *(His voice rising with theirs.)* You're both right—and neither cats nor madmen have use for weapons such as this! Like the man whose trail we followed here, I throw a gun, my knife, my coat into the jungle!

(As said objects crash into the bush...)

Now, Carmen, if you want my wife, try to take her!

JANIS: You were listening—you heard!!

ARCHIE: I only heard what I've known for weeks, and was afraid to admit to myself! We're in the jungle, Carmen, where there's only jungle law—that law says two males cannot share a mate between them and, of those who try it, one must die! One of us is going to die tonight.

BRITT: You little fool, I can break you in two!

ARCHIE: *(Madly)* Ha ha—suppose we see! Suppose we—*(His voice changes to the snarl of a jaguar.)*

JANIS: *(Screams in horror.)*

BRITT: *(Terrified)* Good God!

(Two heavy bodies meet, as though a jaguar had sprung upon a man, snarling and tearing.)

JANIS: He snarled like a jaguar!

BRITT: *(Cries in agony.)* He's clawing my eyes—his teeth are at my throat!!

(He struggles, then is still.)

JANIS: *(Cries)* Dr. Henderson! Manuel! Help—come quick!!

HEND: *(Distant)* I hear the beast! Rifles, Manuel—a jaguar!!

MANUEL: *(Distant)* Si, Señor! Si, si!! *(He shouts orders in Spanish.)*

HEND: *(Coming up.)* Where is the brute??

JANIS: *(Hysterically)* It's Archie—ha—ha—Archie! He's killed Britt!

(The Mestizos murmur in rear as they arrive.)

HEND: *(Arriving)* Archie—? Good Lord!

JANIS: He tore his throat with his teeth—killed him as a cat kills! A great cat—ha ha—a cat!

ARCHIE: *(Softly)* And the taste of blood was sweet.

HEND: *(In horror.)* Dexter!

JANIS: Don't let him spring at me—he'll kill me too!

ARCHIE: No. Another jungle law is that males do not make war on females—and jungle law is all that I have now. *(Turning away.)* Take care of her, Henderson.

HEND: Where are you going?

ARCHIE: Into the wilderness, where the rest of my kind live.

(Jaguars roar in the distance.)

           You hear? They're calling me to join them.

HEND: Are you feigning insanity to cover what you've done? You don't have to with me. I don't blame you—and neither do these Indians. We knew he had it coming.

ARCHIE: I'm not playing a part, Henderson. When I bowed to the Lord of the Jungle today, I became his subject—and he takes care of his own—in his own way.

HEND: What do you mean?

ARCHIE: This shirt binds my body—I'll rip it off and let you see. *(Ripping the shirt open.)* Look!

HEND: God!

JANIS: The spots of a jaguar!

ARCHIE: On my back and in my heart. *(Going)* Goodbye, Janis—my breed of cats and yours is different now.

HEND: *(A pause.)* He's gone.

(Distant roar of jaguars.)

JANIS: To them—forever.

(Musical conclusion.)

EPILOGUE

NANCY: He he he...(CAT) Weel, that's th' end ov a perty stury 'bout some relatives o' your'n Satan. In two weeks, on m' buthday, we'll have another perty year t' spin you folks. He he he he he..(CAT)

(Musical signature.)

ANNOUNCER: This concludes the 305th weekly presentation of The Witch's Tale, written and produced by Alonzo Deen Cole and starring Mr. Cole as Archie and Miss Marie O'Flynn as Janis. Carmen was played by Mr. Mark Smith, Henderson by Mr. Alan Devitt, Manuel by Mr. Thomas Hoier, Maria by Miss Miriam Wolff and old Nancy and Satan, as usual, by themselves. The next drama of this series will be brought to you two weeks from tonight at this same hour.

EPILOGUE
by Miriam Wolff
"Nancy" 1935-38

SATAN: (*Long howling meow as Nancy's laugh fades in.*)

NANCY: Well, that's the end of those ones, Satan. Isn't it great to shiver, shake and quake again?

SATAN: (*Approving meow.*)

NANCY: Well, I'm off on my broomstick to pick up a few hints on haunting for my future birthdays...so tell these folks g'night, Satan..(*He does.*) Happy dreams, everyone! Oh yes...and happy nightmares too when you remember The Witch's Tale! Yes...remember... THE WITCH'S TALE...

(*Fade out on cackling laughs and meows.*)

Program Log ©

Notes: 1) When stories were repeated, the number(s) in parenthesis following the title indicates the program number which aired the repeat.

2) When Cole borrowed plots from other sources, the original source is indicated under the title.

No.	Date	Day	Time	Title/Source
1	5/28/31	Thu	10:15-10:45	The Queer House
2	6/11/31	Thu	10:15-10:45	The Were-Wolf (216) (Fredrick Marryat)
3	6/18/31	Thu	10:15-10:45	The Lady Of The Guillotine (54)
4	6/25/31	Thu	9:45-10:15	The Clock Strikes Four (45)(267)
5	7/2/31	Thu	9:45-10:15	The Bronze Venus (57)(208) (Prosper Merimee: The Venus Of Ille)
6	7/9/31	Thu	9:45-10:15	The House Of The Living Dead
7	7/13/31	Mon	9:15-9:45	The Elixer Of Life (Honore de Blzac: Don Juan)
8	7/20/31	Mon	9:15-9:45	The Victim (96)(249)
9	7/27/31	Mon	9:15-9:45	The Lava Cast (117)(284)
10	8/3/31	Mon	9:15-9:45	Frankenstein (40)(203) (Mary Shelley)
11	8/10/31	Mon	9:15-9:45	The Troth (101)(273)
12	8/17/31	Mon	9:15-9:45	The Lake (81)(228)
13	8/27/31	Thu	8:15-8:45	The Evil Eye (106)(252) (Theophile Gautier: Jettatura)
14	8/31/31	Mon	9:15-9:45	The Firing Squad (113)(311)
15	9/10/31	Thu	8:30-9:00	From The East (Part 1)
16	9/14/31	Mon	9:30-10:00	From The East (Part 2)
17	9/21/31	Mon	9:30-10:00	The Wedding Dress
18	9/28/31	Mon	9:30-10:00	The Cigar Case (Amelia Edwards: 4:15 Express)
19	10/5/31	Mon	9:30-10:00	The Boa God (110)(274)
20	10/12/31	Mon	9:30-10:00	The Oath (128)
21	10/26/31	Mon	9:30-10:00	The Devil And Tom Walker (165) (Washington Irving)
22	10/31/31	Sat	8:00-8:30	The Headless Horseman (218) (Washington Irving)
23	11/9/31	Mon	9:30-10:00	The Corsican Brothers (239)(240) (Alexander Dumas)

24	11/16/31	Mon	9:30-10:00	Honeymoon House (76)(204)
25	11/23/31	Mon	9:30-10:00	Doctor Jekyll And Mr. Hyde (294)(295)
				(Robert Louis Stevenson)
26	11/30/31	Mon	9:30-9:45	The Jest
27	12/7/31	Mon	9:30-10:00	The Confession (92)(234)
28	12/14/31	Mon	9:30-10:00	Solange
				(Alexander Dumas)
29	12/21/31	Mon	9:30-10:00	Procrastinatin' Willie's Rent Receipt(202)
30	12/28/31	Mon	9:30-10:00	The Transplanted Souls (Part 1)
				(Theophile Gautier: Avatar)
31	1/4/32	Mon	9:30-10:00	The Transplanted Souls (Part 2)
				(Theophile Gaulier: Avatar)
32	1/11/32	Mon	9:30-10:00	To Share And Share Alike (71)(223)
33	1/18/32	Mon	9:30-10:00	Kamohoalii (207)
34	1/25/32	Mon	9:30-10:00	The Mysterious Sketch (153)
35	2/1/32	Mon	9:30-10:00	The Flying Dutchman (145)
				(Legend)
36	2/8/32	Mon	9:30-10:00	The Image (197)
37	2/15/32	Mon	9:30-10:00	From Dawn To Sunset (230)
38	2/2/32	Mon	9:30-10:00	Rappaccini's Daughter (195)
				(Nathaniel Hawthorne)
39	2/29/32	Mon	9:30-10:00	The First Of June (86)(235)
40	3/7/32	Mon	9:30-10:00	Frankenstein (10)
				(Mary Shelley)
41	3/21/32	Mon	9:30-10:00	The Wonderful Bottle (184)
				(Robert Louis Stevenson: The Bottle Imp)
42	3/21/32	Mon	9:30-10:00	The Last Waltz (99)(247)
43	3/28/32	Mon	9:30-10:00	The Hand Of Glory (229)
44	4/4/32	Mon	9:30-10:00	Snake House (172)
45	4/11/32	Mon	9:30-10:00	The Clock Strikes Four (4)(267)
46	4/18/32	Mon	9:30-10:00	The Madman (Part 1) (200)
47	4/25/32	Mon	9:30-10:00	The Madman (Part 2) (201)
48	5/2/32	Mon	9:30-10:00	Undine (Part 1)
				(Friedrich de la Motte Fouque)
49	5/9/32	Mon	9:30-10:00	Undine (Part 2)
				(Friedrich de la Motte Fouque)
50	5/16/32	Mon	9:30-10:00	Rat In A Trap (181)
51	5/23/32	Mon	9:30-10:00	The Curse (Part 1) (286)
				(Rosa Mulholland)

52	5/30/32	Mon	9:30-10:00	The Curse (Part 2) (287)
				(Rosa Mulholland)
53	6/6/32	Mon	9:30-10:00	The Mummy Case
54	6/13/32	Mon	9:30-10:00	The Lady Of The Guillotine (3)
55	7/4/32	Mon	9:30-10:00	Hangman's Roost (190)
56	7/11/32	Mon	9:30-10:00	The Spider (178)
57	7/18/32	Mon	9:30-10:00	The Bronze Venus (5)
				(Prosper Merimee: The Venus Of Ille)
58	7/25/32	Mon	9:30-10:00	Rockabye Baby (158)
59	8/2/32	Tue	9:30-10:00	The Ruby Ring (Part 1) (231)
60	8/9/32	Tue	9:30-10:00	The Ruby Ring (Part 2) (232)
61	8/16/32	Tue	9:30-10:00	Clairimonde (222)
				(Theophile Gautier: La Morte Amoureuse)
62	8/23/32	Tue	9:30-10:00	The Great Green Stone
63	8/30/32	Tue	9:30-10:00	The Witness (185)
64	9/5/32	Mon	9:30-10:00	Don Juan (215)
				(Legend)
65	9/12/32	Mon	9:30-10:00	The Magic Skin (Part 1) (210)
				(Honore de Balzac: La Peau de Chagrin)
66	9/19/32	Mon	9:30-10:00	The Magic Skin (Part 2) (211)
				(Honore de Balzac: La Peau de Chagrin)
67	9/26/32	Mon	9:30-10:00	The Hairy Monster (177)(322)
68	10/3/32	Mon	9:30-10:00	The Rada Drums (Part 1) (250)
69	10/10/32	Mon	9:30-10:00	The Rada Drums (Part 2) (251)
70	10/17/32	Mon	9:30-10:00	The Haunted Crossroads (129)(301)
71	10/24/32	Mon	9:30-10:00	Share And Share Alike (32)
72	10/31/32	Mon	9:30-10:00	In The Devil's Name (Part 1) (265)
73	11/7/32	Mon	9:30-10:00	In The Devil's Name (Part 2) (266)
74	11/14/32	Mon	9:30-10:00	The Gypsy's Hand (142)(329)
75	11/21/32	Mon	9:30-10:00	The Martensen House (189)
76	11/28/32	Mon	9:30-10:00	Honeymoon House (24)(204)
77	12/5/32	Mon	9:30-10:00	The Experiment Of Dr. Zahn (Part 1) (226)
78	12/12/32	Mon	9:30-10:00	The Experiment Of Dr. Zahn (Part 2) (227)
79	12/19/32	Mon	9:30-10:00	Tanhauser (263)
				(Legend)
80	12/26/32	Mon	9:30-10:00	The Will (176)
81	1/2/33	Mon	9:30-10:00	The Spirits Of The Lake (12)(228)
82	1/9/33	Mon	9:30-10:00	Castle Terrible (Part 1)
83	1/16/33	Mon	9:30-10:00	Castle Terrible (Part 2)

84	1/23/33	Mon	9:30-10:00	The Deserter (196)
				(Ambrose Bierce: take off/Owl Creek Bridge)
85	1/30/33	Mon	9:30-10:00	Le Loup-Garou
86	2/6/33	Mon	9:30-10:00	The First Of June (39)
87	2/20/33	Mon	9:30-10:00	A Happy Ending (166)
88	2/27/33	Mon	9:30-10:00	The Priest Of Sekhet (244)
89	3/6/33	Mon	9:30-10:00	Graveyard Mansion
90	3/13/33	Mon	9:30-10:00	The Fortune Teller (238)
91	3/20/33	Mon	9:30-10:00	The Bell (256)
				(Frederick Marryat)
92	3/27/33	Mon	9:30-10:00	The Confession (27)
93	4/3/33	Mon	9:30-10:00	The Things In The Woods (Part 1) (236)
94	4/10/33	Mon	9:30-10:00	The Things In The Woods (Part 2) (237)
95	4/17/33	Mon	9:30-10:00	Dangerous Curve (192)
96	4/24/33	Mon	9:30-10:00	The Medium (8)(249)
97	5/1/33	Mon	9:30-10:00	Peter Schlemihl (Part 1)
				(Adelbert von Chamisso: German Legend)
98	5/8/33	Mon	9:30-10:00	Peter Schlemihl (Part 2)
				(Adelbert von Chamisso: German legend)
99	5/15/33	Mon	9:30-10:00	The Last Waltz (42)
100	5/22/33	Mon	9:30-10:00	The Statue Of Thor (278)
101	5/29/33	Mon	9:30-10:00	The Troth Of Death (11)
102	6/5/33	Mon	9:30:10:00	The Vampyre (Part 1)
				(John William Polideri)
103	6/12/33	Mon	9:30-10:00	The Vampyre (Part 2)
				(John William Polideri)
104	6/19/33	Mon	9:30-10:00	The Rattlesnake (259)
105	6/26/33	Mon	9:30-10:00	The House Of The Bridegroom (304)(306)
106	7/3/33	Mon	8:30-9:00	The Jettatore (13)(252)
				(Theophile Gautier)
107	7/10/33	Mon	9:45-10:15	Zanoni (Part 1)
				(Edward Bulwer-Lytton)
108	7/17/33	Mon	9:45-10:15	Zanoni (Part 2)
				(Edward Bulwer-Lytton)
109	7/24/33	Mon	9:45-10:l5	Zanoni (Part 3)
				(Edward Bulwer-Lytton)
110	7/31/33	Mon	9:45-10:15	The Boa Goddess (19)
111	8/7/33	Mon	9:45-10:15	The Toy Maker (225)
				(Fitz-James O'Brien: The Wondersmith)
112	8/14/33	Mon	9:45-10:15	The Perfect Crime (248)

113	8/21/33	Mon	9:45-10:15	The Firing Squad (14)
114	8/28/33	Mon	9:45-10:15	The Tiger (253)
115	9/4/33	Mon	9:45-10:15	The Old Littleton House (241)
116	9/11/33	Mon	9:45-10:15	La Mannequinne (258)
117	9/18/33	Mon	9:45-10:15	Children Of Venus (9)(284)
118	9/25/33	Mon	9:45-10:15	The Golem (Part 1) (260) (Legend)
119	10/9/33	Mon	9:45-10:15	The Golem (Part 2) (260) (Legend)
120	10/16/33	Mon	9:45-10:15	The Bulldog (269)
121	10/23/33	Mon	9:45-10:15	The Devil Of Witzenstein (285)
122	10/30/33	Mon	9:45-10:15	All Hallows Eve (303)
123	11/8/33	Wed	10:30-11:00	The Altar (310)
124	11/13/33	Mon	9:45-10:15	Doctor Basilius (Part 1) (297) (Alexander Dumas)
125	11/20/33	Mon	9:45-10:15	Doctor Basilius (Part 2) (298) (Alexander Dumas)
126	11/28/33	Mon	9:45-10:15	Doctor Basilius (Part 3) (299) (Alexander Dumas)
127	12/4/33	Mon	9:45-10:15	The Reunion (330)
128	12/11/33	Mon	9:45-10:15	The Oath (40)
129	12/18/33	Mon	9:45-10:15	The Haunted Crossroads (70)
130	1/8/34	Mon	9:45-10:15	The Devil Doctor (270)
131	1/18/34	Thu	9:30-10:00	The Bed (293)
132	1/25/34	Thu	9:45-10:15	The Amulet (281)
133	2/1/34	Thu	9:45-10:15	The Fairy Girl
134	2/8/34	Thu	9:45-10:15	The Invisible Wound (279) (Karoly Kisfaludi)
135	2/15/34	Thu	9:45-10:15	The Shining Ghost (264)
136	2/22/34	Thu	9:45-10:15	The Power Of Lucifer (307)
137	3/1/34	Thu	9:45-10:15	Baby Face
138	3/8/34	Thu	9:45-10:15	The Ghost Of The Storage Vaults (Part 1) (319)
139	3/15/34	Thu	9:45-10:15	The Ghost Of The Storage Vaults (Part 2) (320)
140	3/22/34	Thu	9:45-10:15	The Priest Of Egypt (Part 1) (Edward Bulwer-Lytton)
141	3/29/34	Thu	9:45-10:15	The Priest Of Egypt (Part 2) (Edward Bulwer-Lytton)
142	4/5/34	Thu	9:45-10:15	The Gypsy's Hand (74)

143	4/12/34	Thu	9:45-10:15	The Wildman (Part 1)
144	4/19/34	Thu	10:30-11:00	The Wildman (Part 2)
145	4/26/34	Thu	9:45-10:15	The Flying Dutchman (35) (Legend)
146	5/3/34	Thu	9:45-10:15	The Violin (316)
147	5/10/34	Thu	9:45-10:15	Circumstantial Evidence (288)
148	5/17/34	Thu	9:45-10:15	The Compact Of Chester Rand (309)
149	5/31/34	Thu	9:45-10:15	The Hungry God (Part 1) (314)
150	6/7/34	Thu	9:45-10:15	The Hungry God (Part 2) (315)
151	6/14/34	Thu	9:45-10:15	The Murder Of Uncle Bije (318)
152	6/21/34	Thu	9:45-10:15	The Treasure (Nicolai Gogol)
153	6/29/34	Fri	10:30-11:00	The Horrible Picture (34)
154	7/5/34	Thu	9:45-10:15	Germelshausen (Part 1) (289)
155	7/13/34	Thu	9:45-10:15	Germelshausen (Part 2) (290)
156	7/19/34	Thu	9:45-10:15	Ladies' Man (Part 1)
157	7/26/34	Thu	9:45-10:15	Ladies' Man (Part 2)
158	8/2/34	Thu	9:45-10:15	Rockabye Baby (58)
159	8/10/34	Fri	9:30-10:00	The Roll Call (296)
160	8/17/34	Fri	9:00-9:30	The Alligator
161	8/24/34	Fri	9:00-9:30	The House Of The Gargoyles (Part 1) (331)
162	8/31/34	Fri	9:00-9:30	The House Of The Gargoyles (Part 2) (332)
163	9/7/34	Fri	9:00-9:30	The Puzzle
164	9/14/34	Fri	9:00-9:30	Devil Hands (325)
165	9/21/34	Fri	9:00-9:30	The Devil And Tom Walker (21) (Washington Irving)
166	9/28/34	Fri	9:00-9:30	A Happy Ending (87)
167	10/5/34	Fri	9:00-9:30	The Alchemist
168	10/12/34	Fri	9:00-9:30	The Great White Wolf (Fredrick Marryat)
169	11/8/34	Thu	9:00-9:30	The Physician To The Dead
170	11/15/34	Thu	9:00-9:30	Faust (Part 1) (Marlowe & Goethe)
171	11/22/34	Thu	9:00-9:30	Faust (Part 2) (Marlowe & Goethe)
172	11/26/34	Mon	9:00-9:30	Snake House (44)
173	12/3/34	Mon	9:00-9:30	The Resurrection Men (History)

174	12/10/34	Mon	9:00-9:30	The Wooden Stake
175	12/17/34	Mon	9:00-9:30	The Punishment
176	12/24/34	Mon	9:00-9:30	The Will (80)
177	12/31/34	Mon	9:00-9:30	The Monster (67)(322)
178	1/7/35	Mon	9:00-9:30	The Entomologist (56)
179	1/14/35	Mon	9:30-10:00	The Golden Idol (Part 1)
180	1/21/35	Mon	9:30-10:00	The Golden Idol (Part 2)
181	1/28/35	Mon	9:00-9:30	Rat In A Trap (50)
182	2/4/35	Mon	9:00-9:30	Suicide Hall (Part 1)
183	2/11/35	Mon	9:30-10:00	Suicide Hall (Part 2)
184	2/18/35	Mon	9:00-9:30	The Wonderful Bottle (41)
				(Robert Louis Stevenson:The Bottle Imp)
185	2/25/35	Mon	9:00-9:30	The Witness (63)
186	3/4/35	Mon	8:00-11:00	Carnegie Hall Presentation
187	3/11/35	Mon	9:00-9:30	The Walking Dead (Part 1)
188	3/18/35	Mon	9:00-9:30	The Walking Dead (Part 2)
189	3/25/35	Mon	9:00-9:30	The Rocking Chair (75)
190	4/4/35	Thu	10:30-11:00	Hangman's Roost (55)
191	4/11/35	Thu	10:30-11:00	The Guardian Of The Tomb
192	4/18/35	Thu	10:30-11:00	Dangerous Curve (95)
193	4/25/35	Thu	10:30-11:00	The Lynching Tree (Part 1)
194	5/2/35	Thu	10:30-11:00	The Lynching Tree (Part 2)
195	5/23/35	Thu	9:15-9:45	Rappaccini's Daughter (38)
				(Nathaniel Hawthorne)
196	5/30/35	Thu	9:15-9:45	The Deserter (84)
				(Ambrose Bierce: take off/Owl Creek Bridge)
197	6/6/35	Thu	9:15-9:45	Man Beast (36)
198	6/13/35	Thu	9:15-9:45	The Devil Mask
199	6/20/35	Thu	9:15-9:45	Mrs. Hawker's Will
200	6/26/35	Wed	10:30-11:00	The Madman (Part 1) (46)
201	7/3/35	Wed	10:30-11:00	The Madman (Part 2) (47)
202	7/12/35	Wed	10:30-11:00	Procrastinatin' Willie's Rent Receipt (29)
203	7/17/35	Wed	9:30-10:00	Frankenstein (10)(40)
				(Mary Shelley)
204	7/24/35	Wed	10:00-10:30	Honeymoon Cottage (24)(76)
205	7/31/35	Wed	10:00-10:30	The Nightmare (Part 1)
206	8/7/35	Wed	10:15-10:45	The Nightmare (Part 2)
207	8/14/35	Wed	10:15-10:45	The King Shark God (33)
208	8/22/35	Thu	10:00-10:30	The Bronze Venus (5)(57)
				(Prosper Merimee: The Venus Of Ille)

209	8/27/35	Tue	9:00-9:30	The Knife Of Sacrifice
210	9/3/35	Tue	9:00-9:30	The Magic Skin (Part 1) (65)
				(Honore de Balzac: La Peau de Chagrin)
211	9/10/35	Tue	9:00-9:30	The Magic Skin (Part 2) (66)
				(Honore de Balzac: La Peau de Chagrin)
212	9/17/35	Tue	9:00-9:30	The Golden Goddess
213	9/24/35	Tue	9:00-9:30	The Butcher
214	10/1/35	Tue	9:00-9:30	Four Ten-Rouble Pieces
215	10/8/35	Tue	9:00-9:30	Don Juan (64)
				(Legend)
216	10/15/35	Tue	9:00-9:30	The Were-Wolf (2)
				(Fredrick Marryat)
217	10/22/35	Tue	9:00-9:30	The Mirror
218	10/29/35	Tue	9:00-9:30	Headless Horseman Of Sleepy Hollow (22)
				(Washington Irving)
219	11/5/35	Tue	9:00-9:30	The Shooting Gallery
220	11/12/35	Tue	9:30-10:00	The Bloody Countess (Part 1)
				(Legend - history)
221	11/19/35	Tue	9:00-9:30	The Bloody Countess (Part 2)
				(Legend - history)
222	11/26/35	Tue	9:00-9:30	Clairimonde (61)
				(Theophile Gautier: La Morte Amoureuse)
223	12/5/35	Thu	9:00-9:30	Share And Share Alike (32)(71)
224	12/12/35	Thu	9:30-10:00	The Devil's Number (326)
225	12/19/35	Thu	9:00-9:30	The Toy Maker (111)
				(Fitz-James O'Brien: The Wondersmith)
226	12/24/35	Tue	10:00-10:30	The Experiment Of Dr. Zahn
				(Part 1) (77)
227	12/31/35	Tue	10:00-10:30	The Experiment Of Dr. Zahn
				(Part 2) (78)
228	1/7/36	Tue	10:00-10:30	The Spirits Of The Lake (12)(81)
229	1/14/36	Tue	10:00-10:30	The Hand Of Glory (43)
230	1/21/36	Tue	10:00-10:30	Vampire Village (37)
231	1/28/36	Tue	10:00-10:30	The Ruby Ring (Part 1) (59)
232	2/4/36	Tue	10:00-10:30	The Ruby Ring (Part 2) (60)
233	2/10/36	Wed	8:30-9:00	The Cage
234	2/17/36	Mon	8:30-9:00	The Confession (27)(92)
235	3/3/36	Tue	10:30-11:00	The First Of June (39)(86)
236	3/10/36	Tue	10:30-11:00	The Things In The Wood (Part 1) (93)

237	3/15/36	Sun	10:30-11:00	The Things In The Wood (Part 2) (94)
238	3/22/36	Sun	10:30-11:00	The Fortune Teller (90)
239	4/3/36	Fri	9:00-9:30	The Corsican Brothers (Part 1) (23) (Alexander Dumas)
240	4/10/36	Fri	9:00-9:30	The Corsican Brothers (Part 2) (23) (Alexander Dumas)
241	4/17/36	Fri	9:00-9:30	The Old Christopher House (115)
242	4/24/36	Fri	9:00-9:30	The Magician (Part 1)
243	5/1/36	Fri	9:00-9:30	The Magician (Part 2)
244	5/8/36	Fri	9:00-9:30	The Priest Of Sekhet (88)
245	5/15/36	Fri	9:00-9:30	The Doctor Of Souls (Part 1) (Theophile Gautier)
246	5/22/36	Fri	10:00-10:30	The Doctor Of Souls (Part 2) (Theophile Gautier)
247	5/29/36	Fri	10:00-10:30	The Last Waltz (42)(99)
248	6/5/36	Fri	10:00-10:30	The Lorelei (112)
249	6/8/36	Mon	10:00-10:30	The Medium (8)(96)
250	6/22/36	Mon	10:00-10:30	The Rada Drums (Part 1) (68)
251	6/29/36	Mon	10:00-10:30	The Rada Drums (Part 2) (69)
252	7/6/36	Mon	10:00-10:30	The Jettatore (13) (106) (Theophile Gautier)
253	7/14/36	Tue	9:00-9:30	The Tiger (114)
254	7/21/36	Tue	9:00-9:30	The Dead Who Do Not Die (Part 1)
255	8/4/36	Tue	9:00-9:30	The Dead Who Do Not Die (Part 2)
256	8/11/36	Tue	9:00-9:30	The Bell (91)
257	8/18/36	Tue	9:00-9:30	The Caretaker
258	8/25/36	Tue	9:00-9:30	The Mannekin (116)
259	9/16/36	Wed	10:00-10:30	The Debt (104)
260	9/24/36	Thu	8:00-8:30	The Golem (118) (Legend)
261	12/11/36	Fri	10:00-10:30	The Treasure Of Alstone (Part 1)
262	12/18/36	Fri	10:00-10:30	The Treasure Of Alstone (Part 2)
263	12/25/36	Fri	10:00-10:30	Tanhauser (79) (Legend)
264	1/1/37	Fri	10:00-10:30	The Shining Ghost (135)
265	1/8/37	Fri	10:00-10:30	In The Devil's Name (Part 1) (72)
266	1/15/37	Fri	10:00-10:30	In The Devil's Name (Part 2) (73)
267	1/22/37	Fri	10:00-10:30	The Suicide (4)(45)
268	2/5/37	Fri	9:30-10:00	The Glowersby Secret
269	2/12/37	Fri	9:30-10:00	The Bulldog (120)

270	2/19/37	Fri	10:00-10:30	The Devil Doctor (130)
271	2/26/37	Fri	10:00-10:30	The Operation (Part 1)
272	3/5/37	Fri	10:00-10:30	The Operation (Part 2)
273	3/11/37	Thu	10:00-10:30	The Troth Of Death (101)
274	3/18/37	Thu	10:00-10:30	The Boa Goddess (19)(110)
275	3/25/37	Thu	10:00-10:30	Fallon's Folley
276	4/1/37	Thu	10:00-10:30	The Substance And The Shadow (Part 1) (Adelbert von Chamisso)
277	4/8/37	Thu	10:00-10:30	The Substance And The Shadow (Part 2) (Adelbert von Chamisso)
278	4/22/37	Thu	10:00-10:30	The Statue Of Thor (100)
279	4/29/37	Thu	10:00-10:30	The Invisible Wound (134) (Kiroly Kisfaludi)
280	5/6/37	Thu	10:00-10:30	The Tenant
281	5/20/37	Thu	10:00-10:30	The Amulet (132)
282	5/27/37	Thu	10:00-10:30	The Scar (Part 1)
283	6/3/37	Thu	10:00-10:30	The Scar (Part 2)
284	6/10/37	Thu	10:00-10:30	Children Of Venus (9)(117)
285	6/17/37	Thu	10:00-10:30	The Devil Of Witzenstein (121)
286	6/24/37	Thu	10:00-10:30	The Curse And The Charm (Part 1)
287	7/1/37	Thu	10:00-10:30	The Curse And The Charm (Part 2)
288	7/8/37	Thu	10:00-10:30	Circumstantial Evidence (147)
289	7/15/37	Thu	10:00-10:30	Germelshausen (Part 1) (154)
290	7/22/37	Thu	10:00-10:30	Germelshausen (Part 2) (155)
291	7/29/37	Thu	10:00-10:30	The Sign Of The Peacock (Part 1)
292	8/5/37	Thu	10:00-10:30	The Sign Of The Peacock (Part 2)
293	8/12/37	Thu	10:00-10:30	The Bed (131)
294	8/19/37	Thu	10:00-10:30	Doctor Jekyll And Mr. Hyde (Part 1) (25) (Robert Louis Stevenson)
295	8/26/37	Thu	10:00-10:30	Doctor Jekyll And Mr. Hyde (Part 2) (25) (Robert Louis Stevenson)
296	9/2/37	Thu	10:00-10:30	The Roll Call (159)
297	2/9/37	Thu	10:00-10:30	Doktor Basilius (Part 1) (124) (Alexander Dumas)
298	9/16/37	Thu	10:00-10:30	Doktor Basilius (Part 2) (125) (Alexander Dumas)
299	9/23/37	Thu	8:30-9:00	Doktor Basilius (Prt 3) (126) (Alexander Dumas)
300	9/30/37	Thu	8:30-9:00	The Genius
301	10/12/37	Tue	10:30-11:00	The Haunted Crossroads (70)(129)

302	10/19/37	Tue	10:30-11:00	Four Fingers And A Thumb
303	10/26/37	Tue	10:30-11:00	All Hallows Eve (122)
304	11/2/37	Tue	10:30-11:00	The House Of The Bridegroom (105)(306)
305	11/16/37	Tue	10:30-11:00	Lord Of The Jungle
306	11/30/37	Tue	10:30-11:00	The House Of The Bridegroom (105)(304)
307	12/7/37	Thu	10:30-11:00	The Power Of Lucifer (136)
308	12/21/37	Tue	10:30-11:00	The Queen Of Spades (Alexander Pushkin)
309	12/30/37	Thu	10:00-10:30	The Compact Of Chester Rand (148)
310	1/13/38	Thu	10:30-11:00	The Altar Of Hate (123)
311	1/20/38	Thu	10:30-11:00	The Firing Squad (14)(113)
312	1/27/38	Thu	10:30-11:00	The Dead Bring Death (Part 1)
313	2/3/38	Thu	10:30-11:00	The Dead Bring Death (Part 2)
314	2/10/38	Thu	10:30-11:00	The Hungry God (Part 1)
315	2/17/38	Thu	10:30-11:00	The Hungry God (Part 2)
316	2/24/38	Thu	8:30-9:00	The Violin (146)
317	3/3/38	Thu	8:30-9:00	Tourists Accomodated
318	3/8/38	Tue	9:30-10:00	Uncle Bije (151)
319	3/15/38	Tue	9:30-10:00	The Ghost Of The Storage Vaults (Part 1) (138)
320	3/22/38	Tue	9:30-10:00	The Ghost Of The Storage Vaults (Part 2) (139)
321	3/29/38	Tue	10:30-11:00	The Wedding Gift
322	4/5/38	Tue	10:30-11:00	The Monster (67)(177)
323	4/12/38	Tue	10:30-11:00	The Grail And The Spear (Part 1) (Legend)
324	4/19/38	Tue	10:30-11:00	The Grail And The Spear (Part 2) (Legend)
325	4/26/38	Tue	10:30-11:00	Devil Hands (164)
326	5/2/38	Mon	9:30-10:00	The Devil's Number (224)
327	5/9/38	Mon	9:30-10:00	The Snake (Part 1)
328	5/16/38	Mon	9:30-10:00	The Snake (Part 2)
329	5/23/38	Mon	9:30-10:00	The Gypsy's Hand (74)(142)
330	5/30/38	Mon	9:30-10:00	The Reunion (127)
331	6/6/38	Mon	9:30-10:00	The House Of The Gargoyles (Part 1) (161)
332	6/13/38	Mon	9:30-10:00	The House Of The Gargoyles (Part 2) (162)

Program Index ©